I found myself jogging beside the bride, whose face was a knot of worry. I heard the maid of honor say, "I knew something like this would happen!"

I arrived just in time to see the groom collide into the top of a tree with a loud crack, roll several times through the branches, and come to an abrupt stop about a hundred feet from the ground, hanging like a puppet from his parachute.

"David!" screamed the bride. "David, are you all right?"

There was a brief silence, and then a muffled reply came from the limp, dazed body of the groom that sounded like "I'm fine." But then again, it might also have been "I'm dying."

I looked over at one of the firefighters, who was standing to my left, and saw him shake his head.

"You'd be surprised at how many weddings I've been called to," he told me. The tag pinned to his red suspenders read NICK CORONA.

"Funny, I haven't seen you at any of my weddings." I smiled, but he didn't seem to get the joke. I looked up at his face, which up until that moment had been shrouded behind the shadow of his helmet, and my mouth fell open. He was quite possibly the most beautiful man I'd ever seen.

I Do (But I Don't)

A Novel

Cara Lockwood

doWn
tOwn
press

New York   London   Toronto   Sydney   Singapore

An *Original* Publication of POCKET BOOKS

 A Downtown Press Book published by
POCKET BOOKS, a division of Simon & Schuster, Inc.
1230 Avenue of the Americas, New York, NY 10020

ISBN: 0-7434-5753-6

First Downtown Press printing June 2003

10 9 8 7 6 5 4 3 2 1

DOWNTOWN PRESS and colophon are
trademarks of Simon & Schuster, Inc.

For information regarding special discounts for bulk purchases,
please contact Simon & Schuster Special Sales at 1-800-456-6798
or business@simonandschuster.com

Printed in the U.S.A.

Acknowledgments

I had so much help writing this book. Daren, my husband, kept me inspired and kept me writing. Stacey Causey, Stephanie Elsea, Cyndi Swender, and Elizabeth Kinsella, the bridesmaids' posse, gave me tons of material and inspiration. Thanks, guys! Much gratitude goes to my agent, Deidre Knight, whose tireless efforts got this book published. Thanks to Jo and Bryce Lockwood for being my copyeditors. Thanks to Dad, who has always been my best publicist. Thanks to my editor, Lauren McKenna, and everyone else who helped me along the way.

For my mom, who kept the car light on, and for
Shannon Whitehead, who wouldn't let me stop writing.

I Do
(But I Don't)

One

I have seen two brides trip and fall down the aisle; one topple into a reflection pool; one whose violent sneeze catapulted her tiara into the front row during vows, gashing the eye of the father-in-law to be. I have witnessed one groom run from the altar, one bride run from the altar, one father of the bride fall asleep, and one flower girl whose nose bled the entire length of the ceremony. That's not including several fistfights, a half-dozen drunken and slightly insulting toasts from best men, and one collapsing tent in the middle of a seven-course dinner reception.

I am a wedding consultant, which means that despite all of my firsthand knowledge, I'm expected to reassure you that everything about your wedding will be absolutely perfect. And although you might not believe me, I'll tell you that usually, despite little snags (ahem), everything typically does work out all right at the end of the day. *Most* of the time.

And, let's face it, that's why I do it. You can't help but get a heady little rush when you see two people, obviously in love and happy, stand up before all their friends and family and pledge to make a go of it in a world where most people are divorced twice before they see grandkids. And just because I've heard the wedding march somewhere in the neighborhood of 324 times (four times on bagpipes) doesn't mean that I still don't get goose bumps when I hear it, just a little bit, because, well, I think in some sense it symbolizes hope and happiness, and, of course, love, if you'll pardon the string of sappy clichés. (I mean, we are talking about weddings, for goodness' sakes. Sappy clichés come with the territory.) In my experience, during every wedding, even the ones involving catastrophic blunders of the fainting kind, there's a moment, or even two, when everything bad in the world is suspended and you see pure, unadulterated goodwill. That's what keeps me coming back like a junkie, really, knowing that I had a hand in creating that second or two of perfect harmony.

Although, to be fair, I probably should say that for a rather small minority, a second or two of harmony simply isn't enough. It's odd, really, that so many people who don't strive for perfection in any other arena of their lives (professional or personal) have no qualms about demanding a flawless, magical ceremony celebrating (more often than not) a rather imperfect union, witnessed by two less than functional families. (It's a universal truth that relatives will not be on their best behavior just because you've spent ten thousand dollars on food. If that were the case, then psychologists would prescribe surf and turf instead of Prozac.) At a wedding, the smallest thing (a misplaced step, a bit too much wine, the appearance of a long-lost, estranged relative) can turn everything into a drunken, humiliating mess.

Weddings, by their nature, are fraught with peril.

This is why you need me.

Because I worry and fret for you. I troubleshoot, problem-solve, and (on occasion) work miracles (I intercept the drunken maid of honor before she blurts out her undying love for the groom or separate bickering divorced parents). I straighten that errant bridal train, shore up the leaning third tier of the cake, and fix that broken heel.

Being a wedding planner requires far more than just a flare for planning a shindig with champagne. I don't mean to sound snooty or anything, but I believe it takes a certain kind of person to be a wedding planner. Organized, yes. Patient, certainly. But a planner must also possess an unnamed quality: the ability to laugh in the face of a looming crisis.

I won't go so far as to say I possess all that, but I do strive for those qualities.

But then again, my ex-husband always said I had a flare for melodrama. Oh yes, I'm divorced. Did I mention that? Separated a year ago this month, and divorced officially six months ago (not that I'm counting or even paying attention, mind you, I just happen to know that it's been exactly 182 days and six hours since I signed the divorce papers).

Speaking of once-in-a-lifetime occasions, no one ever thinks about divorce in that way (you definitely don't have to worry about whether or not your slip is showing when you sign *those* papers). I certainly didn't pay a photographer $350 an hour to come and take my picture at the courthouse. If I had, I would've been immortalized forever as a red-nosed, blubbering, pathetic loser, because I was a bit unhinged at that particular moment. I suspect I even had a bit of Häagen-Dazs fudge on my chin, since I ate nothing but pints and pints of the stuff the weeks leading into the finalization of the divorce.

Not that I was sorry that I divorced Brad. (I'm not in the least bit sorry!)

I was sad more for the fact that marriage had not turned out the way it was supposed to (or the way I hoped it would). It didn't help that my parents had been married thirty-three years, and my mother took every opportunity to remind me that no one in our family except her cousin Louise in Houston (a notorious flirt) and I ever got divorced. Of course, my parents are absolutely miserable, so it's not like I had a great relationship model there. Somehow, I resisted the very pessimistic idea that in order for a marriage to succeed one had to be completely wretched. Can you blame me for holding out hope for a fairy-tale ending? I mean, for goodness' sakes, I'm a *wedding planner,* so you know I've got a bit of the romantic in me (that or I very much like a high level of stress and abuse, but I prefer to think of myself as a romantic optimist).

I should say that perhaps I was a bit hasty to marry Brad (and that's as far as I'll go to admitting fault on my part). But, you have to understand, I was attending a wedding a week, and the brides seemed to get younger and younger, and, well, I just kept thinking more and more: *Why not me?* I was twenty-six (in my head, I was closing in on thirty), and my mother had begun hinting that she'd like some grandkids soon, and Brad seemed to be willing (at least with a lot of forceful persuasion on my part; that, too, I admit perhaps was wrong of me, but for the very first time in my life I really, *really* wanted to be married).

And, had I not been required to actually live, talk, or interact with Brad, marriage would've worked out just fine.

I suppose I should have been suspicious of his spending habits from the first. But when we were dating I thought it refreshing that he had expensive taste and took care in the way he dressed. Now, I realize that as a general rule you should always question a man who has more shoes in his closet than you do. But I was "in love," or thought I was, and he was incredibly handsome, or at the very least very stylish, and what he lacked in brainpower he certainly made up for in smoothness. Without a doubt, he was a charmer.

It just so happened that he didn't like to work so much, or pay bills, or do anything except borrow my MasterCard and go to the mall. He had a particular affinity for all things Kenneth Cole, especially when they were frightfully expensive and magnificently impractical. He owned no fewer than three leather jackets, although it's common knowledge that here, in Austin, Texas, winter temperatures rarely get below 40 degrees, and you're never more than two weeks away from a 75-degree day even in the middle of January.

It didn't help our relationship, according to *him,* that I was such a detail-oriented and organized person. (So sue me if my idea of bill paying includes actually sending the payment in on time.) Then there's the little issue of the house payment, as in, I paid it. All of it. Every single month. Brad would do charming things like forget to pay the phone bill (the one responsibility I hadn't taken away from him), and then act outraged when the phone company shut down our line. He also held the infuriating belief that credit-card statements were simply suggested payments and not actual bills. "Minimum Payment" to him was nothing more than a polite, unbinding request for money, like a solicitation from the March of Dimes. So, you can understand that I was glad when he finally moved out. Relieved, really. At least he stopped eating all the food I bought, turning up the air-conditioning I paid for, and sleeping in the house I owned.

So I wasn't sad to see him go, but I was very disappointed in how the marriage thing had turned out (even if, admittedly, I hadn't been the best judge of character). Any wrong I did, I've more than paid for it, believe me. Shattered dreams and the fifteen thousand dollars I spent on the ceremony and reception aside, there's the daily occurrence of a client or an acquaintance learning that I'm divorced, and then the inevitable exclamation: "But, you're so young!" As if bad judgment and horrible marriages are reserved for people aged thirty-five and over. It's not like I worked all my life to be part of the exclusive "Divorced Under Thirty" club. (Trust me, the dues are way overpriced and the perks are lousy.)

You might assume I'm a bit bitter, but I like to think I'm a bigger person than all that. Just because Brad monopolized the three years of my life that I could actually squeeze into a size 6 doesn't mean I can't let bygones be bygones. I won't say it has been easy to hold back telling young, nervous brides and terrified grooms to run for the door while they still have their dignity, but I have managed, so far. My boss, Gennifer Douglas, who owns the consulting company I work for (Forever Wedding), has her own doubts (has actually had nothing but doubts since she hired me three years ago, given that she thinks that anybody under the age of forty must by default be an idiot).

So. I'm sure you're curious. About my job, that is. My "office," if you want to be so generous as to call it that, is situated in the small breakfast room of an old antique house. As I mentioned, our business is located in Austin, perhaps not nearly so glamorous or sophisticated a place as, say, New York, but a city where women take their weddings very seriously. ("We don't do just any weddings," G likes to say, "we do *Southern* weddings.") Our office sits on an old residential street that's slowly been converted to law offices and shops. We're located about a half a mile from the University of Texas campus and two miles from the heart of downtown. On clear days, you can see an unobstructed view of the campus tower, which is often lit up in burnt orange (the university's unfortunate color). I once did a wedding for a couple who were very loyal alumni, so much so that the bride insisted her bridesmaids wear burnt orange (this is a color, mind you, that was never fashionable, except perhaps in the seventies). The pictures, as you can imagine, didn't turn out very well, as the bridesmaids all looked particularly disgruntled. Not that I blame them.

G's office sits upstairs in what used to be the master bedroom, which is almost but not quite out of earshot of my little corner. G prefers bellowing down the stairs when she needs me. We have phones, you know, but she doesn't use them. My personal theory is that the Transfer and Hold buttons intimidate her.

Anyhow, back to my cubbyhole. I sit behind a little writing desk, wedged into the corner, and wispy curtains filter the sunlight, which is actually quite bright in the mornings. I have a computer (albeit an ancient one . . . predating the invention of Windows of any kind), which isn't good for much except making me crazy. I keep a huge appointment book (one must if one is to keep up with a number of clients) and a color-coded file system under which I systematically divide our clients by color choice, season, and, of course, name.

I did tell you I'm a bit of an organizational nazi, didn't I? You have to be in my line of work, but I know what you're thinking, of course. I'm one of *those* neat freaks, the iron-my-pajamas, match-my-underwear-with-my-shoes types. The kind of person who spends Saturday nights on her knees in the bathroom, scrubbing tile with a toothbrush. (For the record, I only did that *once* and you wouldn't believe the grout buildup. I *had* to do it.) You're thinking that I am probably impossible to live with, that it's no wonder I'm divorced at twenty-nine. I mean, *what did I expect?* A husband who leaves the toilet seat down? Who doesn't drape his dirty black tube socks across the couch and coffee table? (It so happens that Brad did leave his dirty pairs of briefs in various corners of our apartment, but that's not really why things didn't work out. Really.)

And for the record, it *was* a mutual parting. He didn't want to go on living with me and I didn't want to go on supporting his Tommy Hilfiger habit, and that was that. Just because the man happened to be the last one to ever see me in a bikini on a public beach doesn't mean I'm bitter. Or at least, not *that* bitter.

What was I talking about again? Oh, yes. Neatness. I'm not that bad, really. Honestly, I'm not. I am organized, yes. I am neat, that's true. My closet right now is color-coded and divided by season. My bed is made, with a chorus of matching pillows and shams piled high. I own a handheld carpet cleaner (and I don't even own an animal that might poo on the carpet, making such an appliance necessary). I admit that it bothers me when people put the toilet paper on the roll with the sheet facing inward, and I will fix that hanger that is hung up backward, against the grain of all the other hangers in the department store. But these are things I simply can't help, and I try not to inflict them upon perfect strangers. I am not the kind of person who will honk at you if you throw a cigarette butt out your window. I do not think neat people are in any way better than messy, disorganized people. I don't pass judgment on the woman at the grocery store checkout counter, the one pulling out crumpled coupons from her fat, torn, overstuffed wallet.

I prefer to see my borderline obsession with neatness as a small neurosis that can actually be a positive thing for busy people who hire me to try to instill order in their messy lives. Besides, being neat is really a necessity working where I do. If I misplace a single invoice, G is likely to make me pay for the catered salmon dinner for five hundred. That's probably half of what I earn in a year, since G is a little stingy with the money I earn her. I put her annual income at somewhere in the comfortable six figures, while mine barely has a toehold in five. But, to be fair, she has been in this business for twenty years and has had to survive close to three thousand psychotic and semipsychotic brides, so she probably deserves it (this won't stop me, however, from complaining loudly and often).

But, I digress. And there is a point to all this, so I'd better get back on track.

On a recent rainy and extremely humid Friday morning I was

sitting at my desk, in my tiny cubbyhole, cursing at my computer, since it had crashed again for the third time that morning, taking with it all the files and schedules I had yet to save.

G took this moment to yell down the stairs something I couldn't quite understand, forcing me to get up and trudge up the stairs to her office. Now, G has an expansive office with plush ivory carpet, dark blue velvet curtains, and an old mahogany desk whose chair is so large it could pass for a loveseat. On this gigantic desk of hers sat one new laptop (why, I don't know, as she never takes it anywhere or even turns it on as far as I know) and three stacks of papers (her profits for the year, her bridal magazines, and her pile of *Cat Fancy*). G looked like a cartoon villain, complete with a white shock of spiky hair, bloodred Revlon lips, and big, gaudy rings on her fingers. She even owned a suitably evil white Persian cat, Whiskers (original, I know), who loved to perch on one of the loveseat's plump arms, lazily swinging her fluffy tail back and forth. Whiskers and I do not get along, as said animal has a habit of pooping underneath my desk when she's let loose to run about the house. On seeing me, Whiskers leapt down from her lofty perch and slinked purposefully from the room. I resisted the urge to step on one or another of her paws as she passed me.

"Lauren, dear," G began, and I knew I was in trouble, because G never called me "dear" unless there was a very ugly job to be done. "I need a favor from you. A very old and very close friend of mine has a daughter who is getting married in three months, and I'm afraid their old consultant made rather a mess of things and they need someone to help them sort things out."

A wedding in three months?! Impossible.

G apparently didn't think so. She seemed perfectly calm about the whole thing—naturally, since she wouldn't be doing any of the real work.

G continued.

"My friend is coming in an hour and I want you to meet her. And for goodness' sakes, girl, do something about that hair of yours!"

My hand went up to my head, where I could feel the dark strands hanging loose from the clip I had naively thought would hold the Medusa-like mess atop my head. I smiled uneasily and began tugging and poking at the thick wavy wires as I backed slowly from her office.

At that moment, the corner of the door jumped up from nowhere and slammed into my elbow. I yelped. G only clucked at me, raised her eyes heavenward, and shook her head. G always had a knack for making me feel like a fourteen-year-old with her jeans pockets stuffed with shoplifted lipsticks, and as a result, I always bumped into things when she watched me. It must be her critical scrutiny that makes me so uncomfortable. I'm not usually so clumsy.

I padded down the hall rubbing my elbow (it really did hurt) and ducked into the master bath to fix my hair. G could hardly expect me to do so in the tiny little half bath near my cubbyhole, now, could she?

The master bath had the best lighting, but unfortunately also had six mirrors in a semicircle, which enabled me to see my entire butt all at once (not exactly a sight anyone wants or needs to see, let me assure you). I wasn't sure how G stood the glass shrine of self-doubt (as I liked to call it), being slightly plump in the hips, even for a healthy fifty-five-year-old. I assumed her incredible powers of self-actualization made such petty self-esteem issues moot. I wished I had more of a talent for self-delusion.

But then, I haven't told you what I look like, so you don't know. I suppose I could lie to you. Tell you that I'm a younger, shapelier Cindy Crawford. But I'm afraid I simply wouldn't be able to pull off *that* ridiculous lie. I mean, if my life story were ever turned into a made-for-TV movie, it's not like there would be a host of A-list stars lining up to play me, if you know what I mean. The best I could hope for would be Shannen Doherty. Diane, one of my best friends, says Minnie Driver or Andie MacDowell would be better fits, but I think she's just being nice and lying like good friends are supposed to do.

I'm of average height, dark-haired (jet black, really), and very white-skinned. It's appalling how little I actually tan (I consider wearing shorts a danger to society, since my stark white legs have been known to blind passing motorists). I've got big brown eyes and thick eyelashes, admittedly my best features, a nondescript, forgettable nose, an average mouth that's neither pouty and sexy nor sleek and thin. I have straight teeth, thanks to two sets of braces in adolescence that probably did more harm to my self-esteem than a slight overbite ever would. I am, I guess, reasonably average in weight, but not thin by any means. I have one of those bodies that simply failed to respond to exercise of any kind. I'm convinced I could run a marathon and still weigh exactly the same. My muscles, if I do have them (and that's a fact in serious con-tention), don't understand the concept of self-improvement. They staunchly refuse to tighten up, grow stronger, do anything but sit there, all soft and formless, craving potato chips and French fries.

And then there's my hair. My own mother called it a bird's nest all the while I grew up, partly because she couldn't get a comb through it despite all her best efforts. If a bird had taken up resi-dence there, I'm sure I wouldn't have been able to find it, as my hair is so thick and curly that shampooing it effectively takes an hour. Using clips or pins is a losing battle, but one that I never really had the heart to stop fighting.

I looked into one of the six mirrors and assessed the hair situa-tion. It had sprung free of the new assortment of clips I had used to clamp it down, and was hanging in curly handfuls here, there, and everywhere. These weren't pretty, perfectly formed curls, mind you; these were straggly, frizzy, half-dead snakes. I looked like a member of Poison after a night of debauchery. I sighed, shook my hair free, wrestled it back into a knot at the back of my neck, and barely managed to contain it with a rubber band. "Stay," I told it sternly, though it never listened to me, no matter how often I threatened to cut it all off.

Back at my desk, I found Whiskers had left me one of her presents, a particularly large and gruesome specimen, and I only just managed to get it cleaned up before G's friend arrived.

Her name was Missy Davenport. I am surprised to say that I liked her almost immediately, but not for any of the reasons one should like a person. Ms. Davenport was abrupt, bossy, and, technically, rude. And she wore fur, for goodness' sakes. (Ludicrous on two counts: 1. It was June and 95 degrees outside, and 2. Hadn't wearing fur pelts long since gone the way of leg warmers and frizzy perms?)

I didn't think anybody remotely with a conscience wore fur, but then again, I also couldn't imagine anyone finding the courage to douse this old lady bulldog in red paint. She looked just like the sort who ate Greenpeacers for breakfast.

Ms. Davenport was taller than me, stouter for sure, and had an amber-colored, shellacked helmet atop her head, which I figured must be hair. Her face, stern, wrinkled, and absent of humor, reminded me strongly of the football coach from my high school, and at any moment I thought she might tell me to drop and do fifty.

Instead, she barked, "You must be Lauren."

"Ur, yes—" I began, but she cut me off.

"Quit babbling, girl," she huffed, impatiently whipping her mink stole around her large and, I must say, manly neck. "I don't have time for empty-headed remarks."

Empty-headed? I was shocked and prepared to dislike her immensely, when Whiskers ran into the room, catching her eye.

"You again," she said, turning to the animal. "I haven't forgotten what you've done to my Persian rug you little ninny." Ms. Davenport stomped her foot hard against the floorboards near where the cat was standing. Whiskers let out a frightened hiss and burst from the room as if she'd been electrocuted.

"Thanks," I said, smiling. "You probably saved my desk from another desecration."

Ms. Davenport grunted in what I thought might have been amusement, and then bellowed up the stairs: "When are you going to get rid of that filthy thing, G?"

When no answer came, Ms. Davenport yelled again.

"G? Where are you? Get down here!"

G poked her head around the corner at the top of the stairs and smiled.

"Missy! How good to see you."

"Stuff the nonsense, G. I really can't take any more today."

I admit that what I liked most about Ms. Davenport was how she put G and Whiskers in their respective places. It's terrible, I know, but I have such few pleasures at work, you must allow me this one.

"How's your daughter?" G said, changing the subject. "Is she looking forward to her wedding?"

"Daughter? Wedding?" Ms. Davenport looked baffled for an instant, then recovered. "G, you've got it all mixed up again. It's not Jenna who's having the problems; it's Darla, my niece, who's had the wedding from hell. Lord, G, I don't know how you ever got this agency off the ground with you mixing up everything like you do."

G flushed slightly, and Ms. Davenport let out a gruff laugh. I thought she might lean over and punch G good-naturedly in the shoulder, like Coach Sanders would, but she didn't. "I'd say you're losing your memory faster than any of us, if you had a memory to lose!"

I understood immediately that G realized it had been a mistake to have Ms. Davenport here in my presence. It went a long way toward undermining G's authority. G managed to amble on uncomfortably, sending me out of the room whenever she could, to fetch coffee or albums or some other such nonsense, so I only managed to hear bits and pieces of the conversation.

The problem, as Ms. Davenport explained it, was the world was full of idiots, her niece and niece's fiancé included. I don't know exactly why she thought they were idiots, because I was sent out of the room to find an old photo album, but I do know that they had hired and fired one wedding consultant so far, for reasons I didn't get to hear. I became suddenly wary, because people who have a habit of firing wedding consultants aren't exactly the ideal clients, especially if they're related to an old and dear friend of one's boss. Needless to say, I had a very bad feeling about the whole situation.

By the end of Ms. Davenport's visit, it was decided by G that I would call the niece and set up lunch with her within the week, tomorrow if possible, as time was running out, if we were to bring about a wedding in three months. Meanwhile, at the mention of lunch, Ms. Davenport declared that she wanted an early one. As it was 10:30 in the morning, I couldn't imagine where they might find a restaurant open, but with the will of the two ladies, I was confident they would succeed in bullying some poor waiter into tossing them a salad.

Left alone, I decided it would be best to make the dreaded call to Ms. Davenport's niece, Darla Tendaski. Darla, according to Ms. Davenport, might be an idiot, but she was a successful and very wealthy idiot, being the founder of her own public-relations firm, one of the youngest such executives in the nation at twenty-eight. A graduate of Harvard, Darla came from a successful family, her father being a U.S. senator and her mother a famous philanthropist who had been profiled in *Vanity Fair*. I tried very hard not to hate her on principle.

"Ms. Tendaski's office, how may I help you?" A deep male voice answered her number. She had a male secretary? I stomped down another tiny surge of envy. I imagined him looking like a Hugo Boss model: broad chest, tight black T-shirt, dark hair, chiseled chin, sexy tortoiseshell glasses.

"I'm Lauren Crandell, from Forever Wedding. Ms. Davenport suggested I call . . ." I didn't get to finish.

"Yes, Ms. Crandell, Ms. Tendaski has been expecting your call. She would like to have lunch with you today, if your schedule allows."

"Well . . ." I hesitated. G would be furious if she was left out of the meeting.

"Ms. Tendaski has quite a busy week this week and next. We have a major promotional campaign with Dell to finish by next Friday, and I'm afraid today is the only time she'll be able to meet with you."

"In that case . . ." What choice did I have? "Where would she like to meet?"

"The Four Seasons at noon."

I pulled into the Four Seasons' driveway downtown, and stepped out of my tiny Honda hatchback, sheepishly handing the keys over to the valet, a clean-cut college student who probably made more in tips in one Friday night than I made in one week picking through bridal veils. I sighed.

Inside, the lobby was impressively intimidating, with thick

marble tables and pretty tiled floor, and it smelled like rich-people smell, all leather and cinnamon. The only things that made it bearable were the design attempts at being rustic and Texan—the chandelier made of steer bones, the longhorn orange leather couch in the foyer. It's impossible for the rich to be snobby while sitting on a couch with deer antlers for feet, I decided, and felt better about the whole place.

The hostess in the dining area smiled at me, recognizing one of her own, I thought, as she had hair almost as wild as mine, except hers was red with icy blond, Farrah Fawcett streaks. I smiled back. "I'm here to meet someone, a Ms. Tendaski."

"Oh, you mean Darla!" The hostess beamed. "Follow me."

Hmmm. The bride-to-be was on a first-name basis with the hostess at the Four Seasons? I didn't know what to think about that.

The hostess led me to a table outside, in a shady part of the patio, with a nice view of Town Lake and the perfectly manicured lawn of the hotel.

Darla Tendaski sat with one slim, tan leg crossed over the other, with a cell phone pressed against one ear and her Executive Palm Pilot on her lap. I knew before I saw her that she had to be pretty, because incredibly successful and wealthy people are almost always better-looking than average, but Darla was more than pretty, she was beautiful, the kind of tall, thin, enormous-cornflower-blue-eyes beautiful that put Gwyneth Paltrow to shame.

"The thing of it is," she was saying into her cell phone, "is that we just can't wait that long on the proofs, Joel." She motioned for me to sit down, then ran a hand through her ridiculously shiny and bouncy blond hair. She looks like she could be in the middle of a shampoo ad, I thought bitterly.

"I'd consider it an enormous favor, Joel, if you could get the proofs to me this afternoon," she continued, oozing charm from every syllable. I could feel Joel melting on the other end of the line. She broke into a warm smile that I'm sure Joel could feel through the phone. "I knew you could come through for me, Joel. You're the best!"

She flipped her phone closed and turned her full attention to me, studying me without distraction for the first time. I squirmed under the scrutiny, imagining my hair poking out in all directions and the pallid complexion of my skin looking wan and washed-out in the sunlight. She, of course, wore a healthy, golden tan.

"Lauren," she said sweetly. "It's nice to meet you. I've heard good things about you."

She extended a well-manicured hand, and shook mine firmly and with confidence.

I smiled, feeling tongue-tied and awkward. Good-looking people always made me think I was back in high school, sitting at the band table in the cafeteria with the other clarinet players, hoping no one would throw food at me.

"I heard you've had some troubles with the wedding planning," I blurted without much grace. God, where did that come from? If G were here, she would be rolling her eyes at me, stumbling over herself to apologize to Darla.

Darla, however, laughed. "Have I ever!" she said, leaning forward. "Let me tell you one time . . ."

Before she could finish, her lap started ringing. I thought it was her cell phone. It was her electronic organizer.

"Oh! I forgot about my twelve-thirty," Darla said, peering at the tiny screen. "This thing has saved me more times than I can remember!"

I didn't have a Palm Pilot. Not because I didn't want one. I knew, as an organization freak, that I really *ought* to have one. G, however, didn't pay me enough to buy brand-name cereals, much less the latest gadgets.

"Basically, Lauren," Darla said, leaning forward, "my fiancé and I need help. We've already bungled one ceremony and, well, we need someone who will just make things happen."

"Bungled?"

"Botched," Darla said, whipping her shiny blond bangs from her eyes. "If I had more time I'd tell you the whole story, but it would take a half hour alone."

I found myself staring at the perfect eyeliner line across the top of her eyelids. How did she keep it from smudging like everybody else? By the end of the day, I always found dark smudges in the crease of my eyelid, and sometimes, on a particularly humid afternoon, it would seep and run out the corners, slipping into the laugh lines or underneath the bottom fringe of my eyelashes.

"Do you think you can help us?" Darla said, blinking her two perfectly lined lids.

"Of course," I said, with the sure confidence of someone who doesn't really know any of the details.

Darla reached down below her chair and pulled out a filled-to-bursting portable accordion file and dumped it with a clang on the glass-top table.

"If you really think you can do this," she said, "take a look at these files and they'll bring you up to speed on where we are with planning. The new date of our ceremony is June twenty-eight."

I did a quick calculation. Five weeks? Was that right? There was no possible way I could pull this together in little more than a month!

Darla just looked at me.

"Is that going to be a problem?" she challenged.

"Er, no. No," I said, smiling feebly. It was *so* going to be a problem.

"Is there anything special . . . ?" I trailed off, not really sure what I was asking, and I was distracted by the disorganized and crumpled papers seeping out of the file. I couldn't stand to see the wrinkled corners sticking this way and that. The urge to open the case and start rearranging the papers right there at the lunch table was almost overpowering.

"Oh, sure, it's all in the file. The last consultant working on this made quite the report on my likes and dislikes, right down to shoes the flower girl should wear."

Darla's lap rang again, but this time it was her cell phone. "Don't say it, Joel," Darla said. "Don't tell me what I think you're going to tell me. Stop right there. Joel? Joel! I said stop talking. I'm coming over."

Darla snapped her cell phone shut and let out a deep sigh. "I'm going to have to go, everything's gone to hell. Doug, my assistant, can help you with anything you need. Oh, and Lauren . . ." She paused. "Good luck."

Why did I suddenly feel like I would very much need it?

Two

"Get over here *right now* or I swear I'm going to eat this entire gallon of Blue Bell rocky road."

The hysterical voice on the other end of my cell phone belonged to Diane, my best friend since ninth grade, who happened to be getting married in four weeks and was a complete wreck. She had asked me to be her maid of honor (in other words, to be a wedding consultant for free). But I owed her (in brief summary: four messy breakups, one false pregnancy test, one semi-eating/dieting disorder, one wedding [self], and one divorce of first husband [also self]), so I couldn't say I really minded. Besides, I wasn't looking forward to telling G that I had gone and met with Darla without her, nor was I feeling up to the task of tackling Darla's horribly overstuffed file case. The thought of the crumpled disorganized papers made me shiver. I put them in my trunk and tried (mostly unsuccessfully) to forget they were there.

When I arrived at Diane's apartment, she was sitting in the middle of the floor surrounded by open bridal magazines, and as usual, things in her life were chaos. To give you a bit of background about Diane, she's one of the truly sweetest people I've ever known and because of this she has a history of people taking advantage of her. Take her fiancé, for example. I didn't like him. For one thing, he reminded me a little of Brad, but then again, every man I don't like reminds me of Brad. Seriously, I thought Robert, her fiancé, was, how to put this delicately . . . a pig. The evidence: 1. He went to strip clubs with his friends every Friday night. ("They have great rib-eye," he said. Right.) 2. He told Diane she was fat. 3. He walked around their apartment wearing only his boxers . . . *when company was present.*

I had fought with Diane about him in the past, and had urged her to break up with him, but she wouldn't have it. In fact, the whole argument had almost tanked our friendship, so I'd promised her to try to like him, and to be happy for her because all she really wanted was to marry Robert and be happy (while I believed those desires were diametrically opposed, Diane assured me that Robert was actually very sweet and considerate, though I had never seen any such tendencies in him). So, I'd stopped talking badly about him, and I'd done what any best friend would do in that situation: wish for his untimely death. I rather thought a stroke of lightning had a nice ring to it, or sudden and deadly cardiac arrest. Something that wouldn't endanger anyone else, mind you. I wasn't really a horrible person.

"I am so fat," Diane said, slapping her hand against her thin, StairMastered-to-death thigh.

"What are you talking about? You are not fat. If you're fat, then I'm horribly obese."

Diane smiled, unconvinced. "Robert said I could lose a few pounds off my butt."

"Robert is a . . ." I was about to say "pig" but caught myself in time. "Er, you aren't fat. And if you lost anything from your butt you'd have two nasty pelvic bones sticking out of your jeans. Very unattractive."

Diane smiled. "I'm being a psycho bride, aren't I?"

"It happens to the best of us."

It's common knowledge that the worst part of a wedding consultant's job is dealing with psycho brides, or PBs, not to be confused with PBMs (perpetual bridesmaids). Psycho brides are people who completely lose touch with reality and perspective during the wedding planning and wedding event. Of course, every woman experiences a certain amount of stress and craziness during the planning of her own wedding. PBs, however, take that anxiety to a whole other self-serving level. The sneaky thing about them is that they masquerade as perfectly nice and well-adjusted human beings, until they get engaged and begin planning their weddings. There's just something about weddings that can turn reasonable women into fork-tongued, head-spinning she-devils. The signs of a PB are simple. You know you're one if:

1. You demand of bridesmaids that they perform fantastic tasks in the name of friendship, including, but not limited to: plastic surgery, abortion, and/or quitting job to help full-time with wedding planning.
2. When bridesmaids refuse requests, you burst into tears and scream, "It's supposed to be my day!"
3. You often go around bursting into tears and screaming, "It's supposed to be my day!"
4. You are incapable of talking about anything except your own wedding, even at the most inappropriate times, such as funerals or wakes.
5. You have an unreasonable paranoia that everyone who cares about you is out to ruin your wedding day.
6. You have a reasonable paranoia that everybody who hates you also is out to ruin your wedding day.
7. Your obsession about weight leads you to ask everyone

involved in the wedding, including your seventy-year-old grandmother, to lose five pounds.

8. Despite more than a millennium of wedding ceremonies, you believe that no one before you has ever planned and successfully executed a wedding, and that you are the only person on the planet to make the weighty decision of hiring a caterer.

9. You don't care anything about the groom (Groom? Who's he? Who cares?), because you are caught up in this elaborate, self-indulgent orchestration of your own girlhood fantasies.

10. You forget (or never understood) that a wedding is supposed to be the celebration of a serious, long-term commitment between two people, and not a stage for you to show your friends (and enemies) how fabulous you look in satin taffeta and a rhinestone tiara.

Now, I couldn't imagine Diane ever turning into a PB. She's far more likely to go into the other direction and be a bride-who-wants-to-make-everyone-happy (or a bride who believes she can accomplish the impossible). The only trouble with brides-who-want-to-make-everyone-happy is that they tend to make a lot of speeches imploring friends and relatives to be noble and put aside past differences for one day. Enough of those speeches can make one feel very selfish and petty (more so if it's actually the case that you *are* being selfish and petty). But I decided that I'd be able to handle those speeches from Diane.

"Diane, you look gorgeous," I said. "You don't have anything to worry about, because for one thing, you'll be standing right next to me, and I'll make you look at least twenty pounds thinner."

Diane rolled her eyes. "I don't want to hear another word about you being fat. You so aren't fat."

But Diane was smiling, so I could tell I had made her feel better, and that's really the number-one responsibility of a maid of honor.

I dreaded going back to the office, because I would have to explain to G about the meeting with Darla, and G tends to ask questions rapid-fire, interrupting you in midsentence of your answer, so that you never really get to explain the whole of anything. So, after leaving Diane in a happier mood, I stopped by the drugstore to pick up a new lip gloss (because it's common knowledge that finding that elusive perfect shade of lipstick will change your whole life forever). I also picked up my dry cleaning (which shows how much I didn't want to go back to the office, because I never pick up dry cleaning unless I absolutely have nothing left in my closet to wear).

When I finally got back to the office (about 2:45 P.M.), G was waiting for me.

"Where *have* you been, Ms. Crandell?" G bellowed down the stairs as soon as the door closed behind me. It was obvious she was perturbed, because she never used formal titles unless she was. "Your phone has been ringing off the hook!"

"Meeting with clients," I shouted, which was mostly the truth. "Let me check my voice mail and I'll come right up."

There were four messages for me, and two of them were from Alyssa Darvis—a rather spoiled twenty-two-year-old who wasn't getting married for five years, but still felt the need to call me on a daily basis. One message was from my mom, and the other was from my sister, Lily, who never called unless she needed money (being a perpetual student, she took turns asking members of the family for loans, and I figured I must have been next on the rotation). Reluctantly, I trudged up the stairs to face G.

When I got there, G was acting uncharacteristically sheepish, avoiding eye contact.

"Ms. Davenport, as you know, is an old friend." G cleared her throat. Was she nervous? "I want us to do what we can to help her niece."

I blinked. Was G still embarrassed about this morning? G rearranged some papers on her desk, still not looking at me.

"I think it would be best if you took a leadership role with this one," G continued. "I don't think I need to meet with Darla Tendaski. I'm just swamped this week and anyway it will be a good growth opportunity for you."

Swamped? I thought, With what? Had she fallen behind on her reading of *Cat Fancy?*

Fortunately, I quickly concealed my skepticism.

"I understand," I said, relieved. Now I didn't have to explain about the Darla meeting at all. Or the fact that the nuptials were only one month away. What a stroke of luck.

Hmmmm. I wondered suddenly what sort of terrible thing would happen in the near future to offset my good fortune. I am not a lucky person, as a rule. Good luck only happens in the case of something awful being just around the corner.

In this case, I thought that something awful was the second gift Whiskers left for me underneath my desk. Distracted by my near miss with G, I actually stepped in it, potentially ruining my favorite pair of platform Nine West loafers.

It was clear I needed to go home. It was almost four, and I had two weddings on Saturday I had to mentally prepare for, and, besides, I'd already logged about a thousand overtime hours this month alone. (Does it sound like I'm making excuses? I am. If there's anything Mom and Dad taught me, it's to feel guilty if you're not working.)

•   •   •

"Lauren, is that you? My, you are home early. Are you sick?"

This was my mother, who had called my house just as I had walked in the door.

"Hi, Mom. I'm not sick, I'm just home early."

"Early? Were you . . . what do they call it . . . laid off?"

"No, Mom, I just—" Call waiting beeped. "Hold on a second, I've got a call on the other line."

"Hello," I said.

"Hey," said my sister Lily.

"I've got Mom on the other line."

"Oh! Don't tell her it's me," Lily said, sounding slightly panicked or slightly high, I couldn't tell which. "I owe her a hundred dollars from last month."

"OK, but—" Lily hung up before I could finish. I clicked back over to Mom.

"Mom?"

"So I told your father that . . ."

"Wait, Mom, I didn't hear the last part, I had another call."

"What was that, dear?"

"Another call. You know, call waiting."

"Call what?"

"Never mind."

"So I told your father he better pay for it."

"Pay for what?"

Mom sighed irritably. "Your sister's car."

"What's wrong with it?"

"Didn't you hear a word I said? She's wrecked it again."

I didn't bother to try another explanation of call waiting.

"So it's up to your father . . ."

Call waiting clicked. "Hold on for a second, Mom, OK?"

I clicked over. A telemarketer wanted to sell me bikini wax that swimsuit models use. I told the poor saleswoman that it would take far more than hot wax to change me into a super-model.

I clicked back.

"Mom?"

"That's the plan at any rate. . . . So, I'll look forward to seeing you Monday for dinner."

"Huh?"

"A lady says hmmmm or what but not huh, dear. . . . Frank!" She shouted at my father in the background. "Leave that pie alone. That's for my Women's Republican Club. . . . I'm sorry, dear. Now, I wanted to tell you that I saw Brad's mother the other day . . ."

Oh, boy. Here it comes. Mom never fails to slip in some mention of Brad.

"And we were both talking about what a shame it is that you two split up," Mom was saying, as she let out a long, plaintive, guilt-inducing sigh. "She still has a lot of fond feelings for you, Lauren."

Too bad her son didn't.

"Look, Mom—"

"Lauren, now, it's not too late to reconsider this divorce thing."

"The papers are already signed!"

"Well, you shouldn't be so hasty, dear. If I had given up on your father, well . . . I haven't. Marriage isn't a vacation, you know, it's something you have to work hard to keep together. . . . Hold on a minute, dear. Frank!" she barked at my dad. "Frank! You're dribbling crumbs all over the floor. Use a plate for goodness' sakes. Oh, dear, Lauren. I have to go."

And with that, she hung up.

For the life of me, I could never understand how my parents ever got together. My dad, whose only passion in life was barbecuing various kinds of dead mammals, shares no common interests with my mom, whose single most important pursuit in life has been perfecting etiquette. She cherishes her very extensive collection of Miss Manners books and has never, as far as I know, eaten anything with her fingers. My dad, on the other hand, still tucks his napkin into the collar of his shirt before he eats and has been known to burp loudly at the end of a particularly satisfying meal. Don't get me wrong. I love both parents, and they love me, and I wouldn't exchange them for any other parents (at least, I don't think I would), but they are after all *my parents,* which means they drive me crazy.

As far as I can tell, the entire foundation of Mom and Dad's relationship relies on Dad ignoring everything Mom says, and Mom ignoring everything Dad says. Forget good communication as being a cornerstone to any lasting marriage. In my parents' household, single-minded deafness seems to work much better. A typical conversation between my parents goes something like this:

Mom: Would you please remove your feet from the coffee table?

Dad: Hmpf.

Mom: Frank, I said would you please remove your feet from my coffee table?

Dad: Hmpf.

Mom: FRANK!

Dad: What?

Mom: Your feet!

Dad: Huh?

Mom: Your feet are on the coffee table.

Dad: Uh-huh.

Mom: PLEASE move them!

(Dad moves his feet a smidgen to the right . . . believing Mom's request has something to do with them obstructing her view of the TV.)

Mom: NO! Off the coffee table!

Dad: (unintelligible grumble)

Mom: Your shoes are going to scuff the table.

Dad (eyes glued on the television and not listening to a single word): Um-hmm.

Mom: FRANK!

Dad: WHAT?

Mom: Your feet!

Dad: Huh?

The argument goes around and around much like this for the next half hour, until Mom gets so frustrated she pushes Dad's feet off the table herself, only to find a half hour later he's put them right back on the glass top in the exact same place. My parents have been married more than thirty-three years, and after all this time, my dad has never learned to keep his feet off the table, and Mom has never figured out that despite the first three hundred attempts, Dad *never* listens. This is the bedrock Mom keeps referencing every single time she lectures me on the evils of divorce.

Unfortunately, that's every single time I talk to her.

My stomach growled loudly, and so I went to the kitchen to look for something to eat. Despite my mother's assertions that I'd never get a man unless I learned to cook, I never managed to bother to figure out the most rudimentary cooking tasks, like how to brown ground beef. I'm not a vegetarian, per se, but the thought of handling raw meat makes me want to gag. Ground beef, in particular, I find repulsive. I know secretly you thought I might be a Martha Stewart, pie-baking type, but that's not me at all. For one thing, cooking is entirely too messy for me. For another, my philosophy on cooking is that if it takes longer for me to cook it than eat it, I'm not going to make it. That pretty much means my diet consists of frozen dinners, PBJs, and takeout. This night, I nuked a rather soggy frozen dinner (I swear those chicken strips weren't chicken at all but some form of space-age, barely digestible plastic) and fell asleep on the couch watching a documentary on the migration of geese on the Discovery Channel.

Expected more glamour? Sorry to disappoint. Friday nights before weddings are strictly at-home affairs.

Three

The sky was perfectly clear, with only the whisper of white clouds at the horizon's edges. A few ducks skittered across the horizon, some dipping their webbed feet into the calm surface of the lake. A crowd of about 150 had gathered on the shore, dressed in their wedding finest, and all craning their necks, eyes fixed on the plane that glided overhead. From the plane, a sky-diver, a speck no bigger than a flea, plunged into a heart-stopping free fall. He pulled the cord on his parachute, which instantly fanned out into a pattern of red and white hearts. Everyone on the shore cheered.

This was wedding number one of Saturday, and yes, that was the groom jumping from twenty-five hundred feet, dangling from a piece of thin nylon material by a few strings. I looked over at the bride, who was nervously biting her lower lip. I glanced at the maid of honor and she was grimacing. I thought she must think the groom was a pig like Robert. (I mean, what other kind of groom but a pig upstages the bride in such an extreme fashion?)

I also was wondering why I agreed to be a consultant for this wedding, when it was obvious that the kind of consulting they needed, I couldn't provide. I had, of course, tried everything to convince the couple that such extreme sports had no place in a wedding ceremony (I mean, danger aside, the groom's tuxedo would be irreversibly wrinkled from the parachute harness, and how would *that* look in pictures?). The groom was determined, however, and refused to budge. The bride was a bride-who-wants-to-make-everyone-happy, and so they decided the groom would parachute from above the outdoor ceremony and land somewhere near the aisle (there had been plenty of jokes about avoiding a "splashdown" in the lake, but I didn't find them at all funny). The groom was so excited about incorporating skydiving as a theme in the wedding that their invitations were engraved with the words TAKING THE PLUNGE. I shuddered thinking about it. I suppose it could have been worse. The bride could have insisted on jumping as well, and I don't know of any silk veil made to stand up to 90 miles an hour of high-velocity winds. And I hate to even think what her hair would look like on landing. I suppose you could call her wedding pictures Bride of Frankenstein.

The unusual nature of the groom's entrance meant that I had to make some interesting additions to the guest list, in the form of four paramedics and six firefighters, who were all watching the groom's descent with bored expressions on their faces. I suppose they saw this kind of thing all the time. The groom swooped in a little closer now. You could make out the outline of his arms and legs, and if you squinted, you could almost see the white front of his tuxedo shirt and the sunlight reflecting off his goggles. I looked away from him for a second, checking to make sure that the champagne fountain was still flowing. Suddenly, the bride drew in a sharp breath. I glanced up and found the groom again, and while I don't pretend to be an expert on skydiving, I'm pretty sure that free-falling men attached to parachutes are not supposed to be falling horizontal to the ground.

"It's a crosswind," I heard the best man hiss.

Whatever it was, it was tossing the groom around like an empty grocery-store bag. He zagged right, then back left, then bounced around in the middle for a few seconds. Several guests on the lawn gasped. Then he began drifting west, about two hundred feet from the ceremony from what I could tell, far from the relatively soft water of the lake and toward the sharp and pointed wooded area of trees. Almost at once, the entire wedding party began sprinting toward the thicket of trees, followed by a majority of the other guests. The paramedics and the firefighters, who perked up slightly at this new development, tagged behind.

I found myself jogging beside the bride, whose face was a knot of worry. I heard the maid of honor say, "I knew something like this would happen!"

I arrived just in time to see the groom collide into the top of a tree with a loud crack, roll several times through the branches (with lots more snapping and loud popping noises from the breaking tree limbs, or, at least, I hoped they were branches and not bones), and come to an abrupt stop about a hundred feet from the ground, hanging like a puppet from his parachute.

"David!" screamed the bride. "David, are you all right?"

There was a brief silence, and then a muffled reply came from the limp, dazed body of the groom that sounded like "I'm fine." But then again, it might also have been "I'm dying."

I looked over at one of the firefighters, who was standing to my left, and saw him shake his head.

"You'd be surprised at how many weddings I've been called to," he told me. The tag pinned to his red suspenders read NICK CORONA.

"Funny, I haven't seen you at any of my weddings." I smiled, but he didn't seem to get the joke. I looked up at his face, which up until that moment had been shrouded behind the shadow of his helmet, and my mouth fell open. He was quite possibly the most beautiful man I'd ever seen.

Of course, I know what you're thinking. It doesn't take a lot for a man in a firefighter's uniform to be attractive. I mean, you don't even have to be average-looking to be a hunk in those suspenders and those manly oversized coats (insert sigh filled with longing). But Nick Corona would have looked incredible in a plumber's jumpsuit (of this, I had no doubt). Yes, he was wearing the navy blue T-shirt of the Austin Fire Department, worn tight across his considerably fit chest, which I saw before he swung on the baggy firefighter's coat. He was especially well built, with defined (but not overly puffed up) muscles in his arms. I put his age somewhere in the early thirties. He was tall, or more than a head taller than me, but being about 5'3", I'm not the best judge of height. He had short, cropped hair, big brown eyes, and a strong, slightly squared chin.

I closed my mouth just in time not to embarrass myself by drooling.

Luckily, he wasn't my type, or I might be in trouble. He was probably a himbo, who'd skated by his whole life on his looks. Aren't all rugged, macho types missing brain cells? You know, nature's way of balancing out resources.

I watched him as he made his way back to his fire truck, where his fellow firefighters were already unhinging the long rescue ladder. He directed the other firefighters, as if he were a captain of some sort; most of the others seemed ready to take commands from him. Except one: a man who looked remarkably like him in build and features, except for the lazy slope of his shoulder and the permanent smirk engraved on his face.

I knew his kind. A professional heckler, the sort who lived to ruin a perfectly good wedding reception.

"You think you can handle this one, Nickie?" he taunted, obviously believing he couldn't.

Nick remained silent.

"Shut up, Jay," barked a woman with cropped red hair, suited up in firefighter gear.

It took a half hour for the firefighters to cut David down from the trees, as the parachute had tangled itself up in the many branches, and the harness strap was too taut to unhook easily. In the end, Nick Corona was the one who dragged the semiconscious groom from the top of the ladder, and by the grunts and groans he made, I guessed the groom was a bit heavier than he looked.

The professional heckler seemed more intent on making life miserable for Nick than actually helping, piping up with inane comments every now and again, including his own badly performed rendition of "Here Comes the Bride."

I was beginning to feel sorry for Nick Corona.

It was about that time that the first media camera crew showed up. It took me a minute to realize that they weren't the wedding videographers (the size of the cameras and the fact that they didn't have a separate sound person clued me in). The news cameraman swung his camera to his shoulder, just in time to record the comical picture of the rather pale-looking groom being held in the large and well-muscled arms of the firefighter.

Once Nick realized he was being filmed, he gave a celebrity-worthy scowl to the camera. (Which didn't detract from his good looks, I might add, as it gave him the brooding aura of a bad boy. Mmmm. Bad Boy Firefighters. That sounded like a hunk calendar, if I ever heard of one.) Nick Corona declined to comment to the reporter, who kept chirping inane questions (like "Is this your first rescue of a groom?" and "He looks heavy! Is he heavy?"). Nick's face flushed red, as the heckler barked out an obnoxious laugh.

The groom was helped to a waiting ambulance, and the

reporter, a short, dark-haired woman with a bright, white smile filled with too-big teeth, made a direct line for the bride, who looked, by all rights, shell-shocked. I intercepted her just in time.

"My name is Lauren Crandell," I said, smiling. "I'm the wedding consultant for this wedding and I think perhaps the bride needs a few minutes of recovery before she's asked any questions." I was very proud that I sounded so official and calm.

The reporter, however, just blinked at me, then nudged the cameraman to her right, who swiveled around, turned the camera lens on me, and flicked on the camera's light. It was extremely bright, and now I understood why so many people looked shifty on the six-o'clock news. How could you do anything but squint with that kind of wattage in your eyes?

"Marissa Murray for Channel 36 News. You were responsible for planning this wedding?"

"Yes," I said, putting up a hand to shade my eyes from the light.

"What went wrong here today?"

"I believe the wind carried the groom a little farther west than he expected."

"Is he hurt?"

"I don't think he's seriously injured, but the paramedics are looking at him now."

"Are these kinds of wedding stunts becoming more common, Ms. Crandell?"

I paused.

"I am not sure if you could say they're becoming common. I think most people like to make their weddings unique, but that doesn't usually mean jumping out of planes."

"So you don't approve of grooms jumping out of planes?"

"Well," I said, trying to choose my words carefully. "I think you always have to weigh the risks of adding something like this to your wedding. I don't think most people give it enough thought. But the groom was an experienced skydiver, and I suppose these things sometimes happen. Kablam!" I said, laughing nervously. "Luckily, though, it appears no one was hurt."

It was then the groom wandered by, looking a little dazed, and the reporter grabbed him and began asking him a whole series of questions. It was pretty chaotic after that, and it took me another twenty minutes to steer everyone back to the ceremony area, where the bride and groom assured me they wanted to proceed with the wedding. It was a beautiful little ceremony, ultimately, despite the fact that the groom's lapel was torn and his hair was rumpled, and he looked a little like he'd just fallen a thousand feet into a thick cluster of trees. Afterward, I gave the paramedics and the firefighters some wedding cake to take with them, along with my thanks. I didn't give the camera crew any, but they took some anyway, along with more than their share of the French toast and other assorted goodies in the buffet meant for guests.

G called me on my cell phone to ask how everything was going, and I was forced to tell her a little about the parachute incident. "Didn't I tell you about wind shear?" she said, tsk-tsking in my ear. I hadn't realized that the understanding of wind patterns was part of a wedding consultant's job, I thought, but said nothing. I mentioned the media crew and my brief interview, and G immediately brightened. "Did you mention Forever Wedding? Did you give our contact numbers?"

"Uh, no."

G sighed in frustration. "Didn't they teach you anything in that college of yours?"

"Do you really want a consulting firm mentioned in conjunction with a near-disastrous parachute wedding?"

"Don't be melodramatic," G said. "Any publicity is good publicity. Everybody knows that."

•   •   •

As the day started so well, I figured things must get better by afternoon. I even allowed myself to think: How could they get worse? That was my first mistake.

My second was showing up at the location of the next wedding, the Saturday-afternoon affair, a more traditional, church ceremony without the unwelcome addition of any kind of extreme sport. You can't blame me for believing this event would go more smoothly. I mean, not having any of the wedding party plummeting from high altitudes lulled me into a false sense of security.

The first sign of trouble came about an hour and a half before the start of the ceremony, when the bride arrived at the modest-sized Methodist church. Now, brides are usually nervous on their wedding days, and this anxiety can take many forms—minor irritability, nervous pacing, upset stomach, or even panic. On the day of a wedding, a wedding consultant's job is to reassure the bride that everything will run smoothly and to do what he or she can to calm the tightly strung nerves of a bride-to-be. At first, this bride, Leslie Wentworth, a twenty-eight-year-old high-tech recruiter, normally a gregarious and friendly person, seemed like an average bride with a slight case of nerves. She asked me a lot of questions (mostly normal ones about the reception and the music chosen for the ceremony) but she also asked some peculiar ones like "How would we check to make sure anyone not on the guest list was excluded from the festivities?" I figured she must mean the usual party crashers, people who mooched free champagne or cake, and I said that I would try to keep a lookout for anyone who looked suspicious (for those of you keeping count, this was mistake number three).

Now, to be fair, Leslie didn't tell me to look out for a specific person. For example, she failed to tell me that the groom had a mentally deranged ex-girlfriend, who for the past three months had been stalking the couple and filling their answering machine with obscene messages. I was blissfully ignorant of said person and of the (rather important) fact that the happy couple had obtained a restraining order against said emotionally unstable ex-girlfriend. You would think that most rational people would feel compelled to inform their wedding consultant of such a potentially devastating problem. For whatever reason, Leslie chose not to tell me. Perhaps she was hoping that nothing would happen, or maybe she was embarrassed about the messiness of the situation. Who knows? (G later said I should have asked about potentially psychotic ex-girlfriends. "It's part of the ABCs of wedding planning," she said. Whatever.)

I pride myself on getting to know the brides I work with, and I must say I was very disappointed not to have been privy to this information. I also must admit that I blame myself a bit for not picking up on the fact that something serious (beyond the usual exchange of vows of a lifetime commitment) was bothering Leslie. At the time, I thought she was a typical bride-who-wants-to-make-everyone-happy transformed into a day-of-the-wedding psycho bride, which happens on occasion. The stress is too much for some people. The PB behavior came out in short bursts—the verbal explosion when she found out there were bones in the chicken she ordered from the caterers, the yelling at the maid of honor when a speck of lipstick ended up on the corner of her veil after a well-intentioned hug went awry. Leslie even made her mother cry after ranting about the poor gene pool that gave her small breasts (which don't show up in anything, she wailed, even in the padded bodice of her wedding gown). In short, the hour leading up to the ceremony was very ugly behind the scenes. Honestly, I wasn't too concerned about it. Most of the bad behavior caused by pre-wedding jitters is usually forgiven by the time cake is served at the reception, and being the target of verbal attacks by a bride comes with the territory of being a wedding consultant. (After the chicken incident, Lily told me that her sock drawer was better arranged than this wedding. Being the calmer and more rational person, I let it slide.)

When I went to check on the groom, I found him in comparably high spirits and reasonably composed. Only the slight shaking of his hands showed that he was nervous. As the guests started filing in, I went to stand by the ushers to make sure, as I had promised, that no party crashers made it into the ceremony.

It's very simple how I missed her. It could have happened to anyone. When she walked in, I was engaged in a conversation with a suspicious-looking college-age couple who were in the process of sitting down in a back pew (a notorious place for party crashers). I was probing them gently to find out if they were, indeed, friends of the bride. I believe the ex-girlfriend slipped in behind me then, or at least I think that's probably what happened. She took a seat on the third pew on the groom's side, and blended in perfectly until the end of the ceremony . . . and . . . well . . . I'm getting to that part.

The organist began playing the opening music for the ceremony, and everything proceeded as planned. The groom, the best man, and the pastor made their way to the front of the chapel, the flower girl came, a cute four-year-old with dark curls, followed by the two bridesmaids, and then the maid of honor, dressed in an elegant light blue floor-length Vera Wang shift. Then the bride made her grand entrance, in a swirl of white silk and lace, with a fairly respectable rendition of the Wedding March on the flute and harp. The pastor said some nice words about marriage being a love bond between two people, and the couple exchanged their vows, and the mother of the bride began crying (from joy or because she was still stewing from the earlier outburst from the bride, I couldn't tell), and everything went beautifully. Then the music played, and the couple turned to walk down the aisle as husband and wife. It was then that the ex-girlfriend stood up.

What I hadn't noticed about her when she was sitting on the pew was that she wore a wreath of flowers in her hair—the exact same flowers (periwinkles and daisies) that the bridesmaids were wearing on *their* headdresses. Of course, the similarities didn't end there. She also wore a light blue, floor-length Vera Wang shift (an exact duplicate or close copy of the bridesmaids' dresses). In other words, *she looked exactly like a bridesmaid.* In fact, at first glance, I thought she might be a bridesmaid who was mislaid somehow during the ceremony, but a quick count of the wedding procession found none of them missing.

Leslie, the bride, turned a paler shade of white than her dress, rolled her eyes in the back of her head, and fainted, nicking the corner of a pew with her head on the way down. The groom, equally stunned by the appearance of the unwanted bridesmaid, didn't react quickly enough to catch his bride. The best man and one of the groomsmen took a step toward the woman, either to escort her from the church or to talk with her; I don't know which, because they didn't exactly get to do either. One of the bridesmaids screamed, "You bitch," and leapt from her position in the wedding-party progression, going straight for the woman's throat. The two women collided, and rolled together in a heap of light blue taffeta, swiping fingernails and pulling hair. (By the way, it was only later explained that the bridesmaid had her own grudge against the deranged ex-girlfriend, because she also happened to be the bridesmaid's deranged ex-roommate, who had destroyed the bridesmaid's favorite leather skirt and slept with her boyfriend in retribution for moving out.) The best man and the groomsman looked on, their mouths agape for a few seconds, and then moved to action, separating the two women, with the best man dragging the impostor straight down the middle aisle of the chapel.

Meanwhile, the groom and the maid of honor were busy trying to bring round the bride, who was unconscious and, I fear, bleeding from the head.

I ran to the foyer to call 911, told them about the situation, and had them dispatch help. I feared what G would have to say, given the monstrous two weddings of today. Somehow she would find a way to blame me, I knew for certain. I told the guests to remain calm and seated, until we sorted through what had happened. Within a few minutes, a fire truck pulled up in front of the chapel (firefighters often respond first even to medical emergencies), and I saw Nick Corona jump off the back of the truck, pull up one suspender, and stride purposefully toward the church. He wasn't lying: he did get a lot of calls to weddings.

"Hi," I said to Nick, and he jumped, more than a little surprised to see me. Or perhaps it was my hair. Humidity and complete catastrophe tended to have a frightening effect on my do.

"You sure do get around a lot," I said, sounding a bit standoffish. I always did have trouble acting normally around good-looking people.

"I could say the same for you," he replied, neutrally.

The heckler, I saw, had positioned himself at the back of the fire truck, and seemed in no hurry to move.

Nick, however, was busy asking me what had happened.

I gave what I hoped was a coherent explanation, although I did have trouble sticking to my train of thought, staring at me as he was with those big, brown puppy-dog eyes.

Looks aren't everything, I kept reminding myself, even though I was having trouble concentrating on that thought, being caught up in a whirl of other distractions: his strong jawline (that happened to have the sexiest hint of five-o'clock shadow), his taut, broad chest, and the flat, hard stomach. I was beginning to think seriously that I might need hormone therapy. I never was the sort of person who got hot and bothered. Not unless we're talking about the sort of hot and bothered you get when the AC breaks down in a stuffy church in the middle of a heat wave in August.

Nick directed two other firefighters (including the heckler, who protested this call to work loudly and with some profanity) to go see to the real and false bridesmaids, who were sitting at opposite ends of the church, panting and glaring at one another. Nick went to care for the unconscious bride. As he passed me, one of my hands absently went to my head, confirming that it was indeed, a frizzy, frazzled mess. I admit I shouldn't have been worrying about my hair at a time like this, or noticing how good-looking firefighters are, but I'm human, after all. Just because I didn't go for good-looking guys didn't mean that I wanted him to think I looked like Medusa, either.

Nick knelt beside the limp bride, putting down his medical kit. He felt for her pulse and checked her breathing, and then pulled a light from his pocket, which he flashed in her eyes while he held open her lids. (I noticed, by the way, that he wasn't wearing a wedding band on his left hand, or any rings of any kind. I admit, it gave me hope—silly, I know, since I had about as much of a chance with him as with, say, Brad Pitt.) About this time, the bride began to come around, and asked groggily what happened.

"You hit your head," Nick said, helping her sit up. "Easy, now. It's quite a bump you've got there."

"Honey, are you OK?" the groom asked anxiously, rubbing her hand.

"My head hurts," she said.

"It's OK, ma'am," Nick said (he actually said "ma'am," if you can believe it). "I don't think you have a concussion, but you may need a few stitches."

The bride turned her attention to Nick (I mean, he's hard to ignore) and smiled brightly at him. The groom frowned.

"I think we'll handle things from here," he said, giving Nick a subtle but firm nudge.

"Yes, I'll be fine," the bride said, and began to stand, but wobbled to the left, where Nick caught her firmly with one arm. I was beginning to wish I had been the one who fainted. I sighed.

"Careful," he said, steadying her. "You should really rest. And perhaps have a doctor take a look at that lump. We can take you to the ER."

"I'll take her," the groom said quickly, pulling his new wife away from Nick.

"Whatever you'd like." Nick shrugged. "Just make sure she doesn't fall asleep for another eight hours at least, just in case. And, she shouldn't drink any alcohol for at least twenty-four hours." He squatted, snapped his medical case shut, and then straightened to his full height.

"Good luck," he said, then began walking back to the fire truck parked outside. The two other firefighters were already waiting for him there, since a cursory examination of the other two women found them perfectly fine (minus a few handfuls of hair and a couple of broken nails).

"Thanks," I called from the door of the church. He didn't say anything, just flung a hand backward in a wave and threw a heart-stopping smile over his shoulder, as he slung his lean form into the front seat of the fire truck. The truck pulled away, and that was that.

The reception, needless to say, was canceled, as the bride and groom spent the rest of the evening at the local emergency room. The police arrested the ex-girlfriend (for violating the restraining order and for being a public nuisance). The wedding photographer got a picture of the girl being stuffed into the backseat of a squad car, thinking (wrongly) that the wedding couple might like to see what happened after they left. I talked to the caterer and, given the unusual circumstances, he refunded most, but not all, of the couple's deposit. I got word around nine in the evening that the bride had fully recovered, and the couple was happily settled in the hotel room, glad they were married and safe in the knowledge that the psychotic ex-girlfriend was locked up in the county jail and wouldn't be making any impromptu appearances during their honeymoon. I was relieved they seemed to be in such good spirits, because more brides than you'd think would blame their wedding consultants for mishaps like these.

I didn't manage to stumble home until close to ten o'clock, by which time I was starving. My modest house (two bedrooms, one and a half baths) was located on the edge of a very good neighborhood downtown (Hyde Park), which meant it was also on the edge of a rather not-so-good neighborhood (old airport). The house, a quaint light blue one-story with white trim, was built in 1950, and had the worn lime linoleum on the kitchen floor to prove it. I liked my house, mostly because it was all mine, leaning foundation and all, and partly because Brad had hated it, and anything he hated, I love.

I dragged myself to the kitchen, rummaged around and made some popcorn (my favorite dinner in the whole world, preparation time 2.3 minutes), grabbed a Coke from the fridge, and plopped down on my sage green couch. In this relatively safe environment, I flicked on the television (which, by the way, was my final mistake of the day).

A too-happy news anchor with frosted eye shadow and coral lipstick was talking about the "Wedding of Errors," and suddenly there I was, on *television*. The first thing I noticed, of course, was my hair, which looked like a cross between the fur on a chow and Cher's do in *Moonstruck,* and apparently I had styled it that morning by sticking my tongue in an electrical outlet, because it stood a good six inches up from the top of my forehead. I was grinning like an idiot and squinting, looking so pale and unkempt that I might as well have been one of the mole people escaped from the sewers.

"Kablam!" I said, and laughed like a fool.

The camera cut to the toothy reporter, who said, "Kablam, indeed, is what happened when this young groom fell into a grove of trees instead of landing in the arms of his bride. A crosswind caught the parachute of this groom, taking him off course. He landed in a patch of trees and had to be rescued by firefighters."

The television showed the weak groom being lifted in the arms of Nick Corona and carried down the ladder to safety. Nick, I noticed, looked even better on TV than he did in person.

The reporter was saying, "No one was seriously injured, however, and the bride and groom did exchange vows. Both say they don't have any regrets and that they would do it again."

The camera cut to a picture of a dazed-looking groom. "Yeah, I'd do it again," he said. Then the camera cut back to the reporter.

"Sue, back to you," the toothy reporter said, showing all her big teeth.

I choked on a piece of popcorn and coughed until tears came into my eyes. That was it? That was all! I had said so many intelligent things, hadn't I? The phone rang just as I was able to breathe again.

"Oh my god, you were on TV!" Diane did nothing lately but talk at loud volumes. "What happened today? What's the deal with that fine fireman? *Spill it.*"

"You won't believe me if I told you," I said.

My call waiting beeped. "Uh, hold on a second, I've got another call." I clicked over. "Hello?"

"Lauren, what in the world happened to your hair, dear? Have you been using the hairstyling products I've sent you?"

"Mooooom," I said, unable to prevent myself from whining like a fourteen-year-old. "I've got to call you back. I've got some-one on the other line."

"Just a—"

I clicked back over to Diane, but before I could say much of anything, my call waiting beeped again.

"Just what do you think you're doing, young lady? Hanging up on your mother? Have I not taught you any manners at all?"

Inwardly, I groaned. I clicked back over and told Diane I needed to call her later. When I clicked back, Mom was in mid-sentence, as usual. ". . . not the only golden rule, there's also the second most important rule, which according to Miss Manners is . . ."

Sigh.

Four

I spent most of Sunday in a complete funk. Diane tried to cheer me up by taking me shopping.

"How can I afford to buy anything?" I whined. "G's going to fire me on Monday. I know it."

"If she does, you'll get unemployment checks and have a whole lot more time to shop," Diane said, pulling me in the general direction of a group of sale racks. "Let's go look at shoes. They're the only things that don't depress me when I try them on."

As it turned out, G didn't fire me. She didn't even yell at me. What she did was much worse. She pitied me.

"What am I going to do with you?" G said, sighing. "You're such a pitiful mess." Whiskers flicked her tail and looked disdainful.

"You'll just have to redeem yourself with Darla's wedding," G said, dismissing me with a wave of her hand.

Darla's wedding! In the commotion of the weekend, I had forgotten all about Darla and her overstuffed file folder. Yet another unpleasant task I would have to do today. I put that on my list with all the others, including two meetings with overzealous mothers of the bride, and one dinner at my mother's house.

Diane called then.

"How much do you love me?" she asked, sounding uncharacteristically upbeat.

"I love you more than Whiskers," I said, decidedly.

"I have three tickets to the Fireman's Charity Ball next weekend."

This took a moment to register.

"Robert, you know, being on the city council, always has to go to these stuffy things, but by the looks of the firefighter I saw on TV, this one will be anything but stuffy."

"I can't just go to a fireman's ball," I said, horrified by the idea.

"I think the right response is 'Diane, how will I ever repay you?'"

"But . . ."

"No buts. You're going. You know you want to."

Well, I suppose a small part of me did. Not that I usually went for hunky, himbo types. I wasn't the sort of person who usually dated men who looked like they belonged in a hunk calendar.

This, however, didn't stop me from slipping into a few harmless daydreams. Nick rescuing me from the top of a tree. Nick saving me from my wrecked car. Nick bashing down the door to my office, carrying me to safety from a blazing fire. Whiskers, of course, would not survive. Nick would say, "I'm so sorry I couldn't save her," and I would say, "She's in a better place." Awed by my poise and grace, Nick would gather me in his arms and say, "Lauren, I've never met a woman like you." Then he would give me the most passionate and meaningful kiss of my life (insert dreamy sigh of contentment here).

I got so carried away, I'm afraid, that I spent another half hour dreaming up ways I might be able to see him again. Some were perfectly harmless (say, launching Whiskers into a tree, where she'd be in need of rescue), while others were less than innocent (just how bad would it be to accidentally set a small fire? hmmmm).

"You've got it bad," Diane told me at lunch, over a pair of Cobb salads. I noticed that she had picked out everything remotely containing fat (cheese, avocados, bacon bits, even olives) and pushed them neatly to one side of her plate.

"I have no idea what you're talking about," I said, taking another bite of avocado. "You need to eat more than lettuce," I added.

"I have the rest of my life to eat," snapped Diane. "I have only two weeks to get my arms in shape for the photographs."

"Who said anything about your arms? Your arms are fine."

"Please. I look like Nell from 'Gimme a Break.'"

"You look like Halle Berry," I corrected.

Diane snorted and rolled her eyes.

"Why did I go sleeveless?" she wailed, throwing her fork on the table. This was her continuing mantra since picking out her sleek Carolina Herrera with spaghetti straps and formfitting bodice four months ago.

She looked at me, and must have seen the flat look on my face.

"But here I am going on and on, and you're miserable," she said, softening.

"I think 'miserable' is a strong word."

"I think it aptly describes five months of celibacy."

After lunch, I had the (not so pleasurable) pleasure of meeting Martha Wallergang, a fifty-seven-year-old, and her daughter, Chastity Wallergang, a twenty-five-year-old kindergarten teacher and most definitely a bride-who-wants-to-make-everybody-happy. Unfortunately, Martha, her mother, was a mother-who-wants-to-relive-her-youth-through-her-daughter, one of the worst kinds of mothers of the bride.

In bridal consulting, MOBs (mothers of the bride) are the second most difficult element to deal with next to PBs. They typically fall into one or more of these categories: relive-youth, mother-who-wants-to-control-everything,   mother-who-hates-the-groom, mother-who-weeps-constantly, and mother-who-can't-believe-her-daughter-is-all-grownup. As you can imagine, there are plenty of MOBs who fall into several categories at once. Martha, as I mentioned, wanted to relive her youth, which meant that she was also a mother-who-wants-to-control-everything.

"When I was a bride," Martha said, as she exhaled a small, wistful sigh, "I always wanted ivy garlands around every table."

The three of us, Martha, Chastity, and I, were standing inside the flower shop where I had taken them to discuss color schemes for the arrangements.

"Green has always been my color, you know," Martha was saying. "I have never looked well in blue or yellow, but green has always suited the color of my eyes."

As her eyes were a dull brown (as I have a similar eye color I can say this), I couldn't imagine anything that wouldn't make her eyes look, well, dull brown. I glanced over at Chastity, who was staring off into space, probably imagining herself anywhere but here.

Mark Stewart, the florist, made his appearance then, apologizing for keeping us waiting. Now, when people first meet Mark, his looks often surprise people. I think it's because you have a particular stereotype in your mind of florists; they must either be warm grandmotherly women or pudgy short grandfatherly types. Mark, who was a second-round draft pick for the Dallas Cowboys before he blew out his right knee, stood over six feet four. He was blond, good-looking, and athletic, and looked like he would be more at home on a construction site using heavy and manly tools rather than rearranging tulips and gardenias. There was nothing effeminate about him, yet flower arranging was his passion, and he never saw anything wrong with it. If any of his buddies teased him about it, he would simply shrug and say, "It's a living." He was the only man I ever knew to complain that his wife simply didn't understand how flowers change the dimensions of a room.

I chose Mark for the Wallergangs because he could be very firm with pushy MOBs, and he was more than a little physically intimidating. Also, Mark is very good at what he does. He's been featured twice in an Austin bridal magazine (partly, I think, because the editor has a rather large crush on him, not that she would ever get anywhere, since he's head over heels for his wife and oblivious of other women).

Martha, I saw, was rendered speechless upon his introduction, which I took as a good sign. Perhaps she would be too taken aback to say much of anything, which I hoped would allow Chastity the opportunity to voice her own opinion. Mark, bless him, turned straight to the bride and asked her what kind of colors she wanted in her arrangements, ignoring the gaping MOB.

"P-p-peach and cream," the bride managed, seeming very embarrassed to be stating her own opinion. Her mother looked aghast.

"Peaches and cream? That's an ice-cream flavor, not wedding colors, Chastity. I thought you wanted green. What about the ivy garlands?"

Mark and I exchanged glances, and he immediately understood the problem.

"I think peach would complement Chastity's skin tone better than green," Mark offered, further stunning the MOB. (The image of a six-foot-four football player giving his opinion on color schemes is always a bit shocking.) "Why don't we take a look at some blushing roses, and see if we can't find a shade you like."

●　　　●　　　●

Because of the length of the meeting with the Wallergangs, I didn't have a single minute to spare for Darla's file folder before running to my 2:30 appointment, with a weepy MOB who seemed unable to even look at invitations without sobbing uncontrollably. By the time I finished looking over invitations, running back to the office, and answering a few voice mails and E-mails, it was time for dinner at my mother's house.

Now, I must tell you that after dealing with two trying mothers of the bride in one day, it was very hard to get excited about visiting my mother's house. It's not that I don't love my mother. Of course I do. I just prefer to love her at a distance—of, say, a few hundred miles.

For example, when I arrived, she gave me a stilted, measured hug (not to induce any wrinkles in her blouse), and then immediately handed me a can of styling mousse.

"I thought it would help tame the wild beast atop your head," she said, and laughed deliriously. She thinks these "jokes" help us bond. It's not entirely her fault. When I was fifteen, I accused her of not having a sense of humor.

"Really, Lauren, do you use a blow dryer?" She had her hands in my hair now and was attempting to part it straight down the middle—the exact place my hair never wants to go. I slapped her hands away.

"Mom, please."

"I'm sorry," she said. "But you did get your father's hair. If I had had anything to say about it, I would have given you mine."

I rolled my eyes. She says this every time she sees me. I don't see how I would have inherited Dad's hair, considering that he's bald. My mother does have very nice hair, though. Shiny, auburn strands, board-straight, with a healthy gleam. She wears it cut to a chin-length bob, curled under at the ends.

"Have you been eating chocolate again?"

"No."

"I think you have. You're breaking out on your chin."

My hand went reflexively to my chin. "I am not. Besides, chocolate has nothing to do with pimples."

"So you have been eating some. You know it goes straight to your hips, dear."

She turned to stir the spaghetti sauce. She handed me the salad bowl to put on the table and said, "Lauren, dear, stand up straight and don't slouch."

This was dinner at my mother's house.

"Where's Dad?" I asked, hoping to guide the conversation topic away from me and my posture.

"Where do you think he is? Golfing," Mom said, stirring the tomato sauce with unusual vigor. "You'd think he'd take time to visit with his oldest daughter, but nooooo. Swinging a stick at a little white ball is more important to him."

Mom thumped the wooden spoon with some force against the rim of her pot.

"But, I just have to stick it out," she said, pointedly.

Uh-oh. Here it comes.

"Marriage is not something you can take back, like a sweater that doesn't fit. When I told your father 'until death do us part,' I meant 'until death do us part.'"

I glanced at my watch. Four minutes since I walked in the door and Mom was already talking about the divorce. I believe that was a record.

"And poor Brad. I just hate to think what he's going through."

I choked on the iced tea I was drinking and hacked for a solid thirty seconds.

Mom has a fondness for Brad that goes against all natural feelings a mother should have for a son-in-law. (Correction. *Ex*-son-in-law.) He won her over with his impeccable table manners. He was the only thirty-year-old man she knew who understood how to properly wield a fish knife. After meeting her for the first time, he actually sent her a thank-you note and flowers, which completely sealed my mother's affection and loyalty.

Mom indicated I should sit down, and so I did, managing to constrain my urges to run for the door when she was distracted with draining the spaghetti.

"Have you spoken to Brad lately, dear?" Mom said, slipping into her chair, daintily placing her linen napkin in her lap.

I sighed. "No, Mom. We're divorced, which means we don't talk to each other."

"Aren't there things still left to settle?"

"No," I grumbled.

"What a shame. I still consider him my adopted son."

I coughed. Loudly.

"Lauren, dear, you're dribbling spaghetti sauce on your nice blouse. Be more careful, sweetheart."

"Where's Lily?" I said, because if there's one subject that can distract her from Brad and me, it's Lily.

"I invited her to come tonight, but you know she never does." Mom let out a mournful sigh. "I just don't know what to do about that girl. She thinks she can stay in school forever. She's signed up for another year of classes. Another year, if you can believe it. And then there's her wrecked car, which I don't know how we're going to fix . . . and . . ."

I had successfully diverted her, and she didn't mention Brad again. In fact, she seemed to lose interest in me altogether, which I much prefer, to be honest. I even managed to coast through the rest of the evening without her mentioning my hair again, which I consider a victory.

Tuesday morning, I plowed through the mess of Darla's file folder, and by the end of it I felt I understood a little more about the woman. For example, her favorite colors were daffodil yellow and iris lavender. She preferred salmon to chicken or beef entrees. White wine to red. Cool Whip–based icing on cakes instead of the traditional butter icing. Traditional invitations to modern. Slim-line dresses to A-line, no trains, and no cathedral-length veils. Morning ceremonies to afternoon or evening events. Indoor to outdoor. Sit-down to buffet. Six bridesmaids and six groomsmen, including one flower girl and one ring bearer.

With so many of the major decisions already made, I had a hard time figuring out why she had had so much trouble. By all accounts, she wanted a fairly traditional, elegant, and tasteful wedding, which most bridal consultants live to create. There was nothing in the papers she had given me to indicate the cause of any serious problem. I was left wondering if Darla was perhaps a PB in disguise, which would neatly explain the firing of the previous consultant, and the current demand to have everything re-planned in the span of a mere month. I made a mental note to be careful around her, since PBs can attack unprovoked, with little or no warning.

Alyssa Darvis called, interrupting my train of thought, to ask about whether or not she and her fiancé could be the subject of a gigantic ice sculpture placed in the middle of their reception hall. Since her wedding date (in five years) was in August, I thought an ice sculpture was probably a bad idea. "Think about how you would look when you started melting," I said sensibly.

At 2 P.M., I mediated a buffet vs. sit-down dinner debate between a bride and groom who might very well need marriage counseling *before* their actual wedding. Then, at 3 P.M., I convinced another client she probably didn't want to ride a horse and carriage through her wedding reception (first, think of the smell; second, the risk of a runaway horse barreling through the wedding cake was enough to give any bride pause). An hour later, I negotiated a tentative truce between a clueless but vocal groom (one who was suffering from the common delusion that this was *his* day, too) and his future mother-in-law, who was very close to strangling him. (I couldn't really blame her; he was insisting they have pork rinds at the reception.) By 4:30, I had taken my sixth aspirin and was beginning to wonder whether or not it was possible to overdose on Motrin.

Whiskers, who had crept up beneath my desk, attacked my right leg, causing me to fling the Motrin bottle into the air, scattering what remaining pills I had all over the carpet.

The phone rang then.

"I have found your *soul* stylist," Diane said, sounding excited. "I just came from a salon downtown and you've *got* to go."

"I don't really need my hair cut right now," I lied. I did, and in a big way. I had more split ends than I did actual intact hair shafts. But going to the salon is always a bad idea. I've never found anyone who knows how to properly style or cut curly hair and inevitably I always end up looking worse (believe me, it *is* possible).

"Don't give me that, Lauren. I just *saw* you yesterday. Besides, didn't you tell me you wanted to cut in some layers?"

"Yeah, I guess."

"Come on. I'll even go with you. Let's make it a girls' night out. We'll head straight to the bars afterward."

The thought of being able to drink myself silly was appealing. Besides, I definitely would need a drink after getting my hair done.

Five

Sitting in the salon chair, watching the stylist study my hair with a puzzled expression, I really wished I had drunk a margarita *before* I came. I told Diane this, and she just laughed.

"Relax," she said. "It'll be fine."

I looked at the stylist again, a man in his twenties, wearing a tight black shirt and loud blond highlights in his otherwise dark wavy hair. I was hoping very much that he was gay; otherwise I might be in for a truly terrible cut. (I hate to admit that I do have a bias against heterosexual male stylists, but I do.)

The stylist (Bobbie to his friends) picked up a brush and ran it through my hair, and I cringed. The first thing anyone should know about curly hair is that you don't comb it like that, because you shatter all the curl, and are left with a frizzy, ugly mess (in my case more of a mess than usual). I shrank further in the seat.

"You're a very attractive woman," Bobbie said, winking at me. "I mean it. I don't say that to all my clients."

I nearly jumped up from the chair right then and bolted from the salon. He absolutely was not gay.

It's not that I discriminate against heterosexual stylists, exactly. But I have found, on the whole, that straight male stylists tend to be a little obsessed with letting everyone know they *aren't* gay, given the stereotype, and tend to be far more likely to hit on their clients. Now, I just may be another bitter divorced woman, but I've never met a man who could multitask, and stylists are no exception. Men cannot hit on women and do something else as complicated as cutting hair at the same time. It simply isn't possible.

"Help!" I mouthed silently to Diane, who shook her head. She retreated discreetly to have her nails done, and left me at Bobbie's mercy.

Bobbie was still studying my locks, scissors in hand, with that puzzled expression on his face as if he were trying to figure out a really complicated math problem, when a blond woman in her forties came by, wet nails in the air. She wore a black robe smock, canvas Coach pumps, and a bunch of gold bangles on her wrist that jingled when she walked. But her most surprising feature was her hair. Shorn an inch from her head, it was spiking up in all sorts of odd directions, and though I tried not to stare, I couldn't help but fixate on the fact that her bangs came to a sharp, triangular point at the center of her forehead.

"Bob-bie," she said in a singsong flirty voice, "I've gotten *so* many compliments on my new do."

She had? I thought, amazed. She had to be lying. She looked like a blond version of Count Chocula.

"I knew it was the right cut for you," Bobbie said, oozing confidence. The blond woman with the fright wig put a hand on Bobbie's arm and purred, "You don't suppose you can fit me in for a style this afternoon?"

"Sure thing, darling," Bobbie said, winking.

OK. Not only was he not gay, but he was one of *those* guys. The sleazy, hit-on-anything-with-boobs guys.

"He's going to do *wonders* for you," the woman told me, inspecting my hair.

That's it, I thought. *There's no way this is going to happen.*

Bobbie picked up a handful of hair and prepared to cut off a large chunk of it with his scissors. *"Wait!"* I shouted, suddenly, causing Bobbie to jump.

"What?" he asked, glancing around my chair, as if he'd accidentally stepped on my foot.

"Um," I paused, hoping to think of an excuse. "Uh, I've got to go to the bathroom. Do you have a bathroom?"

I sat in the second stall of the salon's two-stall bathroom and tried to think of some sort of excuse that would enable me to flee without seeming like a lunatic. Business emergency? Lord knew I had enough of those, so it wouldn't be much of a stretch. If the black smock I was wearing wasn't so conspicuous, I might just be able to sneak out the back. Make a run for it.

I was considering this possibility when the bathroom door opened, and I heard the padding of feet on the bathroom floor. They stopped in front of my stall, where ten perfectly painted pink toes in pedicure slippers stared up at me. My stall door flung open, and on the other side was Diane, one hand on her hip.

"What are you doing in here?" she said, immediately sounding stern.

"Hiding," I said.

"Don't you think he's cute?" Diane said.

"Cute? *Cute?* Diane I am going to kill you. Did you know he wasn't gay?"

"Of course. I thought you two might hit it off."

"You were trying to set me up?" I was flabbergasted.

"Of course, silly. He seemed just your type."

"What type is that? Incompetent or moronic?"

"Uh-oh. You didn't like him."

"Diane. You know the cardinal rule about heterosexual hair-stylists."

She shrugged. "Well, you seemed desperate for a lay," she joked. "I thought you wouldn't mind."

"If I get out of this alive, I'm going to kill you."

"Why don't we go get sloshed instead?"

"Now, *that* we can agree on. You're paying."

I wanted to go to a place that had particularly strong drinks and no lights, which ruled out half the bars Diane likes, and left one we could agree on: Club de Ville. A little on the run-down side, it's a two-room bar located downtown, with a large patio full of half-broken furniture. What Diane calls Shabby Chic. I ordered a vodka martini (the drink I drink when I'm serious about drinking) and sat back in the tiny square of space we found in the corner of the patio. I tried not to think about today's near disaster. I'd barely escaped a permanent bad-hair day.

Diane had redeemed herself by staging a distraction in the salon (knocking over a tray of perm curlers), allowing me to sneak into a closet, grab my shirt, and make a run for the door. Bobbie, who was busy talking to the woman with triangle bangs, didn't see me leave.

"You're buying me a second round," I told Diane, even though I'd barely begun on my first.

"You are such a drama queen," Diane sighed at me. "I mean, you'd think I'd just tried to have you killed."

"Well, if I'd let Bobbie cut my hair, I have no doubts the results would've given me a heart attack. So theoretically, you did try to kill me."

"You're impossible," Diane said, but she was smiling. "Isn't a bad haircut worth a good lay?"

"That's up for debate," I said, just as a man (and I use that term loosely, because he couldn't have been older than twenty-two) ambled up to our table and said, "Evening, *ladies,*" looking straight at Diane.

This happens all the time when we go out. Men (and boys) fall all over Diane. It's been happening since college. Diane has a kind of exotic beauty: olive-skinned, with dark hair that she wears cropped short, like Halle Berry. She's tall and slim and exudes sassiness (that is, when Robert isn't around, another reason I think he's a pig).

I excused myself to go to the rest room. Diane hates it when I do that, but I felt like she had some payback coming, and so I left her to smile politely at the college boy.

I had only just made it around the corner when I collided with what I thought at first was a wall. Then the wall took a step back, and I looked up and found myself staring into the (stunningly gorgeous) face of Nick Corona.

I felt a bit of liquid running down my arm, and I realized that he had been holding a drink when I had run into him.

"Oh, I am so sorry," I said, patting helplessly at the front of his shirt, which was wet to the touch (soaked in what had been his beer). "I, er, didn't see you there." (It was very dark in that bar, you know.)

"That's OK. It's my fault," he said, giving me one of his hundred-watt smiles. My heart flopped.

"I didn't recognize you at first, uh, out of uniform," I sputtered awkwardly. He was wearing a button-down oxford and jeans, managing to look even more charismatic than in his firefighter uniform, which I thought would be impossible. I frantically searched for something witty to say. All I managed was: "Do you come here a lot?"

"Often enough. The firehouse is two blocks from here."

"Oh. I see."

An awkward silence fell, during which all I seemed to be able do was think about my recurring Nick Corona rescuing fantasies, which made my cheeks burn. It didn't help that he was actually better-looking than I remembered him, which was very good-looking indeed. He seemed to get taller and more muscular every time I saw him. And did I mention the puppy-dog eyes? (Insert deep drawn-out sigh of longing here.) I smiled nervously.

Before I could think of anything else inane to say, we were interrupted by the appearance of a tall, slim blonde, who curled her arm around Nick's waist. "Did you get my drink?" she asked lazily.

She looked familiar. I squinted, and then she moved into a dim patch of light. I recognized her then. Darla Tendaski.

"Darla!" I said, surprised and horrified all at once. She must be engaged to Nick. Of course he would be marrying someone as gorgeous and put-together as Darla. *Look at her hair,* I thought. It was shampoo-ad perfect, as usual. A self-conscious hand went to the top of my head. I really did need a haircut.

She turned to me slowly, not recognizing me at first.

"Oh! Laura!" she said, realization dawning.

"It's, uh, Lauren," I said.

"Right. Whatever. Good to see you. Have you met Nick?"

"We've met before," Nick said quickly.

"Oh?" Darla glanced from him to me and back again, a speculative look in her eye.

Great, I thought. *Way to hit it off with a client. Be seen flirting with her husband-to-be.*

"It was nice to see you," I said hurriedly. "I should go, I've got to . . ." I was about to say "meet friends" when two hands came up behind me, entangling themselves in my hair.

"Hi, beautiful," said a slightly slurred male voice behind me.

"Now, why'd you go and run away?" I spun around, ready to punch or slap the stranger or do some other form of bodily harm, when I was stopped by a jolt of recognition. It was Bobbie, of course.

"Good to see you, Lauren," called Darla, who was pulling Nick away from the bar with one hand. "We'll talk again soon."

"Uh, bye," I said to her, before turning my attention back to the now semi-drunk, straight male hairstylist. At him, I hissed, "What are you doing?"

"I've been looking all over for you, I thought we could . . . we could . . . uh . . . you know . . . party."

He grabbed me then, and pulled me close, as if he might kiss me. I pushed against him. When he didn't seem to budge, I stepped hard on the instep of his foot. He yelped and sprung back.

"Go party by yourself," I said, stalking past him. He wasn't hard to lose in the crowd, given that he was drunk *and* he was a moron. I found Diane still talking to the college kid. I elbowed in between them.

"Diane, we're leaving."

"What?"

"Now," I said between clenched teeth.

"You've got to give him credit for having balls," Diane said at the bar at Waterloo, where we ended up after Club de Ville.

"Who? Nick?" I was confused.

"No. Bad Hairstylist Boy."

"The only credit I'm giving him is for being a complete asshole."

"So he put the moves on you," Diane said. "He's pretty cute. Not as fine as the firefighter, but close."

"They're not even in the same species."

"Yeah, one is available and one isn't."

• • •

I don't remember much of the rest of the evening (either the last vodka martini I drank obliterated it, or the depression that set in once I realized Nick Corona was engaged wiped it from my mind, I don't know which). I do remember falling into bed mostly clothed, and thinking to myself it would have been a good idea to take a couple of aspirins and a glass of water as a pre-hangover precaution. I congratulated myself on being not too drunk that I thought about such a practical thing. Unfortunately, I was too drunk to actually do it, so I awoke with a pounding headache and a mouthful of sticky sour taste.

That is the last time I go out drinking on a weeknight, I decided, as I rolled out of bed, missed the landing altogether, and hit the floor with a thud.

"Ow," I said to no one in particular, rubbing the hip that had made contact with my wooden floor. I lay there a minute, sprawled out on the ground, suddenly too tired to do anything but breathe—and even that took effort.

"I am not going to take another drink as long as I live," I swore to my ceiling fan, which looped lazily about in slow circles, obviously doubting my conviction.

I managed to pull myself from the floor, only to have the blood rush suddenly from my head, causing my vision to cloud over with white stars. I stumbled about my bedroom and landed in the bathroom, where I took my first look in the mirror.

If that wouldn't sober up a person, I don't know what would.

For one thing, I think I was pretty much a shoo-in for the "Woman Who Looks Most Like Cousin It" award. My hair is always particularly vocal in the mornings. And the fact that I was long overdue for a haircut helped it reach new levels of frightening.

I put my hands to it, trying to smooth it down a bit, and I cooed at it, as one would to a hysterical woman in the next seat on an airplane. It didn't do a bit of good. Only something as drastic as a strong shower would make a dent.

Once I showered, I started feeling more in control. Bits and pieces of the night before came back to me, and I was able to reason through most of the ugly parts. A. Bobbie was a moron with bad manners, but I should find it flattering (if slightly) that he found me attractive. B. Nick Corona was never going to go out with me in the first place, and so discovering that he was engaged only made it easier to dismiss him completely from the might-happen-in-a-thousand-years list (which already had a number of long shots—Keanu Reeves and Christian Bale being two of them).

Numbly, I got dressed (a very dangerous thing to do while hungover, I might add). I suppose I should be grateful that I actually put on a skirt and a shirt in the same color family (blue), so I can't be too upset that instead of the usual sleek, strappy sandals I wear with skirts I chose clunky, awkward loafers. I considered it a victory that in my fuzzy state of mind I remembered shoes at all.

Thankfully, I had sunglasses in my purse, or I would have never made it to work. The sun had an unusually piercing quality that morning, which made it impossible to see. I had to occasionally peek over the rim of the sunglasses to make sure I was actually wearing them, since the world seemed in no way muted by the dark lenses.

Eventually, I just forgot that I had them on at all, which was why I sat in my little cubbyhole at the office wearing them.

"If you have pinkeye, I want you home this second," G said as she passed my desk on the way to her office. "I mean it," she called down from the top of the stairs.

I was tempted to lie and slink out. How can you not think about it when your boss gives you the perfect excuse? But I knew myself. I wouldn't be able to live with the guilt of it.

Still, being as groggy as I was, I don't know how much I actually accomplished that morning. My mind had trouble focusing, and all I could seem to do with any success was stare blankly out into space for several minutes at a stretch. I had Darla's folder open before me. Every time I started to read, the words just floated by me without sticking. After fifteen minutes, I realized I'd been staring at the same sentence and hadn't managed to make any progress.

I flipped to the invitation sections, where I saw the official confirmation of the union between Darla Emily Tendaski and James Nicholas Corona. I understood immediately why Nick preferred his middle name as his first. I couldn't imagine anyone seriously calling him James. James to me was a name that belonged to bookish types with skinny frames (excluding James Bond, of course, but even he says his last name first upon introduction . . . Bond, James Bond).

I made a few calls to reception halls that had been on Darla's list, and found that only one of the five could accommodate us, and even that one was a last-minute cancellation. I booked it hurriedly, and then turned my full attention to caterers, but didn't get far down my list before Diane called, asking for me to meet her at DSW Shoe Warehouse for lunch (not to eat, but to shop, of course). I nearly jumped up right then and ran from the office, I was so in a hurry to get away from the head-splitting caused by Darla's folder. Besides, nothing I knew of cured a hangover better than shoe shopping. (Except maybe bacon-egg-and-cheese breakfast tacos with plenty of salsa. Mmm. Mmm.)

I will say that there's nothing like thirty rows of stacks of shoe boxes with discount prices to make a girl feel instantly better about what would otherwise be a very crummy day. I took in the smell of leather and savings, and made my way down the row of slides and mules (because the best part of shoe shopping is trying on shoes you'd never wear but look fabulous on your feet).

I pulled out a pair of high-heeled snakeskin mules, slid them on, and did a twirl beside a foot mirror. I decided that if everyone just looked strictly at my feet, I'd never be anything but sexy. My feet are normal-looking, if slightly on the small side (size 6 ½ and sometimes 6 on lean, nonswollen days), but I never have to worry about them looking fat, mushy, saggy, or any of the other things that come into play when one is trying on pants.

"Buy those right now!" Diane squealed when she saw me wobbling about in the higher-than-I-usually-wear heel.

"Where would I wear them?"

"Who cares?"

"What would I wear them with?"

"A sleek nightie and black feather boa." Diane paused for dramatic effect. "I'm just kidding. Jeans. You can wear them with jeans."

"Or Daisy Duke shorts?"

"Exactly."

"I was kidding."

"I wasn't."

"Like you'd ever wear Daisy Duke shorts."

"Well, of course not, look at my *thighs.*"

I looked at Diane's sticklike legs. There's no way she had even a millimeter of cellulite on her.

"What about them?"

"Three words: flabby, fat, and ugly."

"Please!"

"My ankles are even fat."

"Diane, you're *not fat.*"

Diane shrugged, obviously not believing me. She could be so annoyingly insecure sometimes. Honestly. I couldn't help but think it was Robert's influence at work.

By the end of the lunch hour, she had three boxes of shoes she was prepared to buy, including two pairs of black platform slides and one pair of hot-pink leather strappy heels. It seemed a shame not to buy anything, so I did get the snakeskin mules (they were on sale for thirty dollars, after all), promising myself that I would return them tomorrow, after I spent one night at my house wobbling around on the heels. I had some doubt that I could wear them without welcoming a gaggle of blisters and the soreness of scrunched toes. Though, they *did* look incredible, and I do suffer from recurring shoe delusions (i.e., that shoes that are horribly uncomfortable by design will somehow magically transform themselves into comfy, feet-friendly wear simply because I look fabulous in them). These same delusions in the past have led me to buy shoes that I can't traverse the shoe section of a department store in but believe will carry me satisfactorily through a three-hour wedding reception.

"Those shoes will be perfect for Friday night," Diane said.

"What's Friday?"

"Don't tell me you forgot."

"Forgot what?"

"The Fireman's Ball?"

"Oh no," I said. "No. No. No."

There's no way I could go now.

"So what if he's engaged. If he's indicative of the firefighter species, then there are bound to be others." Diane gave me a sly smile.

"I'm not going." I handed the lady behind the counter my box of snakeskin mules and my credit card.

"Look, you can say no all you want, but we're going to pick you up at seven. End of story."

"I don't know . . ." I said, trailing off as I signed the credit-card receipt.

"Look," Diane said, "how long has it been since the divorce? A year?"

"Six months. A year since the separation."

"And how many guys have you slept with since Brad?"

"One."

"Lauren," Diane said in her best lecturing tone, "ex-boyfriends from college that you meet at a mutual friend's wedding reception after three glasses of champagne don't count."

"They don't ?"

"Of course not. For one thing, you've slept with him before. For another, you woke up hating yourself and swearing off champagne forever."

I couldn't say much to that, since it was true.

"So. What I'm trying to say is that it's been more than enough time for you to get over Brad. The whole point of being single is meeting new men. And, pardon my saying so, girl, but you really, really need to get laid."

I went back to the office and moped for the rest of the afternoon. I made calls, but none of them connected. G left early for a vet appointment for Whiskers, and I was left alone to brood. I didn't know what to make of Diane's words. They stuck with me, because for one, I had been thinking the same thing, but a part of me just didn't know if I felt ready, yet. I'd been married three years, and Brad and I had been monogamous three years before that, and it had been so long since I'd been with a new man, I just couldn't remember how it was done. Of *course* I remember the mechanics, but the idea of getting into bed with someone that you didn't already know how their skin felt against yours—I just couldn't imagine it. The thought of having to bare my body to a new person, well, it was more than a little disconcerting. After you've been in a relationship awhile, you get comfortable with your partner, and your partner gets comfortable with you. There's a certain established rhythm in an established relationship. You already know what it means when they move a little to the left, or when they make that little sound. You know when to do what, because you've done it so often before. And they know how to read you, too. I suppose this is how sex becomes boring to some people, and I guess sometimes it is, but when you think about being outside that safety of familiarity, it can be frightening. Not that I don't want new relationships, I just still have a hard time seeing myself in one. Unless, of course, we're talking about Nick Corona, but then maybe, I thought, maybe I had fixated on him because I knew it wouldn't be possible to have him (regardless of whether he was single). I considered that for about a half second before I dismissed it completely.

Nah. It was unadulterated, old-fashioned lust, I reasoned, plain and simple.

Six

I fear I have failed to mention that for bridal consultants there is a worse thing than a psycho bride.

And that's an indecisive bride.

As I watched Darla pick up one gown and then another, hemming and hawing, stuck in an infinite circle of debating the merits of alençon lace, Chantilly lace, and guipure lace, I wondered if there was a way I could break one of the plastic hangers and slash my wrists with it.

"I think the Empire waist makes me look too tall," Darla whined, doing a twirl before the three-way mirror. "But then again, maybe the drop waist makes me look too short."

Both were lies.

Darla looked gorgeous in every single dress she'd tried on (approximately twenty). She could be a wedding-dress *model*, I thought sourly.

What had gotten into me? Darla hadn't so much as mentioned the night before (and she had every right to be angry, finding me flirting with Nick). I should be relieved, not grumpy.

"I liked the first one," I ventured, hoping to move her toward a decision. We had only been standing in the dressing room for a mere four hours. For a woman who was so incredibly busy, she sure could waste a lot of time in front of a mirror. As soon as I thought it, I felt guilty for seeming so mean. What was *with* me today?

"The first one?" she questioned. "Hmmm, maybe. . . . If only I didn't have that stupid conference in New Orleans this weekend, I could shop through Sunday."

I kicked myself mentally again for agreeing to come along. Of course, I had to, because this was a special, super-rushed order (given she needed it in three weeks, which would have been impossible, except I had a nice connection with the owner of this shop, who would do it for a not-so-modest fee). I feared what would happen when we managed to move on to veils and shoes. That would take another week at this rate—a week we didn't have, especially with Darla rushing off nearly every week on one business trip or another.

"I think I'm going to try on the A-line dress again," she said, picking up the dress she had tried on six times.

The saleswoman standing next to me let out a long, mournful sigh.

Once I extricated myself from the Purgatory of Fine Bridalwear, the rest of the week sped by in what I can only call welcomed inactivity. I managed to make progress on Darla's florist and caterer, and there were no looming catastrophes, no bickering couples, just the usual routine.

When Friday night arrived, I was feeling more and more confident that a night out was exactly what I needed. I had been feeling run-down lately, and it had been so long since I'd dressed up and gone out, I was finding myself even looking forward to it. And that had nothing at all to do with the fact that Nick would be there, I reasoned. Nothing at all. Remember, I don't like hunky, himbo types. Really.

I did wear the high-heeled mules (at Diane's strict orders) and a slinky, strapless silver number. (If you must know, a modified bridesmaid's dress. I often feel it's necessary to prove that you *can* indeed wear the things again.) This was only the third outfit I tried on, which I considered a good omen, because once you get to the fifth, you know you're going to have a terrible-clothes day. After the fifth, the part of my brain that understands that plaids don't go with stripes just shuts off completely (in frustration with the pathetic lack of selection in my closet). I get so disgusted by that point that I start digging in the back of my closet and pulling out clothes that I stashed back there for a reason (a tear in the left thigh or a skirt that I'm too fat now to fit into), which only causes more frustration. I end up in a downward fashion-faux-pas spiral with a bedful of discarded clothes, and the conviction that no clothes on this earth could be made to fit my irregular body.

So I considered myself lucky to find this dress before the fifth try-on, and found myself feeling pretty good about how I was looking (an unusual thing, let me assure you). My hair, for once, was only mildly disappointing, instead of horribly frightening. It actually resembled ringed curls (not exactly, but as close as my hair gets). I didn't have one blemish on my face that didn't hide neatly under concealer, and I even had a new plum shade of lip gloss, which other than being on the slightly too-shiny side, I thought was very becoming.

Diane and Robert came to pick me up, and even Robert's not-so-subtle attempts at making me feel like a third wheel didn't work (though he made of point of sighing and rolling his eyes and generally making it clear my presence was decidedly unwelcome).

Luckily—or unluckily—the drive to the ball wasn't long. We arrived all too quickly at the auditorium on the University of Texas campus. Outside, there was a mix of tuxedos and suits, and tons of women in sequins and seemingly endless variations of the black cocktail dress.

"I'm not feeling so good," I whispered to Diane. It wasn't a lie. My stomach felt like it had eaten itself from the inside out and was now at work on my small intestine.

"You're being ridiculous," Diane said. "We're going to have a great time."

Robert coughed. I scowled at the back of his head.

"You look fab, and I'm not just saying that," Diane said, turning around to face me.

Robert coughed again. I could swear he was doing it on purpose. I was tempted to thump him on the back of the head, but managed to restrain myself. It was clear that if I asked to be taken home now, Robert would never let me hear the end of it.

I let out a long breath and got out of the car. I wobbled a little on the uneven concrete (I don't think it was the shoes, but then they were a little unbalanced, as the heels were narrow and sharp). I steadied myself and followed Diane through the front door.

Inside, the auditorium's high sweeping ceilings and low light, its regal lines and distinctly curved walls, reminded me why it was one of the best places in Austin to hold a wedding reception. It didn't make a bad setting for a fireman's ball, either, I had to admit. Rounded tables filled the main room, and at the front was a large space cleared away for dancing. A jazz band played, now and again slipping into renditions of modern songs.

For a split second, I was glad I came.

Then, I saw him.

Nick, of course. In a tuxedo. And I thought he made firefighters' suspenders look good.

He was standing to the left of the dance floor, talking to another man in a tuxedo, and was making that man laugh. With much effort, I looked away.

"Why don't we go see where our table is?" Diane said.

"Good idea," I answered, until I realized that would bring us closer to Nick Corona, who stood at the edge of the groups of tables.

Since I couldn't very well run for the exit without attracting undue attention, I had no choice but to follow Diane and Robert. I decided to walk behind Robert, hoping that he would hide me with his girth (which, I noticed, had expanded a bit since the last time I saw him—it seemed that as Diane got thinner, Robert got fatter).

"Here it is, number six," Diane said, indicating a table roughly six feet from Nick. I prayed silently he would move out to the dance floor, or to the bar—anywhere but here.

"I don't understand," Diane was saying. "Where's Lauren's place card?"

I tore my eyes from Nick long enough to see that something was wrong.

"It's there," Robert said, pointing.

"No, that says 'Elsea.'"

"Let me see," Robert grumbled, exasperated.

As the two fought over how to read place cards, I noticed with growing dread that the round table was quickly filling with other couples. I did a quick count and realized there would be no room for me.

Just as I was about to say something, Nick intervened.

"Is there a problem here, Councilman?" Nick asked politely. "Something I can fix?"

I felt my heart sink.

"Our friend doesn't seem to have a seat for dinner," Diane explained.

By now, I had no choice but to step out from behind Robert and show my face.

"Lauren!" Nick said, surprised.

My stomach flipped. He had remembered my *name*.

Then, almost immediately, an inner voice said, *Of course he did, stupid. You're planning his* wedding.

"Why don't you come sit at my table? We've got room."

"Oh, I couldn't."

"No, really. I insist."

So, that's how I found myself sitting at the table with Nick, a fire-fighting woman named Jan and her husband, and a state representative and his wife. There wasn't, I decided, a hole big enough in the ground that could swallow me.

I decided I would be fine if I could just not look at Nick, which was decidedly difficult, since he was sitting right next to me.

Deep breaths.

Deep, long, deliberate breaths.

The waiter brought bread, and another filled up our wineglasses. I gulped down half a glass before I realized what I was doing and deliberately slowed down.

I attempted to join in the conversation with the state representative, who was talking to Jan, the redheaded firewoman, about the problems with keeping up his horses at his ranch in Blanco County.

I didn't know much about horses, or ranches, so I was at a bit of a loss. Still, I tried valiantly to listen.

Then the state representative's wife told him to stop talking about the horses, and turned to ask me what I did for a living, and suddenly I was the focus of the table's collective attention.

The women couldn't get enough of hearing about my wedding stories. The husbands at the table, predictably, looked thoroughly bored with the subject, although I even got a grudging laugh from them, when I told about some of the more outlandish ceremonies I'd put together. Nick, however, seemed to be unusually interested in what I had to say, because throughout the time I spoke, I could feel his eyes on me. Unnerving, to say the least. Even when I stopped talking, I still caught him staring and could feel my face flush. My hand went subconsciously to my hair—surely it must be sticking up somewhere. Why else would he be staring?

"That's a lot to be responsible for," Nick said, suddenly, startling me.

"Well, not like saving people's lives," I felt the need to point out.

Nick just shrugged.

"Lives aren't worth living without good relationships and celebrations," he said. "Besides, somebody's got to look after the details, since so many people can't do it themselves."

It took me a minute to realize he wasn't poking fun at what I did for a living. On the contrary, he seemed to approve. Not just approve. He *understood.*

That was a first. Brad couldn't tell other people about my job without a patronizing little laugh. Brad thought I did wedding planning because I liked flowers and lace. He didn't understand about helping people tie up loose ends, or the patience required for putting together a huge orchestration of satin, flowers, and music.

The main course came, and I felt relieved to focus on my food, which gave me a much-needed distraction.

Nick seemed like a man who chose his words carefully. Unlike Brad, Nick waited until he had something smart or relevant to say before opening his mouth.

I was beginning to suspect Nick was no himbo at all, which was a very disconcerting thought altogether. Himbos were so easy to dismiss out of hand.

• • • •

Midmeal, I excused myself to go to the bathroom. I really needed to see what my hair was doing—it must be something spectacular to keep Nick's interest. Jan, the redheaded firewoman, followed me.

"I think we may have to move our table closer to the fire extinguisher," she said to me, as I reapplied lipstick at the sink.

I felt slow.

"What are you talking about?"

"Oh, I think you know."

I did?

"The way Nick's been looking at you, I don't think there can be any doubt."

I laughed nervously.

"My hair can be distracting," I said.

"I don't think it's your hair he was looking at, sugar," Jan replied.

OK. Something was most certainly wrong here. Calendar-worthy hunks did not find me attractive. What alternate universe had I slipped into, anyhow? This had to be just a typical case of groom's panic syndrome (GPS), where most engaged men start psyching themselves out over the old "I'll never sleep with anyone else again and won't be able to stand it" fear. A man wrapped up in that sort of panic could find a lamp attractive.

It was time, obviously, for me to leave.

I skirted the dance floor on my way back to the table, attempting to think up excuses why I'd have to leave immediately, when someone grabbed my wrist and gave it a yank.

The heckler. The one who had given Nick such a hard time on those calls. The guy who'd sung "Here Comes the Bride" when poor Nick had extracted the groom from the trees. I'd almost forgotten about him.

And now he had me by the hand and was swinging me around the dance floor, with little concern for the integrity of my joints.

"Stop . . ." I sputtered, trying to get my arm back.

"You don't like the way I dance?" the heckler asked, tugging me close. He smelled like beer and sweat.

"I don't want to dance," I said, trying to free myself, but the more I struggled, the more he tightened his grip. He was as tall as Nick, only a bit heavier and thicker.

"But you *need* to dance," he slurred. "You need to loosen up."

"Let me go," I said, trying to remain calm. Yelling never works with drunken hecklers. His eyes were red and watery, and I suspected I could get a contact buzz just from the alcohol content in his breath.

"Looshen up, honey," he stuttered, wriggling against me.

That was it. I could only take so much, and at this point, extreme measures were called for. I aimed my heel for the interior of his left foot and connected with bone. He jumped back with a yelp.

"Christ!" he sputtered, hopping on one foot. "Whaddaya go and do that for?"

"Because you asked for it," Nick said, stepping between us. He put a hand on the man's shoulder. "It's time for you to leave."

"Stay out of this, Nickie," the heckler growled.

"Jay, why don't you go home and sober up?" Nick retorted, his whole body tense.

"Here you go with the good-brother routine," Jay the heckler spat.

"No, it's the sober-brother routine," Nick replied, his voice cold.

Brothers? These two were brothers?

I looked from one man's face to the other, and saw a superficial resemblance. Their personalities were so starkly different, however, I couldn't imagine them growing up in the same household.

I watched as Jay's face flushed red with anger. Jay wiped his lip, contemplating, no doubt, hitting Nick in the face. Another man touched Jay on the shoulder then, and said, "Let's go, man, the bar's out, anyhow."

Jay waited a beat or two in silence.

"Yeah, this party is dead," he said after a minute, looking at Nick.

"I'm so sorry," Nick said, after his brother limped away. "Are you really all right?"

"Fine," I said, moving back from his hands, which were on my shoulders.

"Jay is a good man when he's sober, but sometimes he just gets out of hand. I really am sorry."

"That's OK," I said, unable to think of anything relevant to say.

A rather tipsy couple nearly collided with us then, and I realized that Nick and I were standing together almost in the middle of the dance floor, looking a bit out of place since we were standing still and everyone around us was moving. Nick noticed, too.

"Want to dance?" Nick asked. "We should, for our own safety," he added, a tentative smile tugging at the corners of his mouth.

I looked up at Nick's face, fully intending to refuse.

But when I opened my mouth, I said "Yes" instead of "No" and took his hand.

What was one harmless dance, anyhow?

Nick didn't know the steps. At least, not like Brad knew the waltz (Brad did everything with precision), but Nick had something better than expertise. He had confidence. He put a firm hand on my lower back, grasped my fingers, and steered me deftly into the crowd.

"You're not so bad at this," I said, surprised. I was acutely aware of the light pressure on my back, and the solid way he gripped my hand.

"What? You thought a rough-around-the-edges guy like me couldn't dance?"

"Well, you didn't seem the waltzing type."

"I will take that as a compliment," he said, drawing me closer.

Still, I reminded myself, it was just an innocent dance. There was nothing going on here.

All I had to do was ignore the faint scent of Nick's aftershave, the feel of his breath against my neck, the fact that I was so close to him that I could reach up and touch my nose to his chin.

"I have to admit, you've really surprised me," Nick said, startling me out of my aftershave-induced haze.

"How's that?"

"You're feisty."

"Feisty?" I wasn't so sure that was a compliment.

"I don't know many women who can hobble my brother with one kick."

"Obviously, you haven't met many wedding planners."

Nick laughed, a deep, warm sound. The hairs on the back of my neck stood on end.

I looked up and met his eyes, and for a moment we just stared at each other, and for a split second I had trouble remembering why I had reservations about dancing with him. Then, after another second or two, I was having trouble remembering much of anything at all.

Dumb, I know.

What can I say?

I'm a *wedding planner*. I'm particularly susceptible to romantic drivel.

And, suddenly, it hit me like the maxed-out balance on Brad's MasterCard.

I wanted Nick to kiss me. To pull me even closer. To take me to some seedy hotel room and have his way with me. Anything. Everything.

And it wasn't a passing fancy, or the idle curiosity you feel when you see Tom Cruise or someone attractive and unattainable, as in what would *that* be like. It was far more than the kind of indifferent desire for something pretty.

I'm talking about the sort of pull that's so strong you're helpless. I'm talking mounds of chocolate or French fries two hours after you've sworn off fat forever. The gleaming, expansive floor of obscenely expensive but so stylish handbags at Saks Fifth Avenue, designer labels that cost half your mortgage. The smell of leather and chrome on a car that costs double the debt of your student loans. That model's body on the billboard, the one you can't ever have, no matter how much plastic surgery you get, or if you have your stomach stitched up, or whether you exercise twenty hours every day.

It's the kind of thing that as an adult you know, logically, you simply cannot have. Because this is life, and you don't always get what you want, and nothing about it is fair.

But this doesn't stop your inner brat from whining, "But . . . I *want* it."

And what can you say to that?

Reluctantly, I pulled back from Nick.

"I've got to go," I said. Inside, my brat was throwing a tantrum, a full-out, fists-against-the-carpet fit. I felt like doing that right now: throwing myself on the floor and crying.

"Go? You sure?" The look in his eyes said he knew for a fact that I didn't.

"Positive."

"Want me to drive you home?" he asked.

"*No,*" I said too quickly—before the inner brat could respond first.

"You sure you don't want to stay?" Nick asked.

That was a question I didn't even want to consider.

"I should go," I repeated firmly, taking a step away.

"Wait," Nick said, catching my arm. "How can I reach you, you know, in case I have a pressing wedding-etiquette question?"

"Darla has my number," I said, gloomily. "But, here's my card if you want it." I handed over a Forever Weddings card with my name on it. And it's not what you think. It's my duty to be available to the bride *and* the groom. I couldn't very well keep my work number a secret. And no, I didn't write my home number on the back.

Nick looked at the card a moment, and then slipped it into his pocket.

"You are in so much trouble, there isn't even a word for it," Diane said, shaking her head. Robert, who was sitting next to her in the front seat, snickered.

"I didn't do anything," I protested.

"Yet," Diane amended.

"I don't recall you saying anything when Nick asked me to sit at his table," I said, sullen.

"You're right, I should've asked the mayor and his wife to move down so there'd be room for you."

"I'm just saying . . ."

"That you had a fine time, and don't have one regret."

"I don't want to talk about it."

"That's code for: I'm in big trouble."

"No, it's code for: Shut up."

"Whatever you say."

•   •   •

I woke up the next morning with the bitter certainty that I would die miserable and alone. Diane and Lily would be the only two people at my funeral. And my sister would arrive late, because she's never on time for anything. The pastor would give a generic speech, because I don't go to church except on Christmas Eve and Easter (and weddings, of course, but do those count?), and Diane would cry a little and would say how she tried desperately to help me meet single men.

"If only she hadn't gone lusting after her clients," Diane would sob, right before she would have to leave early to pick up her three beautiful daughters from soccer practice. Robert, of course, wouldn't have the decency to even show up at my funeral, since it would be on a Sunday in November when the Cowboys would be playing.

I poured myself a bowl of cornflakes, feeling like I was the unluckiest and most pitiful person on the planet. The cereal tasted soggy and stale at the same time. I almost cried, thinking how I missed those Saturday mornings when Brad and I were first married, and how he would fix his famous scrambled eggs and cheese, and I would wake up to the smell of bacon and the sound of it sizzling on our stove. He would come in with a heaping plate, saying, "You're going to need your strength today if you're going to spread joy and love for today's lucky couple."

I would frown at him, of course, because he'd be making fun of me. But there were rare times like that when I could pretend he was the perfect husband, because no one brings you breakfast in bed on a Saturday unless they love you, right?

I managed to dress (rather sloppily for me: choosing slacks over a skirt, which I rarely do on a Saturday), and I dragged myself to my car. This wedding was small (at sixty-five people) and there weren't any acrobatics or extreme sports on the agenda, so I felt certain we wouldn't need to call Nick Corona, which I reluctantly admitted was a good thing, since I was having trouble keeping my inner brat in line. She was being particularly loud on Saturday, whispering things like it was all right to be bad, and she was tired of being good, and why was it that other people did rotten things all the time and didn't care, but that I always had to do the right thing?

She could say these things with ease, of course, because she didn't have to face Guilt afterward. That's something only Grown Up Me dealt with. I imagined my inner brat looked something like Pippy Longstocking, only her hair was brown instead of red.

I went through the pre-wedding preparations wearing my self-pity like a shield. I imagined I exuded the aura of a long-silent-suffering Anna Karenina, but after the fourth person asked me if I was coming down with something, I decided maybe the act was working a little too well and tried to be a bit more upbeat. It didn't help that the wedding went perfectly, without the appearance of psychotic ex-girlfriends or fistfights among the groomsmen.

On a normal day, I would have been extremely pleased by everything, because you rarely have a perfect wedding (without so much as a melted cake top or half-wilted flowers). It should have been a moment of pride and accomplishment for me, but I felt only envy and sourness. *Why should they look so happy?* I thought. *What makes them so worthy of this perfect wedding?*

Then again, Brad and I had a perfect wedding.

Textbook-perfect.

Six bridesmaids, six groomsmen, in the lofty, stain-glassed cathedral church where Brad's parents were devoted members. We had pink hydrangeas and white roses at the pews, and I wore sleek satin, strapless, with a cathedral-length sheer veil, and tried not to cry tears of happiness as I walked unsteadily down the aisle, because after so many other weddings, it was finally, *finally,* happening to me.

When I got up to the altar, Brad had sent me one of his sharp smiles and said, "Is it too late to run for the fire exit?"

I thought he was kidding, so naturally, I laughed. At the time, I admired his uncanny ability to break the tension and put me at ease. Only later, I realized he was half serious.

I decided I should visit my mom, because I wouldn't be able to wallow in self-pity for very long there, and no matter what your relationship is with your mother, when you're feeling low and run-down, sometimes you just want the comfort of knowing that somebody really does care about you (even if they show it in peculiar ways). This should also tell you exactly how low I was feeling, because visiting Mom was a last resort for me.

When I got there, Lily and Mom were hugging in the kitchen, and Mom was crying.

"What's going on?" I said, unable to figure out why they were hugging if they were fighting (as they never did anything but fight, I couldn't imagine any other scenario). Besides, this wasn't just any hug. This was a bone-crushing, wrinkles-be-damned hug.

"Oh, my other child!" Mom said, turning toward me and hugging me, too. "It's so nice to have everyone together."

I looked at Lily, but she shrugged.

"Mom, what's happened?" I said, pulling back.

"Your sister is finishing her women's-folklore thesis this year," Mom said, wiping bright tears from the corners of her eyes. "And . . . and . . ."

"And?"

"And I'm dedicating it to her," Lily finished for Mom, who was blowing her nose loudly into the corner of her cloth apron (a faux pas I'd never dreamed I'd see from Mom).

"Tell her what the title is," Mom said.

Lily sighed. "'The Maternal Spirit as Eternal Life Force: A Study of Strong Mother Figures and the Legacy They Create in Their Daughters as Seen in Central American Folklore.'"

"Wow," I said, still puzzled.

"A lot of people dedicate these papers to their mothers or to Mother Earth," Lily explained. "I'm doing both."

"Isn't it wonderful?" Mom said.

Needless to say, I didn't get the comfort I was looking for from Mom. I couldn't even cash in on being the "good daughter," since Lily had temporarily dethroned me. I didn't understand what was happening. Nothing was as it should be. I felt all disjointed and out of sorts.

"It's because you're turning into a hoochie-mama," Diane announced. "Honestly, I didn't think you had it in you."

"What do you mean?"

"You know exactly what I mean. You. Him. I believe 'home wrecker' is the correct term."

"Technically, there's not yet a home to wreck. . . ."

"See? You *are* thinking about it."

"I *am* not. I wouldn't *do* that. I was just making a point. . . ."

"Uh-huh. Sure. I believe psychologists call that denial."

"If you say it isn't a river in Egypt, I won't be your friend anymore."

"Ouch."

Seven

"Where have you been?" This was G, tapping her foot on the carpet before my desk, poised with her hands placed firmly on her hips.

I looked at my watch. It said 8:30 A.M. I watched the second hand move, so I knew the battery still worked. I looked back at G. She was never in the office before 10 A.M. on Mondays. In fact, she was never in the office before 9:30 A.M. on *any* day. This could only mean bad news.

"Uh, traffic was terrible," I said, giving a weak smile. I should have reminded her that I had been at a wedding on Saturday, but instead I just kept quiet, hoping whatever storm brought G to my desk would soon blow over.

"Didn't you get the message I left for you on your answering machine?"

I shook my head. I rarely checked my answering machine these days. It had become so depressing hearing that computerized voice saying, "No new messages." Every time I heard it, it sounded like the machine was getting more resentful. It might as well have been saying, "No new messages, loser," with its tone being what it was. So I had just stopped checking it.

G exhaled loudly and looked to the ceiling.

"*Modern Wedding* called," G said. "They want to do a piece on us."

I was silent, which seemed to infuriate her even more.

"*Modern Wedding. The* national magazine! The most widely read bridal magazine in America! They. Want. To. Profile. Us." G had her hands on the arms of my chair and was shaking it.

"That's great," I said, showing about a tenth of the level of excitement G felt the situation merited.

" 'That's great'? That's all you have to say? This is the break-through we've been looking for!"

I hadn't realized I had been looking for a breakthrough.

"Do you realize what this might mean?"

A raise? I hoped.

"This will raise our profile to a national audience," G said. "We'll be able to expand, and perhaps even hire more consultants. It means more clients!"

It means the same salary. Inwardly, I groaned.

"We've got to prepare," G said, giving me a list of things I needed to do before Friday, when the reporting crew planned to arrive.

Correction, I thought. *More work, same salary.*

Among the chores G assigned me were: cleaning the carpets, the windows, and the staircase banister, repapering the walls in the first-floor bathroom, reorganizing our scrapbooks, photo books, and library, phoning our best clients and setting up interview times for them, making hair and nail appointments for G and one grooming appointment for Whiskers. As far as I could tell, the only preparation G planned to do herself was rearrange her desk (specifically replacing her stack of *Cat Fancy* magazines with a dozen issues of *Modern Wedding*).

Now, the waxing of the floor in the main foyer was one thing. And the wallpapering of the bathroom. And the rearranging of the library. You might argue that it somehow fit into my job description (I was Forever Wedding's Junior Bridal Consultant and Assistant to Gennifer Douglas). But stuffing Whiskers (who has very sharp claws and is very spiteful) into a cat carrier and taking her to the groomer's, well, I have to say that was worse than anything G had ever asked me to do. G also asked me to pick up the cat, who in my absence had nearly taken out the eye of one of the groomers. (He charged me a hundred-dollar fee for the hassle and threatened me with a lawsuit if I ever brought Whiskers back again.)

Whiskers, for her part, hissed at me, and then busied herself gnawing on the pink bow the groomer had tied around her neck. She looked like a giant powder puff (she had obviously been fluff-dried), and I couldn't help but snicker a little, which Whiskers heard. She gave me one of her evil-cat looks, but I didn't much care.

When I brought Whiskers back to the office and set her free, she bounded straight for a chair and began licking her fur maniacally (in an effort to get the poofiness under control). She stretched her claws into the seat of the chair, and I noticed the groomer had painted them red (at least I hoped that was nail polish and not blood).

"There's my little angel," G cooed, in her most irritating baby voice. Whiskers didn't appreciate it either, apparently, because she flattened one ear to her head and looked disdainfully to one side. "Oh, don't be mad at Mommy," G said, and then carried on with some more nonsense. I couldn't stand to hear the rest. I much preferred wallpapering the bathroom.

When Friday came, I was still trying to remove the wallpaper glue from my fingers, which seemed to be a permanent addition to my skin. (I was slowly shedding it, in tiny feathered strips.) I felt like a human lizard, with a lizard's sticky claws, and while I didn't try it, I suspected I might be able to climb the walls. The dried glue made it difficult to do my work, because my fingers were constantly picking up unwanted pieces of paper and sticking to the keys of my computer's keyboard.

The morning of the much-anticipated visit, G asked me to prepare tea for our guests (hot tea served in G's best china, which she brought to work just for this occasion). She wanted to show them Southern hospitality (Texan style), which meant that we were also to have jalapeño scones from the bakery down the street. (I didn't know for sure, but I could guess G planned to pass them off as her own.) Making tea proved difficult with my sticky hands. I kept walking off with teabags attached to one or another of my fingers. I'm not sure why G had her heart set on hot tea, given that the traditional Texan beverage is iced tea (and it was almost July, for goodness' sakes), but for some reason she insisted on using her china. (She wanted an excuse to tell the writer how many generations it had been in her family, no doubt.)

The writer and photographer were late. They had told G they would be there at 11:30, but 11:35 came, then 11:45, and still no sign of them. G's nerves were so frayed, she actually snapped at Whiskers, who looked startled, and then resolved, as she slunk from the room (I assume to leave G a gift under *her* desk). The delay forced me to put the kettle back on, because despite all my best efforts to keep the tea warm, it was quickly becoming iced tea in the cool, air-conditioned kitchen.

When a knock came at the door, G jumped up from the Queen Anne chair in the lobby and sprinted toward the foyer. From my position in the kitchen, I heard a muffled exchange, and then G calling my name in undisguised annoyance. I wiped my hands (which were now wet *and* sticky) on a paper towel, but only succeeded in covering my palms with lint. Unthinking, I swiped them across my skirt, but as it was black and fitted, it soon became covered in white bits of paper-towel lint. Trying to pick them off only added more, and so I quickly gave up.

I turned the corner toward the lobby and expected to see per-haps a delivery person, or even a MOB (they drop by unexpectedly on occasion), but instead saw Nick Corona standing there, look-ing a bit uncertain and out of place in his jeans and his firefighter's red suspenders. He seemed stiff, as if he didn't want to move for fear of knocking into the large array of knickknacks (crystal and otherwise) that G had strewn about the place for the *Modern Wedding* photographer's benefit.

"Hi," Nick said, clearing his throat. He seemed distinctly uncomfortable, but then G was staring at him with almost out-right hostility. "I know this is short notice, but I just got off my shift, and I thought you might like to grab some lunch."

"She most certainly does not," G said before I could answer. "Lauren, I told you that you were not to have personal visitors dur-ing the workday. And today of all days!"

"It's not, uh, all personal," Nick said quickly. "I am in Darla Tendaski's wedding."

"Darla? Our Darla?" G said, realization dawning. She looked at me, and I nodded knowingly.

"You must forgive me," G gushed. "I didn't know who you *were.* Of course you can speak to Lauren. I'm sure you have lots of questions for her. Too many people overlook how *important* grooms are in the orchestration of the perfect wedding. Unfortunately, now is not the best time, my boy. We were expect-ing some visitors just now. Why don't you and Lauren schedule a time to discuss, uh, the issues that concern you."

Nick looked a little baffled (G's violent and erratic mood

swings often cause that reaction in people). "But I'm . . ." he began.

"Oh, no need to give excuses," G ran on. "I know more grooms want to take an active role. You don't need to explain."

"But . . ." Nick started.

"I'm very sorry," I said, figuring that the sooner I got him out of here, the better off we'd all be. G had wandered away from us to look out the front window, but she was straining to overhear, I knew. "If you and Darla would like to talk about the wedding, I'm free for lunch on Monday."

"Well, er, I was hoping to talk about something else," Nick said. I willingly ignored the innuendo. "How about tomorrow?"

"I have two weddings tomorrow," I said, which was true.

"What time are they?"

He was being unusually persistent, I thought. I was beginning to think he might be one of those overly aggressive grooms.

"One is at noon. The other at 6:00 P.M."

"Why don't I tag along for the second? You know, to see how you work?"

I hesitated. I didn't know if I needed that kind of distraction (and he was most certainly a distraction—even with him just standing in the same room I was having a hard time focusing my thoughts).

"What a marvelous idea," G said, making the decision for me (also confirming the fact that she had overheard every word). "And tell Darla she's more than welcome to come, too." G looked at me. "Lauren!" she barked. "Don't just stand there like a ninny. Go and get this young man an invitation so he knows where to meet you."

Feeling more than a little unsure, I went and fetched an invitation for him. He took it from me, and smiled. "See you tomorrow, then," he said cheerfully. (Perhaps a little too cheerfully. I had never known a groom who was so enthused about wedding planning, and that scared me.)

G shooed him out the door (as only she can), and within a half second he was outside on the porch (probably wondering why the invitation I handed him had sticky fingerprints on it, no doubt).

I didn't have time to think much about this new development, since not five minutes later, another knock came at the door. This time, it was the photographer and writer from *Modern Wedding*. The writer, a woman who looked quite a bit like G, only a little younger, with brown hair instead of white, seemed extremely well put-together (so much so, one might be justified in calling her prissy). She was wearing what looked to be a Chanel suit, or a very close imitation, and shiny patent-leather pumps, and large, heavy gold bangles on her wrists. She smelled overwhelmingly of some potent (and no doubt expensive) perfume, and because her nose turned up at the end and she liked to stand with her head tilted slightly backward, she looked a little like a prig. The photographer, however, I liked immediately. He was shaggy, tall, and lanky, nearing forty or forty-five, with an unfashionably unkempt mustache. He wore a worn and spotty baseball cap along with jeans (frayed at the cuffs) that looked to be splattered either with paint, or perhaps peroxide. This was obviously a man who wouldn't care that I had tiny white fuzz balls all over my skirt. He smiled at me, and I smiled back.

G, recognizing what she thought might be a kindred spirit in the younger woman, immediately set to work on ingratiating herself into the writer's good graces, simultaneously ignoring the disheveled photographer.

"Please come in and visit with us," G said, extending her hand. "I am Gennifer Douglas, owner of Forever Wedding, and I'm so glad you're here."

The writer reluctantly took G's hand, shaking it limply and

then dropping it quickly. "Jules Evermore, *Modern Wedding.* This"—she lifted an indifferent hand in the direction of the photographer—"is Larry."

"Er, how do you do," G said, sparing him little more than a distracted glance. She turned to me as if I was an afterthought. "And this is Lauren Crandell, my assistant."

"Pleasure to meet you, Lauren," Larry said, taking hold of my hand and shaking it vigorously. I don't think he even minded the paper-towel lint. I smiled back at him. Jules Evermore simply gave me a nod, but didn't extend her hand (of this I was secretly glad, because I would have hated to see her nose wrinkle at the touch of my sticky palm).

"Would you like some fresh tea?" G asked.

"No, thank you, ma'am," Larry drawled (he had a very heavy East Texas accent). G ignored him, as she was looking expectantly at Jules Evermore.

"No, no, thank you." Jules said, her tight voice leaving no room for much argument. G's face fell. She had really wanted to show off her china. But G recovered quickly, ushering the two into the sitting room, where (in between the knickknacks) she had strategically placed photo albums of past clients. Almost at once she launched into her philosophy of wedding planning ("The bride is always right"), and I almost began to pity Jules Evermore, as I couldn't see how she would manage to get a question in edgewise. After ten minutes, however, Larry had no problem interrupting. He wanted to take a few test shots, he said, using me as a subject in my work area. As G had already dismissed him as unimportant, she agreed it would be a good idea. I wasn't wild about having my picture taken, but I was less enthused about hearing G's speech *again,* and so I was happy to have an excuse to leave.

"Does she always go on like that?" Larry asked as soon as we were out of earshot.

"She's just very excited to have you both here," I said, neatly sidestepping the question. Honestly, she *does* go on like that almost all the time. "She's very eager to make a good impression."

"Oh," Larry said, thoughtful, as he scribbled something in his notepad.

He was a little disappointed in my desk (and I couldn't blame him, because it was pitiful), and when he asked me to show him G's office, I didn't see the harm. He asked me little questions along the way, like how long had I been working for G, and how many weddings had I consulted on, and what were my best experience and my worst (I told him about the parachuting incident, since I figured it was already a matter of public record thanks to the local news). He told me he needed to check the light in the room, and would I mind modeling for him in G's chair so he could make sure his equipment was on the right settings. I said sure, and he snapped a few pictures, talking to me all the while.

It turned out that he was a freelance photographer who worked in the city, and his wife was a professor at the university and they had two kids (eight and fourteen) whom they loved dearly but who were always in trouble. He didn't live in New York, where the magazine was published, but he had done some work for them in the past, and they often called upon him for freelance work.

"It must be nice not to have a boss," I said. Click, click went the camera.

"Most of the time," he said. "At least I know that I've got great job security. I couldn't fire myself."

Click. Click. Click.

"There, I think I've got the settings all right," he said. "Perhaps you should go rescue Jules from your boss's enthusiasm."

G was in the middle of showing Jules one of many photo albums, and Jules was listening in a polite but frigid way, and I noticed that the notebook on her lap was open but she wasn't writing anything in it. Her hand had probably cramped a half hour ago. I told G the photographer was ready to take her picture, and she immediately ordered me to go and find Whiskers (because she felt there wasn't anything as noble as having a long-haired cat poised on the arm of her chair in a portrait). I spent the next ten minutes combing the house, without so much as a single pile of poo as evidence of Whiskers' trail. As a last resort, I took to opening cans in the kitchen, because if there's one sound that can summon the feline, it's the sound of chow soon to be served. Pouting obviously hadn't taken the edge off Whiskers' appetite, because the (still very fluffy) cat came bounding into the kitchen when I was only halfway done opening a can of tuna. I scooped her up (letting her take a good portion of the tuna in the process) and lugged her up the stairs, depositing her into the lap of G.

The cat was still licking pieces of tuna from her whiskers when Larry started shooting. I noticed with annoyance that Whiskers had left a trail of hair on my skirt (which made a terrible addition to the lint). I swept at it furiously, but only succeeded in getting cat hair stuck to my fingers.

Larry ignored the animal, so I assumed he ran into this sort of thing pretty often. Whiskers squirmed relentlessly. It was obvious that, tuna or not, she hadn't forgiven G or me (the cat kept sending me those evil, plotting looks of hers when she wasn't being blinded by the camera's flash). Larry took another few shots and then stopped, saying he had all he needed.

"Don't you think you should get my left side?" G said, tilting her chin in that direction.

For his part, Larry said he had plenty of her left side. G seemed only partially satisfied, and more than a little skeptical of Larry's talents as a photographer (given his appearance, no doubt), but as she didn't want to offend anyone from *Modern Wedding,* she let the matter drop.

"Are you sure you don't want tea?" G said plaintively as the two gathered their gear.

Both declined. Jules Evermore shook G's hand and told her she could probably expect the article to run in six weeks or so.

After the two had left, I wasn't able to accomplish much, between my phone ringing off the hook and G asking an endless stream of rhetorical questions ("Was my hair like this when the pictures were being taken?" and "Was my lipstick even?"). I rushed off to a rehearsal dinner at four, and spent the next two hours herding bridesmaids and groomsmen into their respective places. I didn't get home until nine, and by then I was too exhausted to do much of anything except collapse on my couch and then drag myself off to bed around eleven.

Eight

I didn't have any time at all to think about how I would deal with Nick. Of course, the next morning it was the first thing I thought of when I woke up. I actually came to full alertness sitting straight up in my bed, without so much as the hint of an alarm, my stomach churning. I tried to push the whole worrisome thing out of my head, but it kept sneaking up on me in panic-inducing attacks (in the shower; at the breakfast table, watching New York tourists yell on "The Today Show").

Nick was just another client, I told myself, although not even I was buying it. And Darla, again being out of town, shouldn't matter, either. So why did I feel like I was running around behind her back?

Worst of all, the most urgent concern of the morning seemed to be what I was going to wear, because nothing I tried on seemed nearly good enough, when it really should have been, because, after all, it was only another day of work with another *client*. If I repeated this enough times, maybe I'd come to believe it. I found myself tossing onto my bed most, if not all, of the contents of my closet. I couldn't help it. Every single article of clothing made me look too fat. Or too short. Or too pale. Or too old. Or too (insert undesirable characteristic of your choice here). What happened to the closetful of tasteful, stylish clothes I once thought I had? All that was left were ill-fitting, hideous excuses for outerwear.

Eventually, I settled on a black Banana Republic dress and the slinky snakeskin mules, because that was the only thing I found in my closet that I wasn't embarrassed to be seen wearing in public. Now, I know the etiquette. I'm a wedding planner, remember? I know you're not supposed to wear black to weddings (at least according to tradition, a tradition that was fast becoming obsolete), and that's why I added a silver silk scarf to my outfit (one with a snakeskin pattern similar to my shoes'). So, technically, I wasn't wearing *all* black, and the dress *was* a summer dress, being sleeveless with a hem at my knees. G wouldn't have approved of the shoes, but she wouldn't see them, now, would she? She hadn't been to a wedding in a year ("I've earned my Saturdays off, Lauren," she often said, "and now you have to earn yours").

The fact that I hadn't quite perfected walking in said high-heeled mules didn't dampen my enthusiasm for wearing them. They *did* look incredible, blisters be damned.

I said I was compulsively neat and organized; I never said anything about being practical.

So, I had my outfit together, but I still needed to do something about makeup and hair. Makeup took about a half hour longer than usual, because I seemed to be especially clumsy with my makeup brushes. I kept flinging lavender eye shadow in inappropriate places (my eyebrow, the far corner of my eye, my hairline), and only after several unsuccessful attempts did I get the stuff properly on my lids. Then there was the eyeliner (my recurring makeup disaster). On the first attempt, my liner pencil tip broke, leaving a chunky, smeared mess near my eyelashes, forcing me to use remover which basically took off the liner and everything else (including the eye shadow I had so valiantly fought to get on). On

the second try, a part of my lid repelled the liner with such effi-
ciency that none of it would stick with any kind of thickness
(resulting in a broken, uneven line across my lid).

By this time, my eyes were getting red with all the rubbing of
the tissues, and I began to believe they would soon swell up, making a third attempt at liner pointless. I somehow managed to pull
everything together (or perhaps I gave up; it's hard to say which).
This meant, of course, that I lacked any strength to deal with my
hair, and so I spritzed it with taming conditioner and yanked it
hard into a knot at the nape of my neck. "Stay or I'll let Bobbie
actually have a go at you," I told it sternly.

I told myself as I walked out of the house that the extra hour
spent getting ready had nothing at all to do with Nick. I almost
managed to believe it.

The first wedding went extremely well. But that had very little to
do with me. I was too distracted to pay attention to the things I
normally pay attention to (like whether or not the flowers are in
place before the guests arrive or double-checking to make sure the
organist understands the point at which she should begin playing
the Wedding March). No, I didn't check on either of those things
before the ceremony, and only managed to halfheartedly answer a
few questions from a very anxious maid of honor before the processional music began. I kept staring off into space and twisting
my hands together (acting like a bride myself, but without the reasons for self-absorption), and I kept thinking about what I would
do with Nick (not what I would *do* with him like *that*, but how I
would see to a wedding *and* entertain him).

I was so distracted, I missed an altercation between the bride's
divorced parents, which, according to witnesses, had the potential
to be very ugly, except that it was quashed by a quick-thinking
usher, who broke the two up and sat them at opposite ends of the

pew. Troubleshooting was supposed to be my responsibility, so I felt a little embarrassed that a groomsman interceded for me. Of course, I suppose the morning proved that I could do very little and still oversee a wedding (G would kill me for even so much as implying that consultants sometimes don't make an impact on the Big Day). Still, everyone at the morning reception seemed perfectly happy and content. (Except for the MOB, who kept asking me if I needed a glass of water. "You look a little pale, dear," she kept saying.)

By the end of it, I was feeling a bit guilty, as if I deserved something bad to happen to me for my selfishness and lapse in attention (something small but humiliating, like having a bit of food caught in my teeth the whole of the time I would be talking to Nick). At the thought of that, I whipped out my compact mirror and checked just to make sure. This began a whole series of nervous tics (the rubbing of my nose to make sure there wasn't anything hanging out of it; the constant checks to make sure no bra straps peeked through my sleeveless sleeves; the sprints to the mirror in the ladies' room to make sure there wasn't string or paper stuck to my rear). This lasted all of about an hour (the last hour of the first reception), and then I became too tired to keep up that excessive pace. Besides, I had very little time between the end of the first reception and the start of the second ceremony, and at some point I had to stop worrying about what I looked like so I could start worrying about the possibility of being late.

I must have failed to spend adequate time worrying about being late, because I *was* late, by about twenty minutes, which meant that I arrived only an hour before the start of the ceremony. Very late indeed, by consulting standards. (The caterer, the florist, and the photographer had all arrived *before* me. Very embarrassing.) Luckily, Nick was nowhere to be seen, which meant that I had a little bit of time to do some real work before the true distraction arrived.

Wedding two was supposed to be a relatively simple production. The couple had planned to have the ceremony in the quaint little chapel where the bride's parents were married thirty years before, and the reception that followed would be on the church's rather spacious lawn under a giant white tent. I must admit I am a bit wary of tent receptions, because I haven't always had the best luck with tents or their setup (try two collapsing tent poles, about a dozen uneven sides, and two tent flaps that refused to stay securely out of people's way). But on this particular evening, the tent was already in place when I arrived, along with the tables, the tablecloths, and the chairs (all of which looked very sturdy and well put-together). I waved to Mark Stewart, who stood in the middle of the tent directing his helpers as they graced the tables with his beautiful lilac and violet centerpieces. He smiled back at me and gave me a thumbs-up sign, which I took to mean everything was OK.

I glanced back toward the front of the tent, where the caterers (a mother-daughter team who served a mouthwatering almond-crusted salmon with new baby potatoes) busied themselves setting up the serving tables. A small commotion broke out when the mother of the team realized the daughter had forgotten the tray of hand-rolled bread, but even that minor disruption was quickly solved when the mother dispatched one of her helpers to fetch them.

Everything was so calm and peaceful, I was beginning to think there wouldn't be anything for me to do but entertain Nick when he arrived (a thought that made me more than a little anxious and a little giddy all at once).

That's when I heard a screech from the general direction of the bride's dressing room.

I caught Mark's eye and he nodded at me, as if to say, "Things here are fine, so you'd better go."

I went.

Another, more plaintive wail went up before I reached the dressing room in the chapel (which was actually the Sunday-school room, converted for the day). I knocked frantically at the door, and when no one answered me, I turned the knob and went in, not sure what I expected to see. The bride unconscious on the floor, perhaps? A rabid, psychotic ex-girlfriend of the groom strangling the maid of honor?

I didn't find any of those things.

Instead, the scene looked, well, normal.

The bride was sitting in the corner, wearing her headdress and veil but only a slip and bra, as if she was preparing to get dressed, and her mother was sitting across from her, weeping. (Let me assure you, this is a fairly common scene an hour before a wedding.)

"Look at it!" cried the bride when she saw me, pointing across the room. "It's ruined!" It took me a second to realize what she was pointing at, because at first I thought she meant her mother, but then I realized she had indicated the white lump draped across the loveseat that sat between them. The Dress. Of course.

"What's wrong?" I said, a number of different problems flashing into my mind. Wrinkles. Stains. Loose trains. Broken buttons. Torn lace. Stuck zipper. Severed straps. Too-short hem. Too-long hem. Too-tight waist. Too-big waist.

I will let you in on a little-known fact. Few if any wedding dresses worn down the aisle are entirely pristine and orderly. One can hardly expect so many yards and yards of glaring white fabric to manage to keep themselves spotless on such an important day. Wedding dresses, anyone will tell you, have personalities, and while they are all a little different, they share one common trait: a penchant for self-destruction. More than anything else, you can count on a wedding dress to crumble under the pressure, spitting out an odd thread, loosening a button, or attempting suicide in a far more dramatic way, like hurtling itself toward an oversized, full glass of red wine. It is my greatest wish that someone would decide once and for all that no one is to ever be married in a white dress again, because it would save a good number of brides (and bridal consultants) a fair amount of stress.

In my experience, I had seen quite a number of very weak-spirited wedding dresses fall prey to the usual temptations (smudges of makeup being the most common). I carried a bottle of club soda for this purpose, along with special instant stain-removing towelettes for fine fabrics. I had a sewing kit in my purse filled with fifteen variations of white and off-white threads, and over the last couple of years I had gotten pretty good at stitching torn lace, ripped hems, and severed straps. In any case, my experience has also taught me that brides tend to exaggerate the general condition of their wedding dress when something goes awry (sometimes a pinprick stain of foundation can cause a perfectly reasonable woman to tear off the dress and cry, "It's beyond repair!"). Needless to say, I was fairly confident I could fix the problem.

I went over to the dress and began leafing through the yards of satin, looking for a small stain or tear, taking my time in searching for it, because I thought it might be small enough to miss. In fact, the problem was so large that I passed right over it at first, not realizing that it wasn't part of the initial dress design.

There, in the middle of the front skirt, beginning at the hemline and moving upward, lay a gaping hole larger than my head. The edges of the hole hung frayed and uneven, as if something had chewed its way through the satin. The cloth, I discovered, was also slightly damp.

Before I could ask the bride what had happened, a tiny movement in the corner of the room caught my eye. A scruffy-looking lapdog yipped anxiously once and then fell silent, its small pink tongue poking out of its mouth innocently.

"The dog?" I asked, incredulously, unable to conceive of how the little thing had managed to eat what must have been close to its own body weight in satin taffeta.

The bride nodded solemnly.

"How?" It simply couldn't be possible.

"The dog attacked me," the bride said calmly. "I put it on and the dog attacked me."

"Bunny thought the skirts were drapes," the mother said, as if that explained everything. "I shouldn't have brought him here," she added, growing hysterical. "It's all my fault!"

"Mother!" snapped the bride. "Stop it."

"Yes, stop it," I echoed. The dog yipped once, as if to agree. "Everyone just stop," I added, mostly for the dog's benefit. I had to think before I started to panic. Yes. Think. Think.

I knew where the dress had been bought, and for how much, and that it had been altered very slightly (the straps had been taken in at the sides and the hem had been shortened by an inch and a half, barely anything at all since the bride was very tall). I also knew it would be impossible to have the dress fixed, and that the only hope would be to a) find a means of covering it up or b) get a replacement dress. I looked at my watch. Forty-one minutes until the ceremony. I quickly calculated in my head the time it would take to drive to the closest seamstress (probably twenty minutes) or back to the bridal shop (about thirty, but they closed in five). I picked up the phone in the room and called Sylvia, the owner of the bridal shop, catching her just as she was heading out the door.

I explained the situation hurriedly, having to repeat the fact that a dog *did* eat the dress, which Sylvia took at first to be a joke. Once she understood the gravity of the situation, she put me on hold and ran to check her dress racks. She came back on the line to tell me she had one of the exact same style of dress on the rack in a size 12, the very same size the bride ordered, amazingly (since she usually kept size-16 samples on the floor), and that she would meet me halfway between the dress shop and the chapel at the gas station on the corner of Duval and Forty-fifth streets. "Let's worry about compensation later," she said, adding, "I'll be there in fifteen minutes."

I told the bride and her mother to stay calm, that I was going to get a replacement, and I'd be back in less than half an hour. I sprinted out of the chapel and to the tent, explaining to Mark there was a problem which needed my attention for the next half hour, and that if he needed anything to page me. I told the caterer team the same thing, and then rushed outside, where I ran straight into Nick.

"Hang on there," he said, putting his hands on my shoulders. "You're always running into me. I don't think my toes can take any more abuse."

I managed a weak smile, as I quickly pulled myself back. "Sorry. Dress. Emergency. Got to go. Back soon," I managed to spit out in broken syllables, as I hurried past, leaving him looking a little bewildered.

"What should I do?" he yelled after me.

"Anything you want," I yelled back, jumping into my car and starting it.

I felt bad about leaving him there, especially since he didn't know anyone, but I figured that given his great interest in weddings, he'd manage to find his way around. I didn't give him much more thought. I had a crisis on my hands, and I could only worry about so many things at once.

Sylvia was right on time, pulling into the gas station five minutes after I did, efficiently unloading the giant white garment bag and handing it over.

"Keep this one out of the dog's reach," she said. "And take a picture of the hole—I want to see it."

I stuffed the dress into my backseat and raced back to the chapel. When I pulled up to the back of the church, I glanced around, but didn't see Nick on the lawn, and assumed he had wandered inside the church or into the tent. I slung the heavy dress over one shoulder and ran up the stairs to the church and back to the makeshift dressing room.

It was exactly fifteen minutes until the ceremony.

I knocked once and the maid of honor threw open the door and said "Thank God!" as she helped me carry the dress into the room.

The bride sat where I left her, dressed in a slip and bra, looking a little paler in the cheeks. She brightened slightly when she saw me.

"Will it fit me?" she said, her voice barely giving away a slight tinge of hope.

"It will," I said. "We'll make it fit you."

Ten minutes later we had the dress on her (it had quite a few of those button decorative snaps up the back, and besides, we had to be extra careful not to get any makeup smudges or lipstick on it as we slung it over her head—the fitted bodice made it impossible to step into). The MOB and I managed to pin the straps in place (tucking them in about a quarter of an inch), and the only thing left was the hem. It was, as I expected, one and a half inches too long.

Four minutes until the ceremony.

I dug around in my special emergencies duffel (the larger bag that had such necessities as jumper cables, hand wrenches, and double-A batteries) and pulled out the industrial, fast-drying fabric glue (the superglue of the fashion world). I had the MOB measure out the proper hem length and pin it in place, while I scooted around on my knees, gluing the fabric in place and taking out the stick pins. The bride looked as if she would start crying at any minute, and so I ordered the maid of honor to get her a glass of white zinfandel to calm her nerves.

"Make it two," I called after her. "And bring a straw!" I didn't want any more dress catastrophes.

One and a half glasses of wine later, the bride looked entirely more optimistic.

"Like I said, you look wonderful," I said. "No one will know the difference."

The bride smiled bravely and looked as if she believed me. (I took this as a good sign.)

The FOB (father of the bride) arrived at that moment and tears popped into the corners of his eyes.

"See?" I said, nudging her.

I made my exit, and told her I would take my position by the entrance to the aisle, where I could be handy to straighten out the train and to make sure her hem didn't stick to her shoes.

I went out the back exit, because there wasn't another way to the back of the aisle (except through the front of the church, which seemed an improper route, since it would no doubt now be full of guests). I also wanted to make sure there weren't any stones or branches along the path the bride would walk. The last thing she needed was a sprained ankle.

I hurried forward, bounced up the steps and into the foyer of the church. I scanned the crowd and after a few seconds saw Nick standing by a back pew on the bride's side. An attractive brunette (probably just out of college, if that) was talking to him (no doubt offering him a seat next to her). My suspicions were confirmed when she patted the seat cushion to her right and smiled prettily. It seemed as if he was going to sit, but then he caught my eye and smiled.

God, he was handsome.

And he was coming right for me.

My stomach did a two-and-a-half somersault with a three-and-a-half twist.

"Hi," he said in that sexy voice of his, when he got close enough to be heard.

"Hi," I said, sounding like a nervous fifteen-year-old. I felt like I might as well have had braces again. "Uh, I'm really sorry I left you alone for so long," I said hurriedly, running over any weird silent spaces. "I had an emergency with the bride."

I told him what happened, and he seemed oddly relieved. "Oh, that's all," he said, with a small chuckle. "In my line of work, an emergency usually means something else."

"Like grooms falling from the sky?"

He laughed. I felt giddy. Then almost immediately guilty. Then justified. It was *only* harmless flirting, I told the puritanical part of my brain (the piece that my mom had so carefully crafted with years of disapproving looks).

"Should we sit?" he asked.

"Oh, I never sit at weddings," I said.

"You stand?" he asked, perplexed.

"I'm faster on my feet and besides, it's easier to spot looming catastrophe if I'm standing."

Just then the music started, and we both fell silent, and I hurried off to fix the line of giggling bridesmaids. I sent the flower girl out first. She began tossing clumps of rose petals on the red carpet. I bit my lip slightly (it looked like the six-year-old was being a little too generous with the petals and I feared she might run out halfway down the aisle). I let out a breath when she made it to the preacher, still tossing flowers. I signaled the other bridesmaids when it was their turn to go (I swear no one ever remembers music queues). But I must say I was very proud of them, because none of them walked too fast, which is the number-one problem with bridesmaids. Then, the music swelled, and the congregation stood in anticipation of seeing the bride.

I saw the bride and her father first, of course, and hurried around them to make sure that her train wasn't twisted or tangled (I saw an errant leaf stuck to the back part of her skirt and quickly bent and whisked it away). I must say that my glued hem looked marvelous (at least, it didn't look like it had been glued, which in this case is the very definition of marvelous). The bride looked radiant (her cheeks a little red from the wine, but fetchingly so). I looked down the aisle to the groom, who watched her approach with a kind of reverence and awe reserved only for those men who are truly and utterly in newfound love. I think I must have sighed, because Nick took my hand and squeezed it. If I hadn't been so captivated by the scene, I might have jumped at the contact, but in the context of the moment, it just seemed right.

The pastor spoke a few brief words on the sanctity of marriage and the importance of love in God's great plan, and then he spoke about the two on a very personal level (given that he had known them most of his life) and said some very touching things about how no two people on Earth would be happier. By the time the vows came, half the congregation was sniffling back tears. When the pastor pronounced them man and wife, he didn't need to remind the groom of his first duty. Said groom reached forward, grabbed his bride, and bent her over backward, laying the most passionate, lengthy, and risqué kiss on a new bride that I had ever seen in any wedding, ever. The crowd gasped slightly at the force of it, and then broke out into thunderous applause as the couple finally broke from their lip-lock and stepped back from each other, glancing at the audience with slightly sheepish looks on their faces. I later learned that the young couple had decided not to have sex with each other before their wedding day (inspired by figures such as John Tesh of all people), and the passion they showed had been real, being the evidence of eight months of pent-up frustration and sexual tension.

I realized that Nick was staring at me rather seriously, and I turned to him (waiting for him to tell me I had some awful thing hanging from my chin), but he didn't say anything. It was the strangest moment, because I couldn't figure out why he was staring, but I certainly didn't want him to stop. I suddenly ceased being able to pay attention to anything else, and I think I lost my hearing, too, because no sounds seemed to penetrate the deep, hazy fog that had settled over everything.

I must have been hallucinating, because it appeared as if Nick was coming closer, leaning in, but certainly that couldn't have been the case, because that would mean that he intended to kiss me, which was absolutely impossible.

The wedding procession came through the hall then, breaking the spell, and the bride came between us and gave me a huge hug.

"Thanks so much for everything," she said to me, tears in her eyes. "It went better than I ever dreamed!"

I smiled back at her, truly happy for her. (And even happier that she gave me the credit, to be honest. Look, if I get the blame when things out of my control go wrong, then I can certainly take the praise when they go right, since they so rarely do.)

"Hungry?" I asked Nick, who seemed back to his normal self, without all that gauzy intensity in his eyes (which I must have imagined entirely).

"Absolutely," he said.

"Good, because I know this great little restaurant in a tent. . . ."

• • •

The reception went well (marred only by the unfortunate dropping of two china plates by catering staff), and even the best man's toast turned out only moderately offensive (he proclaimed that he knew exactly where the groom wanted to be right now, and it wasn't sitting in a tent, eating new baby potatoes). The newly married couple seemed to be having a grand time, but after the cake cutting, barely an hour into the gathering, they seemed anxious and impatient (obviously eager to go to their hotel). They didn't last more than a half hour longer before they rushed off into their limo, showered with bird seed and bubbles. I highly doubt they even made it to the hotel before doing the deed. It was a stretch limo, after all.

The cute brunette who had failed to persuade Nick to sit beside her during the ceremony glommed onto him now, hoping to usurp my position as reception guide by telling him what she thought were secrets: "They hadn't had sex before today," she whispered conspiratorially, as if it weren't obvious to everyone by now (even if the best man hadn't made a point of actually spelling it out in his toast). I must admit, I felt a little sorry for the young brunette. All the while she was speaking, Nick looked bored. The poor thing didn't have a chance, but she wasn't going to let a little thing like that keep her from trying. And trying. And trying.

Even I grew tired with her brave but hopeless efforts. Thankfully, Mark Stewart arrived then, giving me an excuse to leave the conversation, which hadn't really included me to begin with. Nick grabbed the arm of my sleeve as I moved to go, saying, "You're not going?"

"I'll be back," I promised him, but the look on his face said he didn't take much comfort in the sentiment. He reluctantly let go of my sleeve.

"How did everything go?" Mark said, looking around at the remnants of salmon on the few plates still dotting the tables. His centerpieces still looked incredible, and I told him so.

"Well, I *knew* the flowers would be perfect," he said, with an exaggerated sigh. "I meant the *other* parts."

"Oh *those,*" I said, playing along. "I had to superglue the bride's hem, but other than that, things went swimmingly. Would you like some cake?"

"No, just my flowers."

I looked around, and saw that in the five minutes I had been standing there, two-thirds of the people still milling about had left. This is inevitably what happens at receptions where there is no open bar.

I helped Mark gather up a few of his less bulky flower arrangements and load them into his car. I almost forgot about Nick, until I looked up and saw him still being badgered by the brunette, who had somehow managed to corner him near the cake table. He shot me a desperate look, and so I felt the need to intervene. Before I got there, however, I was saved the attempt by an older-looking version of the brunette, who insisted they go home. The brunette's mother, perhaps? How embarrassing. The girl turned beet red and mutely turned to follow her mother from the reception. Perhaps she was even younger than I had thought.

"She has band practice tomorrow," Nick said by way of explanation.

"Band practice?" I didn't understand.

"She's a junior in *high school,*" Nick said pointedly. "Now, don't you feel terrible about leaving her to my corrupting influence?"

I smiled and thought he could corrupt me any time he wanted. Oh! Did I really think that? Bad, Lauren. Bad. Bad. Bad.

Better change the subject.

"Do you have any questions for me, er, as far as the wedding goes?"

"Nope."

"No?"

"Well, just one."

"Yes?"

"Would you like to go somewhere and get a drink?"

Nine

Now, I want to tell you that I did know what the right and moral answer to the question was. I still do. No. Of course it's No. With a capital "N." One doesn't go and have drinks alone, late on a Saturday, with an engaged man, no matter how gorgeous he is. Or how funny he is. The answer still should be no. Emphatically No. Definitely not. I knew that. Without a single doubt.

But I said yes anyway.

I told myself the reason I agreed to drinks had nothing to do with the fact that I was wildly attracted to Nick. I managed to convince myself that I said yes because I deserved a drink. Today had been a particularly trying day and if anyone had asked me out for drinks, I would have gone. I *wanted* to be out on a Saturday night, having fun like all the other normal single (er, and attached) people do. I needed to spend the night celebrating a day of work well done (not poring over accounting receipts and worrying over all the little things that didn't go right). In short, I was sorely in need of a good time.

Besides, I counted myself as a mature, normally trustworthy adult who knew her own limits and wouldn't do something stupid just because of a harmless drink or two. I possessed a measure of self-control, after all. It wasn't as if I were a college sophomore at a frat party who didn't have the stomach or tolerance for alcohol. I mean, you couldn't pay me to drink cheap keg beer at this stage of my life. I drank vodka martinis and gin & tonics for goodness' sakes. I liked to think of myself as cosmopolitan. Composed. Centered. Completely in Control.

(Somewhere, I can hear Diane laughing. She's doubled over and can't breathe for giggling so hard.)

So, I guess I'm not usually any of those things. (Not most of the time. OK. OK. Hardly ever.) Sure, I know that *now*. Right at this moment I can see the terrible flaw in my logic (i.e., that I would have believed anything to convince myself that it would be all right to take just one step on the road to temptation, because I wouldn't *actually* go any further). And I must admit that I think things might (even probably would) have worked out better had I *not* had that third and final shaker full of a very pink but very potent beverage. I suppose hindsight is twenty-twenty.

You probably want to know what happened. I don't want to tell you, but I suppose you do deserve to know (having listened to me drone on thus far).

Nick decided it would be silly of us to both drive our cars downtown and fight for parking, and so given that my house was closer to the chapel, he followed me home and let me drop off my car. We rode together in his jeep (a red, open-topped vehicle, which seemed to fit his personality). The fit in the front seat felt a little snug for my taste. (Despite the fact that the stick shift sat between us, it appeared his knee was in constant danger of bumping into mine.) And because the car had no windows or roof, I couldn't shake a growing feeling of nervousness—the dread of a person who knows she always gets caught doing a bad thing no matter how small. (My mom likes to say that there's a "get caught" gene that runs in our family. No Crandell can ever get away with anything, since we always get caught the first time.) Every time we stopped under a streetlight, I thought for sure we'd be seen. (Not that I necessarily thought we were doing anything *that* wrong. Just a little wrong. A little wrong that could look like a big wrong, if taken out of context—although in context, it's not like it looked so good, either, I must admit.) I didn't know when Darla was expected back in town, but I kept expecting to see her at every intersection. I glanced over at Nick, who looked remarkably calm, which was somewhat reassuring and somewhat disconcerting. I couldn't figure out how I felt about the fact that he didn't think we were doing anything out of the ordinary.

We managed to find a space right in the middle of the warehouse district, on the street no less, so hundreds of people saw us arrive. I scanned the crowd but couldn't make out any faces I recognized (although I knew this didn't matter, since I was convinced I'd be found out in some way). We parked in front of Fado's, one of Nick's favorites, he told me, as we squeezed ourselves into the very crowded Irish, oak-paneled bar. It turned out Nick was a soccer fan and came here often to catch the game (the fact that he preferred the sport of Europeans gave him a more sophisticated aura, I thought).

Nick pushed his way up to the bar and came back fairly quickly with our drinks (a move that impressed me, given that in a crowd like that it always takes me a minimum of twenty minutes to get the bartender's attention). In his short absence, the crowd had managed to grow in size, and a wall of bodies seemed to press against us, pushing us toward a corner. I sipped my vodka soda (thinking all the while I should only have one drink, just to be on the safe side).

"Isn't this a fire hazard?" I yelled over the din of voices.

"What?" Nick said, leaning closer.

I repeated what I said. It looked as if he might have laughed, but I couldn't hear a thing. I thought he was saying something, because his lips were moving, but I didn't hear one word.

"What?" I yelled.

"Could be," he shouted, "but most of the department comes here on the weekends, so if a fire did break out, you'd be in a good place."

I nodded. Just as he finished, a man slapped him on the back and shook his shoulder, saying, "Nick, damn you, how are you, buddy?"

The man, a dark, stout, weather-beaten figure, looked as if he could break a man with his bare hands.

"Juan, you devil," Nick said, grasping the man's hand and shaking it firmly, moving half the crowd as he did so. "Juan, meet Lauren," Nick said, turning to me. "Lauren, meet the most worthless firefighter instructor in all Austin."

"Don't believe a word he says," Juan said, giving Nick a playful shove. "This loser is always the last one in and first one out of a fire."

I liked Juan. A lot. But that didn't negate the fact that meeting him made me anxious. Juan must have known Nick was engaged, but he didn't seem at all surprised to find his friend out on a Saturday with a strange woman. I didn't know what I should think about that. Maybe it was because Nick was a good man who didn't do bad things. He probably couldn't go anywhere without women falling all over him, right? Then again, maybe Juan wasn't surprised because Nick was the kind of man who took advantage of all the women who fawned over him. Maybe he went out all the time with women who weren't his fiancée. That thought made me extremely uneasy. I really didn't want to believe that about him. But a part of me kept saying, *Then why did he ask you out for drinks?* And I couldn't come up with a plausible, innocent answer (hard though I tried), because it just didn't feel harmless.

I gulped down the rest of my drink. Call it nerves, or twinges of guilt. All I know is that I needed some serious emotional fortification. And nothing works better than the liquid variety.

Fado's soon became too crowded and too loud. I practically had to scream in Nick's ear to ask if we could go somewhere a bit more subdued (and before you go getting any ideas, like I wanted to get him to a secluded spot, I'll tell you I thought it would be better to go to a place less tightly packed, since any slight move in the crowd sent me straight into him). After just one drink, I still understood that physical contact (of any kind) was probably a bad thing.

We went a few doors down, past Cedar Street and into a new bar near the corner. It had high chairs and tall, round tables along one wall and shorter, square tables on the other, which stretched almost the length of the large, open room. This bar was far less crowded, so we got a seat right away at one of the high tables, and we had enough room that we could sit without our knees touching (a small comfort to my conscience, but a comfort all the same).

The waitress came by and gave us menus, which were filled with a dozen funny-named beverages. Breaking my one-drink resolution (I was simply too nervous to keep that promise), I settled on the Suzie, a spiked pink-lemonade concoction named in honor of a waitress who loved the drink. (It was only later explained to me that the drink was really named in her honor because she had a few too many one night and got a little out of control. No one bothered to warn me that the drinks were so incredibly and deceptively potent until I was on my third. I say this not as a defense, but as an explanation.)

When the waitress put down my first martini shaker of pink Suzie, I poured some into my glass and took a sip. It tasted like nothing more than pink lemonade with maybe a drop or two of vodka (certainly nothing very dangerous, because it tasted so sweet and light). I remember feeling mildly disappointed, even slightly cheated. The drinks were twelve dollars each! It wasn't until I was midway through my second (what harm could there be, I remember thinking, there wasn't anything in them and besides that, I wasn't driving) that I realized the drinks were quite strong after all. At first, I didn't understand. I mean, hadn't I been drinking mostly pink lemonade? Did I really have such a weak constitution?

I remember telling Nick lots of funny wedding-consultant stories (well, perhaps not entirely that funny, but he did laugh), and Nick told me lots of crazy firefighter stories (like once when he burst into a second-story bedroom of a blazing house only to find the couple inside caught in a rather indelicate position and completely oblivious of the house burning down around them). I seemed to be unable to stop laughing. I couldn't remember the last time I found someone so vastly entertaining, and I felt I could talk to him all night (the only danger being ripping a stitch in my stomach).

So, I was a bit distracted and more than a little tipsy when the waitress brought me my third Suzie. I neglected the tiny voice in my brain emanating from the small section, which was still moderately sober, that said "Beware of Hidden Curves: Drink with Extreme Caution" and proceeded to drain the whole thing. As I looked at the bottom of my empty glass, I remember thinking, *Oops.*

And that's probably the last thing I really recall with perfect clarity.

Now, before you go pegging me as somebody with a drinking problem, I want you to know that this kind of thing normally doesn't happen to me. In the span of the last few weeks, I have had two nights where I drank more than I should, admittedly, but I normally don't do that. Honest. And that's not an I-don't-drink-before-five-except-on-weekdays denial. I'm usually the one sipping at the same drink the whole night, marveling at the degree of reckless childishness of the members of my group. You know I hate sloppiness and disorder, and there's no greater means of ensuring sloppiness and disorder than when a person drinks too much, right? Besides, I tend to fall down (usually on the floor) when I drink too much. I did so with such regularity that in college my roommates called me the Toppler. "Weeble-wooble, she always falls down" was the mantra they would chant every time I found myself sitting on my butt in a pool of sticky spilt beer on the frat-house floor. Hmmm. That's probably not helping my "I don't have a drinking problem" argument, is it?

Ahem. Moving on.

Nick, I noticed, had stopped drinking some time ago, a move I found very attractive as a display of adult responsibility (since he was the one who would be driving). In fact, I don't think he had more than two beers in five hours, but my brain was so muddled at that point, I wouldn't even swear to the two.

Now, if you remember, I was wearing very uncomfortable shoes (the high-heeled mules) and I'm sure my feet were throbbing by this point, only I'd had enough to drink to dull almost any unpleasant sensation. The alcohol did not, however, improve my balance, as you might guess. And if you recall, I had a difficult time walking in said shoes when sober. Given the strong pull to the ground I experience when intoxicated, you probably don't need tarot cards to predict what happened next.

Naturally, I fell.

I didn't so much as make it one step from my barstool before landing in an awkward heap at Nick's feet. If I had been a smidgen more lucid, I probably would have been horrifyingly embarrassed, but given my present state of mind, I found the whole situation incredibly funny. To Nick's credit, he didn't tell me I had had enough, or even freeze me with one of those somber, disapproving looks.

Instead, he said, "You fall more gracefully than anybody I know," as he helped me to my feet. The crazy thing is, I think he was serious.

"I've had lots of practice," I said, and then burst out into another round of giggles.

Nick easily pulled me up to my feet, and kept his arm around my shoulders to steady me, but even this didn't seem to help, because for some reason, my left ankle didn't seem to work anymore. It wouldn't bend, not even a little bit.

"My ankle doesn't work," I said, and it was Nick's turn to laugh.

"I'm sorry," he said. "I don't mean to make fun. The look on your face . . . it was like you were mystified. . . . Does it hurt?"

"I don't know," I said.

Next thing I knew Nick had lifted me up and deposited me on the bar stool, and was kneeling, holding my ankle in his big, strong hands.

"Ow," I said when he turned it to the right and pain shot up, even through the alcohol fog.

"Doesn't look good," he said, turning serious. "It could be broken."

"Broken? It can't be broken!"

"You should get an X ray."

"Is that your professional opinion?"

"Yep. Let's take a trip to the emergency room."

"Oh, no," I said. I hated hospitals. And doctors. And needles. And that weird disinfectant smell wafting up from that creepy white or green tile they always have there. I didn't even have the stomach to watch "ER," much less to actually go to one myself. It takes me weeks to work up the courage to go see my gynecologist, and she has nice carpeted floors and plenty of potpourri. "I'm sure it's fine, I can walk on it." I took a step off the stool and almost fell again, but Nick caught me.

"I don't think so," he said, and with one sweep scooped me up in his arms, and carried me straight out of the bar.

Now, even in my alcohol-induced haze, I was beginning to feel embarrassed. I would have felt it more, if it hadn't been so darn nice being carted around by a big, strong, good-looking fireman. He didn't even seem to be under any strain. Remarkable, I thought, given that I always believed myself to be much heavier than I looked. (And about ten pounds heavier than I should be regardless. All right. All right. Fifteen pounds heavier.) I probably should have fought him just a little bit, insisted one more time that I could walk on my own. But it was *really* nice to be carried. Walking is such a bother. Especially when one has a hurt ankle. Especially, especially when one has ingested too many deceptively sweet-tasting pink alcoholic drinks *and* one has a hurt ankle. It was so easy to lean my head against his chest, wrap my arms around his neck, and pretend he was mine.

The ride to the car was so pleasant that I forgot where it was we were going. I was perfectly content—until we pulled into the circle drive of the Brackenridge Hospital emergency room.

"Oh, no," I said, panic threatening to settle in.

"Why not?" he said, sounding so reasonable.

"Er, well, I don't like hospitals." That was a bit of an understatement. I didn't just dislike them. I happened to be deathly afraid of them.

"Lauren," he said calmly. "You've got to have that ankle X-rayed. Look, I know most of the staff here. We'll breeze right through."

"Promise?" I asked, sounding and feeling like a five-year-old.

"Almost guaranteed," he said.

Well, I couldn't very well flip out and not go in. Nick would think I was crazy (if by some miracle he didn't already think I was a lunatic). Besides, Nick insisted on carrying me again (much to my inner delight).

When we walked through the automatic door of the ER and approached the counter, half the female nurses gave a sigh. I knew how they felt. All of them wanted to be where I was. They knew it and I knew it.

"Clarice," Nick said, smiling at one of the reception nurses.

"Nick!" she said, beaming, happy to see him. "What have you brought us?" she continued, giving me a funny look. "Another one of your strays?"

A stray? I resented that.

"She may have a broken ankle," Nick said.

"Uh-huh." Clarice looked skeptical. I couldn't exactly blame her. I'm sure women did more drastic things than twist an ankle to get Nick's attention.

"I probably don't," I added hurriedly, hoping to salvage what was left of my dignity. "I don't really need to be here." Maybe she would tell me I couldn't go in.

"You do," Nick contradicted firmly, dashing all hope of escape.

I smiled at Clarice uneasily. She didn't smile back.

"Go ahead and take her on back to stall six, Nick," Clarice said, shaking her head. "Lucky for you we're not busy just right now."

The terror of sitting on an actual hospital gurney and worrying about what sort of horrid flesh-eating bacterium might attack me (or was eating its way into my leg at this moment) sobered me a great deal. I'm not saying I became instantly clearheaded, but I certainly wasn't drunk, either. As proof, my ankle was hurting. A lot. Like a constant, dull throbbing (believe me, more throb than dull). Worse, the combination of the receding effects of alcohol and fending off waves of hospital-induced terror left me suddenly shy. I didn't know what to say to Nick. "Thanks for fulfilling my fantasy by carrying me in your fit, muscled arms" sounded a little too forward. "Boy am I stupid" seemed more accurate, but perhaps was a fact I didn't want to mention, given I really hoped that obvious sentiment would eventually slip his mind. The silence was killing me, so I had to say something.

"Thanks, er . . ." I paused. "Thanks for, uh . . ." Carrying me like the baby I am? Insisting I go to the place I hate and fear most in the world? Bearing witness to a very embarrassing lapse of judgment? Rescuing me from my own deadly clumsiness? None of those seemed right. Fortunately, Nick didn't seem to need further explanation.

"Don't mention it," he said.

Then we lapsed back into an uncomfortable silence, made worse by the fact that Nick seemed unable to stop staring at me. When I would glance over at him, he'd quickly look away.

In the seconds that ticked by, I convinced myself he must think I was the most irresponsible, clumsy, dorky person he'd ever met. He couldn't possibly like me now (a conclusion that made me both extremely disappointed and therefore also incredibly guilty at the same time). Worst of all, the best thing I could hope for was that he'd pity me. Frankly, I'd prefer he hate me, or extremely dislike me, over pitying me. The last thing I needed in my life was a fire-fighter Adonis to feel sorry for me. I felt so horribly stupid, I didn't even think I could look him in the eye. If I did, I feared I would break out into humiliating, ugly sobs.

The ER doctor came in then, saving me from the further embarrassment of bawling my eyes out. The ER doctor looked young, probably my age (an age I considered fine for myself, but a little young for a doctor). He could have passed for one of those youngish, hunky doctors in prime time. I'd tell you which one, but as I mentioned before, I'm too squeamish to actually *watch* them. Dr. Patrick (as he called himself, a name that didn't match the one stitched on his coat, I might add) could have also passed for the lost member of 'NSync, being blue-eyed and blond. He wore a woven choker (a guy necklace) around his neck with some sort of charm hanging from it, giving him a little bit of a surfer-boy quality.

"Where's Dr. Davis tonight?" Nick asked, turning the doctor's attention from me.

"And you are?" Dr. Patrick sounded aloof and slightly annoyed. (He might look young, but he seemed to have the doctor act pretty well down.)

"Nick. Nick Corona. I work for the AFD."

"AFD?" Obviously, Dr. Patrick was new to town.

"Austin Fire Department."

"Oh." Dr. 'NSync, er, I mean, Dr. Patrick, didn't appear impressed.

My rear was in danger of growing numb from sitting so long in one spot, so I shifted on the examining table. This, unfortunately, drew the attention of both men back to me.

"Ms. . . ." Dr. Patrick looked down at his clipboard. "Doe?" he finished uncertainly.

"Crandell," I corrected. "Lauren Crandell."

"Oh," he said (a particular syllable he used quite often, it seemed). "That's a relief. At least we know you don't have amnesia."

It was a poor stab at humor, and even Dr. Patrick attempted only a wan smile. I smiled weakly back. Nick didn't smile at all. The look on his face said he seriously doubted the young doctor's credentials.

"Now, what seems to be the problem?" Dr. Patrick continued, unfazed.

I was having difficulty concentrating. (Either because of the alcohol or because I really kept expecting Dr. Patrick to break out in song or at least bust a dance move. Bye. Bye. Bye.)

"Er, well, I, uh, twisted my ankle," I said, snapping back to the present, suddenly remembering that I was indeed sitting inside a hospital, a place where they used needles and other equally (and more) unpleasant things. I glanced quickly to the doctor's coat to see if I could detect any evidence of hypodermic needles. I didn't see any, but I knew they kept those things hidden so they could jab you with them when you least expected it.

"I think I'm fine, really," I said, as Dr. Patrick took hold of my left ankle, which I noticed had swelled to a size far greater than my right. "I don't think I need—*ow!*"

The doctor jumped, dropping my foot. It hit the table, and I yowled again.

"Hey, watch what you're doing," Nick said, sounding a bit perturbed.

"I think we'd better get an X ray," Dr. Patrick said, ignoring him while scooting cautiously away from me as if I was the kind of patient who had the tendency to scream for no reason.

"Is that really necessary?" I asked, thinking that all the while I had been worrying about flesh-eating bacteria, I should have been worrying about cancer-causing radiation.

"Definitely." Dr. Patrick was (oh-oh-oh . . . bust-a-move) emphatic.

The X-ray room (if you want to be so generous as to call a closet a "room") smelled funny, like a bizarre combination of melting plastic and fungus. The nurse (excuse me, I mean X-ray technician) had been one of the women loitering in the ER lobby when Nick and I had made our grand entrance. Needless to say, she wasn't very fond of me. Obviously, she believed I was faking. She had asked Nick to wait behind in the ER examining room. Since he was safely out of earshot, the tech could be as mean as she pleased.

"Turn to the left," she ordered none too nicely.

I turned.

"I mean *your ankle.*" She let out a loud, exasperated sigh.

She had me sitting on a chair with my leg resting on the X-ray machine, a big metal contraption with a glass top. She hovered over me, moving the giant camera lens.

"More to the left," she spat out, as she reached over and flattened my foot to the table. I yelped.

"This won't take so long if you cooperate," she snapped.

I really didn't like her, I decided.

She left me and went to work the controls in a separate (and I'm sure lead-lined) room. I saw protective aprons hanging on the wall and noticed the tech had failed to give me one.

"Should I have an apron?" I called after her.

"It won't kill you one way or another," she tossed back.

Ooh. I really, really didn't like her.

Now my mind started conjuring up unique but terrifying ways I could die or be mutated by radiation.

The lights went out in the room and an eerie glow drifted up from the machine (the radiation, no doubt). I found myself wondering if I would be glowing like that afterward. I tried to lean as far away from the glow as possible, but as my foot was sitting in it, I couldn't get far.

The tech came back after a few minutes. (I'm sure she waited for all the radiation to drain from the room, leaving me to baste without so much as an apron for protection.)

"I'd really like an apron," I said when she came close enough.

"Look, you're probably fine," she said. "Maybe a risk of sterility but other than that . . ."

Sterility? Good God, something else to worry about.

I raised my voice. "I *want* an *apron.*"

She looked over at me. "Fine," she said, grabbing one from the wall and tossing it into my lap. Need I remind you how much these things weigh? The apron was lead-lined; ergo, it was very, very heavy.

"Oof," I said when it landed like a brick on my stomach. The tech flopped my ankle over on its side. *"Ouch,"* I said even louder. She didn't say anything, just gave me a look that clearly said, "I'm still not buying your show."

I wanted to stick my tongue out at her, but managed to restrain myself. Just barely. She scurried out of the room and the lights went off as I scrambled into my apron (of course she didn't help me into it). The X-ray light came on just as I had gotten the thing over my chest.

When we were finished, the tech deposited me rather roughly into a wheelchair (probably to ensure Nick wouldn't be tempted to carry me again). She rolled me back, none too gently, I might add, and dumped me into my stall (without even helping me back up to the examining bed). Nick, who had been talking to a paramedic near the nurse's station, came over when he saw the tech bring me back.

"How are you doing?" he said, peeking around the curtain.

"Radioactive," I replied. "Watch out, I think gamma rays may be shooting from my eyes."

He laughed. My heart fluttered a little. Maybe he didn't think I was a complete moron after all. Then again, maybe he was just humoring me.

A few minutes later, Dr. Patrick came back to our little stall with a big envelope tucked under one arm. He had changed his coat, because the name stitched on the front said DOUG PATRICK, M.D., a detail that made me a little more comfortable. If a boy-band reject (he'd have to be a reject to choose a career of medicine over a million screaming thirteen-year-old fans, wouldn't he?) wanted to spend his nights masquerading as a doctor, the least he could do was steal the right coat.

"Do you want the bad news or the good news first?" he said, another obvious and poor attempt at humor.

"The good news," I said. Duh.

"Your ankle isn't broken."

I suppose that was good news, but I didn't take it that way. If it wasn't broken, then why did it hurt like hell? It very well should be broken if it hurt this much and caused me so much trouble.

"The bad news?" Nick asked, still looking skeptical. *He* for one thought it was broken.

"The bad news is that it's one of the worst sprains I've ever seen," Dr. Patrick said (given that he'd probably only been alive for twenty-seven or so years and had only been in the medical field maybe four, I didn't think he could have seen many sprains). "You've torn a major tendon here," he continued, whipping out my X ray and running the top of his pen over one of the gray shadowy areas of my ankle. "I think on Monday you should see a specialist, an orthopedic surgeon."

"A surgeon?" I didn't want to see another doctor, egad. Especially one that used scalpels.

"He can tell you whether or not this tendon will need surgery," Dr. Patrick said, as if it were obvious.

I must have visibly paled, because Dr. Patrick backed away from me, fearing I suppose that I might scream or faint unexpectedly.

"Uh, in the meantime, keep your foot elevated and pack it in ice to keep the swelling down," he said. "Oh, and here's something that should help with the pain."

A nurse materialized by Dr. Patrick's side and offered me a small white pill and a paper cup full of water.

I hesitated. Then I looked down at my ankle, which had turned a dark and ugly purple, and immediately regretted it, because the pain seemed to double once I saw how inflamed and sore it looked. I grabbed the pill and swallowed it, following it quickly with the water. Dr. Patrick looked as if he might leave, a move that put me immediately on my guard. Doctors always poke you with needles right before they flee from a room. This one didn't, however. He just ripped off a piece of paper from the notepad he carried and handed it to me. On it he had written the name and number of the suggested specialist.

After Dr. Patrick left, a nurse I didn't recognize came into my stall carrying a pair of crutches. I think she was supposed to show me how to use them, but instead spent the whole of her time talking to Nick, leaving me to my own devices as I fumbled with the adjustments. In the end, my right crutch sat a little higher than my left, so I wobbled and lurched every time I took a step.

I hobbled on my own back out through the hospital's lobby (going past the nurses, who looked extremely satisfied now that Nick was no longer carrying me about). Nick, for his part, was so popular with the nurses that it took twenty minutes for him to disentangle himself from one conversation or another.

It had been about two hours since my fall, and I had sobered almost completely. With the pain in my ankle and the unnerving possibility that I might have to see a surgeon and might even have to have surgery weighing on my mind, my mood took a turn for the worse. Besides that, I suddenly felt spent. The effort of coordinating the uneven crutches took more strength than I had thought.

Once out in the parking lot (the walk took about triple the time it should have), Nick opened the Jeep door for me and helped me in, taking my crutches and putting them in the backseat, where they were so long they stuck out of the side. Miraculously, Nick remembered exactly where I lived. (He was obviously one of those people who had a great sense of direction. I, on the other hand, could get lost in my own driveway if there was enough fog.) Unfortunately, there were a few narrow steps leading up to my porch, and the thought of having to lug myself over them on two spindly, poorly assembled crutches depressed me. On the first try, the shorter crutch slipped on the slick stone, causing me to flail my arms and fall backward into Nick, who smartly had decided it best to stand behind me, where he could keep an eye on my movements.

"Those things aren't working," he said, standing too close to me. "Why don't you just lean on me?"

I decided to ignore the undercurrent in his voice. The tone that said he'd like to do more than help me up the stairs. The tone that went with that look he was giving me right now. The look that was anything but innocent.

I decided to ignore it all, because I very much wanted his arm around my shoulders.

Nick wrapped me up in his arm, and I slinked one of mine around his waist, and he did most of the work as we made our way up the stairs. Did I mention that Nick has an incredibly firm and fit stomach? You can't always tell from a distance, but given how close I was, I could almost feel the outline of his muscles. I shivered, and quickly tried to think of something else. Like tendon surgery. That was certainly distracting enough.

Once on the landing, I managed to find my keys in record time (a mere three minutes instead of the usual fifteen I spent digging around my purse). I opened the door and Nick helped me inside, as I half sat, half lay on the cushy sofa in my living room. In a role-reversal, given that this was my house, Nick asked if I wanted something to drink or eat. "Water would be great," I said, "but you don't have to get it." I attempted to rise, and he put a firm hand on my left shoulder.

"Stay," he said. "Kitchen's that way?" He pointed to the right. I nodded.

I glanced at my watch. It said 1:45 A.M.

Oh boy. Now I was really in trouble. How would he ever explain this to Darla? I heard Nick opening cupboards in the kitchen, and I tried to remember in what condition I had left the dishes that morning. Of course, my kitchen is almost always clean (I couldn't take it any other way), but the occasional unwashed mug sometimes finds its way into the sink. The thought that I might have left a stray glass out in the kitchen made me itch to get up and check. Before I could, Nick returned with my glass of water and a Ziploc bag full of ice from my freezer.

"Here you go," he said, handing me the glass. While I sipped, he busied himself with arranging my leg on top of a stack of throw pillows. "Let me know if I hurt you," he said. As his touch was incredibly gentle, I doubted that would be a problem. The real issue was that with his hands around my foot, I kept wondering what they would feel like around something else. Bad, Lauren. Bad. Bad. Bad.

"Is it warm in here?" I said, just as he had finished laying the bag of ice on my foot.

"No," he said, suddenly looking worried. He leaned forward and put his palm on my forehead. "And it doesn't feel like you have a fever."

Nick's face was about six inches from mine. I was feeling a little overwhelmed by his close proximity. For one, I seemed to be having trouble breathing.

And he was giving me that look again. The intense one. The serious one.

"Lauren," he said, and there was the tone. He had something terribly bad in mind, I realized with a start. Something Darla wouldn't like at all.

My head suddenly felt light, like it might snap free of my shoulders and float up to the ceiling, trapping itself in a corner like loose balloons do. What had that doctor given me? I was beginning to feel woozy, too, and my eyelids wouldn't stay open, no matter how hard I tried, and believe me I tried hard. I couldn't feel the pain in my ankle anymore, I noticed absently, but then I couldn't feel much of anything at all, since my head was bouncing around somewhere near the ceiling fan. The last sensible thing I did was put my glass on the coffee table.

"I'm very . . ." I wanted to say "tired" but I don't know if I made it that far. I gave up trying to pry my eyes open, and let the darkness come and overwhelm me.

Ten

I woke the next morning to the sound of eggs frying in a pan. Brad must be making breakfast, I thought, feeling all warm and cozy and loved, as I pulled my feather-down comforter up to my chin, fighting off the the air-conditioned chill in my bedroom.

That's about the time I remembered that Brad didn't live here anymore. We were divorced, and he hadn't set foot in the house in over a year.

I sat bolt upright in bed. The motion sent a sharp stabbing pain through my ankle, and snippets of memory from the night before came back in a jumbled slide show, ending with the very last thing I remembered: me lying on the couch and Nick in the chair. But I was in my bed (almost fully clothed, I realized, with great relief) and someone was in my kitchen. The only person besides me who had a key to my apartment was Diane, and she hated eggs. Wouldn't touch them with a ten-foot pole. So it couldn't be her. I threw off the covers, swung my legs over the side of the bed, and gingerly set my feet on the ground. My ankle screamed in pain the second my big toe touched the ground, and so I lifted it up almost immediately, letting out a small curse. My crutches from the night before were leaning against my bedside table, and so I took one under each arm and hobbled out of my bedroom and into the hall.

The smell of bacon, eggs, and toast greeted me like an old friend, and my angry and very empty stomach told my brain that if it was a burglar, I should eat first and then call 911.

I turned the corner and saw that there was a man standing in my kitchen, making breakfast and whistling. Nick Corona.

"What are you doing?" I asked, bewildered.

"Good morning," he said, flashing one of his heart-stopping, lopsided smiles. "Feeling better?"

I took a quick inner assessment: ankle was throbbing, hair felt like it was a horrible heart-of-darkness jungle atop my head, and the implications of seeing Nick standing in my kitchen on Sunday morning were just beginning to sink in. I noticed he wore the same clothes from the night before, except he had taken off the collared shirt and wore nothing but a plain white undershirt and the black pants he'd worn the day before.

Oh my God.

He had *spent* the night. I bit my lip. I didn't remember anything after the couch. Did we, uh, did we . . . ?

"I hope you don't mind," he said. "I crashed on your couch."

Phew. Then we didn't.

"I've got to get to the firehouse by ten." He was still talking. "But I thought I'd make some breakfast, if that's OK with you?"

I nodded, my sleep-encrusted brain still trying to figure out what the hell he was doing here. (Besides whipping up the best-smelling breakfast ever. Those weren't plain old eggs he was frying. Nope. Try an onion and green pepper and cheese omelet!) The crutches bore painfully into my armpits, and so I slid into a chair at my breakfast table.

Oh boy.

I was in trouble. If Darla ever found out about this, there was no way she'd understand. I didn't even understand. What the hell was happening here? I blinked a couple of times, just to make sure he was really standing there, and it all wasn't some elaborate pain-medication hallucination.

Just then, Nick set down in front of me a steaming plate of omelet and toast, with a full glass of orange juice. Were those bits of cilantro on the omelet? Wherever did he find that in my kitchen?

"It looks great." This was my stomach talking, because it didn't care one whit about who the cook was engaged to or why he was standing in my kitchen. I took a bite (my stomach insisted) and almost fell out of my chair (for the second time in twenty-four hours), because it tasted soooo good. Moaning sounds of approval came involuntarily from my throat before I could stop them.

"I'm glad you like it," he said, taking a seat next to me and starting in on his own plate.

I took a sip of orange juice and almost choked.

"Is this fresh-squeezed?" I cried, coughing from the shock of it.

"You were out of orange juice but had plenty of oranges," he said simply.

No way would Brad have ever lifted a finger to squeeze one orange. Not if I were dying and the only thing that would save me was one drop of orange juice. I didn't think he even knew how to peel one.

"It's the best thing for you," Nick said, as if that were reason enough. "Besides, it helps those healing bones. Or tendons in your case."

"This is really, really good," I said, and immediately wished I hadn't. What the hell was I doing *encouraging* him?

"We take turns cooking at the station," Nick said. "You'd be surprised how critical the guys can get. They'll give you grief even if you cook steaks, simply because it didn't require you to chop anything."

"Oh," I said. A part of me recognized that was funny, but I just couldn't seem to laugh. I ate the delicious breakfast in a kind of shell-shocked state, believing that at any moment I would wake up in my bed, the whole thing being a dream. As time went on, and it became clearer and clearer that the whole situation was no dream (the omelet tasted too real, even my stomach attested to that), I began worrying about when Darla would burst through the door, find us at my breakfast table, and demand to know what exactly was going on. I kept hearing noises near the door, and the sounds made me jumpy.

"Are you OK?" Nick said, drawing my gaze from the door to him. "You seem a bit distracted. Is something wrong?"

"Oh no. No. Nothing." God, I even *sounded* guilty. He didn't seem at all nervous, but he did give me a curious look. I was probably acting weird. Then again, I hadn't taken a look at my hair yet that morning. Who knew what it looked like. Frightening, probably.

"Look, I hope I didn't overstep my bounds here," Nick said, a worried look crossing his face. "I, uh, didn't feel comfortable leaving you zonked out on the couch. Besides, you could've ended up with a weird reaction to the painkiller. That happens sometimes."

I was so shocked that I stopped chewing. It took me a minute to remember that it's usually customary to swallow one's food after it has been chewed. I gulped.

At first, I was incredibly flattered. I mean, it's not every day a girl has a gorgeous man looking after her when she's torn up her ankle, or cooking her a gourmet breakfast for the privilege. Don't think I didn't understand how great that all was. That's the problem, really. Nick seemed too good to be true. Saintly, even. Which meant there had to be something horribly wrong with him. And I thought I knew what it was.

"I don't believe you," I said, when my tongue would work again.

"What?"

"Don't get me wrong," I said, beginning to feel as perturbed as I was flattered. The inkling of a suspicion poked from my brain like a tiny flower bud. "I really appreciate everything you did for me, but I don't want you to think that this means anything."

"What do you mean?"

"You and me, that's what."

Nick looked a little taken aback. He probably wasn't used to women talking to him like this. I was beginning to feel like maybe I'd gotten the wrong idea. But the man *did* spend the night at my house, didn't he? He *was* engaged to one of my most important clients, *wasn't he?*

"Are you going to tell me something like you don't date your clients?" he said, a smile itching at the corner of his lips.

I couldn't believe he could sound so lighthearted about the whole thing! Did the man have no scruples?

"Of course I don't!" I exclaimed, sounding as indignant as I felt, though I didn't technically have a policy (it's pretty well a given in all wedding consultant-client relationships).

Nick refused to become the least bit ruffled. His composure continued to rattle me.

"Well, I guess I'll just have to excuse myself from the wedding," he said, lightly, as if the statement held no significance whatsoever. He might as well have been saying "Please pass the butter."

"You can't!" I was horrified. (Later, I would admit that a small part of me continued to be very flattered. Not for long, however. I soon convinced myself he must be either insane or a hopeless unscrupulous player.)

"Why not?" he said, in an annoyingly bemused way. Before I could answer, he got up, taking his dish and mine, and headed for the sink. The man had the gall to begin washing my dishes on top of everything else!

"What would Darla say?" I said, attempting to follow him, but not getting very far on my slick linoleum floor (my lopsided crutches did very poorly on the smooth surface).

"Sit down," Nick ordered. "You'll fall."

I settled for pulling myself up by the nearest countertop and hopping to the sink.

"I said sit down," Nick half laughed, half growled. He put down the dishes in the sink, and faster than I could blink he slung me easily over one shoulder.

This would never do.

"Put me down!" I said, but I doubted he heard me, given that my face was pressed against the middle of his back (my hair dangling in stringy clumps across my eyes). Besides, given that I was bent over one of his broad shoulders, I didn't have a lot of leverage for speaking.

Eventually, he did put me down, but not before walking across my living room to my couch, where he plopped me down on the cushions.

"Stay," he said, with exaggerated firmness, shaking a finger at me. "Or I'll just pick you up again and bring you back here."

He was smiling, but the look in his eyes said he wasn't kidding. I couldn't decide whether or not I actually wanted to test his resolve. What was I *doing?* Imagining being carried around my apartment by some clearly loony fireman?

"Don't do it!" I yelled after him, just as he disappeared around the corner.

"The dishes?" he called back, innocently.

"No! The wedding."

"So you don't want me in the wedding?"

"No! No, I *want* you in the wedding." I could only occasionally see a flash of his arm or leg from my distant perspective on the couch. Maddening! The faucet came on, and I heard the clink of dishes in my sink. I didn't *believe* he was talking about breaking it off with his fiancée while he washed my dishes. Unbelievable.

"Did you hear me, Nick? You can't do this," I said, desperation creeping into my voice.

He said something I didn't quite catch over the sound of water running.

"What?"

All I heard back was the sound of dishes being stacked in the rack. The water shut off, and then Nick came back into the living room, drying his hands casually on one of my dish towels.

"Why don't we talk about this later? Say over dinner?" He tossed the towel on my kitchen table and then grabbed his shirt that hung from my living-room chair.

"Absolutely not."

"How about seven on Tuesday? I'm on shift until then."

"Are you kidding?" What *was* he smoking?

"Tuesday it is," he said, and then dipped and planted a brief but toe-tingling kiss on my lips.

And with that, he slipped out my front door, leaving me staring blankly after him, wondering what in the world I was going to do now.

Eleven

"Screw his freakin' brains out, that's what."

This was Veronica, my wild single friend, the one I could always count on to tell me exactly what I wanted to do, regardless of whether it was (and most especially if it wasn't) morally sound. If my friends were my spiritual advisors, Veronica would be the little red devil sitting on my right shoulder.

"Are you kidding?" I said into the phone, trying to sound as offended as possible (but this was hard, given that I called her for the express purpose of hearing something exactly along those lines).

"Look, honey," she said in her best Karen from *Will and Grace* voice, "this is probably the only time in your straitlaced life that you'll have the opportunity to be the *other* woman. *Take it.*"

Veronica is the only one of my friends who has actually had an affair with a married man. But like all the men she dates, he was quickly eaten up and spit out.

"But how can I *do* that?"

"Any way you want, sweetie. I prefer doggie style, but that's just me—hang on a second, will you?" Then I heard her yell, "Hey, you! Don't touch that Bacardi bottle. Stacey! Are you going to let him drink that?"

"Are you having a party?" I said, looking at my watch. It was 11:00 P.M. on Sunday.

"Nah, just a few people over."

She perpetually had a few people over. Never at any time of day could you find her apartment empty (even when she wasn't in it).

"Listen, sugar," she said. "You sound down about this. Why don't we go out tomorrow? You, me, and a few of the girls. We'll down some beers or Jack Daniels. None of those fruity things you insist on drinking."

"Well, I don't know. . . ."

"Think about it. Call me tomorrow—David!" she shouted midsentence. "David, put your pants back on for chrissakes! You're not *that* well endowed. Sheesh."

With that, she hung up.

Did I mention that Veronica always had people over *and* half of them were usually naked? On two separate occasions the police arrested streakers on her front lawn. Each time, both offenders were men Veronica had broken up with, and both felt they could win her back by serenading in the buff. I suppose it just goes to show what she can do to a man.

I only semi-regretted calling. In the past, I've avoided talking with her because she usually makes me feel like a bit of a loser and definitely old. (Her idea of going out on a Friday night means not coming home before dawn.) On the other hand, if I'm ever in a delicate situation, I can always count on her to put it in perspective (i.e., make me feel that however bad I feel I'm acting, she can always do worse).

I knew I wouldn't be going out with her the next day. The last time I tagged along with her on a weekday, I ended up not getting home until about 7:30 A.M., just in time for me to climb in the shower and dress for work. I spent half the day snoozing at my small desk, being interrupted now and again by G's booming voice. Besides, that was when I happened to be wholly healthy. It wouldn't be possible to keep up with her dance-club hopping on crutches.

After Nick had left, I called Diane first. She insisted on coming right over to view the evidence (my swollen ankle and the rumpled couch pillows). After I finally convinced her that Nick had in fact spent the night and did indeed want to go to dinner with me, Diane had a vehement and firm answer. She told me in no uncertain terms that I should not meet Nick for dinner (because, unlike Veronica, Diane has scruples).

"But you said you loved the fact I was going to be a home wrecker," I said, failing to disguise the disappointment in my voice.

"That was *before* there was any hope that you would be," Diane said, practically. "I didn't think anything would really happen. But this sounds serious."

"I know! What am I going to do?"

"Tell him you don't date married men."

"But, technically, he's not married."

"*Lauren,*" Diane said, giving me one of those looks of hers, the you-know-better-than-that looks my mom often gives me. "You've got to stop thinking like that. He's engaged, and that's practically the same thing."

I sighed, shifting my swollen ankle a little on the stack of pillows on my couch. "I know," I said.

"So, you know what you have to do. Call him. Tell him you can't see him anymore."

Definitely a sound suggestion. A practical, moral, and right suggestion.

So you understand of course why I needed a second opinion. This was why I called Veronica.

But even though Veronica told me what I wanted to hear, I didn't feel any better about the situation. I still had no idea what I planned to do, which scared me to death because I shouldn't even be thinking about going out with him. Why I even hesitated about calling him and canceling the whole thing made me doubt my own scruples.

By midnight, I went to pick up the phone, determined to end this whole thing once and for all. But I realized as I started to dial that I didn't have his number (work number, that is; home number I had in Darla's folder, but as she probably had access to that machine, I thought it wise not to leave a message there). I tried to remember what engine company he worked in, but the number escaped me. I set the phone back on the hook.

I tossed and turned all night, only partly because of the constant throbbing in my ankle. Sleeping with one's foot on a pillow was actually quite a challenge, I found, because it rarely stayed in place when one was rolling around. So I perpetually found myself leaning over one side of the bed or the other, reaching for the pillow that I had inadvertently kicked onto the floor. It didn't help that I couldn't stop thinking about Nick and Darla, and me and Nick, and Nick and, well, Nick. I couldn't figure him out at all. What did he mean to do with me? Why was he so interested? If he wanted to cheat on Darla, I thought, there were plenty of better-looking and more interesting people than me. He could go out with any number of beautiful women with shampoo-ad-perfect hair, so why me?

Could this be some sort of test? Maybe he didn't trust me to plan his wedding and he wanted to challenge my ethics. I dismissed that idea as soon as it popped into my head. What groom in his right mind would cook up such a scheme? Perhaps he desperately wanted out of the engagement and decided to pick the easiest means: cheating on his bride with her own wedding consultant. No, none of it made any sense. Part of me really wanted to believe that Nick wasn't capable of that kind of sinister manipulation. Part of me said he *was* genuinely a good person.

When I did manage to fall asleep, I didn't stay that way for long (waking up every half hour on the hour all night). I jolted awake a last time exactly two minutes before my alarm went off, at 7:28 in the morning. I lay there, staring at my alarm clock, I suppose willing it to somehow rewind itself, go back in time about five hours so I could have another go at sleep. But it didn't, choosing like the fascist it was to tick on to 7:30, when the buzzer came on in short, loud bursts. I hit the snooze button, but as I found myself already wide awake, there wasn't any chance I'd be falling back asleep. So I just lay there, thinking.

As it turned out, I should have probably used all the time tossing and turning to get myself ready for the workday, because it took me twice as long to shower, get dressed, and gather up my things for work than it did when I wasn't hobbling about on one leg. In fact, I didn't actually leave the house until 9:30, as late as I'd ever been to my job in at least four years. To make matters worse, I kept slamming my hurt foot into things (the coffee table, the doorjamb, the table in the foyer), each time sending a white-hot searing pain up my leg. I suppose I wasn't used to holding one foot in the air, and I kept underestimating my turning radius.

I finally did get out the door and down my narrow steps, managing to carry my briefcase and purse over one shoulder while maneuvering the crutches with both hands. I got into my car, using the door to hold myself steady while I tossed my bags and crutches into the backseat. I slid gingerly into the driver's seat (miraculously avoiding banging my foot against the seat or the pedals). When I went to start the car, it dawned on me that I had another serious problem I failed to consider.

My car was a standard. A stick shift, manual transmission.

I touched my left foot gently to the clutch, but recoiled quickly in pain. I attempted to hold down the clutch and gas pedals with my right foot, but succeeded only in stalling my car four times. This was pointless.

I called G and left her a message before calling a cab.

The cab driver, a foggy-eyed twenty-year-old sporting blond dreadlocks and smelling strongly of pot, asked me, as we pulled away from my house, if I injured myself stage-diving.

"My buddy Trent broke his arm stage-diving," he informed me. "Is that what happened to you, too?"

"No," I said, "I was barstool-diving."

"Cool."

We arrived at G's office, and I limped up the stairs to the front door, wobbling decidedly to the left (toward the shorter crutch), and barely had time to wonder how I might work the front door when it swung wide open of its own accord. G stood there, tapping her foot and looking unusually perturbed (even for her).

"Darla's waiting for you," she hissed, trying to keep her voice as soft as possible, which for G usually means somewhere just softer than a shout. "She's been waiting for a half hour. She says it's *important* and she only wants to talk to *you.*"

Gulp.

Somehow, she had found out. I knew she would. And now she was here, ready to confront me, to tell me what a horrible, awful person I was, and there wouldn't be anything at all I could say in my own defense. I felt panic, white-hot, blinding, clammy-palms panic.

"Did she, uh, did she say what this was about?" I asked G, clearing my throat because my guilt seemed to have lodged itself there like a giant ball of phlegm, making it difficult for me to speak. I searched G's face, looking for the smallest clue that would tell me how much *she* actually knew. I couldn't imagine what G would say to me if she ever found out (which could be very soon if Darla planned a fiery confrontation in front of my boss), but I was sure that whatever the speech turned out to be, it surely would include the words "You're fired."

"The wedding, of course," G said, giving me a "what's wrong with you?" look.

That answer didn't help me.

A cold dabble of sweat rolled down the back of my neck (whether from my exceeding anxiousness or from the exertion of wielding the awkward crutches over G's threshold, I couldn't say). Why was this happening to me? I thought desperately. I felt as if I were suddenly back in third grade, walking down that long narrow corridor to the principal's office, knowing that whatever defense I could muster wouldn't matter. The principal would call home and tell my mother I'd been sticking my tongue out at David Masterson.

G took my bag and briefcase and told me to hurry, giving me a gentle but firm shove in the direction of the sitting room, where Darla waited. I swallowed (an action that proved difficult, because all the saliva in my mouth had dried up about thirty seconds before) and began to make my way to the sitting room. Those eight tottering steps took forever.

I saw Darla before she saw me, and the anxiety floating around my stomach, in the form of hyperactive butterflies, turned into a giant lead ball of dread that dropped with a thud into my lower abdomen. Darla, her perfect blond hair wrapped up in a slick French twist, sat with her legs crossed, looking out the window. I wouldn't have believed it, but melancholy seemed to suit her. She looked tragically beautiful, as if she were born to play the woman scorned. A ping of jealousy sounded somewhere in my heart, but it was quickly quashed by the weight of my inexcusable guilt.

"Darla," I said, intending to sound contrite but only managing a kind of croak.

Darla looked up, her big blue eyes glossy, as if she were about to cry, and I almost fell down on my knees and begged her forgiveness.

"Lauren," she said tightly. She knew! She definitely knew.

"What happened to your leg?" Darla added with barely restrained politeness.

"Er, tripped," I said, biting my lip. "Sprained ankle."

"Oh. I'm sorry," Darla said, absently. I was *so* busted. Caught. Found out. Trapped. The room seemed to shrink, and in a few moments I had no doubt it would start spinning.

"Is there somewhere we can talk? Privately?" She glanced over at G, who seemed to be overly preoccupied with the leaves of a fern in the corner.

"How about outside? On the patio?" I felt a momentary rush of relief. At least G wouldn't hear the dressing-down Darla planned for me.

"That's perfect," Darla said, standing, flicking a piece of imaginary lint from her immaculately pressed pants.

I led the way, limping along on my crutches, fearing at any moment that Darla might knock one of them out from under me and I'd find myself sprawling facedown on the tile floor. Maybe she'd kick me for good measure, I thought. Why not? I deserved it.

Once outside, I slid into the closest patio chair, a wrought-iron contraption that didn't allow for much movement, and laid my crutches against the outside window. Darla sat across from me, looking chillingly composed. Gulp: Take Two. I wasn't ready for this.

Then everything changed. Darla, in all her perfect composure, began to cry. Beautiful, round tears dropped from her eyes. (Which I didn't think was fair at all. A beautiful person shouldn't still look beautiful crying. No one looks beautiful crying. Yet, here she was. Bawling and still gorgeous.) I stomped down those obscenely callous thoughts. *You did this,* a voice shouted in my head. *You made her cry.*

"Oh, Darla, I am so very sorry," I said, feeling the worst I'd ever felt in my life.

Darla sniffled, pulling a tissue from her pocket and dabbing gently at the corners of her eyes.

"Don't worry about it," Darla said. "It's not your fault."

"It isn't?"

"Of course not. How could you be late to an appointment I never made? I'm the one who should be apologizing for barging in on you like this."

I was dumbfounded. I was obviously missing some vital piece of information.

"I need your help." Darla sounded, well, desperate.

"You do?"

"My fiancé and I, we had a fight Friday night. It was about the wedding. It's a long story, but he hung up on me, and then didn't answer the phone Saturday or Sunday."

Oh boy. Oh boy. *Oh boy.*

"I just don't know what to do," Darla said. "I think he may be thinking of calling the whole thing off."

"Why would you think that?" I was amazed my voice

sounded so calm and controlled. Inside, my thoughts, which had been buzzing around in reckless circles on the motor speedway of my brain, had crashed together in a big, black, smoky mess.

"He said so. On Friday." Darla sniffed.

This was bad. This was very bad.

"What was the fight about?"

"The guest list."

That didn't surprise me. I didn't know a couple alive who hadn't fought at one time or another about the guest list. The groom always thinks his choices get cut first, while the bride doesn't understand why the groom insists on inviting the whole of his bowling team and their wives.

"Anyway, I know you can help us," Darla said, brightening. "Can you meet with us, both of us, tomorrow? Act as a kind of mediator?"

That was a terrible idea. "What a, uh, great idea," I said. "I'd be happy to." I needed an Alka-Seltzer. Badly. My stomach felt as if it would implode at any minute under the pressure.

"I knew you'd be able to help us," Darla said, smiling. "I know that if I can sit him down and have another reasonable person talk to him, that we can work this whole thing out."

"Uh-huh." I smiled, weakly.

"Oh, gosh, look at the time," Darla said, glancing at her watch. "I've got a meeting in ten minutes! But I'm so glad we talked. I feel so much better."

I'm glad one of us did.

"I'll have my assistant call you with the details for tomorrow. I just know we'll work this out."

"Well?" This was G, hovering over my desk the second after Darla walked out the door.

"The usual," I said, lying with frightening ease. "A guest-list fight."

"Oh! Is that all?" G snorted. "You'd think the wedding was off! She sounded so dramatic."

"Well, she thought it was a serious fight."

"Oh, pooh," G said, wandering off. "When they're fighting about the vows, then come talk to me about serious."

When G left, I put my head in my hands. What in the world was I going to do? I couldn't imagine myself being able to look Nick in the face and tell him he really ought to be a little more flexible on the issue of the guest list, given that he had told me he fully intended to back out of the wedding. Furthermore, I wouldn't be able to hold back much longer, because if I saw Darla again soon I know I'd end up blurting out something horribly incriminating (a nervous habit ground into me by years of knowing stares from Mom).

My phone rang and I jumped. I let it ring twice more, fearing that Nick might be on the line, or worse, Darla, having suddenly discovered I was the reason her dear fiancé didn't come home Saturday and Sunday.

"Are you going to get that?" G bellowed down the stairs. I suppose I didn't have a choice. I picked up the phone.

"Lauren dear? This is your mother."

I never thought I'd be relieved to hear her voice.

"Yes, Mom, I know."

"I just finished talking to Mrs. Baker from down the street."

"Mrs. Baker?" Mom knows an infinite number of people, and she always assumes I know them by association.

"Mrs. Baker. Her son works as an ER nurse."

"Oh."

"Well, she said you were in the emergency room Saturday night! Whenever did you plan to tell me?"

"Mom, it's nothing."

"She said some man carried you in *unconscious.*"

"I wasn't unconscious. I just sprained my ankle."

"Dear. Don't lie to your mother. I know you're deathly afraid of hospitals. You wouldn't go if it were just a sprained ankle."

"Really, it was just a sprained ankle."

"I appreciate you trying to spare my feelings, dear. But I can handle the worst."

"I am sure you can. But it's nothing, really. I just may have to see a surgeon today, but . . ."

"I knew it! It's head trauma, isn't it? Don't let them operate. Did you see what happened to that poor boy on 'Dateline'? Doctors told him he needed surgery, too. Now he can't speak or chew his own food."

I ignored that last part. "It's not head trauma," I said. "It's a sprained ankle."

"Listen to me, don't you dare see a surgeon."

"OK, Mom."

"Do see one if you start feeling dizzy. But don't bother otherwise. Do you hear me?"

"Yes, Mom." (I think the origins of my weird hospital phobia should be clear to you now.)

"Doctors are unscrupulous opportunists."

"Yes, Mom."

"Did I mention that I was engaged to one before I met your father?"

"Yes." She had, many times.

"He had almost convinced me I needed my tonsils out, the scoundrel. . . ."

I had only heard this story about fifty times, so I tuned out for a few minutes.

"Lauren? Did you hear me, dear? Would you like me to bring you some soup tonight?"

"No, Mom."

"You sure, dear? It's no trouble."

"I, uh, may have to work late."

"Promise to call me if the room starts spinning, dear."

"Yes, Mom."

I should have stayed on the phone a few minutes longer. It would've spared me a moment or two of self-torture over this bizarre Darla-Nick-Me triangle of guilt and deception that kept me in a perpetual state of bleakness. The only positive was that I somehow managed to funnel the guilt into motivation for work, making more progress that morning and afternoon than I had for the whole last week. I booked Darla's caterer, reception hall, and florist (all pending her final approval, of course) and busied myself with calling back every single client who had a wedding in the next three months to ask them if they had anything else they'd like me to look into. I even called Alyssa Darvis, of all people, whom I try to avoid calling at all costs, just to see if she had any more leads for me to check out. I figured if I worked hard enough, I wouldn't have time to think about the predicament I was in.

Of course, I couldn't have been more wrong.

Pretending there wasn't a potentially catastrophic problem staring me in the face only made matters worse. For one thing, horrible thoughts I tried to keep bottled kept bouncing to the surface. Nightmarish scenarios ran through my head at top speed. All of them seemed to end with Nick dramatically declaring he'd spent the night at my house and what did Darla plan to do about it?

"I am in so much trouble."

"You're what?" G said, standing in front of my small desk, holding a white paper bag.

"What? Oh, nothing. Nothing." I hadn't realized I'd been talking out loud. I wondered what else I might have said aloud. Disturbing thought. "What's that?" I said, pointing to the bag.

"Your lunch."

I didn't understand.

"I saw you working through lunch, and I know it's hard for you to get around, so I brought you a sandwich. Your favorite. Turkey club."

I was suddenly and deeply touched.

"Thanks, G." Sometimes, the old woman could be very, very sweet. Of course, I reminded myself abruptly, she wouldn't be sweet for long if she found out I was wrecking the marriage of her best friend's niece.

I spent the afternoon at the doctor's office, being told what I'd already known—no broken bones, just a sprain. I got a new ankle wrap and was told to avoid walking, which was fine, since I planned never to leave my house again.

Afterward, Darla's assistant called to tell me that the world as I knew it would implode at approximately 10:30 A.M. the next morning (the time Darla and her fiancé would be coming to visit me).

"Listen, there's only one way to solve this," Veronica told me later. "You've got to come out with us."

"Well . . ." I hesitated. "I'm on crutches." That seemed to be the best excuse I could come up with. It sounded lame and I knew it.

"So?" Veronica said. "All the more reason you need a drink, honey."

"That's what got me into this problem in the first place."

"And that's what's going to get you out. Trust me."

OK. Whenever Veronica says "trust me," you know you're in

trouble. I simply didn't care. As far as I could see, I only had three options: call Darla and confess my guilt, thereby getting myself fired and causing Nick to hate me; call Nick and tell him to stay away from me or I'd get a restraining order against him, thereby saving my job but still causing Nick to hate me; or spend some time with the one person who'd make me feel like there's nothing wrong with doing absolutely nothing at all.

As if there were any contest.

Twelve

"What I want to know," Veronica yelled over the din of dance music playing in the background of a very smoky and very dark club, "was why you didn't just sleep with him to begin with."

"Why do you say that?" I yelled back, scooting my barstool a little closer to the table to avoid overexuberant dancers (somehow, they kept managing to find creative ways to bump into my bandaged foot).

"Well," Veronica explained, "aside from the obvious fact that he's gorgeous and willing, if you're going to torture yourself with this self-imposed guilt, you damn well should've had some fun first."

"So by your logic, I should just go ahead and sleep with him now, since I'm already suffering from the guilt?"

"*Exactly.* Girl, you're finally catching on."

I rolled my eyes.

"Do you wanna dance?" This was directed at Veronica (a gorgeous single girl in her own right—long blond hair, and an attitude that wouldn't quit). The rather unimaginative pick-up line came from a rather cute, if slightly geeky-looking, late-twenty-something with dark hair.

"Where do you work?" Veronica asked. (She never wastes time on moderately nerdy men unless they've got substantial paychecks.)

"Dell."

"What division?"

"Sales."

"No thanks," Veronica said. "Sorry. I don't dance with anyone who works in a department lower than development."

The poor guy looked crushed. Veronica just shrugged.

"He'll appreciate it in the long run," she said. "At least I'm not wasting his time."

"I don't think he'd mind a little wasted time," I said, watching the slump-shouldered figure retreat.

The next hour and a half went on a lot like that. Veronica turning down overture after overture and, in between chewing men up, trying to convince me that what I really needed to do was to have sex more and think about it less.

"You haven't gotten laid since Brad, for godsakes," she said.

"I have so."

"Ex-college boyfriends don't count."

"That's what Diane said."

"Well, she's right. They don't." She took a long sip of beer and sighed. "If you really want to know what's wrong with you, I don't think it has anything to do with Nick or Darla," Veronica continued, flipping back a long strand of blond hair. "I think you're still hung up on Brad."

"I am *not.*" I was appalled. Horrified, that she would even think such a thing.

She shrugged one shoulder. "Whatever. I just call 'em like I see 'em. This all goes back to the fact that Brad cheated on you. You've never dealt with it, and now it's all in your face again. Only this time, you think you might be the other woman, and it's killing you."

"Brad didn't cheat on me."

"Whatever."

"He didn't."

"Look," Veronica said, snubbing out her cigarette and blowing the smoke above her head. "You've got to stop this denial thing. I call screwing the brains out of some young thing *in your living room* cheating."

"Technically, we were separated."

"Technically, he was still your husband and he was doing it with a strange woman on your leather couch. That's cheating. It's an even worse crime than that. It's called divorce settlement sabotage."

"What?"

"Who got the couch?"

"He did."

"See. It was probably part of a master plan."

I hadn't thought of it that way. I suppose I should explain the whole leather-couch incident. Brad and I had been separated a month when I came home early one Friday to find the door unlocked and Brad rolling around on my brand-new leather couch with a nineteen-year-old college sophomore. Certainly, you could say this was a turning point in our relationship, I'm not denying that. (Until then, Brad had been dropping hints that we might get back together. *That* door slammed shut immediately, let me assure you.) Still, I don't consider it cheating with a capital "C." I mean, we were separated, right?

The funny thing about walking in on them is that I remember thinking for just a split second, "God, is that what he looks like when he's on top of me?" I mean, he was wearing his black socks, for goodness' sakes. And he's probably the least limber man I've ever seen. And hairy. Don't even get me started on the back hair. He just looked so, well, ridiculous. Like some kind of horrible science experiment gone wrong. Without his nice clothes, he was just a spindly, white, black-sock-wearing goof. And those stupid gyrations of his, I don't even remember why I ever thought he'd been a decent lover. He had about as much finesse as a dog humping a fire hydrant (and at least the dog has a little passion working for it). I mean, even the ruddy sophomore looked like she might've been faking it. Her eyes were tightly closed, and I imagine she was dreaming of somebody else with a little less lower-back hair.

It was at that moment that I fell, completely and finally, out of love with Brad (which for some of my friends was probably a year too late, but what can you do). But this had absolutely nothing to do with the situation at hand (regardless of Veronica's harebrained theories), and so I'll move on before I disgust you further with the mental image of my bowlegged ex-husband in tube socks.

"Look, my point is Brad did that horrible thing and many horrible things to you and you just rolled over and played dead," Veronica said, lighting another cigarette.

"I did not."

"What did you do?"

"I divorced him," I said, proudly.

"And gave away half your 401K."

"Technically, it was two-fifths," I corrected.

"And all of your good furniture. And your new car."

"He paid for half of it."

"With what? His collection of Polo Sport? Lauren, honey, you gotta toughen yourself up, girl. What you need to do is embrace your inner bitch."

Before I had time to ask more about the "inner bitch" phenomenon, I caught a familiar face in the crowd. Tall, lean, blond, and sickeningly perfect: Darla Tendaski.

"Stop everything," I said, grabbing Veronica's arm. "There she is."

"Who?"

"Darla," I hissed, although I doubted voices could carry over the booming thuds of techno bass. "Darla. The person whose wedding day you want me to ruin."

"Oh. She's not so hot," Veronica said, giving her the once-over. "She's insecure. I can smell a fragile ego a mile away. I'd put five hundred dollars on an eating disorder."

Did I mention that I loved Veronica?

"Wait, honey, who the hell is that with her?" Veronica tapped her cigarette against an empty beer mug without looking to see where the ashes fell. "Don't tell me *he's* the rugged firefighter."

I couldn't see who she was talking about, sitting where I was at the corner of the table. A cocktail waitress and her heavily loaded tray blocked my view. *Move,* I willed her. After a few more heart-wrenching seconds, she did shuffle to the side, clearing my view. There, of course, stood Nick.

I immediately ducked my head, trying futilely to hide behind my almost full pint of beer.

"Hide me," I pleaded to Veronica, who just looked at me and snorted.

"Honey, I'm going to do you a favor and pretend I didn't hear that," she said, scooting a little to the left so had Nick looked my way, he would've seen me clear as day. She gave him another look and smacked her lips. "I'm afraid you're going to have to sleep with him now. I simply can't allow you to let *that* go. God, look at those abs! I think I can see the ripples from here."

"Shhh!" I said, even though they stood a good twenty feet from us.

"Uh-oh, looks like trouble for our young couple. What a pity." Veronica's voice dripped sarcasm.

But there did seem to be trouble. For one thing, Darla kept trying to put her arms around Nick's neck, and Nick kept resolutely shaking her off. They were arguing, that much was obvious, and it looked like Nick told her to leave him alone. Meanwhile, Darla, in a show of remarkable desperation for someone so usually composed and confident, seemed unable to stop touching him, despite the fact that he definitely did not want to be touched. In a last, wholly extreme effort, she leapt forward and tried to kiss him on the lips. Nick ducked and firmly pushed her back, clearly looking disgusted. He plunked down his beer hard on the bar and then turned to walk away from her (which happened, unfortunately, to be straight toward me).

Despite all my best efforts to hide behind one of my crutches (damn them for having so many holes), Nick saw me. Recognition dawned on his face, followed closely by something like horror. But, instead of slowing down or turning in another direction and ignoring me completely as I fully expected him to do, he quickened his pace, heading right for me.

"Oh, shit!" I blurted, fumbling with my crutches and my purse, knowing my only hope was to make a quick escape to the bathroom.

Veronica seemed to find the whole situation vastly amusing, and did nothing but laugh at me as I tried to hobble quickly away from the table. Let me tell you that maneuvering on uneven crutches through a very active dance crowd was no easy task. Needless to say, I didn't make it very far.

"Lauren, wait!" Nick called somewhere close behind me. I stopped, hoping against hope that I might be camouflaged in the bopping heads of the strobe-lit crowd. "Lauren!" he said again, this time putting a heavy hand on my shoulder. I was caught. Damn.

"Lauren," Nick said, jumping in front of me, and at the same time easily deflecting a couple of wild dancers who were on a collision course with my crutches. "Lauren, it's not what you think."

"What do you mean?" I looked around to see if I could catch a glimpse of Darla, but she had conveniently disappeared.

"I mean there's nothing between Darla and me."

OK. I wasn't expecting him to say something like that. I suddenly felt deeply and fiercely angry. Did he forget who I was? Did the very important fact that I happened to be *planning his wedding* somehow slip from his well-coiffed head? Was this the kind of pathetic line he used on empty-headed women who were foolish enough to follow him around like enamored puppy dogs?

"How can you say that?" I said, raising my voice again over the music that just then jumped several decibels in volume. "She's your fiancée. Your fiancée! That means there's everything between you."

Nick shook his head, motioning to his ears in the international "I can't hear you" sign. "What?" he yelled back.

"I said," I continued, yelling louder, "you should be ashamed of yourself." I finished just as the music in the club abruptly stopped.

Nick certainly heard that last part. So did everyone else in the bar. A few heads turned, then the music cranked up again, and the dancing resumed.

I turned away from him, attempting to make a dramatic exit (the crutches severely hindered the ultimate effect, however).

"Wait, Lauren. You don't understand," Nick called behind me.

"I understand everything," I said, trying but failing to remain calm. "I don't want to hear anything else."

"Damn it!" Nick said, next. "My pager!" There was a pause, as he fumbled with the device. Then, he skipped in front of me.

"Look, I've got to get back to the firehouse, but we're not finished here," he said.

I blinked at him. God, it was hard to stay mad at a man that gorgeous. Just look at those giant, pleading brown eyes.

"I want to explain. I'll call you," he said, starting to make his way back through the crowd.

I shrugged.

"I mean it. I'll call you tomorrow!" With that, he disappeared into the sea of people.

Tomorrow. Tomorrow! It dawned on me with all the subtlety of a Mack truck that he would be more than calling me tomorrow. He and Darla would be sitting in my office in exactly fifteen hours.

Gulp times two.

Thirteen

The next morning, I awoke to find that my ankle had miraculously (almost) entirely healed itself, with a tiny trace of soreness as the only evidence that I had ever hurt it in the first place. As a testament to my scattered and occupied state of mind, I didn't even notice the improvement until about an hour after I got out of bed. (I had already walked to the bathroom and then to the kitchen before it dawned on me that I was moving about without the aid of crutches.) I suppose I was too preoccupied with the very worrying appointment I had today. Even the passing thought that my healthy ankle meant I wouldn't have to see a specialist after all didn't manage to raise my spirits.

As I got ready for work, I dreamed up wild excuses to tell G so she'd let me stay home. "I broke my leg" was not only plausible but practically true (given that my ankle is attached to my leg), though G would never buy two separate near-crippling injuries in one week. "I was hit by a car" seemed too extreme and too easily verifiable by one call to the emergency room. "I've come down with a rare and very contagious disease and a group of German scientists are flying in to examine me" had a nice ring to it, but was too much of an embellishment even for me. After lots of pacing back and forth (on my greatly improved ankle), I realized that it would be far worse if I stayed home. The thought of G meeting with Nick and Darla alone made me extremely nervous. What if Nick said something and I wasn't there to at least attempt my own defense? No, I couldn't risk it.

I finally came to the conclusion that there was only one thing left for me to do: Go to work and then fake a fainting spell right before Nick and Darla arrived. With any luck, I'd hit my head on the corner of a table on the way down. At least then I could pretend to have amnesia.

I flung open my closet doors, wondering why I cared what I looked like (the fact that it still mattered to me what Nick thought of how I dressed didn't make any sense, but there the feeling was, just the same). I rifled through my clothes feeling like a man adjusting his wrinkled shirt before the firing squad pulled its collective trigger. I decided on a J. Crew version of my black Banana Republic dress (which had a longer skirt and was made of linen instead of nylon/cotton spandex) and a black blazer over it (symbolically appropriate, I thought, for my own figurative funeral). For once, my hair actually looked, well, good. This, by the way, was just another means it employed to mock me (looking smashing on the very day I'd be fired is exactly the kind of plot my deviant hair follicles dream up while I sleep at night). My makeup even seemed to apply itself easily on the first try, which meant I didn't even have that excuse to dawdle around the house. When typically difficult things start becoming easy for me, I always get suspicious. Karmically speaking, something's got to give.

I pulled up to the office at exactly 8:35 A.M., hoping all the way to the door that I'd find a message on my voice mail telling me they weren't coming. In fact, any interruption would do. Barring a simple cancellation, I would have settled for a small natural disaster (like a tornado or earthquake), or even a man-made debacle (like the crash of a single-engine plane into G's roof). I wasn't picky.

At about a quarter to ten, Whiskers arrived in the office, followed closely by G. Both of them ignored me on the way upstairs, thankfully. The last thing I needed to deal with this morning was cat poo. At five till ten, I poured myself my third cup of coffee. (In retrospect, it was a mistake to ingest so much caffeine on top of my already tightly wound nerves.) The knock sounded on the front door, causing me to choke on coffee. *They're early!*

I put the glass down (rather too hard, because it splashed a little on my old yellow keyboard) and sprinted to the door. I looked through the peephole, preparing to fake a faint if necessary, and saw a woman whom I'd never met before. I decided it would probably be best to remain in an upright position. I opened the door.

"Yes?" I said politely to the woman, who wore a pink halter, a long black skirt, and fabulous open-toed hot pink slides.

"Lauren Crandell?"

"Yes."

"I'm Jenn Jones, Darla's maid of honor. We need to talk."

Until now, I haven't spent much time discussing maids of honor. I suppose this is because I don't have too many negative things to say about them. Having been one, I can say that usually (and I emphasize *usually*) they have the best interests of the brides at heart. Every once in a while, however, you run into a maid of honor who is more selfish (a condition usually fueled by self-pity at not being the one who's actually getting married herself). The worst maid of honor is one who happens to be insanely jealous of the bride, but who would never in a million years admit it (thus being your typical "Who me? Eaten up with envy? Never" maid of honor).

Initially, I suspected Ms. Jones might fall into this category (if only for the simple reason that this was Darla Tendaski we were talking about, and I could only imagine that Ms. Jones must have lost a few boyfriends to her in the past). Ms. Jones settled into the chair, leaning back and putting one well-dressed foot on the ottoman.

"First, did you know that Darla's had two, count them, two attempts to marry James?" She smiled slightly when she said this.

"You mean Nick."

"No, honey, I mean James."

Who was James? And why was she calling me "honey"?

"Did you know that Darla's been engaged to three different men?"

"No." Uh-oh. The warning "Danger: Delusional Maid of Honor Crossing" popped into my mind.

"That's why we need to talk. Can I smoke in here?"

Jenn looked suddenly edgy and nervous. G's antismoking rules be damned. Better to have her smoke than have her whip out a weapon and use it too generously on my person in some kind of nicotine-withdrawal frenzy. I nodded and she instantly lit up, as if a cigarette were a permanent, retractable part of her lip.

"Look, I appreciate your coming," I said while she lit the thing. "But I feel I must tell you that Darla and her, uh, current fiancé plan to be here in . . ." I glanced at my watch. "About fifteen minutes."

Jenn's eyes grew wide. She grabbed her purse and stood. "She can't see me here. She'll kill me."

"Uh, all right." I found myself feeling a bit suspicious. Perhaps she wasn't the real maid of honor, after all. She acted much more like a stalker ex-girlfriend of the groom than best friend of the bride.

"I still think we need to talk. Here's my card. . . ." She rummaged around her purse and pulled out a card with a torn edge. It said JENN JONES: FAMILY THERAPIST on it. "Call me today and we'll meet later."

I made a mental note to lose her card immediately and avoid all of her future phone calls.

No sooner had Ms. Jones left than another knock sounded at the door. I swung the door open. On the porch stood Jay the heckler, looking a bit sheepish.

"Er, hi," he said.

Great, just what I needed. Another run-in with Jay the heckler.

I took a tentative step backward—was he going to maul me again? I sniffed the air, but didn't smell alcohol.

"Look, I'm sorry about, er, the fireman's ball." Jay flushed bright red at the memory.

"Apology accepted," I said briskly. "Now, if you'll excuse me, I have a meeting with a client."

"I know. That's why I'm here."

Huh?

"What?" I just didn't get it.

Now it was his turn to be baffled.

"The guest list," he said. "Darla and I want to talk to you about the guest list."

"I thought that was an issue between the bride and groom."

The wrinkle in between Jay's brows deepened. "It is."

"Er, then, Nick is coming?" I said, fishing for clarity.

"No," Jay said, sounding even more confused. "Not that I know of."

Before I could digest this latest enigmatic piece of information, another knock sounded at the door. Darla, of course.

"Lauren!" she gushed, as if we were best friends. God, I hated it when brides did that. "So goooood to see you." She leaned in and kissed me, European style, on the cheek, but as I wasn't prepared for it, I flinched slightly, causing her lips to land somewhere to the right of my ear.

"Sweetie!" she said to the figure behind me (Jay, I assumed, unless she was speaking to Whiskers, which I doubted). Darla brushed past me, and kissed Jay full on the lips. Was *that* European style, too? I wondered.

I cleared my throat.

"So, are we still waiting on the groom?" I asked.

Both Darla and Jay gave me funny looks.

Then Jay answered with "You don't have to wait. I'm here."

"I know you're here, but where's the groom?"

Darla and Jay looked at each other and then back at me.

"Jay is James, the groom, Lauren," Darla said very slowly, with a worried look pulling at the corners of her face.

"No he's not," I said, laughing nervously. She was joking, right? Jay couldn't be the groom. . . . If he was the groom that would mean that Nick was . . . Nick was . . . single?

"You're not . . . He's not . . . Er . . . Then Nick is . . . uh . . . the . . ."

"Best man," Jay prompted.

OH MY GOD.

How could I have been so wrong? So horribly nearsighted?

"Of *course* you're the groom," I said, exhaling a forced laugh. "Of course Nick is the best man. I was just, er, *kidding.*" Marvelous recovery, I thought stupidly.

Darla and James didn't laugh.

"Uh, ahem," I said. "Would you like to sit down in the, uh, sitting room? I'll be right back."

I whipped around the corner into the kitchen and slumped against the counter. I felt so *stupid*. No matter which way I looked at it, I could not seem to digest this startling new, landscape-altering fact.

Nick wasn't engaged after all. My heart did a short but enthusiastic celebratory tap dance on top of my rib cage. Then the (admittedly rusty and seldom-used) gears of my mind creaked forward another notch. OK. If he wasn't engaged to Darla, then why was she all over him at the bar last night? And at Club de Ville a week ago? What the hell was going on here?

The caffeine in my system was pumping the blood so quickly through my veins that I felt light-headed and slightly nauseated. My heart thumped entirely too fast, skipping through beats, thudding hard, then soft, then hard again. *Wait a minute,* I thought, a sudden realization dawning. *I'm not the stupid one here* (well, not for the obvious reasons, anyway). Indignation welled up and spilled over into annoyance. *I* shouldn't be the one made to feel foolish. What the hell was Darla doing hanging all over her fiancé's brother, anyway? This explained why Nick hadn't seemed so pleased with her at the time. Now it was starting to make sense.

Even Jay the heckler doesn't deserve that, I thought. *He may not be as good-looking or as smart as his brother, but for goodness' sakes, no one deserves a cheater.* A quick and chilling calm came over me (which should clue you in immediately to the fact that I wasn't in my right frame of mind because when am I ever calm?), and I left the kitchen.

"I'm so sorry to have kept you waiting," I said, smiling brightly at the couple, who still looked at me with some degree of wariness.

"It's been such a busy season, you know. I hardly know whether I'm coming or going." I laughed lightly. Darla and Jay joined in.

Look at Darla, so smug in the belief that she's perfect. I couldn't *stand* it.

"Darla," I said, pushing on despite all the warning sirens in my head. "Did I see you at Paradox last night?"

Darla grew pale. "W-what?" she stammered.

"Paradox? You know, the dance club? Were you there last night? I could have sworn I saw you and . . ."

"No," she interrupted, a bit forcefully. "You didn't."

"You sure?" I said. "I thought I saw you and Nick there."

Her mouth dropped open. She couldn't believe I had actually said it. Come to think of it, I couldn't believe I had actually said it, either. What had gotten into me?

Jay saved the situation by laughing.

"Oh, I've got no doubt you saw Nick, and there was probably some woman hanging on him, because there always is," he said, chuckling. "He's got a thing for blondes."

Oh, he does, does he? I felt the temperature of my blood rise about ten degrees.

"He and Darla dated awhile—that is, before I stole her away," Jay continued, giving another out-of-place laugh.

My mind seemed to freeze. Did he say Nick and Darla dated?

"Oh, that was a long time ago," Darla said. "And you're the better catch, honey. You know that."

I looked at her and then at Jay. Was she serious? He was so pudgy. So loud . . . and did I mention he was beginning to bald?

At that moment, Jay gave her a peck on the lips and called her "pookie."

I was going to be sick. Violently ill. And soon.

"Let's get to the matter at hand," I said, breaking up the nauseating exchange. "The guest list."

Darla seemed relieved, but still wary. "Shouldn't we bring Gennifer in on this?" she said, a warning look in her eyes. Clearly, that was meant as some kind of threat.

"If you'd like," I said breezily, refusing to be intimidated.

"I would like," Darla said, sounding calm. Too calm, in my mind. I should have been more suspicious, granted, but what do you expect? I was still reeling from the information that Nick was single. I went to fetch G, who seemed predictably pleased that Darla asked her to be involved (despite the fact that just a week ago she had practically washed her hands of the whole affair).

I thought it best to clue G into the current situation by introducing Jay as "Darla's fiancé, Jay," and to G's credit, she didn't so much as blink an eye. I knew she had been under the same impression I had been (due to my influence), but she managed the new information admirably.

Darla chose this moment to blindside me.

"Gennifer," she began. "My aunt has such faith in your abilities."

G beamed. The more obvious the flattery, the better G likes it.

"But, I do have a concern," Darla continued.

G's brow came together in a worried, pinched way.

Just what was Darla up to?

"My concern is that, well, Lauren's been so busy with so many clients that Jay and I have not gotten very much attention."

"Is this true?" G said, clearly seeming as if she believed it was.

"Of course it's not true!" I blurted, sounding hopelessly childish and defensive, and thereby guilty. I tried to regroup. "Er, I mean, I've already made arrangements for the reception and the florist."

"You have? I wasn't aware of that," Darla said.

G let out a very loud and very aggravated sigh.

"How many times have I told you about the importance of

communication, Lauren?" G said. "You've got to keep the bride in the loop."

Darla smiled smugly. I just managed to restrain myself from clawing her eyes out.

"I am . . ." I wanted to say "appalled at your noxious behavior" but instead said, "I am sorry if I've not kept you properly informed." The apology sounded almost as insincere as I felt. Almost. Though G didn't seem to notice. Neither did Jay, who was managing nicely not to look at me directly, probably worried I might mention the firefighter's-ball incident to Darla. I glanced over at Darla. If she caught the edginess of my tone, it didn't dampen her bout of gloating.

Ooh. I was really beginning to hate her (and not in a "because she's put-together, rich, and beautiful" way, but in a self-righteous, morally founded "she's a major-league bitch" sort of way). The rest of the meeting went on in a similar fashion. Me pretending to be sincere, and Darla manipulating G like pretzel dough. Amazingly enough, I made it through the rest of the encounter without once hurling, a feat of incredible proportions, I thought, given the circumstances.

As soon as Darla and James left, and G finished lecturing me on the importance of customer service (God, I really *despised* that particular lecture, and the fact that Darla was the reason I had to listen to it *again* only made me hate her all the more), I fished out the maid of honor's crumpled business card from my purse and called her. Somebody needed to do some explaining. If it had to be the borderline psychotic with fabulous footwear, so be it.

"What's going on between Nick and Darla?"

Since Jenn seemed to prefer a blunt approach, I decided to use one. We were sitting on the patio at Shady Grove and had just ordered lunch. I couldn't think of a more crowded and public lunch spot (two necessary requirements for meeting with Jenn; I hadn't decided whether or not she would do me bodily harm), so here we were. Besides, Jenn could smoke here.

"So you know." Jenn seemed genuinely impressed. She lit up a cigarette, and took two or three deep puffs. Smoke wafted up above her head, into the branches of the giant tree above us (said tree accounted for both the "shady" and the "grove" in the eatery's name).

"All I know is that Darla is marrying Jay, but she appears to prefer mauling Nick in public places."

Jenn barked out a harsh laugh.

"Well, she always had a thing for him. Personally, I think she regretted picking Jay, given how the brothers turned out."

"What do you mean?"

"I mean, Jay used to be thirty pounds thinner and had a full head of hair," she said.

Jenn smashed her half-smoked cigarette into a stack of sugar packets on the table and then promptly lit another. "Darla can't keep her hands off men. Especially good-looking men. She is, to be frank, a slut."

I choked on the iced tea I had been about to swallow, spewing it down the front of my dress.

"Pardon me?"

"Don't get me wrong. I love her to death. But I love her like I would a friend who is an alcoholic or bulimic—with tough love."

"Oh." I patted down the front of my dress with my paper napkin, leaving a torn trail of soggy lint and bits of paper.

"Like I was saying, Darla is a slut. But she also has this ridiculous idea she wants to be married. It's an obsession with her. She doesn't care who's standing on the other side of the aisle, so long as he'll put a ring on her finger. Even when she's not engaged, which isn't that often, let me tell you, she's shopping for wedding dresses and veils."

I'd heard of this sort of thing before, though not as extreme a case as this. I even had a woman come to me and hire me for consulting purposes only to find out she didn't actually have a fiancé (she figured she'd pick one up sometime before the invitations were scheduled to go out).

"Anyway," Jenn continued, "the same thing happens each time. Darla suckers some poor fool into proposing to her, then she cheats on him. He finds out and the wedding's off."

"Does Jay know?"

"No. Not that he'd care. He's just as much on the prowl as she is. I wouldn't trust him as far as I can throw him, and since he weighs three times what I do, that wouldn't be far."

"Hmmm." Darla was far more of an evil person than even I gave her credit for (and I gave her credit for quite a lot, let me assure you). Of course, Jay wasn't exactly innocent, either, so I couldn't really feel sorry for him. "So why did they postpone the wedding three times?"

"First time, Darla got a weird case of cold feet. She does that sometimes. Second, James went off to Cancún with some ditsy blonde. Third time, she slept with her wedding consultant."

I must have looked at least half as flabbergasted as I felt, because Jenn quickly added, "He's a man," for clarification purposes.

"She was so busy screwing him, he didn't have much time to put the whole wedding deal together," Jenn said, crushing out her second cigarette in as many minutes.

"Oh." Made sense, in a bizarre way, I suppose.

The waiter, who had been hovering a bit too closely to our table, I thought (no doubt lured by our conversation), finally brought us our food: giant bowls of salads larger than our heads.

To my mind, the most important question hadn't yet been answered.

"Is Darla sleeping with Nick?"

Jenn, whose mouth was full of ranch-drenched salad, shrugged. "Look at her," she said after swallowing. "She's gorgeous and she doesn't take no for an answer. What do you think?"

Fourteen

I left Shady Grove and went directly to find Diane. First, I had to tell somebody about what had happened, and second, I didn't want to give G another opportunity to launch into her "bride's always right" speech. If G didn't like the fact that I was taking a two-hour lunch, I decided, she could damn well fire me. At this point, I frankly didn't care.

Diane was at home, thank God. She is a freelance writer, so you never know when she's going to be running off somewhere to do some interviewing. Although, these days, wedding planning had taken a front seat to working, and you were much more likely to find her poring over bridal magazines than writing her own articles. I personally believe that Congress should pass a Wedding Planning Leave Act that would enable all brides-to-be to take off a month from work in order to plan their weddings. It's a universal truth that soon-to-be brides waste at least thirty percent of their workdays in wedding distractions.

"Lauren, thank goodness you're here," she said when she opened her door. She pulled me inside before I could say much of anything.

"What do you think? This one?" She held up a small white,

embossed card. "Or, this one?" Another white, embossed card. They looked almost identical. "For the place cards," she explained. As far as I could see, the only difference was in the placement of a single curlicue (left-centered versus right-centered).

"This one," I said, pointing to the first.

"You think so?" Diane looked doubtful.

"No, the other one," I said. She instantly brightened.

"Yes, I think so, too."

"Diane, I have to talk to you."

"OK. OK. Just one more thing. This card holder?" She held up a tiny silver stand. "Or this one?" She held up another tiny silver stand.

"The second one," I said decisively.

"You think?" Diane hesitated. "God, I have such fat fingers," she muttered, distracted by her hand. "I *hate* my hands."

"You *aren't fat,* for crying out loud!" I said, raising my voice a little. "Now, can I speak?"

Diane jumped, startled.

"What's wrong?"

"Nick isn't engaged to Darla."

"Why didn't you *say* something before now?"

"Can you believe him?" I said, indignantly, after I had finished telling her the whole of the story. "He's *sleeping* with his brother's fiancée!"

"Why are you surprised?" Diane said. "Didn't you yesterday suspect him of hitting on you when you thought *he* was engaged?"

"But that's different."

"Why? Because he was hitting on you and not Darla?"

Hmmm. She might have me there.

"Well, that doesn't matter. I think you should calm down a minute," Diane said. "First of all, you don't know for a fact they're sleeping together. I mean, didn't you see *him* rejecting *her* last night?"

"Yeah."

"There you go. Now, let's get out of here. You, my girl, still need shoes for my wedding, which must I remind you is in two weeks? Besides, I wouldn't mind buying another pair, because my feet are the only part of me not ten pounds overweight."

"You aren't fat! How many times do I have to say it?"

"Yeah, yeah, whatever."

I couldn't concentrate at all on shoes, which shows you just how distracted I really was. Diane gave up after half an hour of trying to entice me with all sorts of cute slides and open-toed strappy contraptions. "Just sleep with him for crying out loud," she told me when I dropped her off at home. "Just do it and be done."

The very thought of *that* sent my head spinning.

It's only natural, then, that I could not do any more work for the rest of the afternoon. Every time the phone rang, I thought it might be Nick (he did say rather emphatically that he would call), and every time it wasn't him I quickly lost interest in the other person on the line.

G came down to my desk around four to tell me something, but I don't remember what exactly, because all the while her lips were moving, I kept thinking, *Nick, Nick, why haven't you* called *me?* Now that I knew he wasn't engaged, everything had changed.

I felt sure that if I could only talk to him, I'd be able to straighten this whole situation out. The more I thought about it, the more what Diane had said made sense. I didn't know for sure he'd slept with Darla, and until I did, I couldn't very well hold that against him. What had he said last night? Something about nothing being between them? Then again, the thought that he might have slept with her made me crazy. I *had* to know. Not knowing was killing me.

"Lauren, are you listening?" This was G, one hand on her hip and the other holding her reading glasses in an accusatory point.

"Uh-huh."

She began speaking again, and immediately my mind drifted.

"Lauren!" G barked after a minute.

"Huh? Oh, right. Sure." I have no idea what I agreed to do.

"Great, then I'm headed out."

What? I perked up. G was leaving? I looked at my watch. Four-fifteen on the nose.

I waited until I heard G pull out of the driveway, and then I quickly packed up my things and turned off my computer. Did you really expect me to stick around?

I was so preoccupied on the way home that I missed my street at first, and had to loop around the block to get to my house. I walked up the narrow path to my front door in a fog, my head down, my thoughts circling around my head like sharks.

So you see why I didn't see him right away. One doesn't usually expect to have men waiting on one's porch, if you know what I mean.

"Lauren?"

"Nick!" I jumped back as if he had been a giant bug. God, he had a way of sneaking up on me. I never understood how he managed to do that. He was so broad. And tall. And firmly muscled. Mmmm. I snapped back into focus. *Get ahold of yourself,* I thought, giving myself a mental shake. He had some explaining to do, didn't he?

"Uh, I wanted to talk to you." He sounded almost, well, sheepish.

"How long have you been standing here?"

"Not long." He kicked the toe of his shoe against the corner of my welcome mat. "Maybe an hour."

"An hour?" A whole hour? I couldn't believe it.

"I didn't want to miss you," he said, looking at his feet. "I didn't want to give you the chance to, uh, lock me out."

"Oh," I said, pausing to digest this new piece of information. "I suppose I should let you in, then." I couldn't believe how cool I sounded. Who knew I had it in me?

I unlocked the door and walked through it, leaving Nick to follow. He did, shutting the door behind him. I tossed my bag and my blazer on the ottoman, took a seat on my couch, and crossed my legs. Nick remained standing.

"What was it that you wanted to tell me?" Listen to the calmness of my voice. I couldn't believe how confident and collected I seemed.

Nick began to pace.

"Lauren, I like you. A lot," he said, looking everywhere in the room but at me. "You're so put-together. So sure of yourself. So capable. So funny and beautiful. Not at all like any of the women I've dated before."

I blinked. Did he say "beautiful" and "funny"? I blinked again. Did he also put me in the official "girls he's dated" category?

"I really liked you and I really hoped we could have a . . . have a . . ." Nick swallowed. "A relationship."

I must be hearing things.

Nick stopped pacing. He turned and faced me.

"I know you must think after what you saw last night that there's something between me and Darla."

At the mention of Darla's name, my hands tightened around the folds of my skirt. I wasn't sure I wanted to hear what was about to come next.

"But I want you to know that there isn't anything between us," he said. "We went out on two dates. Long before she and my brother got together. But that's it. Nothing more. I've tried everything to get her to leave me alone, and she just won't. She's making my life a nightmare."

Two dates? That was all?

How could I not believe him? Look at those earnest, puppy-dog eyes. I let out a small, inaudible sigh. Even my inner brat felt all giggly and warm.

"The worst of it is, she's probably made me lose the one thing I want most," he said, giving me a sincerely pained look. "You."

Nick looked down at his shoes again. My mouth fell slack. When I managed to gain control over my jaw again, Nick had barreled on.

"Darla follows me everywhere," he continued, putting both hands in his hair. "She calls my house four or five times a day. She's shown up at the firehouse and refused to leave. She grabs me in public places, as if she wants to get caught . . ."

I didn't hear what he said next.

I stood, crossed the room, and put my hands on either side of his face. I don't even remember deciding to do it. I just somehow wanted to and I did.

I kissed him.

And not just any kiss. An openmouthed, ain't-nothing-platonic-about-it, let's-get-it-on kiss. And before you go thinking this is the sort of thing I do all the time, let me tell you it isn't. I'm the worst when it comes to being the aggressor in physical relationships. I've never in my life initiated the first kiss. Never. Not once. Not even with Brad. It's just not something I do. I usually feel so horribly shy when it comes to that kind of thing. I'm always worried about what he'll think, and how I might seem, and if my breath is fresh enough. I'd rather die than make the first move. Even if Keanu Reeves were standing in my living room, practically begging me to kiss him, I don't think I could do it. Yet, here was Nick, standing in my living room, looking ten times better than Keanu Reeves, and I was kissing him like a first-rate porno star.

Meanwhile, Nick, who seemed at first taken aback by the kiss, now decided to become an active participant, and began kissing me back with a toe-curling amount of, uh, enthusiasm. Believe me, I felt it from the tip of my scalp all the way down to the silver polish on my toes.

"Stop . . ." I exhaled as our lips touched again. " . . . talking . . ." And again. " . . . about . . ." And again. " . . . Darla."

"OK," Nick said in a hoarse whisper. Then he leaned in, covered my lips with his, and deepened the kiss, shooting it up by about forty decibels (and believe me, it was pretty loud already). All I can say is there was definitely tongue involved. And groping. Lots of groping.

I found my hands roaming over his back, into his hair, over his shoulders. I felt his hands wandering up my back, then back down to my waist and around my hips. He pressed me closer to him, squeezed me into him, so we had full and complete body contact. I can safely say I could feel the ridges of his abs through the thin T-shirt he was wearing (most definitely a six-pack), and, I might add, I believe I felt something else, too, if you get my drift.

I hadn't been so worked up since, well, never. I wanted Nick. I wanted him right now. And if I was feeling what I thought I was feeling, he wanted me, too.

His shirt absolutely, positively had to come off. Now. I tugged at it and it went easily over his head.

Then, Nick scooped me up in his arms, continuing to kiss me as he guided me toward the couch. Now, that just wouldn't do.

"The bedroom," I managed to get out between kisses, as I pointed back in the other direction.

He turned and went that way (managing to maneuver me

through my narrow hall without once hitting my head or legs). He gave my bedroom door a firm kick and it swung open, hitting the wall with a crack (a sound that sent shivers down my spine). He carried me easily over the threshold of the bedroom (how he saw where he was going, I'll never know) and then laid me down on my neatly made bed. Of all the times I'd dreamt of Nick carrying me to my bedroom (and believe me, they were many), it had never been this . . . delicious.

"Are you sure you want to do this?" Nick said, pausing.

The fact that he actually took the time to officially ask my permission drove me absolutely over the edge.

"Uh-huh," I said, as I wrapped my fingers around his belt loops and pulled him down on top of me.

Fifteen

J'm not sure how it happened. One minute we were about to kiss. The next minute, we'd clonked foreheads.

"Ow," I said, wincing, holding my head. "I guess I'm dangerous."

Nick, who was looking at me through one open eye, laughed.

"Maybe we'd better slow down," he said, giving me a sly smile.

His hands were on the buttons of my shirt, undoing each one in seeming slow motion. He spread the fabric deliberately, and then leaned down—slowly this time and with care not to collide—and lined my neck with a trail of kisses, ending at the clasp of my bra. I thought for one fearful moment he'd unlatch it with his teeth, and then I'd have to laugh at him, or run from the bedroom screaming—who does that? And then I thought, *Why am I thinking he's going to undo it with his teeth?* And just as I was trying to tell myself not to worry, and just to go with the flow *for once in my life*, he'd already undone it, the traditional way, with his fingers, and there I was, half naked. But he didn't stop there—he was tugging at my skirt, and before I had time to even think about what underwear I was wearing, it was off, down around my ankles.

Now this is the point where I usually panic. After all, I don't particularly like being naked—especially not in front of a man as good-looking as Nick, and under the bright lights of my bedroom. Being naked usually reminds me that I'm about to have sex, and while I certainly like to have sex, I'd prefer, honestly, to be able to have sex in a set of oversized flannel pajamas. That would be the ideal comfort zone. Then I wouldn't have to worry about the cellulite on my thighs, the way my boobs seemed always to want to drift apart, wall-eyed, the way my stomach paunches in the least attractive way. After a while, when I was with Brad, I'd forgotten some of these insecurities, but here, with Nick, I remembered them all in a rush. Suddenly, I wanted to dive under the covers.

Nick, however, didn't run screaming from the bed. He didn't laugh at me. In fact, he was peppering my stomach with kisses, which I took as a good sign. He worked his way up, greeting each nipple with a flick of his tongue, and my mind, which had been spinning, started to relax into a sort of comfortable goo. *This feels good,* my body screamed to my head. *Shut up and enjoy it.*

Nick was kissing me on the lips now, his body heavy on mine, his lips soft, insistent. My hands instinctively busied themselves unlatching his belt, and the top button of his pants, and just when I managed to get his zipper undone, he moved down again, out of my reach. He was kissing my stomach, my belly button, my lower abdomen. Before I could even think of what it meant, he was kissing my inner thigh, gently pushing my legs apart. I snapped my head up.

"What are you doing?" I asked, shocked, because when Brad did what Nick looked like he was about to do, usually he wanted a ticker-tape parade afterward, a medal of honor. Brad went there so rarely it was like a special holiday when he actually made it, a sexual Christmas. As a result, Brad wasn't very good at it. Horrible, to be honest. It was hardly worth the buildup. I didn't want Nick to fall into that category. I didn't want him to be a fumbler.

"Relax," Nick said, "I want to."

I closed my eyes and braced myself for the worst.

It didn't happen. Nick was nothing like Brad. Nick knew what he was doing.

After a few moments, I completely lost every single coherent thought in my head in the rush of heat that flooded my body. I was close, very close, almost over the edge, my mind too far absorbed to think this was odd, especially on the first go, after so long out of practice. Under normal circumstances, orgasms were elusive things. I had to chase after them, deliberate, focused. This was something else entirely. This was like a wave, an ocean. It had its own rhythm and speed. It was taking me along for the ride.

I was tugging at Nick's arms. I wanted something else. I wanted *him. Inside. Now.* There was a pause, a rustle of paper—the condom wrapper fluttered down into the trash can beside the bed. And Nick was on top again, inside, kissing me with his whole mouth. The urgency and the heat collided, and then all my senses were flooded by a great, crashing wave.

After, we lay panting, together, me beside him, my hand on his chest, feeling the cool air of my bedroom evaporate the thin layer of sweat on my back. And I was still not thinking coherent thoughts when I said, "Wow," blowing out a long, satisfied breath. Nick grabbed me and pulled me close, kissing me, and then I rested my head on his chest and sighed. We lay like that for what seemed like ever.

"You're good," I said, then regretted it, thinking it sounded stupid, even for after-sex talk.

"You too," he said, smiling, pulling me even closer, kissing my forehead, then my nose, then lips. "You want seconds?" he asked, smiling like he'd done something bad.

"Do I ever," I said, climbing on top.

• • •

I've never in my whole life just fallen into bed with a man I barely knew. Especially not one as good-looking as Nick. In fact, one could say with some certainty that I've never slept with anyone as gorgeous (and as talented) as Nick. I only barely resisted the urge after we were done to roll over and call Diane and Veronica. Barely. I mean, who would believe I actually did it? Fortunately, after the second round, I was in no frame of mind to tie my shoes, much less use something as complicated as a telephone. My brain had been transformed into a warm, gooey substance incapable of coherent thought. Diane? Veronica? Who were they?

After a few more scrumptious moments being cuddled in Nick's strong (and particularly well defined) arms, I absently noticed that in our fury, we had made a disaster area of my bedroom. Pillows had been tossed haphazardly in every direction. My comforter clung to the corner of my bed by a small patch of fabric and the sheets had somehow been twisted and pulled and lay predominantly on the left side, having been completely ripped from the right. Clothes lay strewn across the floor, on my night table and the lamp. I looked up and saw my bra hanging by an arm strap from the left post of my bed.

Oh my.

For once, I didn't at all care about the mess. Secretly, I wished I could snap a picture for posterity. Rarely (and in my case never) does one's bedroom become a scene from a bodice-ripping romance novel.

The light in the room dimmed, and I noticed the room had gotten significantly darker since we had first entered it. How long had we been at it? I wondered. I glanced over at my alarm clock, but a strategically placed sock blocked out the numbers.

Nick nuzzled my ear and I shivered in delight.

My stomach chose this moment to let out a loud, bubbling

growl. It, apparently, was the only part of my anatomy not thoroughly satisfied.

Nick laughed.

"Hungry?" he asked, touching his nose to mine.

I nodded. "I suppose I should get dressed and . . ."

"Absolutely not."

"What?"

"Get dressed. I forbid it."

"You do?"

"It took me this long to get that gorgeous figure out of those clothes. As far as I'm concerned, clothes are the enemy." Nick smiled, a big, boyish grin. He grabbed the nearest article of my clothing (the bra) and flung it with relish to the other side of the room.

I laughed. Never in my life had a man ordered me to remain naked. I had always assumed covering up was best for everyone involved. This was a new and decidedly sexy turn.

"What about food?" I asked.

"I've got it," he said. "Don't move a beautiful muscle." He kissed my shoulder and slid off the bed. I watched his delectably firm figure pad out of my bedroom. Shortly thereafter, I heard the refrigerator open, and articles being shuffled around my kitchen. I found myself beaming. I took a ridiculous amount of delight in the notion that Nick was wandering naked around my house.

In another minute, Nick returned, carrying a tray filled with cheese, crackers, a sliced apple, and an open bottle of merlot and two glasses. I must admit, however, that the tray wasn't the first thing that drew my attention, if you understand what I'm saying.

"This is the second time you've made me a meal," I said. "Is this going to be a habit?"

"I hope so," Nick said, feeding me a piece of cheese. For a second or we two both ate hungrily. Then, Nick paused.

"I have a confession to make," he said.

Uh-oh. Was this where he breaks the news that he has a wife and three kids in Arizona?

"I thought I didn't have a chance with you."

"You what?" I said, stopping in midchew. A double life I could handle, but him doubting he'd get me into bed? What was the world coming to?

"First of all, almost every time I saw you, there was some guy hanging all over you."

"There was? When?"

"At Club de Ville."

I racked my brain. Club de Ville? Man hanging on me? Oh! Bobbie. The horny hairstylist. Ugh.

"Then, my brother did a nice job mauling you, so that I doubted you'd ever want to see me again," Nick was saying. "Plus, I figured I'd probably scared you away by insisting you had to go to the emergency room for the ankle and then imposing on you by spending the night. I figured you must think I was the biggest jerk."

I was so taken aback I couldn't speak (that, and my mouth was full of cheese and cracker bits).

"Then, that morning you looked like you kept expecting a boyfriend to come over. And the final thing, of course, was when you saw Darla and me at the club."

It was my turn to confess. I told him that the reason I had been acting so weird was that I was under the mistaken impression that he was engaged to Darla. Any bizarre behavior on my part could be mostly attributable to that. Other weird behavior, I didn't have an excuse for.

"You thought Darla and I were engaged?" Nick sounded astonished. "But she isn't my type at all."

I suppose Jay the heckler had another thing wrong.

"What is your type?" I asked, swallowing another mouthful of crackers.

"You," Nick half-growled, pushing the tray out of the way and pouncing on me in a lusciously primal way. He kissed me as he pushed me down on the bed.

For the rest of the night, we spent precious little time sleeping. Between talking and activities decidedly more physical, sleep didn't play a major role. Around 4:30 A.M., I fell asleep with my head against Nick's chest, and didn't wake up until the sun was streaming brightly through my windows. I was alone in bed, and thought for a second that the whole thing might have been a dream. Then I heard Lily's voice at my front door.

"Who are you?" she was saying.

"Nick Corona," I heard Nick say, in that deep voice of his.

I jumped out of bed (or semi-hobbled, since my ankle, though almost as good as new, was still a bit tender) and scurried to find something to wrap myself in (Nick had made good on his promise to keep me nude) and found a discarded silk robe on the floor. I put it on and rushed to the front room. Lily was standing on my porch, and Nick was holding open the front door wearing a pair of jeans but nothing else (beautifully bare to the waist).

I got there just in time to hear Lily say, "You're much better-looking than the losers Lauren usually drags home."

Ooh. I was going to *kill* her. I cleared my throat. Lily sent me a sly smile. "Hi, sis," she said, coming through the door carrying a large duffel bag. "Long time no see."

"What are you *doing* here?" I hissed at her when she got a little closer.

"The more interesting question is what exactly are *you* doing here?" Lily said, clearly having fun at my expense. Ooh.

Sometimes sisterhood was a great burden to bear. She tossed her duffel in a corner and promptly plopped down on my couch.

"I got evicted," she said matter-of-factly. "Do you have anything to eat?" She stood up and headed to the refrigerator.

"You got evicted?" I said, trailing after her.

"Yup. They took my furniture for back rent."

"*Your* furniture? You mean Mom's furniture."

"Whatever."

"Does Mom know?"

Lily, who was drinking out of my orange-juice carton, choked. "Of course not," she said indignantly. "What kind of idiot do you think I am?"

"A homeless one," I said.

She ignored me.

"So, I was hoping to crash here a few days."

"Oh, no," I said. "Last time you crashed here, so did six of your friends. I'm still finding pot stashes all over the house."

Nick, who was keeping a discreet distance, let out a small cough.

I lowered my voice.

"You can stay, but only if it's just you," I amended, figuring that she'd do what she wanted to anyway, and there wasn't much point in me putting my foot down.

"OK," she said, shrugging.

"And my closet is off-limits," I added.

"Whatever."

"And no drug use," I said.

"OK. OK." She put the orange juice back in the fridge. "Did you really find pot?" she asked hopefully.

"I flushed it."

"Damn."

●　　　●　　　●

Nick, as it turned out, had the day off. I was slowly learning about how firefighters worked. It seemed they had twenty-four- or forty-eight-hour on-duty shifts and then three days completely off in between. I, on the other hand, had to work, and as tempted as I was to call in sick, I decided G probably wouldn't let me stay home (on days I did call in sick, she'd drive me crazy by calling the house every five minutes to ask where some folder or another was). Besides, I had a couple of meetings in the afternoon that I didn't feel it would be fair to cancel.

Loath as I was to do it, I did get dressed for work. Nick didn't help. He kept trying to convince me that I should play hooky (I could see already that he would be a very bad influence on me, but I loved the fact that it was the morning after and he still wanted to spend time with me). I told Nick he was welcome to stay (unlike Lily, who wasn't welcome, but would stay anyway). When I prepared to leave, Nick followed me to the door, refusing to let me go before giving me a very long, very intense good-bye kiss (I think it was his last-ditch effort to convince me to stay home and, let me tell you, it almost worked). I had a difficult time walking to the car, what with my knees having turned into water.

On the way to work, I reapplied my lipstick while waiting at a stoplight (most of it now being on Nick instead of me) and noticed that my lips looked a little on the puffy side (they weren't used to so much exercise, I suppose) and my cheeks had an inert, rosy glow. My eyes looked bright and full of energy, and my hair had a slightly tousled, easily thrown-together look (my hair always looked thrown-together but never easily so). *Sex with incredible-looking men becomes me,* I thought. *I should make a rule to do it more often. Much more often.*

I breezed into G's door an hour late and wasn't even worried about what she might say. I couldn't care less. All I could think was: Nick had made love to me. Repeatedly. That thought, and flashbacks from the night before, kept popping up in my head even while I was doing the most mundane of tasks, like pouring myself a cup of coffee or paper-clipping a file. I couldn't concentrate on anything (so much for sex making a woman clearheaded, I thought, with not a little amount of irony). I found myself putting receipts into the wrong folders and staring blankly for minutes on end at my computer screen.

Distractions aside, nothing, I decided, could ruin my day. Not even Whiskers, who had taken to mewing pitifully from the vicinity of the kitchen. Aside from that, the house seemed remarkably quiet. I went to check G's office, but it was empty and her computer was turned off (although that's not really a sign of anything, since it's so rarely turned on). But her purse, I noticed, wasn't anywhere about, so it was safe to assume she had not yet arrived.

The morning ticked on. Two hours slunk by, and all I managed to accomplish was drawing little doodles on my calendar and misfiling about a dozen receipts. I was overcome by the strongest urge to call home, just to see if Nick was still there, but I managed to restrain myself. The last thing I wanted to do was seem eager and pathetic (most especially because I was). I had that much dignity at least. Noon rolled around and there was still no sign of G. I didn't take much notice. Sometimes she went whole days without coming into the office, but she did usually make a point of telling me, if in passing. But not always. Whiskers, meanwhile, only seemed to get more vocal as the day wore on (mewing pathetically at high pitches). It got so bad, I couldn't even concentrate on my now-based-on-a-true-story Nick fantasies. I finally went into the kitchen to see if the cat had somehow hurt herself.

I found her sitting in the middle of the floor next to one of her bowls, which she had knocked over. The cat put a paw on the underside of the plastic dish and mewed. I guess that meant the thing was hungry. I opened the cupboard and pulled out a bag of cat food and poured the dry mix into the righted bowl. Whiskers just stared at it, flicked her tail disdainfully, and flattened one ear to her head.

"If you're hungry," I told her, "you'll eat it." My phone rang, and so I put the bag down on the floor and went to answer it.

"Hi." At the sound of Nick's voice, my stomach tied itself into a knot and squeezed.

"Hi," I said, my voice dropping about an octave.

"Want to grab lunch?"

"Yes," I nearly shouted, then swallowed. "Er, I mean, uh, that would be great."

Nice recovery, I thought. Nick, however, was laughing.

We decided to meet at the Austin Java Company, since Nick had to run some errands downtown and the place was pretty close to G's office. Parking, as usual, was a mess, and it took me about ten minutes to find a space around the corner. Nick was waiting for me inside, and my heart jumped a little when I saw him. A little bit of gloating glee bubbled up inside me. Less than six hours ago he was lying in my bed naked, I reminded myself. Naked. In my bed!

And if the look he gave me when he saw me was any indication, he was thinking the exact same thing about me. That thought made me blush straight up to my ears.

"Hi," he said, slipping an arm around my waist.

"Hi," I said, leaning into him.

We ordered (we both had turkey sandwiches) and then we sat down in a corner booth right below a rather distorted-looking painting of a woman by the local artist of the week.

"Did you survive Lily?" I asked, as Nick sat down on the other side of the table.

"She's a good kid," he said. Secretly, I was thrilled he called her a "kid." Not that I'm usually the jealous type, but my sister is plenty attractive in her own right. There are tons of men attracted to her free-spirit, no-rules, retro-hippie style.

"What did you guys talk about?" Please not my ex-husband, I inwardly prayed.

"Stuff. She had a wealth of information about you."

Oh lord. I knew it had been a mistake to leave the two of them alone. God knows what she told him.

"Like what?"

Nick smiled his lazy smile, but said nothing. A waiter interrupted us then with the distribution of sandwiches.

"Tell me," I pleaded, taking a bite.

"Nope," he said, shaking his head. "I was sworn to secrecy."

Lily was so dead. So dead.

"You were, were you?" I shrugged. "Doesn't matter." I tried valiantly to look calm and nonchalant. All the while I was dreaming up ways to squeeze out of Lily whatever it was she had told him.

"Your mom dropped by," Nick said.

A piece of turkey lodged itself in my throat and I started coughing uncontrollably. Nick had to come around to my side and tap me on the back before I'd stop.

"What?" I said when I had air in my windpipe again. "My mother!" Horror of horrors! I hoped Nick had a shirt on by then.

"She brought you some soup," he said. "For your ankle," he added. "I told her it was about healed."

What else did you tell her? I thought, worriedly. Or, more important, what did she tell Nick?

"I'm sorry," I said. "I usually save my mother for the fourth or fifth week of a relationship. She tends to have a talent for scaring off boyfriends."

"Not at all. I liked her."

"You did?" No, he had to be lying.

"She loves you and Lily a lot."

"That's true," I said. "Sometimes, she's a little overenthusiastic in that department."

"All mothers are."

"Did my dad drop by, too? Maybe my second-grade home-room teacher? Or my high-school prom date?"

"Nope." Nick laughed.

"Good."

Since Nick had met my mother and my sister in one day, I felt sure he probably wouldn't want anything more to do with me for the rest of the week. Miraculously, he invited me out to dinner that very same night. (I readily accepted. Veronica later said I should have played it cool and put him off, but I was never any good at playing hard to get. In my experience, a woman like me playing it cool with Nick would be like a blind man turning down free sight-restoring surgery: a very dumb idea.)

When I got back from lunch, there was still no sign of G, and furthermore, both of my appointments that very afternoon called to cancel, leaving me free to daydream to my heart's content. Around 2:30, with G still not in the office, I decided that what I really should be doing was shopping for an outfit for tonight.

I called Diane, realizing with a start that she had no idea what had happened overnight, and gave her a quick update. She told me she had to see me, and so we met at Scarborough's boutique. My inner brat was getting her way quite a bit these days, since I was ready to plop down three hundred dollars for a new dress. But, I reasoned, they had great shoes there, too, and I needed to find a pair that wouldn't land me in the emergency room.

"Oh my God. Look at you," Diane said when she saw me. "You look like you just rolled out of bed with him. Was he that good?"

"Better," I said.

Diane humored me through about ten dress try-ons, before I finally settled on a lime green slip dress (not a color I normally wear, but one that Diane said looked incredible as a backdrop to my dark, curly hair). I was a little worried about the slit in the side (it practically went up to the meatiest part of my thigh), and the neckline, which was decidedly lower than I usually wear. You could definitely see a hint of cleavage from certain angles. Diane pooh-poohed what she called my "puritanical critique."

"He'll love it," she said confidently. "Trust me."

Shoes came next, and this time I was determined to choose heels I could actually walk in without breaking (or spraining) an important joint. I picked open-toed slides with a cute, inch-high sliver of a heel.

Then came my next crisis. My toes. The paint on them was so old, it was peeling up along the edges. I looked down, hoping that Nick hadn't taken much notice of them last night. Of course, as I recalled, he seemed more involved with certain other parts of my anatomy. I blushed fiercely at the memory.

"Pedicure. We both need one," Diane said, dragging me off to another diversion. After a pedicure and manicure (Diane insisted on both), it was 5:30 P.M. And I hadn't been in the office all afternoon. I took about a minute to be worried about that fact. That was all the time I could spare, really. The rest of me was too wrapped up in thinking about the coming evening. Can you blame me?

When I got home, Lily was lounging on my couch eating chips out of the bag and dribbling crumbs all over the front of her shirt and into my couch cushions. A half-dozen empty soda cans sat in various locations across the living room, with the heaviest concentration on my coffee table.

"Lily," I said, sternly.

She didn't turn.

"LILY!" I yelled. She sat up slightly and looked over at me.

"What?" she said.

"What did you tell Nick about me?"

"Nothing."

"Really. What did you say?"

"Just that it had been a while since you'd gotten any."

I just barely restrained myself from throttling her.

"You didn't."

"It's no big deal. He seemed to be more interested in the fact that you had been married before."

"You didn't tell him about Brad!"

"How do you think we got on the subject of you not getting any?"

I put my head in my hands, then lifted it again.

"Did you see Mom when she came by?"

"Nope. I hid in the bathroom."

"You let Nick deal with her *alone?*"

"Uh. *Yeah.*" She said it like it was the only reasonable course of action.

"Lily! How could you do that?"

"Do what?"

"Arrgh," I said, throwing up my hands. I had a date to get ready for, and the last thing I needed was to get worked up by Lily's fuzzy logic.

"Wow," Lily said when she wandered into my bedroom an hour later (eating more of my food, by the way—this time carrot sticks).

"'Wow' good or 'Wow' bad?" I asked.

"Definitely 'Wow' good," Lily said, her mouth full. She swallowed. "I take it I'll have the house to myself tonight?" She raised her eyebrows.

I blushed furiously. I had to stop *doing* that, I thought.

"Uh-huh. That's what I thought."

I was busy trying to pull out the clumps in my mascara when Nick came to the door. Lily let him in, instructing him that I was "primping" in the bathroom. Lily didn't wear makeup, because her skin was practically perfect and her eyelashes were naturally thick and curly, so she took digs at me whenever possible. At least she managed to refrain from referring to me as "raccoon eyes," which she did on occasion.

When I emerged from the bathroom and walked into the living room, Nick, who was conversing with Lily about something, stopped in midsentence. His eyes widened a little.

"You look . . ." Nick paused. "Incredible."

I blinked, because that's not exactly what I expected to hear. But I liked it. I definitely liked it. In fact, I thought, I could get used to his compliments.

Lily gave me a "I told you so but you never believe me" look over Nick's shoulder, and I just restrained myself from sticking my tongue out at her. Instead, I wrinkled my nose in her direction, which was just as effective, I thought, but (a little) less childish.

"No parties and no pot," I said over my shoulder as Nick pulled me out the door.

Lily rolled her eyes. "Yes, *Mom.*"

"I am *not* like Mom," I threw back.

"Whatever," she said, closing the door after us.

•   •   •

We didn't make it very far. As soon as we got to the curb, Nick pressed me up against him, and kissed me. My inner brat was jumping for joy. I didn't even have time or the presence of mind to worry about whether Lily was watching from the house.

"I'm beginning to think we should skip dinner," Nick said, a little out of breath, when he finally pulled back. I was thinking the exact same thing.

My stomach, ever the betrayer, loudly voiced its opposition to that plan.

"But it sounds like you're hungry," he said. "Let's eat first."

We decided on Z-Tejas, because they have wonderful fish tacos. Sounds disgusting, I know, but they are actually very good. The restaurant was extremely crowded (as all good restaurants in Austin are at any time of night even on a Wednesday—I believe no one in Austin ever uses their kitchens, and that the population's collective refrigerators and stoves are all for show). The hostess shuffled us to the bar, where we lasted about fifteen minutes before Nick (who kept whispering rather naughty things in my ear) suggested we order our dinners to go.

I'm (only slightly) ashamed to admit we didn't get around to actually eating our dinner until much later on in the evening.

Since my sister was now a squatter in my own house, Nick invited me over to his place, which was a spacious yet quaint two-bedroom renovated carriage house in Tarrytown. Inside, his place was remarkably neat and well put-together (not overly stylish, but well organized, a trait I admired). Almost before I had put my purse down, Nick had his arms around me, and you know where that would lead.

Later, Nick brought me my cold take-out and served me in bed.

"I'm beginning to think you won't let me eat unless I'm naked," I said, taking a bite of my flour tortilla.

"Now, that's an idea," he said, grinning like a fiend.

Nick and I parted ways around 12:30, since Nick said he had to work in the morning. He told me he'd call me in a day or two (as his shift began later that day) and he wouldn't be free again until Saturday night. He told me under no circumstances should I make plans unless they included him. That thought kept me smiling.

Sixteen

I didn't think anything could touch me. That's how completely
happy and content I felt.

But you knew it wouldn't last.

In fact, that feeling of invincible happiness pretty much disappeared the minute I arrived at work.

Everything was in chaos (and I'm not talking the usual bridal
emergencies; this was a mess by any standard). It looked as if
someone, or more likely some thing, had torn through the house
with the force of a cyclone, ripping at curtains, tossing magazines,
trailing bits of trash everywhere. The epicenter of the storm
seemed to be in the kitchen, which had been turned upside down.
Cupboards on the top and bottom cabinets stood open, and a glass
or two (who could tell from the shards) had toppled out of them,
crashing into pieces on the countertop. The cat-food bag, which I
had inadvertently left out, had been ripped to shreds, and bits of
dried cat food pieces were tossed to all corners of the kitchen. I
kept stepping on the crunchy pieces, grinding them into crumbs
as I made my way through. I doubted seriously that a burglar or
human vandal would take such an interest in cat food. This left
only one obvious culprit.

I ventured up the stairs and was hit with a particular pungent smell on the second landing (catbox stink, and the worst kind), and also saw evidence of more damage, including the back of G's chair, which was scarred with Whiskers' telltale claw marks.

For her part, Whiskers sat on top of G's desk, coolly licking one paw, and didn't give me so much as a glance when I entered the room.

"Shoo," I told her, annoyed at the mess she had made. She just stared up at me blankly.

I didn't understand why G hadn't taken the thing home. Whiskers flicked her tail and slowly jumped down from the desk, clearly letting me know it was her choice and not my orders at the root of her decision to leave the desk. When she leapt down, she uncovered G's desk calendar, which had a circle around this week. "Gone to Chicago Bridal Convention," it said, with a line running from yesterday until Sunday.

That's why I hadn't seen G in a while. And, I realized with a start, she had probably told me she was going to the conference day before yesterday (when I had tuned her out). Then, almost immediately, the repercussions of G's being out of town hit me in full force: I could have easily taken off the last two days and spent them with Nick, dammit! She would have never known. Ooh. I never thought I'd be kicking myself for not listening attentively enough to G. Damn.

I looked down at Whiskers, who was trying (unsuccessfully) to extract a sticky note from one of her back paws. I leaned down and easily plucked the thing off.

I recognized G's loopy handwriting immediately. At the top, it read: "Remind Lauren to look after Darling W" (Darling W being Whiskers) and in all caps at the bottom she had written: "DO NOT LEAVE W ALONE IN HOUSE."

Uh-oh. Too late.

"Bad kitty," I told it, belatedly.

Whiskers just flicked her tail once to the right, and put her tiny pink nose in the air.

It was hard not to dwell on the fact that I carelessly lost two luxurious days with Nick, and even harder to keep my spirits up while cleaning up cat poo from all the corners of G's expansive bathroom (a chore that lasted a good forty-five minutes). I decided that the damn cat had pooped everywhere but actually in the litterbox, and it must have crapped twice its own body weight, from the amount I found. I cleaned up the cat food, but I couldn't tell if Whiskers actually ingested any or simply tossed bits all about the house. The cat's food bowl was missing altogether, and despite a thorough search of the downstairs, I didn't find it. I picked up the trash and papers, and vacuumed, and by 2 P.M. everything looked relatively normal, except for a few mangled curtains, ripped cushions, and G's torn chair. I hadn't figured out how to fix those, yet.

Just then, someone threw open the front door (which landed against the foyer wall with a loud bang) and called (or rather yelled) my name. The voice, an older woman's, was one I didn't immediately recognize. I barely had time to peel off the rubber gloves I had donned for the purpose of cleaning before the visitor yelled for me again, sounding as if she were walking freely through the house.

"I'm here," I called to the empty front room, to which the voice answered "Where?" from somewhere near the back of the kitchen.

"Here," I called again, and this time, the mysterious woman emerged, looking more than a little agitated.

I realized she looked somewhat familiar, and then it hit me:

She reminded me of a more ruffled, poorly put-together version of G's friend (Darla's aunt). She must be Darla's mother—a fact that was quickly borne out the minute she introduced herself.

"I am very sorry to be bothering you like this, but I had to speak with you," she continued after informing me that her name was Lynda Tendaski. I removed bits of shredded cushion stuffing from an empty seat, but she declined to sit, choosing instead to pace up and down the carpeted corridor. "This must seem very strange, and I'm not even sure why I feel it's appropriate to tell you, but my sister told me that it's very important to share problems with the bridal consultant, because, after all, troubleshooting is what we pay you for. Ha. Ha." She laughed, weakly.

"Yes, that's my job description in a nutshell." I tried to sound warm but authoritative at the same time. I could read MOBs well, and this one was clearly on the verge of some kind of nervous breakdown. Not surprising, given the fact this was Darla's mother we are talking about.

Lynda Tendaski laughed nervously again. She sat down in front of me, then leapt up out of the chair again as if something had bit her. Nothing had, but she had enough nervous energy to power a 747.

"I don't really know how to begin," she said. "Oh." She sighed and bit one knuckle. "I didn't think this would be so hard."

"Please, have a seat," I said. Clearly she needed to calm down.

"All right," she said, easing into a seat once more, and this time managing to stay relatively put, aside from a relentless stream of anxious fidgeting.

We sat in silence for a second, with me waiting patiently and Mrs. Tendaski looking in dire need of some Valium or Prozac. I, unfortunately, had neither.

"Well, I suppose I should say that I probably am mistaken about the whole thing, because Darla is a wonderful girl," she said. "She's always been special, even when she was very young. She's one of a kind, you know."

Of that, I was already certain.

"What is it that you would like to tell me?" I asked, my patience having been worn more than a little thin by handling cat poo all morning. Plus, I had to admit that talk about Darla annoyed me. Immensely.

"I should just come out with it."

Yes, I thought, *you should.*

"All right, here goes." Mrs. Tendaski took a deep breath. "I saw one of the groomsmen at my daughter's apartment this morning."

"There's nothing too unusual about that," I said, wondering what her point was.

"Er, well, no, not usually," she said. "But—" Mrs. Tendaski cleared her throat. "He was . . . he was . . . ." Her voice dropped to a whisper. "Naked," she finished, turning a brighter color red than the cushions on G's Queen Anne chair.

"Was he there alone?" I was being a little slow, admittedly. No doubt my thickheadedness was the result of inhaling too much cat urine in close quarters.

Mrs. Tendaski shook her head vigorously.

"He was naked and Jay was there?"

Mrs. Tendaski shook her head again.

"He was naked and Darla was with him?"

Mrs. Tendaski nodded, looking very much like she might need to breathe into a paper bag. I was beginning to see the problem.

"Were they, um . . . were they?"

Mrs. Tendaski nodded again, this time slowly.

"Oh," I said, the tiny prick of a very uncomfortable suspicion forming in the back of my mind.

"Do you know which groomsman it was?"

"Er, no. Not exactly," she said. "But he looked like a relative of James's that I've met."

"A cousin?" I hoped.

"No. No. I believe it was a brother. What's his name?"

"Nick?" I said, a feeling of dread and horror stretching my stomach like a flat, heavy stone.

"That's the one," Mrs. Tendaski said with confidence.

Oh. Brother.

This couldn't be right.

It couldn't be.

Could it?

I didn't believe it was possible.

And yet, part of me seemed to think it made sense. Part of me always knew it was too good to be true. It had to be, didn't it? I mean gorgeous, funny men didn't usually find their way to my bed unless there was something horribly wrong with them. I mean, as a rule, I only sleep with men who are a) terminal jerks, b) spend my money, or c) sleep with other women behind my back (that, by the way, is not an admission that Brad actually cheated on me with a capital "C"). So a part of me had been waiting for the other shoe to drop, and now that it had, said, "I told you so. See? I am *not* paranoid."

This half of my brain (the critical, cynical side that usually had control of me but over the last two days had been beaten into submission by my wistful, dreamy, and horny and inner-brat side) now came roaring back to the helm with smug satisfaction, bringing two distinctly unwelcome and bothersome roommates: Insecurity and Self-Loathing. "What the hell was wrong with you?" they whispered in my ear. "Don't you feel stupid? How could you ever think a man like Nick would be satisfied with just you?"

But, then again, he hadn't seemed all that thrilled with Darla, had said he didn't like her, hadn't he? I mean, I shouldn't just assume, after everything he'd done and said, that he was lying. Should I?

Still. Lynda Tendaski had *seen* him there. *Naked.*

I didn't know what to believe anymore.

It didn't help that Diane assumed the worst.

"You said he was naked? *In her house?*" Diane practically shouted into the phone. I had a hard time relaying the iffiness of Lynda Tendaski's account. It came out sounding like I was trying to make excuses for Nick. Maybe I was.

"She wasn't sure," I said.

"You said she said it was the brother. How many brothers does he have?"

"Well, one, I think," I said.

"Look, I don't want to jump to conclusions here," Diane said. "I just don't want you to fall for another Brad."

"Nick isn't like Brad," I said, but even my voice held a pitch of doubt.

"I'm worried about you," Diane said. "Do you want me to come over?"

"No," I said. "I want to mope at home alone tonight."

I didn't have the heart to call Veronica. She'd tell me something that I really wouldn't want to hear. (Like, I should go out and sleep with someone else to make him jealous. Her advice on getting even usually involved strategically placed used condoms.)

One thing I knew for sure: I wasn't ready to talk to Nick.

The thought of him laughing at me, telling me I was a fool, was more than I could bear. I'd much rather pretend it was a nice one-night stand. At least then I'd get to keep what dignity I had left.

Before I left the office, I spent an hour chasing Whiskers around upstairs before I finally cornered her and put her in the carrying case. The fact that she scratched me until I bled didn't faze me one bit. Nor did the prospect of having the cat running about my house at night seem all that bad (I would have to take her home, or the thing would destroy my office). Besides, the worst that could possibly happen to me already had. What's one more disaster here or there?

I, of all people, should have known better. I've got to learn to stop daring fate to take me literally. By now I know fate always obliges. I suppose being slow is part of my growing list of weaknesses.

I knew something was wrong when I turned the corner and saw the flashing lights of the police car in front of my house. My first thought, if I had one, was that perhaps my neighbor's burglar alarm had gone off again (it does that on occasion and every once in a while the police come and check it out). Of course, when I took a closer look at my house, I realized that there were strange people standing on my lawn. A lot of strange people. And they looked dazed and disoriented. Like all of Lily's friends usually do.

Another police car pulled up then, and two policemen got out, looking (as policemen usually do) intimidating and distinctly annoyed.

Have I mentioned lately how much I hate my life? Why can't I ever have enough time to digest one piece of horrible news before something else terrible happens? It just wasn't fair, dammit.

I parked my car across the street (the cop cars were in my usual space) and walked up my lawn. One of the officers was busy telling two of the very high-looking bystanders to go home, when my approach caught his attention.

"Hold on there, miss," he said, turning to me.

"I live here, and I own this house," I said. "Can you tell me what's going on?"

Another car pulled up about this time (a black van with CRIME SCENE UNIT 4 on the side). A band of lab-coat-clad investigators hopped out.

"Talk to Detective Douglas," the officer said, motioning me inside.

Before I got two feet inside my own door, a rubber-gloved uniformed officer told me to stop.

"But I own this house," I said again, trying to juggle Whiskers in her case and my purse at the same time. Whiskers let out a pathetic mew.

"Talk to Detective Douglas in the kitchen," he said, pointing the way (as if I didn't know where my own kitchen was). I put Whiskers down on my foyer table, but chose to carry my purse with me (officers or not, I wasn't about to leave my wallet unattended in this much foot traffic).

In the kitchen, a plainclothes officer was talking to my sister, who was holding a Ziploc bag full of ice against her forehead. When she saw me, she brightened.

"Oh, Lauren, I'm so glad to see you," she said, taking off the ice. Underneath was a very ugly, swollen knot.

"I wish I could say the same," I said. "What the hell happened?" I fluctuated between feeling intense sisterly concern for Lily's welfare and my own bubbling anger at whatever chaos she had brought into my house.

"Michael came by and we got into a fight," she said.

"Who's Michael?"

Lily rolled her eyes. "My ex-boyfriend."

Lily went through boyfriends so quickly there wasn't any point in keeping up with them. She had more exes than Elizabeth Taylor.

"What happened?"

"He had too much to drink and he came over with a couple of his friends. And then he pulled out a gun . . ."

"He what?!?" I dropped my purse on the floor. From the corner of my eye, I saw one of the lab-coated men extracting something that looked suspiciously like a bullet from the far wall of my living room.

"Calm down," Lily said. "He missed me."

"Calm down? Calm *down?* You could have been killed and for what?"

"He thought I stole his stash of pot."

"Did you?" I looked over at Detective Douglas. (A very young detective, by the way. He seemed better suited for drinking fruit smoothies at the mall than investigating an attempted murder. His face was so smooth I seriously doubted he was capable of growing a full beard.) Seeing that there was an officer of the law in the kitchen, I decided maybe Lily shouldn't be tempted to say anything incriminating. "Nevermind," I said. "So why the bruise?"

"Well, Chad—er, Detective Douglas pushed me out of the way when Michael fired his gun, and I hit my head on your coffee table."

"Oh." Now I was really confused.

"I'm an undercover vice cop," Detective Douglas explained. "I was investigating Michael."

"Oh." Good lord. A terrifying idea occurred to me. "Are you, uh, investigating Lily, too?"

The young cop laughed. "No," he said, sending Lily a sly look.

I swear that girl had nine lives. He had some crush on her, since he seemed not to be able to keep his attention away from her for more than a few seconds. Meanwhile, Lily probably had enough illegal substances stashed in her duffel to make his career. Or at least land him a promotion.

It took the half-dozen officers in my house about an hour to leave. Between feeding them cans of soda and Lily's raiding of my refrigerator, I didn't have much left in the way of food when they did finally go.

Detective Douglas ("Chad") promised he'd be back to check on us (read: Lily) tomorrow to see if everything was OK.

When he left, Lily let out a long, protracted sigh and said, "I think I'm in love."

"I'm glad one of us is," I said bitterly.

"Uh-oh," Lily said. "This isn't just about the cops, huh? Something else happened today?"

"How did you guess?"

"For one thing, nothing bad ever happens to you without coming in groups of three," she said. "It's the downside to having Aquarius as your rising sign."

I chose to ignore that last bit. Reluctant as I was to give Lily another means of torturing me, I told her what I found out about Nick.

"What did Nick say?"

"I haven't called him."

"Damn it, Lauren. Do I have to tell you everything about men?" Lily said, looking to the ceiling.

"Like how to have my very own psychotic, gun-toting ex-boyfriend?"

"As opposed to a Gucci-wearing, cheating, loser ex-husband?"

"He didn't technically cheat," I felt compelled to say.

"Whatever, Ms. Denial."

"Hey, is that my J. Crew tank you're wearing?"

"Don't change the subject," Lily said (clearly attempting to distract me). "Call him." She wandered off to the kitchen and stuck her head in my refrigerator. "Oh, but before you do that, you should go get more groceries. There's nothing to eat in this place."

• • •

"Lauren? Dad. Want to talk."

That last little bit wasn't a question; he meant it as a statement of fact.

"Your mother told me about, er, your injury."

He must have meant my ankle. But I liked to think he was talking about my newly crushed heart.

"You OK?"

"Yes, Dad."

"You sure?"

"Yes, Dad."

"Good. Er, get plenty of rest. You need help with the, uh, bill you let me know."

"I won't need help, but thanks for offering."

Dad, being as uncomfortable with mushy emotions as any man I've ever known, always had a hard time expressing his feelings. He once told me he loved me (the morning of my wedding), or at least I think he did, but it came out as a half-garbled cough, so it might have been "Tie your shoes" instead of "I love you." I can't be completely sure. Dad is most comfortable when he's talking about his affection in terms of money (specifically showing me how much he cares by offering to buy me things). Some psychologists might think this is damaging (could even be at the root of my man problems), but I prefer to take a different view. Dad is from an older generation (where men were providers and women cooked meals) and he more than met the requirements for paying for a roof over our heads when we were growing up and stepping in as the stern enforcer of house rules when situations called for it, and so I don't really blame him for keeping his feelings close to his vest. After all, a more sensitive and emotional man would've been eaten alive by mother, which would have been far more damaging to my psyche, I believe.

I actually felt oddly touched by his call. Telephone conversations are, as a rule, difficult for him, and so I appreciated the gesture, even if my ankle was practically as good as new. My heart, of course, was another matter entirely. I told myself I should be grateful that I learned the truth early in the relationship, but I was too busy feeling shortchanged to feel much gratitude. I only had two measly days believing Nick cared for me, which was by all angles a crime.

I let out a long, depressed sigh.

"Stop it, will you!" Lily said, sounding exasperated. "That's the twentieth sigh this hour! I'm trying to watch *Friends* here. Sheesh."

Who needed a gorgeous boyfriend when one had such sisterly affection?

"When is it, exactly, that you planned to move out?" I said, annoyed.

"Shhh," she said, watching the television attentively. Ross made some self-deprecating comment, and she laughed. "God, what a loser," she said—to the television more than to me, but the sentiment could apply to either.

I got up and went to my bedroom, where I promptly began the process of pulling everything out of my already neat and compartmentalized closet. Reorganizing storage space was always a good refuge, though temporary, from emotional stress. When I was done with that, I moved on to my sock drawer, and then my sweaters drawer, and even the box of winter clothes I keep under my bed. After my bedroom came the kitchen. Lily, I saw, had left two more of her dirty cups in my sink (how hard is it to put them in the dishwasher, anyway?) and so I washed those, and then proceeded to clean out my refrigerator, the microwave, the oven, and even my dishwasher (yes, I do clean my dishwasher). Then, I dragged out all my dishes and my pots and pans from the cabinets and reorganized them according to frequency of use. (Before, they had been organized strictly according to size—larger plates down to smaller, etc.)

Next, I went on a dusting spree, finding a way to get behind my stove and refrigerator, and pulled out a nasty clump of hair and gray dust balls. I waxed and then rewaxed the kitchen floor. I shampooed the carpet in the living room and in my bedroom, and then promptly did all the dirty laundry that there was to be done in the house. I went to the bathroom next, getting on my hands and knees and cleaning all the tiny specks of grout from between the tiles on the floor (I hadn't realized there were any, but if I looked closely, I believed I could detect some).

When I had finished my frenzy of cleaning, it was close to two-thirty in the morning.

"You need serious help," Lily said, passing me in the hall on the way to bed. "Serious help."

I woke up the next morning feeling horribly immobilized by a deep and brooding depression (and my painfully stiff back, the result of hours of manic cleaning). It was so bad, I didn't even have the strength to roll over and push the snooze button on my alarm clock, so I listened to the annoying bursts of buzzing for a half hour before Lily came tromping into my room and plucked my clock's electric cord from the wall.

"Shut up," she said (I assume she was talking to the now pow-

erless clock), and then stomped straight out of my bedroom and back to my guest bed.

I realized that there was a rather heavy and furry pillow leaning against my head, and when I reached up and felt it, the pillow meowed. Whiskers, whom I had let out of her cage the night before, must have climbed up on my bed sometime during the night, and now she lay wrapped around my head. One of her paws dropped down over my forehead, stopping just short of poking me in the eye. Even this new indignation failed to stir me.

I found myself staring at the blank face of the unplugged clock while soaking in a pool of self-pity. "Why me? Why does this always happen to me?" the deflated, defeated half of my brain asked over and over. The grumpy, cynical side of my brain shot back with: *"Hello.* Because you're a loser. Duh." And that's the basic gist of the conversations that looped around in my head. Neither side suggested that I actually get up and shower. On that point, both remained noticeably silent.

I finally decided to get up when it occurred to me that I was lying in the bed where Nick had made love to me for the first time (just two days ago), and the sickening, sad feeling that followed that memory pushed me slowly but surely to my feet. Whiskers growled in protest when I sat up, as the sudden motion sent her tumbling down my pillow and into the hollow of the bed near my hip.

"Meow," Whiskers said, which I pretty much figured meant, "You're forgiven only if you feed me."

So I went to the kitchen, dug out a few slices of cheese, crumbled them into pieces, and put them on a paper towel on the floor. Whiskers ate them voraciously, as if I had served her sirloin mouse steak.

I didn't manage to get up enough energy to shower. What would it matter? I kept thinking. I threw on a pair of jeans and a cotton, sleeveless sweater (damn G's dress code, it wasn't like she'd be there to see me, anyway) and pulled on a pair of tennis shoes. When I'm depressed, I always wear tennis shoes. I simply didn't have the energy to squeeze my feet into some terribly uncomfortable high-heeled contraption, and furthermore, I didn't care at all what I looked like (because when you're wallowing in self-pity, looking pitiful is an essential part of the strategy).

Whiskers, amazingly, came when she was called, and went without protest into her carrying case. When we arrived together at the office, I let her out of the case, and instead of running off she took up a vigil near my desk. I figured even the cat knew something was wrong. At one point, she even leapt into my lap and began purring loudly, and so I patted her once on the head and then she jumped down again, somehow satisfied.

At noon, I went to the kitchen to heat myself a powdered Cup-a-Soup (how pathetic is that?) but didn't get a chance to eat it. A loud knock sounded at the front door, and when I went to the peephole, I saw Darla tapping her foot impatiently on the front porch.

The very last person in the world I wanted to see.

I swung the door open, but blocked the entrance with my body.

"Darla," I said in what I hoped was an even but distinctly unfriendly tone.

"Lauren," Darla replied with equal coolness. "I need to speak with you."

"About what?" I said.

"My wedding," she said, betraying a hint of a deeper, less civil feeling.

I moved from the entrance and she glided inside, flipping her thick and shiny blond hair off one shoulder. I resisted the urge to wrap my arm around her neck in some wrestling move. I smiled at the image of me holding her well-groomed head in a sleeper hold. I doubted she could be so dignified then.

"Gennifer isn't here," I said pointedly. (Translation: Your threats won't work today.)

"I didn't come to talk to her, I came to talk to you."

What was she up to now? I wondered.

"I want to get married."

"I thought that was your plan all along," I snapped, then tried to rein myself back in. Losing my composure wouldn't help me. "Er, isn't that what I've been working on all this time?"

"I mean, I want to get married soon."

"How soon?"

"This Saturday."

I stood up. "I'm sure you can accomplish that at the county courthouse. Or in Las Vegas. You don't need my help with that."

"No, I want most of what you've planned, only sooner."

Sure, as if a wedding was something as easy to plan as catching a nearby matinee (could we meet at five-thirty instead of seven?).

"Why can't you wait the extra two weeks?" I was really tiring of Darla. I really was.

"I just can't."

"I'm not going to do this unless you give me a good reason," I said. In fact, I didn't really want to do it at all, and I was on the verge of telling her so (at great peril to my own job, I realized, but I didn't care).

"I'm pregnant," she blurted before I could say anything more.

I blinked. Then, recovered.

"So?" I said, when I had beaten back the puritan surprise that had momentarily gripped me. After all, it wasn't like this sort of thing was unheard of, or even unusual. We lived in a new millennium, right? "I'm sure James will make a fine father."

"It isn't his."

This was said so softly that I wasn't sure I heard properly.

"What?"

"I said, the baby isn't his," Darla repeated a little louder.

"How do you know?"

Darla gave me a cutting look. "I know," she said.

"Whose?"

She shook her head. She wasn't going to tell me, and frankly, I wasn't sure I really wanted to know. A deep, simmering anger that had been hiding just beneath the surface of my depression now rose up and boiled over, taking complete control of me.

"What the hell is wrong with you?" I shouted, catching her off-guard. "You've got everything and you're throwing it all away!"

Darla blinked back surprise. But nothing could stop me now.

"You think just because you're pretty and rich and that all men love you, that gives you the right to treat people as if they're simply actors in your very own personal soap opera? Being beautiful on the outside doesn't make you beautiful on the inside. Not even close."

Darla's face fell a little. But I was just warming up.

"You make me sick. You and the waste of all you have make me sick. I wouldn't be you for all the money in the world. I may not be as attractive or as successful as you are, and I may not be able to manipulate all the people in my life to do my bidding, but at least when I wake up in the morning, I can look at myself in the mirror. I may not always like what I see, but at least I can look myself in the eye. If I were you, I'd never be able to do that."

I paused to take in air.

"So, I'm not going to move up your wedding just because it's part of your latest scheme," I said, reaching a feverish pitch. "I'm not. Fire me if you want to, or tell G to fire me, but I won't do it. You'll have to find some way else out of this mess. I suggest you be honest with the people who care about you, because they don't deserve this. And frankly, they don't deserve you. No one does."

I realized I had nothing more to say. I looked down and noticed for the first time that Darla had begun crying. I now saw the big, fat tears rolling down her face. Her nose was all red and runny, and her mouth was distorted into a mangled "o." Finally, I remember thinking, an ugly cry. It was about time she had one.

Seventeen

all me heartless. Call me a bitch. I don't care. For the first time in my life, I had told someone who had been taking advantage of me exactly what I thought about them and what they were doing, and the freedom of that action felt exhilarating.

I had never before now ever told a client what I told Darla. In fact, I'd never even been so honest with Brad, who of all people deserved a good verbal thrashing. I felt like a new person entirely. A stronger person. More composed and in control. Never again would somebody walk all over me.

Then Darla got a hold of herself. Apparently, women like her had a tear reserve lasting only about sixty seconds.

"You'll be sorry you said that," Darla said, as she dabbed at her eyeliner and mascara, which I noticed with sadistic satisfaction was smudged. "You'll be very sorry."

"If you'll excuse me, I have other business to take care of," I said coldly, turning my back on her.

I heard the front door slam, and let out a long breath. And then all the self-righteous indignation, the confidence I'd had, promptly disappeared.

It occurred to me (belatedly, I admit) that when G found out what had happened, I would probably be fired, and not just fired but completely blackballed from the business. How would I ever pay the mortgage or Brad's outstanding credit debt? The elation over telling Darla exactly where she could put her self-centered, inconsiderate, and tactless person quickly faded and was replaced by a gripping, fearful panic.

I was going to be fired. Canned. Dismissed.

And I could forget my secret dream of opening my own consulting business. G would never tolerate that. She would have all the florists and caterers and bakers in town believing that I was evil incarnate and decidedly bad for business. None of them (with the possible exception of Mark Stewart) would ever do business with me. My life, in short, was ruined.

I needed chocolate. Lots of it. As I was contemplating in what form I'd ingest a ton of the sugary, caffeinated, cocoa goodness (ice cream, frozen yogurt, or pure block bar?) when my phone rang. It was Diane.

"Guess where I have to go?" She sounded excited.

"TCBY?"

"No, but we could stop on the way. Guess again."

"Bridesmaids Shoes R Us?"

"No, silly. Your favorite place in the world."

"Lammes Candies?" I couldn't think of any place that didn't have chocolate not being one of my favorite places at this particular moment.

"No, the Container Store."

"Ooh!" I instantly felt better. "Can I come?" There are few problems in my world that a trip to the Container Store won't fix (or at the very least overshadow for short periods). For a neat, neurotic junkie like me, the Container Store is a compartmentalized, neatly arranged, perfectly filed haven.

•   •   •

When the sliding glass doors opened with a whoosh and the carefully cooled air-conditioned air blew across my forehead, I knew that somehow things would work out. Look at all these gleaming shelves and file cabinets. See the shelves filled with color-coded files, index tabs, measuring cups, and clear, plastic bowls. Marvel at the aisles upon aisles of gleaming wrapping paper and brightly colored storage boxes. A world that could be this organized and orderly simply couldn't be all that bad.

I let out a happy little sigh.

"I knew this would cheer you up," Diane said, pushing a wheeled cart in my direction. "Here, fill this up with whatever you want. It's on me."

"What?"

"Think of it as a thank-you-for-being-my-maid-of-honor gift," Diane said.

I spent an hour and a half traipsing up and down the aisles, and when I finished I had enough shelves, Elfa blocks, and organizational gadgets to spend the next week remodeling my closet.

"Thanks," I said to Diane as we lugged my heavy packages to the car. "I mean it. You're a real friend."

"Don't mention it. Besides, I had an ulterior motive. Now you've got to come with me to get your shoes for the wedding. It's a week from this Saturday, need I remind you . . . ?"

Friday came and went, and I settled into the idea of spending the weekend rearranging my closet. Chad—I mean Detective Douglas—did come by Friday to check on Lily, and he spent four hours interrogating (I mean flirting with) Lily before he finally left around ten o'clock. He might as well have stayed longer, because Lily couldn't stop talking about him after he left. I wouldn't have minded so much except she kept asking bothersome rhetorical questions like "Isn't he cute?" and "Don't you think he's brave?" and more sickening drivel.

I freely admit I was in no mood to be kind or generous to any member of the opposite sex. It was Friday night and the highlight of my evening was screwing bolts into my closet door for my new shoe rack, for goodness' sakes. Lily eventually got frustrated trying to talk to me while I was rummaging around behind my clothes, and she gave up, deciding to seek out a friendlier ear in the form of one or another of her friends.

Saturday came, and my closet was the cleanest, most organized it has ever been (which says quite a lot given that I initiate a makeover every time something terrible happens in my life). I surprised even myself with this new project. It looked better than it did even after the divorce, which I never imagined was possible (I spent three whole days on that project).

Only one thing could dampen my short-lived (and probably illusory) peace of mind.

Nick.

He called twice, disrupting my mediations in front of my closet. He left a message both times, saying he was sorry he missed me and was eager to see me that very night.

I was so upset, I almost ripped everything out of my closet and started all over again. There was only one thing to do. Rip the Band-Aid off. One swipe.

Eventually, I did call him back and thankfully got the answering machine. I was pretty sure I wouldn't be able to talk to Nick in person, but a machine seemed a more moderate (and certainly less guilty) listener. I decided there was only one thing to do, really. End this thing. End it fast. Save what little self-respect I had left.

"Uh," I began, self-conscious at the sound of my own voice. *Sound put-together. Don't be mad. Say something.* Say something.

I froze. And then panicked, slamming down the phone, and jumped back from the receiver as if it were on fire.

"Chicken," Lily said under her breath as she walked through the kitchen.

"Shut up," I said, because she was right. I've never been anything but timid and weak of will, so slipping right back into old habits came easily. They fit like an old comfortable sweater. One that hid all those unwanted bulges and sags.

Eighteen

I awoke Monday morning with a start, as if I'd been having a terrible nightmare. Cold sweat rolled in drops down my back and I felt overwhelmed by that same frightful, heart-pounding dread that usually comes with the realization that one has overslept one's alarm by say, an hour. At first, I couldn't figure out what exactly was wrong. My clock said 7:15 A.M., even earlier than I normally wake up. Whiskers, whom I had let sleep in my bedroom all weekend, was lounging atop my head as usual, and when I shifted on my pillow, she flicked her tail across my nose and mewed in protest. I spat out a mouthful of cat hair and sat up.

Then it hit me.

Today was Monday. And G would be in the office today. In which case she would very shortly hear about how I treated Darla (I assumed in her absence the fiend had left dozens of irate voice mail messages on G's phone). Oh, sure. Why not? Nick left me for Darla. Now G would ruin my professional career. Welcome to "My Life in Shambles: Part Two."

"What's wrong with you?" Lily asked over the breakfast table. I assumed I drew her attention because I was poking at my soggy cornflakes with a fork. (In my depressive and distracted state, I didn't notice at first that I had grabbed a fork instead of a spoon, and even after I realized my mistake, I didn't have the energy to fix the problem.)

"My life is falling apart, that's all," I said glumly.

"When has it ever been together?"

"Don't you have class to go to?" I snapped.

Lily shrugged.

I walked outside carrying Whiskers' case in one hand and my purse in the other, and on my way down my front steps, I saw that Detective Douglas was still sitting in his car across the street. He held a Styrofoam cup and was only partially (if that) disguised by dark sunglasses. I decided not to wave. His presence, after all, was becoming a bit of a nuisance.

When I arrived at work, I saw G's car parked in its usual place, which I took to be a terrible omen. She never arrived at work before 9:30, especially after coming back to town after a trip. She must be here to fire me. Darla must have made good on her threat to make me pay.

I opened the door as quietly as possible, trying every means necessary not to attract undue attention to my arrival, but it didn't seem to matter. The minute I put one foot on her hardwood floor, I heard G bellowing down the stairs.

"Lauren! Here! Now!"

I was so fired. Beyond fired. Terminated without any hope of seeing that last paycheck she owed me.

At G's voice, Whiskers mewed softly (she knew as well as I did what G's tone meant). I let Whiskers out of her cage, and she darted through the house, promptly hiding somewhere in the sitting room. As tempted as I was to do the same, I figured I might as well get this over with.

"Welcome back, G," I said, standing in the doorway of her office.

"What the hell happened here while I was gone?" G demanded, slapping a file of papers down on her desk.

Now, that was an interesting question. I tried but failed to come up with a proper answer.

"I mean look at my chair, for heaven's sake," she said, pointing to the deep (and I feared permanent) claw marks left by Whiskers. It hit me suddenly that I hadn't gotten a chance to fix G's seat cushions after Whiskers' antics last week. Excuses whirled through my mind as I thought of something plausible to tell G.

I decided the best defense was a good offense.

"Don't blame me," I said, in a defiant and stern tone that I have never ever once used to my boss. "Your cat is a mess. She pouted the whole time you were gone. She tore at everything the second I took a telephone call. In fact, I didn't get any work done at all because of all her caterwauling. She scratched me, bit me, and almost took out my eye. And you don't want to see what that feline did to my own house."

G, surprised at the forcefulness of my answer, just stared at me for several seconds without speaking.

Then she did the most amazing thing.

She apologized.

"I had no idea she would miss me so much," G said, looking truly contrite. "I am so sorry if this interfered with your work. And she went after your eye, you say? How awful."

I nodded.

"Well, let me pay for the damage she's done to your house," G continued. "I won't hear of you paying for anything. It's my fault. I shouldn't have left. I suppose the poor dear can't bear to be parted from me."

I nodded again. And resisted the urge to roll my eyes.

As if understanding the danger had passed, Whiskers appeared at the door of G's office.

"There's my precious baby," G said, stretching out her arms. This is usually the moment when Whiskers takes a running leap into G's lap. This time, however, the cat stayed still.

When G got closer, the cat did something she never has: spat and hissed. Then she walked in between my legs, curling her tail around my calves. The damn thing had the nerve to start purring.

"Go to Mama," I said, shaking one foot and then the other, but the thing wouldn't go.

I laughed uneasily.

"Go on. Go to Mama." Nothing. Just more purring and tail-curling about my legs.

G looked from me to the cat and back again. The cat, in all her evil mischievousness, refused to budge.

"It's trying to make you jealous," I said, which happened to be the first lame excuse that came to mind.

G didn't look convinced.

"Go," I hissed to the cat, shaking my foot harder. The thing went away from me, but instead of going to G, she turned and trotted down the stairs.

Whiskers spent the whole of the day wrapped around my feet. She refused to leave my desk, even when G produced a can of smelly (but I'm sure scrumptious for felines) cat food.

"You're not helping me, you know," I told her, but I guessed she already knew that. I suppose she had finally figured out a better means of hurting me than leaving poo under my desk.

G, miraculously, continued to blame herself, saying that she never should have left the poor cat, because in the trauma that followed, Whiskers suffered a self-imposed amnesia.

"I don't think she even knows me," G cried at one point, retreating to her office.

With the crisis of Whiskers' affection, G didn't mention Darla once, and she didn't fire me either, two events that I expected to happen at any moment. But when the entire day came and went, and neither one did, I decided that perhaps Darla had yet to contact her. I'm not completely sure that G knows how to work her own voice mail, anyhow, given that she is severely electronically challenged.

But Monday passed into Tuesday and Tuesday into Wednesday, and then before I knew it, Friday came, and I still had my job. Puzzled and impatient to have the bad news over with, I even worked up the courage to ask G if she had heard from Darla.

"No," she said, considering. "But I did get a call from her mother," G added, almost as an afterthought.

Here it comes. The ax.

"I forgot to mention it before," G said, rather briskly. "She called me to compliment you on your handling of a particularly delicate situation."

I blinked. Surely that couldn't be right.

"She said she was very grateful you handled the problem, but she didn't want to elaborate," G said, attempting to look disinterested when she so obviously wasn't.

"The bride was having a case of, uh, cold feet." This was a bit of a lie, since I don't think Darla's ever had a case of cold anything as far as men were concerned. "So, Darla didn't call?" I asked hesitantly, fearing the answer.

"No, why should she?" G replied, distracted as she flipped through her latest issue of *Cat Fancy*, which had arrived with the morning mail.

"Oh, no reason," I said, wondering what the hell Darla was up to, because she wasn't the sort of person to have a change of heart. If she wasn't getting me fired, then she had to have something else equally awful planned.

My phone downstairs rang then and I had an excuse to duck out of G's office.

"Tell me I'm doing the right thing," Diane breathed on the other end of the line. "Tell me I'm not making the worst mistake of my whole life."

As today was Diane's wedding rehearsal and rehearsal dinner, this first attack of nerves would only be followed by many more before Saturday.

As I hated Robert, I found it difficult to be enthusiastic and truthful in my reassurances.

"The antichrist"—that's Robert's mother—"just arrived," Diane said, at the level of a whisper. This made me believe that said future in-law might still be in hearing distance. "She's pulling out the weeds in my front yard," Diane hissed. "The weeds!"

"Hmmmm." I didn't have much to say to that.

"And she said she wants to dust next," Diane said, her voice high-pitched. "Dust! Can you believe it? She'll be in my closet next."

"Take a deep breath," I said, glancing at my watch. It was 4:45 P.M. "I'm coming right over."

I had figured this might be a problem. Men like Robert are only the way they are typically because they have doting, spoiling mothers who feel that no woman is good enough for their son (hence, Robert's overbearing, intolerable superiority complex). Said mother had refused six months ago Diane's suggestion that she and Robert's father stay in a hotel with Robert's other out-of-town visitors, and instead insisted that she stay with the (until then) happy couple. This had been the first sign of trouble.

Then, there had been the not-so-subtle suggestion that Diane should allow Robert's grandmother (Mexican by birth but American by citizenship) to cook her famous tortillas, tamales, and refried beans for the reception. When she found out Diane had planned an Italian meal instead, Robert's mother had thrown a fit and threatened not to come. Diane acquiesced to the idea of Robert's grandmother cooking food for the reception (along with her concern that the eighty-eight-year-old would have trouble preparing food for 250 people). Then, two months before the wedding, Robert's mother had called and said that cooking would be too much of a strain on the grandmother (a fact that Diane had been trying to explain for eight months) and that Diane would have to find something else.

Then there had been arguments over the guest list (Robert's mother felt 150 was too small to accommodate Robert's large and far-flung family). Diane tried but failed to convince her that a fourth cousin removed doesn't exactly qualify as immediate family. So, the guest list was enlarged to 250 to include relatives that even Robert admitted he had never before met.

I had a particular bone to pick with Robert's mother (besides the obvious fact that she was the reason Robert existed in the world). For the last year, in her many attempts to dissuade Diane from marrying Robert, she only managed to increase Diane's resolve. For one thing, Diane spent so much of her time being angry at Robert's mother that she was too distracted to be peeved at Robert himself (for some reason, her fiancé visiting strip clubs seemed less offensive than her future mother-in-law disagreeing with the color scheme for the reception centerpieces). I felt sure that if Diane hadn't been distracted by Robert's mother, she would have noticed before now that Robert was simply not the man for her.

• • •

When I arrived at Diane's house, Robert's mother had stopped her weeding of Diane's yard (but there were still piles of misplaced dirt here and there) and had moved on to waxing Diane's kitchen floor (given that the linoleum was a no-wax surface, I doubted that this would do much good other than coat the floor with a sticky, cloudy mess).

"Where did she find the wax?" I whispered to Diane, who was watching the older woman with a resigned, depressed expression.

"She brought it with her—along with her own vacuum cleaner," Diane whispered back, inclining her head in the direction of the guest bedroom. I saw an old, antiquated Hoover upright sitting with its bright 1950s cord wrapped thickly around its handle.

This was much worse than I thought.

Robert's mother roughly pushed Diane's kitchen trash can into the hall, and I saw that it was full of unopened frozen pizzas and Lean Cuisine dinners.

I gave Diane a questioning look.

"She brought Robert one hundred and fifty frozen tamales from his grandmother," Diane explained in low tones.

Just then, Robert himself appeared, belching loudly and rubbing his (rather large) stomach.

"At that rate, perhaps he'll eat them before the frozen dinners thaw," I suggested, causing Diane to bark a rude laugh.

Robert's mother turned and gave us both dark stares.

"Let's get out of here," I said, pulling at Diane's arm.

We decided to go to the church. It seemed an appropriately serene and peaceful place (two things Diane desperately needed at this point). We were a half hour early for the rehearsal (but as we had left Robert in charge of driving his mother here, I seriously doubted we'd start the rehearsal on time). Diane spoke to the pastor for a little while, asking about the length of his sermon before the vows and other routine questions.

The other members of the wedding party trickled in (including the other bridesmaid, Robert's sister, a shy seventeen-year-old who seemed a bit underwhelmed by the whole process). Robert arrived (miraculously only five minutes late), acting as his usual disgusting self. He didn't even bother to hold the door open for his own mother, choosing instead to stride ahead into the church, letting the heavy oak door sling back toward the older woman, who staggered slightly under its hefty weight.

A feeling very close to annoyance pricked the hairs at the back of my neck (my usual reaction when Robert entered a room). I glanced over to Diane, but she hadn't seen, wrapped up as she was in her conversation with the pastor. It occurred to me, perhaps for the first time, that she really was going to marry Robert. Robert the Strip Club Regular. Robert the Lazy and Cheap. Robert the Pig.

A dark, ugly feeling somewhere at the pit of my stomach rumbled, yawned, and came to life. Jealousy? I dismissed that immediately. Couldn't be jealousy. Look at Robert, standing there so smug and obnoxious. No, not jealousy.

Dread. It was a deep, bubbling, terrifying dread.

A fierce and sudden imperative gripped me. I could not let her do it.

Sweet, honest, gullible Diane simply could not marry piggish, disgusting, arrogant Robert. It defied the laws of right. Of justice. Of sanity.

It simply could not happen.

I had assumed for too long that Diane would wake up and see where she was, as if after a college night of binge drinking, finding herself wrapped up in a stranger's sheets, her face hot with embarrassment. She was supposed to understand at some point that Robert would not do, that he was far too ugly, in appearance and in spirit, for her. It would be a momentary lapse of judgment that we would both laugh about later down the road over a margarita or a beer when I would tell the story of how Diane almost married the dumbest, rudest, most horrible man in the world.

That was the way it was supposed to happen.

Not like this.

I realized the rehearsal was already under way, and that somehow I had made it down the aisle and was standing facing Diane, watching her make her way toward Robert.

This would not do.

I managed to wait until the pastor finished giving us his final instructions. ("Don't forget to stand with your knees bent," he said. "Or by halfway through you'll topple like rotted trees.")

Then I grabbed Diane and told her I needed to talk to her. Now.

"You can't do this," I whispered urgently, once the rest of the wedding party had dispersed.

Diane, who had completely recovered from her run-in with Robert's mother, started.

"Why on earth not?"

"He's not for you," I said, my heart pounding, sweat breaking out at the back of my neck. I saw her face harden a little bit, and I knew, somewhere I knew, I should shut up, but I didn't. "He's a pig, Diane. You're making a mistake. A terrible, awful mistake."

Not exactly my most articulate moment, I admit.

Diane's face paled and then flushed with color.

I don't know what response I expected. "Oh, Lauren, you're such a good friend to me" or "Thank you for saving me from myself" would have been fine.

That, of course, was not what she said.

"How dare you," she spat, in a steely, lethal voice I never thought she'd use on me. I was her best friend, right? "I love Robert and Robert loves me and you of all people have no right to tell me whom I should and shouldn't marry.

"If Robert treated me half as bad as Brad treated you, then I would leave him in a second," she continued, jabbing her finger hard into my chest, pushing me backward a half step. "And that's more than I can say for you," she added cryptically.

"W-what do you mean?" I was very close to blubbering, and the room seemed to lose its focus. The dark, oily feeling in my stomach expanded, rose up into my rib cage, and wrapped itself tightly around my heart.

"I mean what your friends and your family have known all along, but what you never, ever admitted. You didn't leave Brad. Not when things got bad. Brad left you."

She paused to take a breath.

"It wasn't a mutual, adult parting like you say it was. You never came to terms with how horribly he treated you. You just let it happen. You let everything just happen to you. Your whole life, everyone has walked all over you. Your boss. Your mother. And Brad. He cheated on you and then he left you. He hit on every one of your friends and even your sister, and you refused to see it. He slept with half a dozen different women when he was married to you and you denied it, even when you found him screwing your neighbor on *your own couch.*

"He's the one who filed for divorce. And even then, you didn't do anything except let him take you for everything you owned."

My heart contracted hard, sending an ache across my chest. A great pressure shifted. I wanted to tell Diane to stop, that I didn't want to hear any more, but I seemed to have lost the ability to speak.

"You were the one who would call him dozens of times the week after he left, begging him to take you back," she said, harshly. "That was you. No one else. You."

No. I couldn't hear any more. I couldn't. But it kept coming.

"Even in divorce court, you were so eager to please, so eager for everyone to like you," Diane said, her eyes darkening even further. "You let him take everything, including your self-respect. You never stood up to him. Not once. Ever."

Surely that wasn't right, I thought. That couldn't be right.

"Lauren," Diane said fiercely, zeroing in on the worst possible most horrid thing she could say. "Brad doesn't even know *you're not friends*. He has no idea you don't like him. Worse, he doesn't think he did anything wrong. He's even bragged that he can get you back into bed anytime he pleases."

The lump in my throat grew to the size of a grapefruit. My eyes burned. I was going to lose it and soon.

"You, of all people, should never give advice on men to anyone," Diane said, winding up for the last and fatal blow. "Don't talk to me about Robert. How could you even dare? I know you're miserable. But for God's sake, can't you let me be happy?" Diane finished, her eyes bright with tears. With that, she turned and ran from the room.

Under the weight of a hundred different emotions, my heart staggered, weakened, and then burst, sending a stream of ugly tears down my cheeks, across my nose, and dribbling like drool off the tip of my chin.

Nineteen

I don't know how I made it home. What with tears and snot running down my face unhindered, and me very close to becoming a fully unhinged, blubbering maniac (oops, too late, I was already there), I don't know how I managed to get in my car, start it, and drive home.

It follows, of course, that I didn't make it to Diane's rehearsal dinner.

I don't remember parking the car, or unlocking my door, or crawling straightaway into my bed, fully clothed. I just remember sobbing like a baby, loud and messy and uncontrolled, until I simply ran out of salt tears, and had nothing more to give but wretched, dry hiccups. I fell asleep hiccupping, my nose swollen and my eyes red and watery.

I woke up who knows how much later, in complete darkness, with the smell of chicken soup wafting into my room from the kitchen. Even the hungry rumble of a growl from my stomach didn't motivate me to get up. As far as I was concerned, I never again wanted to leave the safety of my warm, snuggly bed. Anything else seemed too horrible to contemplate. Getting up again I vowed I'd never do. Not when there was so much suffering out there. Not when so many terrible things can happen to you. Not when your own best friend can dredge up the most painful memories that you've never faced. No. The bed seemed infinitely safer. Even the kitchen, at this point, was too risky.

All I wanted to do for the rest of my life was sleep. I shut my eyes and willed sleep back again, but it skipped away from me, mocking me in my efforts to catch it. I began to envy coma victims. If only I could manage a head injury, I thought, then I would never again have to face anyone I knew.

How they must all be laughing at me, I thought, horrified. How all my closest friends must have whispered behind my back. "Pathetic," they must have said. "Pitiful."

And I was. That was the worst thing. I was pathetic two times over. First, for letting Brad walk all over me, and then for denying it ever happened. I never even found the guts to face it, and all this time I'd been pretending I had been the woman I wanted to be: strong, confident, sure. Instead, I was weak, oblivious, foolish.

No, I would never get out of my bed again. Not even to shower.

Just then, the lights flicked on, blinding me with a harsh, garish glare. I pulled the covers up over my head.

"Go away," I croaked, but I don't think it actually came out in understandable English.

"It's time for you to eat something," Lily said.

I pulled the covers down slightly, opening one eye. She held a tray of chicken soup and crackers and a can of Diet Coke.

"No," I said.

"Yes," she said. "You must eat."

"Why?"

"Because I'm going to kick your butt if you don't. I put a lot of time into making this. Besides, you should reward my thoughtfulness so I'll do it again."

My stomach growled even louder and I sat up a little. She put the tray down on my lap.

"I didn't know you even knew how to work a can opener," I said.

"Me either," she replied, her face splitting into a smile.

By the time I finished the soup, I felt strong enough to try venturing into my living room. Mind you, this had nothing to do with the fact that Lily had the TV tuned to an Audrey Hepburn classic-movies marathon. Absolutely nothing. Although, nothing too awful ever happened to Audrey—at least nothing so terrible that it couldn't be fixed by the end of the movie.

I sat down silently on the sofa next to Lily, who offered me some of her freshly popped popcorn.

"You OK?" she ventured.

I shrugged.

"Diane called," Lily said, looking down into the popcorn bowl. "She said she's sorry."

I sniffed loudly, pretending that grammar scene in *My Fair Lady* was especially sentimental.

"Oh, and Nick called, too. He wants you to call him." She paused. "I really think you should."

That was absolutely the last thing I would do (although I couldn't deny that a little attention from Nick would've made me feel much better). But to give in to that temptation would have meant sacrificing what was left of my dignity (which was very, very little, granted). I mean, I didn't want to repeat the same mistakes I'd made with Brad. I promised myself I would not let myself walk around in a fog, letting people take advantage of me.

I perked up a little bit. Things weren't so hopeless, were they? I mean, I had made progress, hadn't I? I told Darla where she could get off and what she should do with herself when she got there, something I never would have done even six months ago. Yes, I had lived in denial about Brad, but that was out in the open, too, and I would deal with it, I was certain I would. Somehow.

Just after midnight, a knock came at my door. I opened it to find a chagrined-looking Diane standing on my porch holding a duffel bag.

"I am such a bitch," she said. "Will you ever forgive me?"

I gave her a big hug.

"It's nothing I didn't deserve," I said, pulling back and feeling a bit teary (not at all surprising given my general emotional state in the last five hours). "I'm sorry for what I said about Robert."

Now, this should show how mature I had become in just the last half hour. I was apologizing for calling Robert a pig.

"I really am sorry," Diane said. "And I'm not just saying that because I want to crash on your couch."

"You need a place to stay?"

"Robert's mom is *still* vacuuming," she said, letting out a long, depressed sigh.

The three of us watched the end of *My Fair Lady* and all of *Sabrina* and then fell asleep in various pieces of furniture in the living room. Unfortunately, none of us set an alarm. I awoke to frantic shoulder-shaking by Diane, who informed me in a panic that it was 11:45 A.M. Her wedding happened to be at 2 P.M.

The next half hour was a flurry of chaos, what with me running about my house looking for my dress and shoes, and packing up anything I thought we would need. I told Diane that I would meet her at the church, and so she sped down my street with the fury of a bride running half an hour late for her manicure. Luckily, Diane's mom had her dress and had made plans already to take it to the church, so all I was responsible for was her makeup kit and shoes.

I jumped into the shower and sponged off, then hopped out again, running around my bedroom like a human tornado, throwing around clothes and bags in search of a clean, run-free pair of pantyhose. This was not unlike looking for a needle wedged underneath a bulldozer. Impossible.

Miraculously, I managed to pull everything together and throw it in the car. I didn't, however, have time to blow-dry my hair (which meant that half of it would be hopelessly frizzy, while the other half would curl out in odd directions). I raced to the church and got there just past 12:50. I flung the makeup bag and everything else into a room and went back out to check on the florist. (It wasn't Mark Stewart—poor Diane couldn't afford him, sadly—and I didn't trust this florist much farther than I could throw her (she was a friend of a friend of a cousin of Diane's mother, of all things).

I introduced myself, but the poor older woman (short, slightly bent, and white-haired) just stared at the top of my head.

After a few moments, she reached up and plucked out a small green twig from the mess of my hair.

"There now, that's so much better," the florist said, smiling. "What was it you were saying, dear?"

There's nothing like a bit of trash hanging from one's unkempt hair to undermine one's authority. I sighed, repeated my instructions, and then rushed back to Diane's dressing room.

She was standing in front of a full-length mirror and her mother was kneeling behind, zipping up the long, straight, strikingly simple gown.

Diane looked so beautiful and perfect. I immediately started crying. Something I seemed to do quite a lot of these days.

Of course, the minute I started, Diane couldn't help but join in, too, and then her mother began (because moms don't need much of a reason to start the waterworks on wedding days), and soon we were all sniffling and laughing and hugging like sentimental idiots, which I suppose we were, God bless us.

The next hour sped by like lightning, and soon the pastor's assistant was telling us we should take our places, and I found myself standing in the vestibule, waiting for my music cue to play. Looking out over the sea of guests seated in the pews, I was struck by how much it reminded me of when I walked down the aisle at my own wedding. I looked down and saw Robert and his best man standing in front of the pastor. Robert looked pale and more than a little nervous, and I realized for the first time that this day *was* a big deal to him. I remembered a stark difference in Brad's face. He had looked almost bored.

Maybe I was wrong about Robert.

The organist struck up the chorus of the Wedding March, and I took a step forward, walking steadily (and slowly! slowly! I reminded myself) down the aisle. All the people turned to look (some I recognized and some I didn't) and even Robert gave me a shaky smile. I took my place on the left side of the altar, and turned back to watch the second bridesmaid (Robert's bored-looking younger sister) make her way down the aisle, and then the music swelled, and the congregation stood, and Diane and her father appeared at the door. Diane was indeed a beautiful bride. Her veil, sheer and trimmed with ribbon, fell to the tips of her fingers, and the pink and peach combination of roses in her bouquet brought out the almond hues in her skin. Her face radiated happiness and excitement, and Robert looked struck and humble, as if he couldn't believe this was the woman who would be his wife. When Diane made it to the feet of the pastor and joined hands with Robert, I felt as if I couldn't have been more wrong about the couple. They were, indeed, in love, and pig or no, Robert was head over heels.

"Give to each other," the pastor was saying, "a gift every day. A gift of patience, of trust and of love."

When it was Robert's turn to say "I do," his voice shook with emotion.

I felt a sudden urge to break into tears—again.

By the time I heard the "to have and to hold" part from Diane, I almost did. The warmth and the love two people share, no matter how flawed or imperfect, could be infinitely beautiful, a fact I had temporarily forgotten.

The pastor pronounced them husband and wife. The couple kissed sweetly, and the audience broke out into loud, approving applause.

The music began again, and Robert and Diane turned and headed down the aisle. The best man hooked his arm in mine (not exactly correct, but I let it go), and we followed closely behind.

I don't know what quirk of fate caused me to look to the left just then, to the back row as I made my way along the processional. I don't like to think I was drawn to that space or that the man sitting there had any power left over me. I just know that I looked there and I saw him.

Brad. Sitting at the end of the pew. Grinning from ear to ear.

Whatever brief spiritual awakening I had experienced standing at the altar dissipated under the weighty descent of panic. *What was he doing here?* Was he going to the reception? What in the world would I say to him? Should I tell him off the way Diane said I never did? But then, wouldn't showing anger just demonstrate that I still had feelings for him? My mind whirled.

I did have the presence of thought to congratulate Diane, tell her that hers was the most beautiful ceremony I had seen in years (including my own). You'll be proud that I didn't even mention

Brad the whole of the time we took pictures on the church steps. I scanned the lingering loiterers, looking for any sign of my ex-husband, but I didn't see him. Maybe I had imagined him altogether. A hallucination. Yes, that sounded reasonable. Perhaps it was only the effects of emotional stress.

I smiled uneasily and the camera clicked again. The photographer waved me off, and I stepped to the side, watching as Diane's parents and the couple posed together.

Someone tapped me on the shoulder and I jumped three feet.

"Now, that's a bridesmaid's dress I can see myself in," Veronica said, tugging at the sliver of silver strap over my right shoulder. Veronica knew Diane from her college days, even though they didn't hang out all that much anymore. I suspected Diane had invited her for my benefit. I'd never been so glad to see her.

"God, you scared me," I said, putting a hand to my heaving chest.

"Who were you expecting? Your ex?"

"Yes! How did you—"

"I saw him, too."

"What am I going to do?"

"I've got a great plan," Veronica said, pulling me toward a discreet corner. "Listen, this is what you should do. . . ."

I wouldn't call Veronica's plan great. In fact, I wouldn't even be so generous as to call it a plan. First of all, it would never work even if I did manage to pull it off, and secondly, I could never pull it off, so it would never work. An entirely circular and predestined disaster. Veronica, in her twisted, bizarre mind, had hatched a plan that would require me to fawn all over *her* date (whom she offered up to me, unconditionally), which would somehow prove that I was completely over and beyond Brad (though I insisted that I really thought I was far along on the over-Brad road already, and not an in-denial recovery, but a true one, marred only by my one notice-able relapse from the night before). Veronica, however, didn't believe me.

"You need to make him jealous," she said.

"But I don't want to make Brad jealous," I said. "I don't want Brad to notice me at all. I want him to *go away."*

Veronica looked skeptical.

"I mean it," I said desperately.

"Then you'll have no problem with the second part of my plan," she said.

The second part involved me being cool and reserved and dis-tant, which Veronica said would drive Brad crazy and make him hotter for me than ever.

"The thought of him touching me is repulsive," I tried to explain, but Veronica only beamed.

"Excellent! That's the attitude I'm looking for. Only bring it down a notch or two. You don't want to be hostile, just indiffer-ent."

I sighed and rolled my eyes. It was going to be one helluva long reception.

The reception was held at the Old Pecan Street Café, housed in an old saloon-era building with quaint wood floors and paneling and long, narrow windows. Diane, for her part, continued to look happy and radiant as she picked her way through the crowd. She never let go of Robert's arm even for a moment, and Robert seemed ready to burst with pride and contentment. A day ago, that scene would have made my stomach turn, but now I think I could safely say that I felt happy (and, more importantly, hopeful) for them both.

For myself, on the other hand, I had no hope whatsoever. Veronica, unfortunately, had sent her date after me probably with instructions to hang all over me, because he seemed not to be able to keep his hands from the small of my back or the tops of my shoulders. The date, a thirty-ish bartender, was, objectively, very good-looking (not as much as Nick, but I was beginning to think no one could be). I am not sure what Veronica told him about me, but I had a sneaking suspicion that it might have been a bit of a lie along the lines of I was in the market for anonymous and immediate sex.

As annoying as this was, I must admit that it did keep Brad at bay for at least a half hour, as he hung by the open bar looking a little uncertain. Not that I was paying attention, mind you (only in the sense that one would be aware of a giant, hairy spider in the far corner of one's living room), but I noticed that Brad had not come to the reception alone. A leggy, slim blonde seemed to hover constantly near his left shoulder, and they seemed to know each other.

I want to make clear here that the tight, knotted feeling at the base of my stomach was not jealousy. Or envy. Or any emotion approaching that caliber. I discovered, quite surprisingly even to me, that I wasn't at all jealous. That I didn't care what the blonde did with Brad. I even felt a bit of pity for her. She had no idea what an ass he was. Without even knowing her, I decided that she didn't deserve him. No woman did.

After the third time I tripped over the feet of Veronica's bartender (he was invariably underfoot at the worst times), I sent him to get me a glass of wine. As the line for the bar was fifteen people thick, I hoped that would detain him awhile, or at least long enough for me to breathe freely for a few minutes. Unfortunately, the very minute the man left, Brad began moving toward me through the crowd. I didn't want to talk to him under any circumstances, and so I discreetly began moving to my left, where I thought I might be able to duck into the women's bathroom.

My escape was cut off by Diane's mother, who stopped me with a great big hug. She wanted to tell me how she appreciated my help with the wedding, and how much she considered me her unofficially adopted daughter, and a barrage of other equally wonderful (and yet movement-delaying) sentiments.

Just as I managed to pull away from her, a hand reached out and snagged my shoulder.

I knew without looking that it was Brad, because I felt a shimmer of disgust and a wave of nausea flow through me.

"Lauren, you look great," Brad said, grinning like the fiend he was. He wore a freshly pressed Banana Republic black collared shirt and khakis and shiny Kenneth Cole loafers on his feet. Brad had always been a man who relied on his good looks and charm to ease his way through life, but all I saw when I looked at him now was a pathetic, shallow creep whose widow's peak had receded about a quarter of an inch since I had last seen him. The fact that Brad might indeed be going bald sent a little shiver of satisfaction through me.

"Brad," I said, my voice devoid of all emotion. Veronica would have been proud. "You look . . ." I paused, cocking my head to one side. "Tired."

A tiny wrinkle appeared on his forehead as he drew his eyebrows together slightly. A flicker of uncertainty crossed his features. He hadn't been expecting that. Good.

"So," he said, smiling again, only this time not quite as confidently. "What have you been up to?"

My gaze slid away from his face and behind him to other parts of the crowd. Diane and Robert were laughing with the best man.

"What?" I said, distracted, finding it remarkably easy and in fact natural to ignore Brad. My eyes slipped back to his face. Was he always so . . . ordinary looking? I wondered. And his nose seemed, well, piggish. It definitely turned up unattractively at the end. And his complexion seemed all blotchy, like he'd been using a wrinkle cream that didn't agree with him.

"I said . . ." Brad repeated his question.

"Oh, the usual," I answered halfheartedly, my eyes drawn back to Diane and Robert. I noticed that some of Diane's train had come loose from the back of her bustle, and I had to fix it. "Excuse me, Brad," I said, pushing past him.

He called "It was good to see you" over his shoulder, but I didn't answer him.

I snuck behind Diane and quickly fixed the errant bit of train. Diane turned then, and looked back over my shoulder, her eyes widening when she saw Brad.

"Yes, I know," I said. "I just talked to him."

"I had *no* idea he was coming. He just crashed. I *swear* I didn't know," Diane said. "Are you OK?" she added, searching my face.

"I'm fine," I said, and I meant it. I was feeling remarkably good. Great, even.

"You sure?" she said, still searching.

"Absolutely," I said. "I mean it. I feel great. I think I'm really over him."

Diane looked a little surprised, then infinitely pleased with whatever she saw in my face.

"I think you really are," she said, sounding a little amazed. "I think you really are."

The reception sped by surprisingly quickly, and I didn't speak to Brad again the whole time. In fact, I even lost sight of him the entire last half, which proved just how little I cared about him. I didn't manage to shake Veronica's date, however, who stuck to me like wallpaper glue. After Diane and Robert left under a shower of birdseed and bubbles to their awaiting limo, the crowd began to break up, and Veronica's date (I couldn't remember his name—it was either Dave or Daren or Doug) insisted he drive me home. I would never have agreed under normal circumstances, but when we went outside, I found my car wedged in behind two long Lincolns, which completely blocked me in. I was far too tired to go searching for the Lincoln owners, and Veronica said she would be happy to drive home my car (since she didn't plan to actually leave Sixth Street for another four hours or so, being that she had more partying to do).

So, Doug or David drove me home, attempting to cup my knee at various stoplights along the way, until I felt I had to be blunt.

"I don't know what Veronica told you," I said as he pulled up in front of my house. "But I don't intend to sleep with you."

Doug or David digested this information.

"How about make out?" he offered lamely.

"No," I said firmly.

"Oh."

"Thanks for the ride," I said, as I hopped out of the car and swung the door shut behind me.

I noticed as I ducked inside my house that there was still an unmarked police car parked across the street, but this one had two officers in it that I didn't recognize. Detective Douglas was out of sight. Maybe he finally went home to shower.

Exhausted and emotionally spent, I peeled off my bridesmaid's dress and pantyhose, and slipped into a pair of fuzzy, flannel pajamas. While it was at least 80 degrees still outside, Lily had dropped the thermostat to somewhere below 60 in the house. But as she was nowhere to be found, I couldn't even take her to task for it.

I collapsed on the couch, flipped on the TV, and promptly fell asleep with the television's blue light flickering on my face.

•　　•　　•

I awoke with a start to the sound of my front door slamming. Sunlight streamed into my living room, catching the corner of my coffee table and illuminating the bits of dust that floated in the air. It was obviously more than a little late in the morning. I sat up and called out for Lily (as she was the only one not on a honeymoon in the Caribbean at the moment who had a key to my apartment), and she answered me with a monosyllabic grunt from the kitchen. I sat up, and realized that during the course of my sleeping on the couch, my arm had fallen asleep and my hand was completely numb.

I shook it, and pins and needles of pain pricked at my fingertips, as I slowly tried to bend and straighten them. A white-haired evangelist in a shiny blue suit stared at me from my TV set, promising he could save my soul for only a very small donation. I fished the remote from underneath a couch cushion and clicked the power off. I heard the refrigerator door open and then shut, and then Lily yell out that I should go to the store and get some milk because she was about to use the very last of it (this was usually her idea of being considerate). I yawned, stretched, and smacked my lips together, tasting that stale, post-wedding-champagne stickiness on my tongue.

A loud knock sounded at my front door then, and I got up, assuming that it would be the mailman. He always drops mail off early on Saturdays, especially if he has a package that I should sign for. As my brain was sluggish and sleepy (and probably a little stiff, like the rest of my body, from a night on the couch), it took me a few minutes to realize that today was Sunday and that the mailman didn't come on Sundays.

I swung open the door and saw Brad standing there, looking more than a little wrinkled and unkempt (which for Brad, is the sign of a complete and total crisis).

He swept past me before I could so much as run a hand

through my unruly hair. I was too disoriented and groggy to feel much of anything except minor annoyance. It would have been the same feeling, I decided, if a telemarketer had called.

"What are you doing here?" I managed, before I was overcome by another, staggering yawn.

"We need to talk," he said, sounding far more serious than he usually was.

Lily took that moment to come into the living room. "What the . . . ?" She didn't finish. On seeing Brad, her face took on a distorted, ugly curve. "What the hell are you doing here?"

"Exactly my question," I said.

Brad looked a little like a man caught between two sides of the enemy. Then he tried what I am sure he thought was a charming smile. Neither of us was very charmed.

"Brad," I said, feeling put-upon and tired. "I don't want to talk to you. About anything. I want you to *go away.*"

"Yeah, Brad," Lily said. "Get the hell out. I'm allergic to that damn Calvin Klein crap you're wearing."

Brad sniffed his own collar. "But it's Nautica," he said, sounding wounded.

Another knock sounded at the door. This time, I looked through the peephole before I opened it.

It was Nick!

My heart dropped two inches in my chest and began beating furiously.

He even managed, I noticed, to look gorgeous through the fish-eyed glass of my peephole.

I glanced back at Lily and Brad, who were both staring at me curiously.

"I'll be back in one second," I said, opening the door a crack and slipping out.

Nick took a step back, surprised.

"Uh, hi," he said, looking right and then left. "Did I catch you at a bad time?"

"Sort of," I said, feeling acutely aware of the fact that I was wearing baggy, wrinkled blue pajamas covered with tiny white clouds, and that my hair was probably a jumbled, awful mess. Nick, on the other hand, looked incredible, in his usual uniform of a T-shirt and jeans.

"I wouldn't have come, but—" Nick paused. Was he nervous? "But you, uh, didn't return my calls."

He actually looked uncomfortable. Obviously, he thought I had been avoiding him, and he seemed a little hurt (that I *had* been avoiding him wasn't entirely lost on me). But seeing him so uncertain and sad made me feel a pang of guilt. (The fact that he was the one who had been romping around with Darla got lost for a minute or two. Or that it sure seemed he had. Hadn't he? Now, looking at him, I wasn't so sure.)

"I'm sorry," I said, and I really, really was. He deserved a straight answer, not my duck-and-cover, avoid-conflict-at-all-cost techniques. "It's been a crazy week. Diane, my best friend, got married last night, and, well, things have been . . . er . . . happening."

Nick looked hopeful, then wary.

I heard voices arguing on the other side of my front door, and then the door swung open, causing me to fall back. Brad stepped forward into the open doorway, pushing me farther backward. When I regained my balance, I saw Nick and Brad staring at each other (or rather Nick looking down at Brad, because he was a good two and a half inches taller).

"Who are you?" they both said at the same time, appearing not unlike male rams, ready to butt heads.

Brad answered first. "I'm her husband," he said with a possessiveness in his voice that made me want to strangle him.

"Ex-husband," I corrected, but I'm not sure Nick heard me. He looked down at Brad's wrinkled shirtfront, and then me in my pajamas and disorderly hair, and drew a horribly erroneous conclusion. Before I could so much as disabuse him of *that* absurd (and might I add disgusting) notion, Nick turned abruptly and stalked away from the house.

"Wait," I called, halfheartedly taking a step forward. Brad was in the way, so Lily gave him a swift kick to the shins. I stepped past him in time to see Nick turn.

"You could have told me," Nick said, flashing me a terribly angry, terribly hurt look. The ferocity of it silenced me completely.

And with that, Nick threw his jeep into gear, and peeled away down the street.

I stood on my porch, hands crossed over my chest, furious and confused and completely unsure what it was I should do next.

Twenty

I can't believe you kicked me," Brad said again for the hundredth time, rubbing the back of his leg as he shifted on my couch. (Not the couch that he had been screwing my neighbor on, I had to keep reminding myself. *That* couch was much nicer and more expensive.)

"Just be glad I aimed for the leg," Lily said, wandering away from the living room toward my guest bedroom. "I'm going to sleep," she announced. "Why don't you do us all a favor, Brad, and get the hell out?"

After she slammed her door, Brad said, "Sheesh. What's *her* problem?"

I chose to ignore that. And him, in fact, altogether. Besides, I was too preoccupied with the terrible look Nick had given me. I felt terrible. And yet . . . *I* wasn't the one jumping into Darla's bed, was I? Why the hell should I care what he thought? Still . . .

"Lauren?" Brad sounded a little annoyed. "Have you even been listening?"

"Huh?" I said, roused out of my contemplative stupor.

"I said I've been thinking . . ." he began.

"Well, that's your whole problem then, thinking. You know

you don't do well thinking unless it's about hairstyling products."

Brad ignored that comment. "I've been thinking about us," he said.

"There is no 'us.'"

"There isn't?"

"No, and there never was. There was only you."

Brad, as usual, looked puzzled. I was beginning to think all that styling mousse he used on his head to help rearrange his widow's peak was seeping into his scalp and eating away brain cells (items that for Brad were already in short supply).

"Brad, you are by far the most self-absorbed, arrogant, shallow, and vain little man that I've ever known."

"What do you mean by 'little' ?" he said defensively, missing most of my point.

"I mean that I'm ashamed I ever married you, and as far as I'm concerned, I'd like to forget I did." I sounded so amazingly calm and reasonable, lacking all heated emotion, as if I was stating a plain fact, which I guess I was. For the first time since the divorce, I managed to feel reasonably detached from the whole situation, as if discovering that I had simply taken the wrong exit off the freeway. At least now I knew it was wrong, and I knew in which direction I was supposed to be heading.

"I guess that means you don't want to have reunion sex," he said, sighing.

"Brad, I don't want to have any sex of any kind with you ever again," I said. "Do I have to add the 'even if you were the last man alive' clause or do you understand what I'm saying?"

Brad swallowed. "I understand." He nodded, and stood, limping slightly as he made his way to the door. He put his hand on the doorknob and looked back.

"Can we still be friends ?" he whined.

"No," I said firmly.

"Oh," he said, looking more dejected.

"Don't worry, Brad," I said as he opened the door. "You'll have another fallback girl before you know it."

"Fallback girl?" He feigned ignorance.

"Don't play dumb," I said. "I know what you thought I was. You're not exactly very clever, you know."

"Yeah," he conceded with a small sigh. "I know."

He paused for a second.

"I'm beginning to think maybe I really should have held on to you," Brad said, almost as an afterthought.

"You couldn't have, even if you'd tried," I said.

I should have felt good. Liberated, even. But I didn't. I couldn't shake the terrible guilty feeling that seemed to haunt me, even though I had not done anything wrong, while Nick clearly had. I just wasn't sure what I should do next. Should I call him? Should I just put him out of my head forever?

In the end, I left a couple of answering-machine messages for him, but I suspected he might just delete them the second he heard my voice.

As Diane was in the Caribbean, I couldn't very well call her for advice. And I didn't want to talk to Veronica (she would only tell me I should run directly out and sleep with the first man I saw).

I found it infinitely irritating that on the first day that I really, truly came to terms with my divorce and regained a measure of dignity, I couldn't sit back and enjoy it. But this is probably the story of my life. All gains in self-esteem are quickly and instantly negated by some other hefty emotional setback. I kept expecting at any moment for Mom or Dad to call and tell me that I had been adopted or that I was an unwanted child. That would certainly obliterate any remaining progress I had made. How is a person ever supposed to become a healthy adult in this emotional mine-field? Just when you feel like you're through the worst of it, kablam! You lose another limb. It just wasn't fair.

I slunk into work Monday morning, dejected. As Darla's wedding was this weekend, and we hadn't even sent out invitations and I had managed to tell the bride she was basically a worthless human being, I felt more certain than ever that I would be fired, and the wedding itself would be postponed (indefinitely, I hoped, for James's sake).

I put down my bag and sat down at my desk only to find a huge box full of tissue-papered embossed ivory invitations and another whole box full of matching ivory envelopes. A third box contained hundreds of single Federal Express Overnight Delivery folders, and on top of this box was a guest list with corresponding addresses and a note addressed to me.

"Lauren," it began in a big bold script. "Here are my invitations. Please address and mail them overnight to the list I've included." The letter was signed: "Darla."

This could not be possible. Could it?

I scanned down the list and saw dozens of Coronas and even more Tendaskis. I pulled out an invitation, and there, plain as day, were the names of Darla and James, and the names of their church and reception hall (that I had booked two weeks ago). Sure enough, the date was this Saturday.

"I see you found the invitations," G said, startling me. When had she become so stealthlike? And what the hell was she doing here before 9:30, *again?* Pretty soon she might actually learn how to work her laptop.

"I don't know . . ." I began, but didn't get to finish (a normal occurrence when speaking with G).

"Well, we knew it would be close, didn't we?" G said, matter-of-factly. "It's not the only wedding I've overnighted invitations for and it probably won't be the last."

"Has Darla talked to you?"

"No, should she have?"

"No, I guess not."

Curiouser and curiouser.

I stretched a foot out under my desk and hit something soft but solid: Whiskers. Apparently the cat's newfound affection had yet to wane. I began sorting through the boxes (made more difficult by Whiskers, who seemed infinitely fascinated by the many ways she could bat around pieces of paper). Every time I retrieved a loose invitation, she would pounce on it with both front paws and gnaw on its corners mercilessly. Not fifteen minutes passed before G came down the stairs and offered her help, nearly rendering me speechless. G never helps with tasks so mundane as invitation stuffing. I began to suspect she used her offer of help as a ruse to be closer to Whiskers, who hadn't spent one full minute in G's office since her return last week.

The whole of the afternoon the three of us worked furiously (G and I stuffing and addressing envelopes, Whiskers clawing them and knocking them onto the floor). By 4:00 P.M., we had finished all the invitations and had loaded them into my car for delivery to the post office. G even gave me her corporate credit card to pay for it until we are reimbursed by Darla.

I did successfully mail the invitations (much to the annoyance of the post office worker, who had never in his life been responsible for 250 overnight letters sent out at once). I heard more than a few restless sighs behind me as I held up the line, and felt several frustrated looks, but frankly I didn't care. My hand was still cramping from all the addressing (not to mention writing the 250 overnight labels), and I suspected at any moment it would soon curl up into a hideous claw and stay that way forever.

I waited my turn and now everyone else could wait theirs.

"Must be mailing the whole city," the postal worker muttered under his breath as he dug through my stack of overnight letters. I gave him an ugly look, but he pretended not to see.

"You know," said a woman to my left who stared at me with beady, narrow eyes, "you really should have come at an off-peak time. You *are* holding up the line."

I was thinking I might hold up something else if that woman didn't take two steps back.

"If I had that kind of leisure time do you really think I'd be paying nineteen ninety-five apiece to overnight wedding invitations? Does that really make sense to you? Maybe you'd like to tell the bride that the reason why no one showed up at her wedding is because a nosy, pushy woman mailing off stupid birthday cards couldn't wait a measly five minutes in line."

The woman, slack-jawed, backed discreetly away from me.

"Hey, calm down, lady," said the postal service man behind the counter.

"Just do your job," I snapped, annoyed at everybody and everything. Hadn't I earned the right to be a little rude? I glanced back over my shoulder and saw a dozen hard, judging faces looking at me as if I were a psycho bride.

Had it come to this? Was I now all the things I despised in my worst clients? Self-centered, self-absorbed, and completely oblivious of anyone else's feelings?

I spent the week in a deep and furious depression. I alternated between feeling sickeningly sorry for myself and being so angry I felt that I would pop an artery in my head. All of this was made ten times worse by the fact that every working hour I had some project or another of Darla's to rush off and finish (often asking old business associates large favors, such as Lynette's Cakes to whip up a three-tiered concoction in less than two days—favors, I might add, that Darla of all people *did not* deserve). Every day, I became grumpier and grumpier. I snapped at G, Lily, and even Whiskers, and I began to wish that G really would fire me, so I wouldn't have to work on Darla's wedding anymore. The thing was killing me. I hadn't gotten home from work earlier than nine at night the whole week! Twice, I picked up the phone to call James and sabotage the whole thing. Once, I got as far as hearing the dispatcher at the firehouse answer before I abruptly hung up the phone.

By Friday morning, I think I had figured out the root of my problem: a lack of personal courage. I simply didn't have the courage, even now, after all that had happened, to step down from this wedding. It was the hypocrisy of the thing that ate away at me. Darla should not be able to go through with this wedding. It was that simple. Doing so went against everything I believed in, and the whole reason I ever got into wedding planning in the first place. Yet every time I picked up the phone to call Darla, I hung up again. And every time I walked toward G's office to tell her the truth about Darla, I never made it past the fourth stair before turning around again and slinking back to my desk. The worst part was that I walked around feeling as if there was a sticky layer of slime all over me. I needed a shower even after I had showered. I began to despair that I had made no personal progress at all. Where was the Lauren that had so easily disposed of divorce baggage just days ago? Or the Lauren who had tumbled confidently into the bed of the gorgeous Nick Corona? I wanted her back, but I didn't know where she had gone.

In her place was a moping, depressed Lauren who snapped at innocent women at post offices and did the dirty work of a very unscrupulous client, who seemed to want to marry one man but have babies with another.

I was growing to hate Darla. Much more than a strong disliking, or even a mild detesting. I'm talking rip-her-eyes-out, wouldn't-mind-if-she-met-a-horrible-death, going-to-hell-but-don't-care, full-fledged Hate. With a capital "H." I doubted I could stand being in the same room with her for five minutes.

Which should make the hour-long rehearsal interesting.

Friday came too soon.

As I stood on the front steps of the Our Lady of Mercy church, I considered fleeing. I went to the front of the church, but that door was locked (an ominous omen, in my opinion). Unfortunately, the second door I tried slid open and I found myself faced with a narrow hallway, which had plenty of nice hiding places, I noticed. I could just hide and pretend I was lost.

I'm convinced old churches were designed with complicated, circling hallways so that none of the parishioners could escape (should they be bored by a particularly dull sermon). In any case, navigating around a strange, large church was always difficult, as small doors tended to lead into large, cavernous vestibules. I went around trying doors (feeling a bit sneaky, I admit) and found a good number of tiny Sunday-school rooms, but no sign of the large hall.

I heard noises from behind one door and assumed that it might be the pastor's office, but when I twisted the knob and opened the door, a quite different scene met me.

There stood Darla with her blouse half undone, flushed and panting, her arms and one leg wrapped around a man. I couldn't see the man's face, because his back was to me, but his hair was the same dark shade of brown as Nick's. The noises I heard were their dueling groans, as each of them was pawing the other with some enthusiasm. Their lips were fighting each other in a passionate, sloppy mess. Disgusting.

I meant to shut the door quietly (the last thing in the world I wanted to do was catch Nick in the act of actually making out with Darla), but in my surprise at finding the two of them in such a shocking state of undress, in a church for goodness' sakes—well, I let out an inadvertent squeak of surprise. The couple immediately broke apart, and my eyes were drawn to the man's face.

A huge tension left me.

It wasn't Nick after all. Though, I must admit, this man did look a *lot* like Nick, and I think I can say that I'm not just being obsessive here. This man looked much more like Nick's brother than Jay did. But this man was younger. Much younger, if the dark, purplish shade of a blush on his almost smooth cheeks was any indication of his maturity. I put his age somewhere in the early twenties, no older than twenty-four, if that. He also looked eerily familiar, but I couldn't quite place him.

"Lauren!" cried Darla, breathless, pulling her clothes back together.

"I didn't see anything and I was just leaving," I said, wanting to beat a hasty retreat.

"No, don't go," Darla said, surprising me and the boy (er, man) both. "I want you to meet Rick."

"Rick?"

"Rick Corona," she said, emphasizing that last name.

"Another brother?" I asked before I could stop myself, I was so bewildered. "Is he a firefighter, too?"

"No, an engineer," Rick corrected.

"How could you?" I added, all inhibitions and good sense going right out the window. "Is there a fourth or fifth brother I don't know about? Have you slept with them, too? God, Darla. Don't you have any class?"

I didn't let her answer.

"Do you even know who the father is?" I said, wanting to take Darla by the shoulders and shake her.

"Father? What the hell . . . ?" Rick said.

"Shut up," Darla and I both said at once.

"It's Rick's, if you must know," Darla said, flipping her hair out of her eyes. I noticed that even after it had been ruffled a bit by Rick, it still looked magazine-model perfect. More so, if that was possible.

I don't think what she said even registered with me, I was so mad. I just couldn't believe that she kept sinking lower and lower. Maybe she was sleeping with James's father, too. I should have asked that. But all I could think of was getting away from her before I ended up doing something that I'd really regret (like perhaps taking out her left eye with my fingernail). So I just turned and stomped out of the room, leaving Rick to fire questions at her, to which she barely mumbled replies.

I found my way to the main congregation hall and almost ran straight into Darla's mother, who was looking even more nervous and unkempt since the last time I saw her.

"Oh, I'm sorry," I said, pulling myself back a foot and steadying myself on the back of a pew. I heard Rick and Darla coming up behind me, with Rick talking and Darla telling him to be quiet.

Mrs. Tendaski grabbed my arm and pulled me away toward a more secluded spot (or at least out of hearing range of her daughter).

"That's who I was talking about," she hissed, her nails digging into the fleshy part of my arm.

"The naked . . . er, groomsman?" I said. "But you said it was Nick!" I was a bit peeved at this turn of events.

"Isn't that Nick?" Mrs. Tendaski looked baffled.

"Oh for goodness' sakes," I said, disgusted with the whole family. *"That's* Rick. With an 'R.'"

"Wait, maybe I should take out my glasses."

She fished around in her purse and pulled out the thickest lenses I'd ever seen. She peered through them, and then said, "Oh, so you are right, my dear."

"Were you wearing glasses the morning of . . . the morning you found . . . them?"

"No, I don't like to wear these glasses, they make me look squinty."

"Good grief!" I exhaled loudly. "How do you even know he was naked? Maybe he was just wearing beige."

Mrs. Tendaski considered this for a moment.

"No, I'm pretty sure he wasn't wearing clothes," she said. "Unless his pants had separate moving parts."

I couldn't take any more of this family. I had reached my limits with the whole bunch. First Nick was guilty, and now he was innocent, and all because of one nearsighted woman who seemed to be able to identify genitalia but not facial features. Darla was sleeping with God knows how many Coronas, and I was supposed to lead this farce to fruition tomorrow. Ridiculous. I had half a mind to quit and walk out, and never have anything to do with any Tendaski or Corona again.

"All the brothers look alike to me," she said, a bit louder probably then she intended.

"That isn't how it always was," said a Corona relative who'd appeared suddenly behind us. "Can you believe Nick used to be the fat one? It was so much easier to tell them apart when they were younger. James was the tall one. Nick was the fat one. Rick was the skinny one. Now they're all the same."

Did the woman say "fat"?

"Nick used to be fat?" I asked, amazed.

"Oh, well, chubby for sure. You know how some kids are. They don't lose their baby fat until much, much later. In Nick's case, I think he was in college."

Nick used to be fat?

"Don't tell him I told you," she said, her voice lowered to a whisper. "He's very sensitive about that. He got teased so much about it. He was the ugly brother forever."

Nick? Ugly? Could it be possible?

I realized then that I didn't know Nick at all. That I'd made the same sort of shallow judgments everyone does. I'd pegged him as the handsome guy who'd skated through life on his looks. I'd never even bothered to ask him about his brothers, about what it was like growing up. I bet they had been merciless in their teasing. No wonder he seemed so much more scrupulous than the rest of them. He'd had to fight them all his life.

I felt like an idiot.

Then Nick arrived.

I didn't even have to see him come in to know he was there, because the energy in the room changed a little bit and I felt an irresistible pull toward the door. When I looked over, my breath caught a little, because that's the kind of effect he had on me. How he managed to take so much oxygen from a room, I'll never know. Nick was wearing the collared white shirt of his firefighter uniform, with the matching black pants, which gave him an added quality of hunkiness (which he had plenty enough of already, believe me). I tried to imagine him younger, heavier, teased constantly. Could he have been really miserable? Was there a time in his life when the girls laughed at him? Turned him away?

Oh, I had been so stupidly wrong about him. I had blown him off, ignored him, and led him to believe I was cavorting with my ex. He must think I was guilty of the worst sort of game-playing. And here he was innocent of wrongdoing. I felt like crap. Total crap.

Nick looked in my direction, and I smiled at him, a tentative, testing smile, but he didn't return it. In fact, he glanced quickly away from me, as if I was no more than a stranger he'd met once or twice. That hurt more than liked to admit, and I could feel my stomach, which was already a little anxious, squeeze itself into a hard, painful knot. It hurt, and all the more so because I knew I deserved it. I glanced over at Mrs. Tendaski, who was squinting off into space looking disoriented, wondering why in the world I had ever thought to trust her eyewitness account on anything.

The rehearsal began, and people took their places, as directed by the minister, who stood at the front of the altar. I probably should have taken a more active role, but I frankly couldn't have cared less. All I could do was sit in a middle pew and watch Nick, and curse my own stupidity for believing Mrs. Tendaski, when I should have just gone and asked Nick about Darla in the first place. Darla, I noticed, fawned all over James as if she hadn't been pawing Rick just ten minutes ago. It took every last ounce of my willpower not to claw her eyes out.

After the rehearsal (that seemed to go on for hours), I was bombarded by questions from Mrs. Tendaski, who was obsessed with the kind of cutlery that the caterers planned to use. By the time I had freed myself from her and made my way through introductions with key players (the remaining bridesmaids and Mrs. Corona—a large, outspoken, beehived woman clad in a pastel polyester blend), Nick had managed to escape me. He hadn't even said hello.

Twenty-One

I moped all the way home, and even turning up my radio to full volume didn't seem to energize me. When I got there, the one thing that should have improved my mood didn't.

I found Lily packing up her clothes and preparing to move out.

"You're leaving?" I asked rather pitifully, thinking that even my sister was now deserting me.

"Yeah, aren't you happy?"

I couldn't very well say no and still save my pride, so I said, "I guess." I played with the frayed edge of her duffel. "Where are you going?"

"I got another student loan, if you can believe it. Somehow, I guess my application slipped past the noses of the credit police."

"How much?"

"Enough for my own apartment and furniture for a few months. Besides, Chad—er, Detective Douglas—told me I should find another place, because Michael's probably going to come back."

"Oh." I paused, and the full meaning of the statement sank in. "Wait a minute, what about me?"

"Michael doesn't care about you," Lily said, rolling her eyes. "He won't harm you."

"That makes me feel *sooo* much better," I said. "I'm glad he's a *selective* lunatic."

Then another disturbing thought occurred to me. "But what if he mistakes me for you?"

"He'd *never* do that. I mean, who would?"

I looked at her long, straight hair, her stark lack of makeup, and the faded, frayed jeans she wore, and I had to agree.

Lily grabbed her bag and headed toward the front door.

"Wait," I said, feeling very much like having company. "Don't you want to stay and . . . eat something?"

"You don't have anything to eat," Lily said.

"That's because you ate it all," I shot back.

"Right. See you later," she said, tromping on out the door and letting it slam with a bang against its hinges. A quietness settled, and then the door creaked opened again and Lily popped her head inside.

"Oh, and thanks for letting me crash here."

And, just like that, she was gone.

I never thought I'd actually be sad to see her go, but there I was, sitting on my couch, staring blankly at the TV screen, feeling like the most unloved, misunderstood woman in the world (not to mention the most threatened, given the not insignificant danger from Lily's crazed ex). I tucked back the edge of the curtain at my front window, but didn't see any cars parked in front or across the street from my house, and so I assumed the police surveillance (such that it was) had been only for Lily's benefit.

I tried not to sigh repeatedly, but I found I couldn't help it. Pretty soon, darkness settled in, and I found myself still sitting in my empty living room feeling immensely sorry for myself. Finally, I decided I would call Nick, so I could clear up this whole thing. Of course, I got his answering machine.

"Nick," I began. "It's me. Er, Lauren." Great start. Way to win him over.

I paused, gripped by the certain knowledge that Nick might very well be sitting there listening as I recorded this message. I pushed that thought aside, took a deep breath, and continued.

"Look, I want you to know that I'm really sorry for the last week, and everything that's happened. There have been a lot of misunderstandings, that I'd like to explain—for one, I am most certainly *not* married, but I understand if you don't want to talk to me. I, uh, well, I understand. But . . . I really do like you a lot. And I really enjoyed the time I spent with you. And I just want to tell you that you've made me feel . . ."

I heard a loud click on the other end of the line, and I stopped speaking, because my heart had lodged itself tightly in my throat. Maybe he was picking up the other end! Maybe Nick was going to talk to me, after all.

But instead of Nick, a banal, emotionless computerized voice came on the line: "You have run out of time for your message. There are . . . ZERO . . . minutes left to record." This was followed by a loud click, and then a fast busy signal. A polished recorded operator's voice informed me: "If you would like to make a call, please hang up and dial again."

Needless to say, I didn't sleep much that night. As much as the intellectual side of my brain (don't laugh—I do have one, albeit a very little-used part) told me that it never would have worked out with Nick anyway, because he was far too good-looking and fabulous to stay with someone like me, a part of me just refused to believe that. Besides, the whimsical side of me kept saying that it didn't matter if he'd eventually break up with me, because who knows how many multiple orgasms I might experience before then? Who cares if the breakup would've killed me? We're talking at least six weeks of pure, unadulterated pleasure. The fact that I actually loved talking and spending time with him was an added bonus. And who knows? Maybe we could've lasted six months or even a year before Nick realized that I was far too plain and boring for him. You never know. It could happen. A whole year with Nick. I simply wanted to weep for the shame of losing that possibility. It just wasn't fair, dammit.

I rolled over on the couch and saw gray light seeping in through the curtains, and realized with a start that it was already dawn on Saturday, and I hadn't slept the whole night. I hadn't even slipped into those light dozes that sometimes sneak up on you during those restless nights. No dozing. No naps. Nothing.

I pulled myself up off the couch and went to pour myself some cereal, but despite the fact that I knew I was hungry, I didn't seem to have the energy to carry more than one or two bites to my mouth before I lost interest in the whole process. I ended up just pushing most of the mushy flakes around in my bowl, swirling my spoon in tight, then loose circles.

At some point, I found the energy to get up and shower, although I didn't do much more than weakly shampoo my hair and spread a few sparse suds of soap along my person. I didn't get behind my ears like I usually do, and I certainly didn't wash my feet. They seemed entirely too far away.

I got out of the shower, dried off, and then pulled the very first dress in my closet out and put it on, without even thinking about what it was that I was wearing. I went back to the kitchen and noticed absently that I had left my cereal bowl (still almost full) sitting in plain view on my kitchen table. I never do that. Not ever. I always rinse out and wash my breakfast dishes immediately after use. I've never left a single dish in the sink after a meal. The truly astonishing thing was that I didn't even care that it was there. I could have really left it sitting out all day and not even thought about it. I must have been suffering from a deep depression to let that go.

Of course, I didn't leave it out. I did scrape out the cereal, but I didn't go so far as to wash it. I just left it mostly rinsed in the sink. Even that was quite a large departure from my usual routine, so it just goes to show the state of mind I was in. I didn't bother to comb my hair or style it in any fashion. Out of apathy, I simply let it air-dry into a frizzy, horrid mess. I didn't care. I ran one hand through it, but it got stuck in a mess of tangles, so I just dropped it, leaving my hair as it was.

I did put on some makeup. In the South, a woman over twenty-five does not leave the house without makeup, no matter how depressed she is. But I only put on a dash of powder, blush, eyeliner, and mascara. I left out the eye shadow from sheer lack of enthusiasm.

It wasn't until I got into my car that I realized I had dressed more for a funeral than a wedding, with a long black sleeveless dress and severe, sleek black heels. I had forgotten a necklace or earrings, and even my watch, which I never do on wedding days. I think this should adequately show you how little I really wanted to do this today, and how little I cared how any of it turned out. I mean, G and her friend Ms. Davenport would be there, and I simply didn't care. What was the point? Darla was a fraud, James an imbecile, and Nick, the most gorgeous man on Earth, hated me.

I pulled my car into the church parking lot at exactly two hours before the scheduled start of the wedding, and G and Ms. Davenport were already there, waiting for me.

"What are you wearing?" G said, disapprovingly, scanning me from head to toe. "And look at that hair of yours! I swear, you don't comb it on purpose just to spite me."

"Hello, G," I mumbled. "Nice to see you, too."

"Stop picking on the girl!" Ms. Davenport demanded, in her very commanding tone. "Come here," she said to me, "I want to talk to you. Alone," she added, when G made a move to follow us.

"How are you?" she said, when we were far enough away from G not to be heard.

"Not very good, I'm afraid," I said.

"Well, it's what happens when you get tangled up in my sister's family," she said, giving me a sympathetic look, which for her was something just less intimidating than a frown. "I wanted to tell you that . . ." Ms. Davenport dropped off in midsentence, her eyes widening, as they focused on something back over my left shoulder. "Oh, good lord."

I turned then, and saw Lynda Tendaski approaching us, looking even more of a mess than usual. For one thing, her hair was sticking straight up. Quite as if she'd had it blown dry by a 747 taking flight. Her face was smudged with some dark and unknown substance. All but two of her nails were broken; the left arm of her beaded sequined jacket hung by a thread, and one heel was completely broken off, causing a pronounced limp to the right. In addition, by the looks of things, either her skirt was extremely short and fitted, or she wasn't wearing any pants.

"Lynda!" exclaimed Ms. Davenport.

"Mrs. Tendaski!" I sputtered, wondering as I did so if she had had a psychotic break (which is not nearly as uncommon as you might think). "What on earth has happened to you?"

Before she could answer me, I saw a man (probably Mr. Tendaski) running up behind her, carrying what I assumed was the lower half of her outfit, bellowing out her name and shouting, "Lynda! My God, woman, put these on! You're indecent!!"

Mr. Tendaski caught up to us both, stuffing his wife into the long, cream-colored skirt beaded around the bottom with matching sequins from her badly battered, and I might add stained, jacket. The skirt's side had been badly ripped, however, and would not stay up on her hips on its own, and Mrs. Tendaski, being too disoriented to hold it there herself, had her husband's big fist clasped resolutely around the material at her side.

"Has Darla arrived?" Mrs. Tendaski blurted out.

"No," I said. "What's happened?"

"Is our deposit refundable?" Mr. Tendaski broke in, keeping a tenacious hold of his wife's waist, as she seemed to want to run off somewhere.

Ms. Davenport let out a snort. "Don't be ridiculous, Tom," she said. "I'm sure that won't be necessary."

"Yes, everything will be fine," Mrs. Tendaski echoed. This from a woman who smelled like a fraternity-house bathroom.

"Can I get you something? A drink?" I asked, nervously, fluctuating between relief (maybe there wouldn't be a wedding after all!) and dread (how would I explain to Mark Stewart that he had to pack up his beautiful white and pink roses?).

"No, no. I'll be fine, really. It was just a little tumble."

"Tumble?" I asked.

"Only from a moving car," Mr. Tendaski said, as he went on to explain what had happened. Apparently, at 8 A.M. (two hours earlier), the Tendaskis noticed that the bride (Darla) and her maid of honor (Jenn) had not returned from the bachelorette party from the night before. Logically, a scouting party was sent out to look for them, consisting of the groom (Jay), the best man (Nick), both sets of parents, and a couple of aunts and uncles. They paired off in separate cars driving to Sixth Street, the Warehouse District, friends' houses, and other likely places a hungover and missing bride-to-be might be found. Now, I want to tell you that I didn't mention at this point that I always tell my clients that it isn't wise to have such parties the night before the actual event, because inevitably you end up looking all green and hungover, hardly the kind of once-in-a-lifetime memory one wants to create. That's beside the obvious risk of getting carried away, passing out, and waking up with a BORN TO BE SINGLE tattoo across one or another of the bride's cheeks (you laugh, this did happen). As a rule, in today's world, bachelorette parties are far wilder than bachelor parties, because grooms-to-be, unlike future brides, increasingly fail to elicit promises from the girls not to include naked people at parties, groping, or excessive drinking. I can only guess that this is because men have no idea what women are capable of, and think their sweet somethings couldn't possibly end up grabbing that cute bartender's rear and asking him for sexual favors, until her girlfriends actually take pictures of her doing just that. And this *was* Darla we were talking about. I was only glad that Austin was not a seaport (otherwise she might have found her way onto some battleship destroyer).

At any rate, earlier that morning the poor Tendaskis were out looking for their daughter when they saw what looked like her car, only the front was all smashed in and the bumper was resting on the curb. They stopped, inspected the car, walked around it, went up to the door of the house, rang the doorbell, and waited. Just about this time, Jay and Nick showed up, having just come from Jenn's apartment, where they found Her Honor stretched out on her couch and mumbling incoherently. They managed to wrench directions of some sort from her, but not much else.

So, the four of them stood on the strange porch, listening. After some shuffling, hushed voices, and a decidedly long pause, the door swung open to reveal an almost entirely naked Rick Corona, wearing (and I use that term loosely) a hand towel. Right about this time Darla appeared somewhere behind him, in what was either her underwear or a white and blue bikini, saying, predictably, "It's not what you think."

At this point, the groom punched his brother in the face, then fell on top of him, followed by Nick, who was either trying to break up the fight or join in. While attempting to intervene, Mrs. Tendaski got her sleeve torn, while Darla, screaming about her lug of a fiancé, leaped over the struggling men, jumped into her battered car, and drove off.

The Tendaskis got into their car and followed, but in her haste to reach the car, Mrs. Tendaski slipped on the curb and broke off her heel, and then, flustered, failed to shut her door completely. Darla was driving much like a maniac, taking turns rather sharply and speeding. Mr. Tendaski did his best to keep up, and on one of these particularly sharp left turns, Mrs. Tendaski's door flew open, and she fell out. Her fall, however, was somewhat cushioned by a row of plastic garbage cans filled with banana peels and used-up diapers (which explained, mostly, the terribly pungent smell).

Now, I wasn't sure how much of this story to believe (given Mrs. Tendaski's horrible nearsightedness and her stubborn refusal to wear glasses), but as Mr. Tendaski nodded on several occasions, I assumed the account was fairly accurate. At the end of the story, even Ms. Davenport was stunned speechless. I was the only one who seemed relatively unfazed (I mean, given the events of the last few days, this one seemed relatively tame).

In an incredibly calm and rational voice I said, "I think it would be best, Mr. Tendaski, if you and your wife went home and cleaned up, and we'll handle things here. I'm sure everything will work out all right." I wasn't at all sure they would work out well, but they would certainly work out somehow, so I wasn't technically lying. None of the three adults looked as if they believed me, but Lynda seemed very much like she wanted to. Her husband was only too glad to have an excuse to leave (and probably herd his wife into the nearest shower).

"Lynda!" barked her husband, tugging hard on the skirt, which looked as if it would not be able to take much more abuse. "Let's go!"

As Ms. Davenport and I watched the rumpled couple get into their maroon Lincoln, she said, "I think that I'm going to get a drink," and walked off in the direction of the parking lot.

Shortly after she left, I saw Jay, in shorts and a torn T-shirt, sprinting across the lawn toward the church. Naturally, I followed him.

When I caught up to him, he was running up the grand oak-paneled staircase in the entry hall, taking the red-carpeted steps two at a time.

"Jay?" I called, but he either didn't hear me or didn't care to, and continued on up to the second floor.

After a pause, he called out for Darla, and I could hear him opening and slamming the antique doors upstairs. He reappeared on the stairs, rushing down them at a dangerous speed.

"She isn't here, Jay," I said, in what I hoped was a calm but stern voice. He noticed me then, looking down at me from the foot of the staircase, and as if my words had knocked all the steam out of him, he stopped and immediately slouched down, sitting awkwardly on one step.

"I've lost her," he said glumly, putting his head in his hands. "I've lost her forever."

Lucky you, I wanted to say, but managed to restrain myself. I couldn't understand why he seemed so *sad*. He should be angry, furious, or at the very least bitter.

"I can't believe she would . . . and now there's . . ."

"The baby?" I prompted.

"The what?" he said, his head popping up.

Oops.

"Er, nothing. Nothing." Well, *I* wasn't going to be the one to tell him. That was Darla's responsibility.

"What am I going to do?" Jay whined. "I've been a first-rate ass this last year, but I'm going to change."

I must have looked a tad skeptical.

"I mean it. I'm a new man. I want her back. I want to make it up to her."

"Do you really want her back?" I was stunned. How could he possibly still *want* her? She was an absolute mess, and furthermore, she couldn't possibly love him.

"Of course," he said, looking pathetically forlorn.

"Oh, Jay," I scolded, feeling immensely wise and worldly. I had *so* been here a year ago. Deep in denial. Wrapping up all my self-worth and value in a person undeserving of the honor. I squatted beside him and put a hand on his knee.

"You're not going to believe me now, but you'll find a way to deal with this. And it'll be the best way for you."

Jay looked so hopelessly defeated, and I saw so much of myself in him that I felt a sudden strong urge to wrap my arms around him and give him a soothing hug. *It's what I would have wanted a year ago,* I thought. *It's what he should have now.* So I did. He still deserved basic human understanding. Even if he was a heckler and smelled vaguely of alcohol.

"What in the world are you doing?" This was G, who had happened upon our little Hallmark moment with all the grace of a bulldozer.

"I'm comforting the groom," I explained calmly, straightening and smoothing out the wrinkles in my skirt.

"Well, don't just stand there. Go see to the musicians. I hear they're arguing over the cues."

The musicians—two violins, a cello, and a harpist—were in the middle of one of those formally schooled versus play-by-ear musical arguments about the best way to play the Wedding March. The lead violin had been saying that the harpist didn't know a four/four time from an old shoe, and the harpist told the violinist that she didn't care how they did it in the city orchestra, she'd been playing the harp and the organ at Our Lady of Mercy for more than twenty years. This caused the cellist to lean over and whisper something ugly about working an organ to the other violinist, which sent the two musicians into a fit of dirty snickers. Luckily, the harpist didn't seem to get the joke and I was able to step in and propose a compromise.

I left the musicians in an uneasy truce in the balcony and went downstairs. Once there, I saw that G had somehow managed to calm the groom (with what looked suspiciously like a full glass of scotch). I didn't ask where G found such a large amount of hard liquor (inside a church, no less). I figured Johnnie Walker Red was a usual part of G's emergency kit.

Marc, the photographer, made his appearance then and informed me that he had arrived early to take pictures of the bride. I had the unfortunate task of telling him there was no bride to take pictures of.

"She'll show," I heard James say behind me.

I gave the photographer a doubtful look. "You might set up anyway, just in case," I whispered, as he and his assistant made their way up the stairs to the second-floor landing, where he had planned to shoot scenes from the ceremony. I glanced at my watch and calculated that it was about forty-five minutes before the early-bird guests would arrive. I felt extremely restless and kept looking around me, and pacing and going in and then out of the church's front doors.

The Tendaskis returned, looking, for the most part, composed (and in Mrs. Tendaski's case decidedly cleaner and fresher-smelling in a new pale-blue gown). Neither had heard anything from their daughter. Five minutes passed. Then ten. G graciously pulled out a tin flask from the inside of her cream-colored jacket and offered them both a shot of whiskey in a paper cup. Both readily accepted.

It was about this time that I caught a glimpse of the maid of honor, who was trying to get my attention from the side door. She was gesturing silently from behind where the Tendaskis stood, obviously hoping to signal me without the seeing. I caught G's attention with a look, and to her credit she summed up the whole situation in half a second. She easily distracted the Tendaskis with another Dixie cup of whiskey while I slipped away toward the beckoning bridesmaid.

"I've got Darla in my backseat," she whispered. "I think I can sneak her in the back way."

"Why sneak her in?"

"It was hard enough to get her here," the maid of honor hissed in my ear. "I think at the first sign of conflict, she's going to bolt."

"Maybe she should," I said.

Jenn thought about this for a moment. "No," she said after a second. "I think she has something planned."

Oh, great. Evil, conniving, self-centered Darla had a plan. I could hardly *wait* to see what that was all about.

I followed Jenn out the back door and to the small circle drive where her Volkswagen Jetta was parked. What Jenn had failed to tell me was that Darla wasn't alone in that car. Nick was with her. Correction: Nick was *under* her (given that she was half lying, half sitting in his lap).

A hot bolt of jealousy shot through me.

"Nick," I said coolly, watching as Darla's head slipped from his shoulder, and lolled back for a moment before swinging forward and finding Nick's arm again.

"Lauren," he replied, with an equal level of coolness.

"Have your hands full, I see." I couldn't help but poke at him.

He frowned at me. I frowned back.

Then the maid of honor stepped in.

"We don't have time to chat," she said. "We've got to get her inside."

I looked closely at Darla for the first time, and realized that she was most definitely out of it. (She was mumbling incoherently and lacked—or was faking—the ability to walk. I suspected she might be faking as an excuse to cuddle up to Nick.) She wore a baseball hat scrunched on her head and dark, mirrored sunglasses over her eyes. She looked very much like a drugged celebrity stalked by paparazzi.

"Darla, we're here," her maid of honor said. "It's time to go in."

Darla answered with a grumble.

"How are we going to get her in?" I asked, stupidly as it turned out.

"I'll carry her in," Nick answered.

Over my dead body.

"*No,*" I said with more emotion than I intended, causing both Nick and the maid of honor to start at the force of it. I brought my voice down a few notches and continued. "It's just that, er, well, you know . . ." I searched frantically for some good excuse. "Th-the pastor would question whether or not she could give her full consent if she doesn't walk into the church of her own accord."

That was a miserable lie, but I was desperate. The very last thing I wanted to see in the world was Nick holding Darla in his arms. Uh-uh. No way. Never.

Nick blinked, then shrugged and said, "Whatever."

"Let's put her between us," I suggested to the maid of honor, and she nodded her head. "It will be less conspicuous that way."

That left Nick to trail behind us.

We made it through the main foyer and to the staircase before Mrs. Tendaski spotted us.

"Darla!" she squealed. "Darla, sweetheart! Can Mommy help?"

"Shhhhhhh," Darla hissed, holding her hand to her head, and then mumbled something incoherent that I thought might be "My head is splitting open."

Upon hearing his beloved's name, the groom rushed into the hall. "Darla!" he said. "Thank God."

"Go to hell, Jay," the bride said, and suddenly infused with a mysterious new energy, she straightened and stomped up the stairs, slamming the first door she found. I heard the lock turn, and the maid of honor and I exchanged glances. She shrugged her shoulders and went up the stairs. I glanced at my watch. T minus thirty minutes to the scheduled start of the ceremony.

Twenty-Two

I want to tell you that I saved the day. That with my amazing organizational skills and human empathy, I swept in and fixed everything, amazingly managed to turn Darla from a spoiled, evil bitch into a humble, loving woman who finally understood the value of her love for Jay and that her sexual exploits were simply a cry for love and attention from the one man she feared losing (Jay). I would like to say that with an eloquent speech on love from me even Nick realized his mistake and forgave me, then spontaneously asked me to marry him, right there, right then, and suddenly a single wedding became a double, and the four of us jetted off to fabulous tropical honeymoons and experienced a bliss that would last the rest of our lives.

None of that happened. But then, you knew that already, I'm sure.

After the door slammed, and Jay and Jenn bolted up the stairs after the bride, the Tendaskis began a heated argument about the origin of the stubbornness of their child (specifically, Mr. Tendaski claimed his wife had spoiled her), and they continued to fight as they wandered off in search of G (and her much-needed silver flask). The groom and maid of honor took turns trying to coax the bride-to-be to open the door. I could chart their progress by listening for the occasional thud that marked another object being thrown at the door by Darla.

That left Nick and me, standing silently together in the hall. While I was working up the nerve to say something to him, he turned and stalked off.

Better and better.

Luckily, I didn't have time to dwell on that. Because Darla asked for me. This from Jenn, who came down the stairs and said Darla refused to talk to anyone except me.

I don't think I need to tell you *that* was the last thing I needed.

I tromped reluctantly up the carpeted steps, trying to tell myself that flying off the handle wouldn't get me anything but fired, and wouldn't make me feel better about losing Nick (even though deep inside, I had a feeling that it would make me feel better, if only for a little while).

I rapped on the door, and Darla asked who it was. After a long banter through the oak door which included me having to swear that I was alone and wouldn't let anyone else in, Darla opened the door and quickly ushered me in. She still wore the jean shorts and the T-shirt, but her hair was at least fixed and twisted up on top of her head. She had been crying—her eyes were red and puffy—but she wasn't wearing any makeup, so at least she didn't have mascara running down her cheeks. I was still enough of a wedding consultant, apparently, to be worried about what the photos would look like. Then I remembered that I hated this woman, and she didn't deserve a wedding, much less beautiful wedding pictures.

"I've been thinking a lot about what you said," she began, as she paced back and forth in the tiny room. She stopped in mid-stride to blow her nose loudly into a well-used Kleenex.

"Which part?" I said. Seeing as how I had said quite a lot to her over the past week, and none of it very favorable, I wanted to make sure we were both talking about the same thing.

"About me," she said. "And Jay."

That utterly failed to narrow it down.

"About him not deserving me," she further clarified.

"Uh, that's not exactly what I said." In fact, that's the exact opposite of what I said, if I remembered correctly.

Darla ignored that. "I thought about it, and I think you're right. He doesn't."

"No one does," I muttered.

"Exactly!" she said, surprising me by taking both my hands. "No one deserves me! I'm just too much for any one man. And to think I thought you wouldn't understand!"

WARNING: Egomaniac bride on the loose. Silently, I counted to ten. I would not lose my temper. I would *not* lose my temper.

"So, I'm going to tell them all."

"You're going to tell them all what?"

"I'm going to tell them all they can't have me."

"Wait. Wait. Wait," I said, pulling my hands from her grip. "What about the baby?"

"What about it?"

"Aren't you going to tell Rick?"

"I have already."

"And Jay?"

"Yep."

"What did Jay say?"

"He said he always wanted a son."

I realized that something wasn't right here. I suspected I might know what it was.

"Whoa. Back up. What exactly did you tell Jay?"

"That I was pregnant." Darla blinked innocently.

"But you didn't tell him Rick was the father."

Darla laughed. "Of *course* not."

Just before I could wrap my hands around her neck and give it a good yank (less than she deserved, believe me), a rather shrill voice on the outside of the door demanded to be let in. I would have laid money on Mrs. Tendaski, but then I could hear what I thought was a screwdriver jimmying the lock in the door, and I realized a beat or two too late that Mrs. Tendaski would not have been that resourceful. The door swung open with a thud and in it stood a rather large, powerfully perfumed woman who wore her blond hair wound up high in a beehive with a tiny curl looped forward on one cheek. It was, of course, Mrs. Corona.

"Now WHAT is this NONSENSE I hear about you NOT MARRYING MY SON?" Mrs. Corona screeched in an octave higher than I think the human ear is supposed to hear comfortably. I suppose this was a rhetorical question, because Mrs. Corona clambered on with "HOW can you for ONE moment even THINK about calling off the WEDDING? We have relatives flying in from VIRGINIA and TENNESSEE and GOD KNOWS WHERE ELSE, and you simply CAN'T CALL OFF THIS WEDDING!"

Mrs. Corona was pacing the room in a flurry of pink and silver chiffon. Darla looked alarmingly pale, and much like she might faint or throw up at any moment.

"I mean, Darla, honey, if you don't marry Jay, then WHO WILL? He's HOPELESS. Lord knows I've TRIED to TALK SENSE TO THAT BOY. He's just a stubborn, selfish, ungrateful . . ." Mrs. Corona trailed off when she saw the effect her speech seemed to have on Darla. You can't expect to woo a hesitant bride by listing the faults of her would-be groom, now, can you? Mrs. Corona changed tack. She calmed the tone of her voice and turned up the Southern lilt to maximum volume.

"Darla, honey-sugar. You know I simply a-d-o-r-e you. I think of you as the daughter I never had, dear. Don't break my heart, sugar. I-I-I just don't think I-I-I-I could t-t-t-ake it."

Then came the tears. I have never in my life seen a woman cry so many tears on cue. Her eyes became rivers, spewing out large, fat drops of moisture in every direction. Darla, who had regained some of her color, rushed forward to give the woman a handkerchief. She blew her nose appreciatively, and continued.

"I'm a lonely woman, sugar," she said. "I just want to see my sons happily married before I, before I p-p-pass on."

Another emphatic blowing of the nose.

"And I don't think it will be long, now. Heart disease runs in our family. My poor husband Herb, rest his soul!"

Another round of protracted sobs.

I looked at Darla, and thought she might give in out of sheer weariness, and I was on the verge of asking her for both our sakes to do so, when Jenn burst through the door and breathlessly spat out, "Fight. On . . . front lawn. Jay and Rick . . ."

All three of us jumped up. We flew down the stairs and out the front door, and collided with a ring of curious spectators (most of them, I'm very sad to say, were caterer and bakery staff—who were supposed to be setting up across the street).

I couldn't see at first what was going on, until I pushed past a waiter and got a clear view. Rick and Jay were indeed fighting. They were both locked in a kind of death grip, rolling about on the grass. (A part of me cringed to see their white tuxedo shirts being rubbed in the dirt. I suppose I should've been glad that they both had the sense to take off their *jackets* before pummeling each other, but that was a very small consolation.) Nick stood nearby, attempting to talk sense to the two men, without physically interfering, although he wasn't making any progress in breaking up the fight. In fact, he didn't even seem to want to break it up.

Rick attempted to wrestle his older brother to the ground, but temporarily lost control of Jay's right arm, which swung around and connected with a loud smack against Rick's right eye. Rick flew backward and landed flat on his back.

I glanced around quickly. Where was G when you actually needed her? She could have broken this up with one shout. As no one seemed to be making a move to stop the two (including their own mother), I felt I had to intervene.

"STOP IT!" I yelled, in my best imitation of G's bulldog persona, which she regularly uses to bark orders at catering staff. "STOP IT THIS INSTANT!" Rick looked up and saw me, and while he was temporarily distracted, Jay took advantage of the moment to leap on him.

That did it.

I pushed my way through the onlookers and went directly up to the two men, attempting to grab Jay and pull him back, but Jay was even heavier than he looked, and no amount of tugging seemed to do any good.

Just then, Jay's elbow whipped back (as he attempted another punch), and connected squarely with my nose. Pain shot up the front of my face, and the force of it caused me to stumble backward. My arms flailing, I couldn't regain my balance and ended up landing with a bone-jarring thud on my butt in the grass. A warm trickle of blood flowed like water from a faucet over my lip and down my chin.

Dazed, I didn't see what happened next, but Nick must have thrown himself into the fray, because suddenly there were three men fighting instead of one, and Nick looked to be winning. Jenn came to my side and pulled me to my feet and out of the way of the flying fists. She sat me in a chair on the porch and pushed a wad of Kleenex in my face.

Eventually the other groomsmen and the pastor managed to

break the three men apart, but not before they had crashed through two bushes and a potted plant and knocked over a giant gardenia-and-iris-laden topiary.

Guests would begin arriving any minute now, and the first thing that greeted them would be the sight of the groom and two of his groomsmen sitting on the church steps, shirtfronts smudged with grass stains and traces of blood. Not to mention, one wedding consultant (me) holding her head backward, with a bunch of tissues stuck to her face.

G, with impeccable timing, came to the rescue.

"Lauren!" she bellowed across the lawn, as she came striding in my direction, the daisy along the brim of her straw hat bouncing erratically with each step she took.

G didn't even wait for an explanation; she just started barking out orders to everyone in the vicinity (catering staff, groomsmen, bride, and me), sending everyone scurrying in different directions. She shouted at the caterers, yelled at Darla to go get dressed, told Mrs. Corona to see to the pew bows, and finished by handing over her entire whiskey flask to Jay and ordering him to finish it in the vestibule.

No one even thought about canceling the wedding—not with G barking instructions.

Wow, I really needed to learn how to do that.

When we were alone, she turned to me and clucked. "Lauren," she said, shaking her head. "You know better than to intervene in a fistfight. Haven't you learned anything at all?"

"But . . ."

"No buts," G said, raising a hand. "Just go and sit in a corner and try to make yourself less conspicuous. I'll take over."

"That's not necessary . . ."

"You can't very well greet guests with a bloody nose, Lauren," G said, giving me a severe look. "And you absolutely, positively

must stay away from the photographer. I don't want any pictures
of you on the roll."

Something about that seemed absurdly funny. Maybe we could
use a picture of me with my swollen nose in our next ad campaign.
"We take hits for you" could be our new motto. I broke out into a
kind of hysterical laughter. G took me by the shoulders and gave
me a hard shake.

"Get a hold of yourself, Lauren!" G commanded.

I couldn't figure out why she was so serious. I mean, after all,
this wedding was beyond hope.

"Drink this," G said, thrusting a large foam cup in my hand.

"What is it?" I said, sniffing the bright red alcoholic concoction.

"Vodka," G hissed.

Hmmm. I didn't believe vodka was supposed to be red.

"Now, drink it and go clean yourself up," G shouted at me over
her shoulder. "And try to stay out of sight."

I drained the contents of G's oversized Dixie cup in four long
swallows (it was so sweet I couldn't even taste the alcohol) and
then got up to look for a bathroom. My nose still throbbed, but
the bleeding had mostly subsided. When I found a rest room, I
locked the door behind me and took a long look in the oval,
golden-rimmed mirror.

What a mess.

Figuratively and literally.

I looked like I had just been in a fight with about a dozen professional football players. My nose had swelled to more than a half
size bigger than normal, and was in the process of turning an ugly
purple color. Torn pieces of Kleenex had stuck to the dried blood
along the left nostril, and my hair was a frizzy, tangled hive with
small bits of leaves and grass sticking out all over. I managed to
clean up as much as I could, picking off tissue bits and powdering

my nose (which helped cover most of the emerging bruise, but did nothing for the swelling). By this time, the music had begun and I heard the chatter of many voices.

The guests.

I took a seat in a back pew of the church on the bride's side in the back and tried to remain as inconspicuous as possible. Only a few people gave me odd looks, so I assumed that I looked as normal as I could, considering the circumstances.

The rows filled shortly, and the organ music swelled and then ebbed, as the mothers of the bride and groom were escorted down the aisle. Mrs. Tendaski looked very much like a deer in headlights, while Mrs. Corona was resolutely and determinedly composed. Then the pastor, groom, best man, and other groomsmen took their places on the right side of the altar, which was covered in gardenias and ivy. No one, I'm sure, was looking at the flowers.

Jay sported a split lip and a deep cut over the bridge of his nose. An ugly purple and red bruise spread itself over Nick's cheek. Rick stood with a cut above his right eye that every so often would ooze a drop of blood (not to mention a frightening amount of swelling). They looked like thugs. Or rugby players. Or both.

I had long ago gotten past the point of worrying about the wedding photos, but the more I thought about them, the more I found the whole situation ridiculously funny. Now all we needed was for Darla to fall into a door, and the whole photo album would be complete! I giggled a little aloud, and an old, blue-haired woman in front of me turned and glared.

That only made it harder to stop. Because the more I tried not to giggle, the more I giggled, and the funnier things got.

I had a fleeting sober thought: What in the world had G put in that drink? That wasn't plain old vodka. That was vodka and something stronger. I felt like I had downed three drinks instead of one.

I looked up and saw Jay stumble a little (and the weird thing was he wasn't even *walking*—he was just standing there, and he tripped). Nick reached out and steadied him, whispering something in his ear. Whatever it was, Jay found it extremely amusing, because he barked out a rather loud laugh that could be heard over the organ, the violins, and the harp. Nick just gave his brother an odd look, which I found even funnier. I remembered that G had given Jay something to drink, too (in fact, a whole flask), on top of the alcohol he'd already consumed before coming to the ceremony. I wondered if he was feeling as woozy and bubbly as I was. Just then, a woman hiccupped loudly from somewhere in the vicinity of the front pew: Mrs. Tendaski. She had had some of that drink, too, I remembered. Oh, now *that* was funny.

We were all absolutely sloshed. Pickled. Drunk off our collective ass. I was laughing so hard my side hurt.

The blue-haired woman in front of me leaned back and shushed at me.

"Sorry," I said, and then broke out into a new round of giggles. Oh, this was funny. This was definitely funny.

The flower girl came down the aisle then, weaving a bit to the right, and swinging her basket a little too hard to the left. Luckily, it was empty, or the pews on the left side would have been pelted with rose petals. I put a hand up to my mouth to choke back another outburst.

The other bridesmaids made their way down the aisle with smiles frozen on their faces, followed quickly by Jenn, who didn't smile at all as she walked down the aisle. Appropriate, given the true nature of this fiasco. Jay, I noticed, found the appearance of Jenn extraordinarily funny, and kept letting out tiny snickers. Nick elbowed him gently in the ribs, but it didn't do a bit of good. Even the pastor, at one point, stepped forward and whispered something to Jay, but this had the exact opposite effect the clergyman intended. Jay just laughed harder, bending over double and slapping his own knee.

Needless to say, I didn't need any more encouragement to start laughing myself, because the whole situation was so ludicrous, and the more I thought about it, the funnier it got. I mean, I was sitting here, about to witness the worst disaster ever recorded in a wedding, and my *nose was swollen*. And probably broken, I thought, as another wave of giggles rattled through me.

By the time the music reached a crescendo, and everyone stood in hopes of seeing the bride, I was howling and tears were pouring down my face.

"Shhhh," the blue-haired woman spat for the third time.

I stuck my tongue out at her, which caused her to gasp in shock, offended, which of course just made me laugh even harder.

I was one of the last guests to stand, and I noticed that my knees seemed a bit wobbly (as if I had downed four tequila shots in succession), and I was having trouble keeping my balance. I had to steady myself by gripping the back of the pew. And why was it so hot in here? Was the air-conditioning even *on*?

When I saw Darla, my mirth cooled a few degrees. She was, objectively, quite beautiful in her silk shift, a cathedral-length sheer veil cascading down her arms, her back, and to the floor in a cloud of white. The veil was anchored by the ornate silver tiara she wore on the crown of her head. Her hair was pulled back in a neat French twist, with not a single hair out of place, as usual. Who would have guessed that someone so evil could be so outwardly *perfect*.

Well, I was never fooled. I knew hair that gorgeous didn't come without a price (like selling one's soul to the devil).

Amazingly, Darla made it to the altar, without once turning and fleeing the church (which is what I expected her to do at any moment). Nick, I noticed, wasn't looking at her, while Rick seemed unable to look anywhere else.

"Dearly beloved," the pastor began. "We are gathered here today to witness the glorious union of this man and this woman in holy matrimony. . . ."

Another loud hiccup escaped the lips of Mrs. Tendaski.

"Marriage is a sacred institution, created by God, honored by man, as a symbol of the strong union between a man and a woman. A union based upon love, respect, and . . ."

At this point, the groom let out a bark, something between a pshaw and a laugh. Rick, meanwhile, pulled at the collar of his white tuxedo shirt, looking very warm and uncomfortable.

The pastor hurried on.

"And their willingness to uphold God's law. The Bible tells us that to make a marriage work, you need three separate partners: the wife, the husband, and . . ."

Jay snorted.

" . . . and, uh . . . their Lord."

Darla, I could see, was squeezing Jay's arm tightly.

I was biting my lip to keep from laughing out loud. It was hard, so hard, not to laugh.

"If anyone objects to this union, please speak now," the pastor said as a matter of routine.

A hush settled over the proceedings in that tense second of silence that followed this sentence. I kept expecting someone—Darla, Rick, anyone—to say something. Even Jay looked around, as if he expected someone to jump up and declare the wedding a fake. Darla, for her part, just stared straight ahead, and Rick continued to look overheated and uncomfortable.

Then someone hiccupped. Loudly.

A few people turned to stare at me, and I realized that I had done it.

"Sorry," I told the lady with blue hair.

"I believe we will move on to the vows," the pastor said, turning to Nick. "The rings?" he asked.

Nick reached into his pocket and handed the pastor the two platinum wedding bands. The pastor held them up for the audience to see.

"These rings symbolize commitment and fidelity . . ."

Jay was overcome by another fit of hysterics. In reaction, Darla stepped on his foot and whispered something harshly in his ear.

"James," the pastor said, clearing his throat. "James," he said again, to make sure he had the groom's attention. "Do you take Darla Tendaski to be your lawfully wedded wife, to have and to hold, from this day forward, in sickness and in health, until death do you part?"

A long, unpunctuated silence met his question. Then Jay's shoulders started shaking. He was *still* laughing, and apparently he thought the pastor's question was the funniest he'd ever heard in his life. Darla, who had turned and was looking at him expectantly, now just stared at him, baffled.

"Oh, boy," Jay said, clutching his side. "Oh, that's rich."

Mrs. Tendaski let out another squeak of hiccup, which sent Jay over the edge. He was howling now, and very close to rolling on the floor. "Oh . . . Stop . . ." he said. "I can't take any more. . . ."

Confused murmurs rippled through the onlookers.

Jay clutched his side, and then straightened. "Oh. Sorry about that," he said more to the pastor than to Darla.

"My son, would you like a glass of water?" the pastor said.

"No. I'm fine, really."

"Would you like me to repeat the question?"

"That won't be necessary," Jay said. He drew in a deep breath. "I don't."

"I'm sorry, my son. What was that?"

"I said, I don't take Darla to have and to hold and all that. I don't. I don't want her. I changed my mind."

The audience let out a collective gasp.

"*What?*" Darla and Mrs. Corona said at the same time (as the latter jumped from her seat).

"You can't break up with *me*," Darla said, batting back her veil, so she could have a clear view. "Because *I'm* breaking up with *you.*"

Another gasp came from the audience.

Jay just shrugged. "Whatever," he said.

"Wait, wait," Darla said tugging on his arm. "You're ruining the speech I had planned. . . ."

Jay stopped and rubbed his nose, looking more than a little drunk.

Darla cleared her throat. "I wanted to say that *I'm* breaking up with *you*. . . ."

A hushed silence fell over the guests.

Rick looked decidedly pale and unsteady. Like he might faint.

"I would never have had the courage to state my real feelings if it hadn't been for Lauren Crandell . . ." She pointed directly at me as she said this. ". . . who taught me that I should honor my inner feelings."

I said no such thing!

Everyone was staring at me, and it took me a minute to realize that I had actually spoken that last bit out loud. I was even standing, swaying a bit on my feet.

"Darla," I scolded. "I didn't say *that*. I *told* you to quit being such a selfish, evil, nymphoma—" Hiccup!

Oh my, but I was drunk.

"The *point*," Darla said, unruffled, "is that I'm breaking up with Jay. Because I'm in love with his brother."

The audience let out another collective gasp.

"Nick?" someone called from the audience.

"No, Rick," Darla answered.

Jay made a blah-blah-blah sign with his hand, rolling his eyes.

"I'm sorry, I'm a bit confused," said the pastor. "Who is Rick?"
The audience, dumbfounded, sat silently.

"Darla," Jay said, tapping her on the shoulder. "Are you done?"

"Well, I—" she began.

"Good. Because now I want to tell *you* something. I've cheated on you, too, not that I'm as proud of it as you are. You're a selfish, mean, petty, and awful person, and I should know, because I've been a selfish, mean, petty, and awful person, too. The difference is, I know what I am, and I'm tired of being it. Well, no more. I'm turning over a new log."

"Leaf, you mean," someone from the audience yelled. Probably a Heckler.

"Right, leaf or whatever," Jay said, tugging at his bow tie. "I don't want to spend the rest of my life with you. In fact, I don't even want to spend another minute with you. Rick can have you, and good riddance."

And with that, Jay tossed his bow tie on the ground at Darla's feet and stalked down the aisle, through the church doors, and out of sight. Darla threw down her bouquet of flowers and proceeded to stomp on them. Rick tottered, his eyes rolling back in his head, and fainted dead away, landing facedown on the church's plush red rug. Someone in the audience (my guess is Ms. Davenport) exclaimed a loud, impatient "Good lord!"

At that moment, I felt sharp fingernails in my arm and looked up to see G standing next to me.

She cleared her throat. "Lauren," she said calmly, without a hint of anger, retribution, or bitterness. "You're fired."

Twenty-Three

I knew that was coming.

I had been expecting it for more than a week, but actually having it happen came as a bit of a shock. Had I been a tad more sober, I have no doubt my reaction would have been appropriately somber. However, being far past tipsy, that's not exactly how I came across. Quite the opposite, actually, but I think I should say for the record that it wasn't really my fault.

G made the mistake of feeding me, James, and the Tendaskis incredibly potent drinks. I later discovered G served us all hard liquor diluted with Red Bull energy drink, which happened to be the only thing on hand she could find to mix with the stuff. James drank most of her whiskey, and so she fed me and the Tendaskis Everclear and Red Bull. While it's not scientifically proven, some people have said that herbal energy drinks tend to deliver alcohol at a faster rate to the brain, leaving you feeling like you've drunk far more than you actually have. Before you go and think G kept up with the latest in cocktail trends at frat houses, I should mention that she stumbled upon this impressively strong concoction by accident.

But, back to the story.

So, there was G telling me serenely I was fired, as if she were simply making an innocuous comment about the weather. I don't fully remember everything I did next, but Mark Stewart (who was lingering on the edges of the crowd) later told me that I threw my head back and cackled. I don't exactly remember doing that, but then I don't remember a lot of the rest of that afternoon, either. Apparently, G then said that she wasn't kidding or joking and I was *really* fired, to which I replied, "That's what makes it so *funny.*" G lost a little of her composure then, and stalked off in the direction of Darla, the now red-faced and ranting bride.

I somehow made it to the reception (across the street at a large old Southern house complete with gazebo), and proceeded to drink five flutes of champagne in succession (or so says a waiter, but I very much doubt that I drank *five;* three, probably, but five?!), and then stumbled over to the buffet line and proceeded to help myself to a bit of roast, stuffed chicken, and green beans without the help of a plate or utensils. I mean, half the guests were milling about confused and bewildered, so most of the food would wind up going to waste, wouldn't it?

Soon tiring of the food, according to more sober witnesses, I then went around to complete strangers introducing myself as a recently unemployed wedding consultant. "Know anyone that wants to get hitched?" I'd say. "If they want a ceremony just like this one, tell them to call me," and then I'd laugh like a maniac, leaving whoever I was talking to looking confused and uncertain. (For the record, I really don't think I did this, but as I don't remember, I can't say for sure.) At one point, I reintroduced myself to Mrs. Corona, who told me in no uncertain terms that she planned to sue me for breach of contract and fraud. At which point, I snorted loudly and told her that the layer of lacquered

Aqua Net holding up her beehive must prevent the movement of thoughts through her brain—assuming that she actually had one to begin with.

As far as rude, obnoxious behavior goes, I was just getting started.

I found Rick next, who had sufficiently recovered from his fainting spell, and told him he needed to grow up and learn the meaning of what it means to be a real man, a father, and a brother, and that he should be ashamed of himself and all the trouble he'd caused (at this point I was slurring my speech badly, some said, but while my words weren't clear, my message was). I told the Tendaskis that perhaps they should have thought of having Darla spayed when she was fifteen, and mentioned to Ms. Davenport that she was correct in her analysis that her sister and their whole family were idiots (I said this loudly and in range of all of said relatives).

When I wasn't seriously offending people, I found the time to lose my left shoe, steal a plate of food from another guest, and upend the groom's cake (witnesses said I proclaimed I was looking for a "surprise prize" underneath it). Nick found me when I was digging through the remains of the chocolate icing and dragged me away from the table.

"I've been fired," I informed him, with a bit too much glee. "I'm *fired*," I said loudly for the benefit of anyone else in the near vicinity. "F-I-R-E-D. Fired!" I then kicked off my right shoe, broke from Nick's grasp, and did a cartwheel, right there on the lawn of the old house. (Unfortunately, I can't deny I did this, because I do sort of remember doing it.)

"That's enough," Nick said, or something like that, putting an arm around my shoulders and steering me toward the parking lot.

"Spoilsport," I slurred, trying to push myself away from

him, but as he was hopelessly strong, I couldn't manage to break free. The lawn was so large, it seemed we had been walking forever. I suddenly felt overcome with fatigue. So I sat. Just stopped walking and sat, cross-legged, on the lawn. "I'm tired," I said, throwing my head back and lying down in the grass.

Nick let out a frustrated sigh.

"Come on, Lauren," he said, sternly. "You need to go home."

"I want to sleep," I said, curling up in a ball.

"That's why you need to go home," he said, taking hold of both arms and tugging until he got me in a sitting position. He was squatting in front of me, so close I could smell a faint trace of his cologne. I put a hand on his arm.

"Nick, I . . ." Even in my alcoholic fog, there were so many things I wanted to say to him and I didn't know where to start.

He paused, looking me in the eye.

"I'm . . . uh . . . I'm . . ." I couldn't seem to keep a straight thought in my head while fixed by his big, brown eyes.

"I'm . . . uh . . . going to be sick."

And I was, horribly so, all over Nick's shiny black tuxedo shoes.

If that wasn't a low point, I don't know what was. Even now I'm horrified thinking about it. It's not like one can recover any measure of dignity after puking all over a gorgeous guy. I mean, what do you say? "Oops"? "Sorry"? Cracking a joke would be even worse ("I didn't know I ate *that,*" you say as you point to an amorphous, smelly glob). I don't care if you're the most beautiful, sophisticated, chic model on Earth, you simply cannot be cool during or after barfing. It's just not possible.

Luckily, I was extremely drunk at this point, which was the only thing that saved me from sinking into the earth from the sheer embarrassment of it. More stupefied than mortified at that very moment (I couldn't really comprehend why it was I had thrown up), I wiped my mouth, looked up at Nick, and said, "That's not what I meant to say."

I thought for sure Nick would be disgusted. I mean, it doesn't get much worse, does it? Not unless I had puked in his lap, which would have been slightly more revolting. Nick didn't seem at all fazed. He just shrugged and said, "Don't worry about it. They're rentals," as he kicked off most of the stuff from his shoes into the grass.

"I really think we should get you home," he added, gingerly helping me to my feet.

I was no longer in a position to argue.

Nick drove me home (despite the great risk of my ruining the interior of his jeep—I didn't, by the way) and helped me inside my house. Even in my less than coherent state of mind, I really hoped he might stay, but he didn't, saying that he had some other things he needed to go take care of. Unfortunately, I don't remember anything else he said, because as soon as he got me to bed, I collapsed on my stomach on top of my flowery comforter and promptly passed out.

Unfortunately, I didn't stay that way for long.

Around 2 A.M., I awoke sitting straight up in my bed and was sick again all over my clean sheets. I stumbled to the bathroom and proceeded to heave for several hours until it was no longer possible to retch anything but air. While sitting on my bathroom floor I made a number of promises to my creator, including but not limited to: the swearing off of all alcoholic beverages, devoting my life to charity work, and beginning regular church attendance again. All I wanted in return was the immediate and permanent cessation of the rolling of my stomach and pounding of my head so that I could sleep.

Eventually, I became stable enough to leave the bathroom, and strong enough to pull the sheets off my bed and toss them into the washer (you didn't expect me to leave them, did you? I'd have to be dead or dying to do that). I stumbled out to my couch around 6 A.M. and half fell, half lay on it, slipping into a shallow, fitful sleep.

Twenty-Four

An awful, thunderously loud crack woke me later that morning, and it took me several full minutes to realize that it was the sound of someone knocking at my door. I sat up, and immediately regretted doing so. Blood rushed from my head, which was already in grave danger of caving in under some fierce but invisible pressure, and my stomach, a tightly twisted knot, felt sour and sore from all its unaccustomed exercise the night before. My mouth was a dry and pasty desert, and I felt like if I coughed I could exhale a handful of sand.

I was confused. What was happening? Why was my head splitting open? And what the hell was wrong with my nose? Had I stopped a train with it? It hurt. Badly.

Then the bits and pieces came back to me. Throw-up on Nick's shoes. The botched wedding. G and her damn Red Bull and vodka. Me being fired and then making a complete ass out of myself.

Still more pounding came at the door (was someone trying to break it down with a sledgehammer, for crying out loud?). Groggily and with much resentment, I pulled myself to a standing position. The room instantly took a spin, and stars flooded my eyes. I stumbled, caught myself, and then made my way to the door, one hand trailing along the wall for balance.

More insistent knocking came, along with an ear-piercing female shout.

"Lauren! It's your mother, dear, open up."

My life was a nightmare.

I arrived at the front door by taking very small shuffling steps and shielding my eyes from the blinding sunlight brazenly pouring in through my gauzy white curtains.

"I'm coming," I croaked, but I doubt she heard me. I slipped open the bolt, turned the knob, and opened the door a tiny crack.

The sunlight from outside pierced through my eyes and zeroed in on the most hurting part of my anatomy: my brain.

"What is it?" I mumbled, squeezing my eyes shut against the agonizing brightness.

"It's you, dear. It's you!" Mom said, bustling past me and into my living room. I shut the door and leaned against it.

Who else did she expect to open my door? Was senility finally settling in?

"Lauren," she said in a disapproving tone. Apparently having quickly recovered from the shock of finding me at my own house, she decided to scold me. "It's 9:30 in the morning, dear! It's more than past time to comb one's hair. And what happened to your nose, my dear? Did you have an allergic reaction? You know you mustn't eat shellfish."

I just stared blankly at her, my eyes hardly focusing. "What do you want?" I finally said when the creaking gears of my brain pushed ahead a notch. I pressed my hands to my temples to hold my brain in. It seemed in danger of bursting out of my ears.

"Look!" She held up a copy of *Modern Wedding*.

"Mom, I know the magazine."

"No, look!" She pointed to the picture on the cover. "I saw it as I was in the checkout line of the grocery store this morning."

The cover showed a woman sitting in a desk. Beneath her were the words: "Junior Wedding Consultants: The Real Experts." I still didn't get it. Although the woman's hair certainly was a tangled mess. Maybe mom was trying to console me.

Wait a minute. Wait a damn minute. I looked closer.

That was *me*. Sitting in G's office and grinning like an idiot.

I flipped the magazine open, thumbing quickly to the start of the article. There was another picture of me, looking as if I were riffling through pictures. In the corner was a photo of the disastrous parachute wedding, along with the several more generic wedding shots.

The headline read, "Today's Renaissance Woman: Junior Wedding Consultants Breezily Handle Everything from Torn Veils to Plummeting Grooms."

I scanned the article in disbelief. A full half of it was about *me*. I was quoted four times, and numerous former clients raved about me (even the parachuting groom!). G wasn't even *mentioned*. Not so much as a single word.

G would be livid!

Served her right. A weak laugh escaped me.

"What's funny, dear? I think it's wonderful," Mom was saying. "Hurry up and get dressed. I want to take you out for brunch."

I believe there's little worse in the world than trying to disguise a severe hangover from your own mother while attempting to follow her twisted attempts at conversation. I had a hard enough time focusing enough so that I could drink my coffee without spilling all of the cup's contents down the front of my shirt (I dribbled quite a lot, believe me). But actually keeping up with what my mother was saying—well, that was downright impossible. For one thing, she never stayed on track for very long, and when she did it was usually about some fault she found with my appearance. Secondly, there wasn't much she expected in the way of an answer (a few um-hmm's and really's go a long way). So, you can't blame me for tuning out for a few minutes (all right, all right, a half hour). This explained why I was taken completely by surprise when I realized she was talking about Nick.

"I'm so glad you're dating a real gentleman again, like Brad," she was saying, giving a little sigh of longing after Brad's name.

"Who? What? Who, Nick?"

"You sound like an owl, dear."

"Moh. Ther."

"Yes, of course, I was speaking of Nick. I didn't realize your dating life was so full that you were going around with more than one man."

"Mo-*ther,*" I said again.

"That was a joke, dear."

"That's the scary part," I muttered, but I don't think she heard me.

When the waiter brought our food, I was surprised to discover that I was actually hungry. Famished, actually. I ate every last crumb of French toast on my plate, downed a third cup of coffee, and began to feel a little less like a battered suitcase and more like a human being.

"So, I was telling Nick how sad I was when you and Brad decided to divorce," Mom said, buttering a small piece of her blueberry muffin. "And how much I'd like to see you two back together again."

I almost spewed coffee all over the white tablecloth.

"Mom, you didn't."

"Lauren, I always say what I mean and do what I say."

"No wonder he got the wrong idea," I muttered.

"Speak up, dear, I can't hear you."

"That's the idea," I mumbled.

"Well, I heard *that* clearly enough. Lauren, don't be childish."

"Mom, I'm going to say this once and I want you to listen to me."

"Dear, when one is in a conversation, one should always listen."

Good enough. I continued.

"Brad is an awful, two-timing, cheating, shallow, mean person. Just because he sent you a thank-you note doesn't mean he's a good guy."

"Lauren, I think you're exaggerating."

"I am not. He tried to get Lily to sleep with him *while* he was married to me."

"He did not."

"Ask her. He stole money from me. He used my credit cards without my permission. He is, in short, a very bad man."

Mom stopped chewing.

"Lauren," she said, touching my arm. "Why didn't you *tell* me this sooner?"

"I only just came to terms with it recently myself."

Mom sniffed and her eyes clouded as if she might cry. She wiped her nose with the corner of her napkin (an etiquette faux pas that demonstrated her extreme emotional reaction).

"All this time I thought . . . that he was . . . that you were . . . Oh, I am sorry. I was so wrong."

I had never seen Mom look so flustered, or for that matter, so contrite.

"Don't worry about it, Mom."

"But it's my job to worry, dear. Don't you know that?"

We ate in silence for a couple of minutes. This was as close as I'd get to a bonding moment with Mom.

"What about this Nick character?" Mom said after she had recovered. "Is he what he seems?"

"Nick is a very good man," I said. "He saves people for a living. He's thoughtful, kind, and considerate. He's everything Brad isn't and will never be. But, I don't think it will work out between us."

"Why ever not?"

Uh, because I puked all over him? Didn't return his calls? Offended every last member of his immediate family?

"He thinks I'm back with Brad," I said, as a simple way to deflect that answer.

"You aren't, are you?" Mom looked horrified. She really did care, I realized. She really didn't know how terrible he was. And how could she, I thought, when I wouldn't even fully admit it to myself?

"Of course not," I answered, sipping at my coffee. "It's all a misunderstanding, but he won't talk to me long enough for me to explain."

"Do you want me to call him for you, dear? I will, you know."

That was a terrifying thought.

"No, God no," I said, emphatically, setting my coffee cup down a little too hard in its saucer.

"The Lord's name, dear! Don't take it in vain," Mom scolded.

When we finished brunch and Mom dropped me off back at my house, I went into a fury of post-spring cleaning. By my standards, my place was a mess (two dishes to do, a bed to remake, and my carpet in sore need of a vacuum). I knew I should begin looking for another job, or do something equally constructive, but cleaning was a means of not coming to terms with reality, and I was all for that at this point. If I sat still long enough to really think through the repercussions of events that had unfolded over the last forty-eight hours, I might just slip down into a quagmire of self-pity and take to my bed for three days.

That night I went to bed early (since I had never completely recovered from my hangover). My alarm sounded as it does every weekday morning at 7:30, and I had the great (but short-lived) pleasure of turning it off for good. I mean, where did I have to be? Nowhere! I was unemployed. I resolved to spend the entire day in my pajamas. And eat peanut butter from the jar. And watch soaps. And do all those other sinfully uncouth things that unemployed people do.

When I did finally get out of bed (near the late hour of 9:45 A.M.), I found myself in a surprisingly good mood. In fact, one could say that I was almost, dare I even think it, lighthearted. I began to understand what a hefty weight I'd been carrying these last four months or so. The weight of dreading going to work, of hating your boss, of despising half your clients. Instead of fighting that awful sense of panic and dread that usually greeted me every morning, I felt uncharacteristically positive and upbeat.

I could definitely get used to sitting home and watching daytime television (I had forgotten how raunchy the soaps are, and how crude the talk shows are). I found, too, how wonderful it is not to have a tyrannical boss lording over you all day and not to have to deal with dozens of hysterical or psychotic women who spend too much time planning the wedding and not enough time thinking about what marriage really means. The mistake too many brides (myself included) have made is putting so much effort into the one day while failing to think about the next ten thousand days after that one. Do you really want to be married to this person? Or do you really just want a great big party in your honor? It's a question every bride-to-be really ought to think about.

I decided that if I continued with bridal consulting (which was a big if, given that G would do her best to blacklist me), I resolved to ask every single one of my clients whether they'd still be so excited to marry their fiancés if they had to exchange vows in the back of someone's garage. Or in the middle of a hurricane. Or on the Las Vegas strip. Because a wedding shouldn't be about the cake toppers, or lace or cocktail napkins. It should be about the mutual love, respect, and commitment between two people. Never, I thought, should the pomp and circumstance on the big day get in the way of that.

For the first time in a long while, I felt something approaching peace. I didn't dare call it contentment, but it felt nice all the same. I even managed for short periods to put Nick out of my mind, though he kept creeping back in throughout the day. Given my Saturday performance, I knew I should call him, but I simply failed to muster the courage to do so. I had made an ass of myself, and I needed some time to deal with the humiliation before I attempted to talk to Nick again. Besides, I reasoned, things would all work out. Somehow.

Right. That's a good one.

Maybe I'll win the lottery, too, and become wildly rich and famous, and start my own consulting firm.

I mean, come on, it's *me* we're talking about here. If I feel good about things, that's because there's a tornado or hurricane rumbling up behind me and I just haven't seen it yet.

The first bad thing that happened occurred sometime around 5 P.M., when I heard a scratching sound at my back door. I went to investigate and found Whiskers, sitting on my porch with one paw raised and mewing pathetically.

This simply could not be good.

First of all, I had rather hoped never to see G or her cat again as long as I lived. (Though, I had to admit, the cat *had* grown on me in the last week or so. It was pathetically sweet that it had come and sought me out, and a small part of me was pleased it cared . . . I mean, at least something did.)

But this did mess up my plan for a late-evening stealth mission to my office to collect my things, at a time when there would be no chance of meeting G. Whiskers, of course, changed all that, because it was clear I had to give her to G personally.

The minute I opened my door she sprinted in, wrapping herself and her very furry tail around my legs (which left a trail of white cat hair on my fuzzy pink pajamas—the price of cat love, I guess). I knew I would have to return her, and soon, since G would probably be in a fit of worry, but I simply couldn't make myself go—just yet. It was hard enough simply putting on a T-shirt and a pair of jean shorts, and after that, I was simply drained of all energy. How I had ever managed to go to work all day I'd never know. Now that I didn't have to, even the smallest thing (i.e., making myself a sandwich) seemed like too formidable a task. Putting on shoes? Forget it. I'd much rather lounge on my couch and watch "Shocking Secrets Revealed!" on a bevy of daytime talk shows.

I was in the middle of one such show (a woman was about to tell her husband of ten years that she moonlighted as a prostitute and that she wanted to leave her upstanding man for her swarthy-looking pimp) when I heard a loud crashing sound toward the back of the house. My first instinct was that Whiskers had gotten herself into something (or more likely knocked something all over my kitchen floor), but when I sat up, I saw Whiskers sitting on one of my armchairs, licking her left paw. Even this conniving feline couldn't be that quick. The neighbor's dog, maybe? The giant brown boxer was always jumping their fence and roving the neighborhood looking for expensive flower beds to destroy (luckily I had a black thumb and didn't have anything but the stoutest shrub grass growing in my yard), but I did have a potted plant or two, and I hated to think of them in pieces on my porch. I went to my back door, and sure enough, one of my clay pots had been knocked over, and shards lay scattered beside the mangled corpse of a begonia. The dog, however, was nowhere to be seen (but that's not surprising, given that the speed at which he completes destruction is neighborhood lore). I picked up the biggest pieces of pottery (when we're talking about mess you know I can't let it go), and I went inside to get a dustpan and broom.

Suddenly, I heard the telltale creaking of footsteps on the wood floor.

In my house.

Heavy ones, from the sound of the creaking boards.

And they definitely weren't mine.

My blood, for lack of a better description, ran cold, like ice, and my heart manically doubled its beating, thumping hard against my breastbone. My frantic brain searched for a legitimate, nonthreatening reason that someone had sneaked into my house and was now walking freely through it.

My mother? No, she knocked. Always. My dad? He'd never just let himself in. Diane? On her honeymoon. Veronica? Never kept her mouth shut long enough for one to hear her walking.

Lily? Maybe it was Lily!

"Lily?" I called, my voice little more than a scratch.

No answer.

It definitely wasn't Lily. She wasn't that heavy, anyway. The footsteps stopped abruptly, and I sucked in a breath and held it.

This wasn't happening.

Another creak.

It *was* happening. Oh, God. Help! I needed help!

I grabbed the phone's receiver on the kitchen counter and began dialing 911.

Now, I probably should have sprinted right out my back door. Sure, that sounds like the reasonable thing to do. If I were you, reading this, I'd be yelling at me to do the same thing. I can't explain it, but I seemed to be absolutely frozen to the spot. And I didn't happen to have a cordless phone in my kitchen, which would have made a free sprint more difficult, given that the trail of cord would have told the intruder exactly where I was anyway.

My fingers, ice-cold, fumbled with the buttons of the telephone keypad.

"Nine-one-one. What's your emergency?"

"Th-th-there's someone . . ."

I didn't get to finish. I had been looking in the direction of my living room and not the back door. After all, I had assumed that's how he came in, and as he was already inside, there didn't seem to be a good reason to keep an eye on the door.

Something heavy and flat hit me on the back of my head, hard enough to throw me to the ground. Shortly after that, everything went black.

While under, I had an incredibly vivid dream. First, my house was burning. Flames licked my curtains; smoke was everywhere. I heard Whiskers mewing plaintively some yards away. I remember thinking how odd that I would choose *this* dream. Hadn't I fantasized about being rescued from a fire?

The dream, as I said, was incredibly real. I could smell the smoke, feel it itching my throat and causing my eyes to water. I heard the crackle of my couch catching fire, and the snapping of glass and plastic popping in the heat. It was spectacularly hard to breathe, and I was impressed that I had managed such an incredibly vivid dream. The concussion, I figured, must have caused it.

Then two large, strong arms grabbed me, hauled me up, and held me, and I rested my head against the thick veneer of a fireman's coat. Nick's, I thought, dreamily. Rescuing me from imminent peril, saving me from certain death because . . . he loved me. Yes, he loved me. This was my dream, wasn't it? If it was my dream, then he loved me and wanted me back. He was frantic with the thought that he might lose me forever, and that had made him realize the depth of his feeling for me.

Mmmm. I liked that.

I really should get knocked out more often.

Cool, fresh outside air hit my face, but still I clung to Nick, who was walking swiftly toward a waiting ambulance, carrying me with the strength and authority of a person who has done this many times before. He laid me down and threw off his own helmet and mask. His face was wrinkled with worry, and the edges of his cheeks were ringed with black dust.

"You're going to be fine," he said to me, squeezing my hand. "You're going to be just fine."

Then I was on a gurney, a plastic oxygen mask on my face, listening to the wail of sirens and the rush of the ambulance wheels through traffic.

Twenty-Five

I didn't want to wake up.

I wanted Nick to carry me again, valiantly save me from the dangerous blaze. I wanted him to tell me he loved me. I was sure if I could stay asleep a little longer, he would. Certainly he would.

In the end, I didn't have a lot of choice about waking up.

My head decided that for me. Specifically, the dull, thudding ache at the base of my head and neck.

Have I been drinking again? I thought groggily. But I'd sworn off alcohol, hadn't I?

The sheets around me felt stiff and scratchy, like polyester fiber. I didn't own any such sheets. I'd never buy anything with less than a three-hundred-thread count.

"Lauren?"

"Huh?" Who was calling me?

"Lauren! You're awake!"

I cracked open my eyes and immediately saw my family crowded around my bed: my mother, my father, and Lily all studying me with such concern and worry on their faces that it made me wonder what the hell was wrong and what in the world they were doing in my bedroom. And who put these cheap, artificial-fiber sheets on my bed? I tried to speak more than a simple grunt, and I realized that my throat was on fire. It felt cracked and dry, and I discovered that I could speak only in a kind of croak.

"W-w-hat?" I was so confused. Belatedly, it dawned on me that this wasn't my bed. For one thing, it was a single, not a queen, and had large, shiny metal bars on each side. Besides, my house would never have that kind of fleshy, salmon-colored wallpaper.

"Oh! It's my fault!" Lily cried, and I saw that her eyes were puffy and red, as if she'd been crying.

I still didn't understand.

"There's been an accident," Mom said briskly, because she is always particularly brisk when she fears getting emotional.

"It wasn't any accident," Dad spat.

"It was Michael!" Lily declared. "He broke in."

"There was a fire," Mom continued.

"He hit you on the head!" Lily wailed. "He thought you were me. You could have been killed!"

"The police botched the whole thing if you ask me," Dad said, knowingly.

"They did not! Chad's the one who caught Michael!"

"But who set the fire?" Dad said.

"That was Michael, Dad," Lily said, sounding exasperated.

"Then why did Detective Douglas run off?" he answered.

"To catch him," Lily snapped.

"Damn it!" This was my mother, whose bottom lip was trembling. "You two shut the hell up!"

My mother never, as long as I've lived, uttered a single curse word. Not ever.

We all stared at her, disbelieving.

"My baby!" she wailed, bursting into tears and throwing her arms around me in a massively tight, shirt-wrinkling hug.

•   •   •

A nurse broke up the emotional moment, pushing her way through and demanding that everyone leave so she could read my vital signs. I blinked up at the dark-skinned nurse in the pink and purple scrubs and let the shock of it sink in. I was in a *hospital*. I had survived a fire and a madman! Had Nick really saved me? Or was that just wishful hallucinating?

"You've got a concussion," the nurse informed me. "And smoke inhalation. But you'll be fine in a few days." She wrapped a plastic cuff around my arm, looking at her watch.

"Blood pressure is good," she said, releasing my arm from the cuff and setting it back down at my side. "Somebody was sure looking after you."

I drifted back to sleep (whatever they fed me through the IV seemed to be tugging at me like a heavy weight, keeping me perpetually under). I had another dream. This one, with Nick holding my hand at my bedside. He was so tender and sweet. Sigh. He really did care!

Then I woke up.

It was dark outside, and Lily, not Nick, was sitting beside me, holding my hand.

"Mom and Dad went to get food," she said. "How are you?"

"Mad as hell at you," I teased.

"If you're giving me crap then I know you feel better," she said, blinking hard.

"Whiskers!" I exclaimed, remembering the cat for the first time.

"She's safe," Lily said. "She ran out of the house after the fire started. Nick caught her and gave her back to your boss."

"Nick?" My heart fluttered a little. He *was* there, then. "Did he . . . uh . . . help?"

"He only knocked down your front door, rushed into the

house, and dragged your heavy butt out of there," Lily said. "None of my boyfriends would've done that."

My ears and face grew warm.

"Or stay at a hospital all night long," Lily added.

"H-he's here?"

I felt a rush of panic. My hand instinctively went to my hair, but I felt only a great big stiff bandage around my forehead and some tufts of unruly curls sticking through.

"He was," Lily said. "He paced the halls all day and half the night, but I think Mom finally convinced him to leave."

I felt a strong, flattening disappointment.

"So?" Lily said.

"So . . . what?"

"So what's the deal with you and him? Is it serious?"

"I don't know."

"Do you want it to be?"

I thought about that. "Yeah, I guess so."

"Yep, just like I thought." Lily stood, stretched, and then declared she was going to go home and get some sleep.

The next morning, a short, balding doctor with large, plastic-frame glasses took off my head bandage and examined the stitches at the back of my head. (They had shaved a small square there, but I discovered that my hair was so jumbled and long that it neatly covered the bald spot.) He shone a light in my eyes, put a stethoscope to my chest, and then declared that I was well enough to go home.

Unfortunately, I didn't exactly have a home to go home to. What wasn't touched by fire had been severely damaged by smoke and water, so much so that my dad estimated they would have to level the place and start over. I couldn't bear yet to see it, given the blunt and awful descriptions from Lily, who nonchalantly informed me that the whole thing was a soggy, black, sooty mess. "If you go home, you'll just be compelled to start cleaning again and you won't stop," she said, making a remarkable amount of sense. "Get dressed and then we're going to my place."

Lily, bless her, had taken out all the clothes she had ever borrowed from me (which were a good many, let me tell you) and had brought them all to the hospital so that I would have my choice of what to wear. I figured that her unscrupulous borrowing probably saved the very best of my clothes from being destroyed in the fire. How's that for irony?

Lily insisted I come and stay in her new apartment, which to my surprise was a spacious two-bedroom, one-and-a-half-bath, in a sprawling, gleaming new apartment complex in northwest Austin.

"I have four pools," she boasted, taking me through the gates.

"How did you afford this?" I said, immediately suspicious. Was she selling pot now?

"Student loans," she said. "The suckers!"

"No pot then?"

"*Hel-lo,*" she said, giving me a "I'm so over that" look. "Chad's convinced me of the error of my ways."

"So . . . you two are . . . ?" I trailed off.

"We most definitely are," Lily finished for me, winking.

Lily showed me to my room (and it was little more than that, since the only piece of furniture in it was a futon). "I'm still in the process of decorating," she said. Despite the lack of furniture, the place still had a good amount of clutter. Some of it, I noticed, wasn't Lily's, unless she wore size-11 men's shoes. Chad's, of course. He spent more time here than at his own house, Lily informed me.

In fact, he arrived shortly after we did.

He wanted to take my official statement, although he ended up telling me much more than I told him.

For example, I discovered that the strange man in my house roaming the living room had not in fact been Michael. That was Chad, of all people, who had been watching the house all day and had seen Michael sneak around to the back. Knowing that I was inside and could be in danger, he had let himself in through an open window near the guest bedroom and was quietly (not so quietly, I corrected) making his way to the back. He suspected that Michael might do something drastic (like set the house on fire) because he had made some such threat the night he had attacked Lily.

I was a bit peeved that no one had bothered to tell me that some wacko had vowed to burn my house to the ground, and said so (I mean, I never would have lain around in my pajamas all day if I had known), but Chad just shrugged. "It would only have worried you," he said. "Besides, I and a few other officers took turns staking out your place. You were never in any real danger."

"Then how did I get this bump on my head?" I was furious. Being clonked on the head and then left in a burning building certainly seemed like danger to me.

"That was . . . er . . . my partner's fault," Chad said, sheepishly. "We got our signals crossed, and he didn't realize he was supposed to go around back. We're very sorry about that."

"And why didn't one of you pull me from the fire?" I asked, so angry I could barely grind out the words.

Chad laughed uneasily. "We didn't know he had set fire to the house. We did call medical response," he added quickly, as if that's supposed to make up for overlooking such a life-threatening, major detail. "But we had to catch Michael, or he'd be free to do it again."

I was seething. He had left me in a burning house, for crying out loud, and that's in addition to letting that thug give me a concussion.

"We did catch him, and he's facing three felony charges," Chad finished proudly.

"Lauren," Lily said, trying to divert my attention. "Remember that Nick was with the first-responder team, and he knew just what to do."

"Hmpf," I grumbled, still a bit perturbed. I mean, Michael could have as easily shot me as hit me over the head.

"I'm starved," Lily declared. "Let's go eat." She tugged on Chad's arm.

"Want to go out with us?" Chad said to me. Somewhere out of Chad's line of sight, Lily shook her head deliberately at me, telling me my answer should be no.

"No," I said, though I didn't need her prompting. I thought it best if I stayed away from Chad just now, or I'd be tempted to do him bodily harm.

"Good," Lily said a bit too eagerly. I later figured out that this was not a magnificent showing of unsisterly coldness but actually the execution of a very devious plan.

Just then, Lily's doorbell rang.

"I wonder who that is," Lily said in a tone that meant she didn't wonder at all.

She opened the door, and Nick walked in.

"We were just going," Lily added, dragging Chad out of the apartment.

That left Nick and me, staring at each other.

He seemed rather reluctant to be there, which took me off guard. Why would he come if he was still angry at me? Granted, I had insulted every living member of his immediate family at his brother's wedding. Thrown up on him. Ignored him. Not to mention the fact he believed I was in the middle of a torrid affair with my ex-husband.

Then again, I reminded myself, he had saved my life.

I owed him a great big apology.

"How are you doing?" he said, staying at a discreet (and disappointing) distance.

"Fine," I said. "Thanks to you."

He shrugged. "Just doing my job," he said, sounding awfully detached.

"Oh," I said. Was that all? Just doing his job? I felt my heart sink. "Look, I feel terrible about everything that's happened," I said.

"Everything?" Nick wasn't talking about misunderstandings now. He was talking about something else altogether. Oh, those eyes. Those big brown eyes.

Why couldn't I seem to keep my thoughts straight when he was standing in the same room? And he was so tall and broad and . . . strong . . . and . . . muscled.

"Er . . . I mean about the wedding and insulting everybody," I hurried on, trying vainly to focus on something else in the room. Nick was far too much of a distraction. "And throwing up on you and then getting into a mess where you had to come and save me . . . and . . ."

I was babbling now. I sounded like a complete dork. Nick just stood, listening patiently. His coolness infuriated me. If he was mad at me, then he should be mad. If he didn't care about me, then why was he here at all?

"I didn't sleep with Brad," I blurted suddenly, involuntarily, defensively. "Well, not recently. I mean, I did sleep with him when I was married to him, but that was a long time ago, and he wasn't really very good. . . ." I was blathering on, my mouth running at speeds I hadn't thought it capable of. So much so that when my mind heard what was actually coming from my mouth, it could simply point and think, "Is she really *saying* that? Abort! Abort! Abort!"

". . . during the act he was always trying to look at himself in mirrors, which isn't really what making love is supposed to be about, and I felt like he was making love to himself half the time and it didn't matter that I was there . . . and . . ."

Nick crossed the room and with a sudden urgency, grabbed me by the shoulders, and pressed me to him, shutting me up in the most direct and efficient way possible: with a perfectly passionate, intense, mind-melting, openmouthed kiss. When he finally pulled away some minutes (five, ten, or fifteen, who's counting?) later, he growled, "Stop . . . talking . . . about Brad."

I stood, baffled, with my knees all wobbly and my arms like jelly, and said, "Brad? Brad who?"

In answer, Nick rewarded me with another heart-pounding, tongue-twisting kiss, and this time I somehow ended up pushed straight back against a wall, which turned out to be a door, and somehow the doorknob turned and the door fell open, and then Nick half pushed, half carried me into the room with the futon, kicking the door shut behind us.

It turned out that Nick didn't hate me after all. In fact, he quite liked me, and spent a few hours showing me just how much (in creative and deliciously naughty ways). I must admit I didn't realize the variety of gymnastics that can be performed on a futon (and I'm not even including what we did on the floor). It turned out that Nick had been eaten up with jealousy about Brad. In fact, he told me that my mother had led him to believe that a reunion was imminent, and he was heartbroken about it.

In fact, once he'd figured out that that had not been the case at all (follow-up conversations with Lily and my mother in the hospital proved this beyond a reasonable doubt), he felt awful for giving me the cold shoulder. About my drunken escapades at the wedding, Nick secretly found them hilarious (he couldn't stop laughing remembering the look on the Tendaskis' faces when I suggested Darla should have been spayed at age fifteen). After leaving the wedding, Jay checked himself into rehab, which he never would have done sober, so Nick had a special thanks in mind for G, who had served us all those potent drinks.

I also discovered from Nick that after I left, other interesting developments occurred, including the fact that Rick told Darla he wanted nothing more to do with her, and that he was deeply ashamed of his conduct. So Darla got dumped not once, but twice, and at her own wedding! Darla's pregnancy also had been a sham—just another one of her compulsive lies. Nick and Darla had dated, however, if briefly. It took Nick only two dates, in fact, to realize what sort of woman she was.

"I still can't believe you'd ever think I'd go for Darla," Nick said, pulling me close. "Especially when you're in the same room."

"Oh, really?"

"You're a hundred times the woman she is."

"Oh, do go on. . . ."

"You're a million times more clever, funny, witty, dazzling, and sexy, I can't forget sexy . . ."

Mmmmm. A girl could definitely get used to this.

"And charming, beautiful . . ."

Oh, yes indeed.

Later, Nick insisted that I come and stay at his place for my own safety (he, like me, didn't necessarily trust Chad's assertions that Michael really wouldn't get out of jail). Not to mention the very practical fact that he had a king-size bed, and the two of us were having a lot of trouble sleeping (and doing more active tasks) on the tiny futon. Nick didn't want to let me out of his sight (as much because he feared he might have to rescue me from a burning building as the fact that he didn't want any more stupid misunderstandings to get in the way of . . . well, I think you know). Unfortunately, living with Nick meant that I wasn't in any kind of hurry to repair my house. In addition to keeping me in a perpetual state of glorious dishevelment, he also cooked me the most scrumptious meals. Breakfast, as it turned out, wasn't his only specialty.

He was in the middle of cooking a particularly yummy batch of his spaghetti sauce when his phone rang. He answered it while lifting up a wooden spoonful for me to taste.

"It's for you," he said, handing me the phone, and leaning over to wipe a drop of sauce from the corner of my mouth. Ooh. He could make the most ordinary thing sexy. I was contemplating jumping him, when I put the phone to my ear.

"Hello?" I said, fully expecting Lily.

"Lauren! Thank God I found you," G said frantically. "You've got to come back."

Before I could even answer, she rushed on with: "The phone's been ringing off the hook. Everyone has read the magazine article and dozens of new clients are asking for you!"

Nick, who had lost interest in his tomato sauce, fixed me with a look and then wrapped one arm around my waist, tugging me closer to him. He planted feather-soft and very distracting kisses on the nape of my neck.

"I don't know . . ." I said, pausing, trying to digest this startling new development. Hadn't I waited for years to hear G begging for my help? But I couldn't think clearly, not with Nick's lips on my throat. Mmmmm.

"I'll pay you!" G was saying. "I'll pay you anything you want! Six figures. You name it. You can have your own assistant."

My own assistant?

Nick, who seemed more than eager to assist me in more personal ventures, was unbuttoning the top of my blouse.

"Five weeks' vacation a year," G continued. "Your own office. You name your hours. Anything you want."

What I wanted was for Nick to kiss me on the lips. He did.

"Lauren? Lauren, are you still there?"

"G," I said, a bit out of breath. "I'm going . . . to have to call . . . you back . . ."

Nick pulled the phone from my hand almost before I finished this sentence and dropped it haphazardly on the countertop.

"Lauren? Lauren!" G shouted to empty air.

By then, Nick had swept me up in his arms and we were already halfway to his bedroom.

Epilogue

The white roses in the bouquet were a tiny bit askew, and I couldn't help but straighten them. It was a habit, really.

"Stop it," Lily commanded. "You are not allowed to fuss over anything at your own wedding."

I smiled. I supposed this was true. I'd have to let go.

"You look beautiful," she said, looking over my shoulder at the reflection of us together in the floor-length mirror. I was wearing a simple, ankle-length silk sheath. I wasn't wearing a veil, or petticoats, or a giant A-line skirt. I wasn't wearing a tiara, or a cathedral-length train. It was a much more subdued version of me, this second time around. My hair, which never much liked bobby pins anyway, I kept free. It was long now, far past my shoulders. Nick liked it that way.

This time, I wasn't worried about the caterers, or if the floral arrangements had arrived, or if the guests would like the favors. This time, I didn't have three-hundred guests, or a three-tiered cake, or twelve bridesmaids.

This time, though, it felt right.

"I think I'm going to cry," my mother said, sniffling behind me, because since the fire she hasn't been able to put a rein on her emotions. She cried at telephone commercials now. It was like she'd opened a faucet.

"Here," I said, whipping a tissue from my sleeve, because old habits died hard.

"Thanks," she sniffled, dabbing at her eyes. Now she always wore waterproof mascara.

"Mom, you're being sappy again," Lily scolded, but she was smiling.

"I'm just giving Lauren some practice," Mom said, blowing her nose. "Now that Lauren has opened up her own bridal-consultant office, she'll have tons of nervous-wreck mothers like me to deal with."

"And then some," I said, just as Mom enveloped me in a huge hug. She hugged all the time now—bone-crushing hugs.

Strains of music drifted up from downstairs, and my dad appeared in the doorway.

"I'm no expert, girls, but I think we'd better get a move on," he said.

Mom released me from her grip and scurried out the door. Lily gave me a peck on the cheek and followed.

"You ready to do this thing?" Dad asked.

"Ready as ever," I said, smiling.

G's old house made a great setting for a ceremony. The guests (only thirty this time) were arranged neatly in the front sitting room as we descended the stairs. I saw G first—directing Lily and Mom to their proper places. She had a clipboard, and a headset on, and she looked like she meant business. When she saw me, she gave me a wink. I smiled back. Mark Stewart was there, too, standing beside one of his particularly impressive orchid topiaries. And

Veronica and Diane were already at their places, standing at the front, by the fireplace. Lily, the last to join them, waved at me.

When the harpist played "Here Comes the Bride," and Dad led me down the aisle, I only had eyes for Nick, who was standing at the far end, in a linen suit and no tie, looking as perfect as ever. He smiled at me, and my stomach jumped. I didn't even think about what my hair looked like as I walked down the aisle, and then looped my arm through his.

Because true love isn't about sheet music or embossed invitations or lace. It isn't about the size of your bridal party or the expensiveness of the food. True love is what you find when you aren't expecting it. True love is taking the risk that it won't be a happily-ever-after. True love is joining hands with the man who loves you for who you are, and saying, "I'm not afraid to believe in you."

A love like that has legs. A love like that will survive most anything.

Even a less-than-perfect wedding.

Up Close and Personal With the Author

WHERE DID YOU GET THE INSPIRATION TO WRITE
I DO (BUT I DON'T)?

Like many women in their twenties, I was surrounded by friends who got swept away by the wedding pagantry. Everyone knows a Psycho Bride. They seem normal, and then they get engaged and suddenly there's no topic of conversation more important than whether or not they have tulle on their dresses. I wrote this book for fun, and to show the lunacy of a worst-case scenario wedding.

IS THERE SOMETHING WRONG WITH WANTING
YOUR WEDDING TO BE PERFECT?

Not at all. Everyone wants their wedding to be perfect, but it shouldn't be an excuse for excessive self-indulgence. There's a real danger in seeing a wedding as a goal, rather than as the start of a journey. Weddings should be fun. They shouldn't be status symbols, or an excuse to indulge yourself beyond what's reasonable. Marriage is not an easy or a lighthearted commitment. Ultimately, whether or not your cake melts won't make or break your marriage.

HOW MUCH IS LAUREN LIKE YOU?

Well, I am the opposite of a neat freak. Ask my husband. My mother once apologized to him because I turned out to be such a slob. Beyond that, I think there is certainly part of me in Lauren. I don't have curly hair, but I do have more bad hair days than good. I think we all share some of Lauren's insecurities, even if we don't want to admit it. Lauren is ultimately very competent at her job, and very conscientious, and she wants to succeed, even though circumstances conspire to thwart those desires. I care about my work, like Lauren, and I want to be a success, even though I often feel, like Lauren, that some things are out of my control.

THERE IS A REAL DICHOTOMY BETWEEN HOW LAUREN SEES HERSELF, AND HOW OTHER PEOPLE SEE HER. HOW DO YOU SEE LAUREN?

I think she's far more put-together, both physically and mentally, than she lets on. I think she's actually quite pretty, even though she'd be the last to admit it. I think she's also quite capable, even though she is constantly fighting to establish her credibility. I think the root of Lauren's insecurities stem from the fact that she feels so much like an outsider most of the time. Being a wedding planner allows you access to people's lives, but at the same time, keeps you apart. You plan the details of the wedding, but you don't actually take part in the ceremony. I think this leaves Lauren with a feeling that she's more of an observer than an active participant in life.

LAUREN REALLY LEARNS TO BE MORE SELF-ASSERTIVE BY THE END OF THE BOOK. WHAT IS THE PIVOTAL MOMENT FOR LAUREN?

I think it's a slow change for the most part that occurs in her since her divorce from her first husband, which causes her to reevaluate the facts she took as truths (that marriage means happily ever after, that getting married is a destination, not the start of a trip). But the real breakthrough point for Lauren comes when she speaks her mind to Darla, whom she sees as a person who's carelessly throwing away opportunity. Lauren knows from experience that life is often unpredictable, and she sees Darla's reckless behavior as a fundamental waste. It's the last straw for Lauren. After Lauren breaks that final rule, of not only arguing with, but shouting down, a client, she's much more free to assert herself in other ways.

LAUREN AND HER MOTHER HAVE AN INTERESTING RELATIONSHIP. EXPLAIN HOW YOU THINK THIS RELATIONSHIP CONTRIBUTES TO THE DEVELOPMENT OF EACH CHARACTER.

Lauren's mother is probably the single most important influence in her life. She steered Lauren to her neatness tendencies, and gave her an appreciation of etiquette. I think the tension between Lauren and her mother comes from the fact that the two are actually very much alike. I think Lauren's evolvement over the course of the book actually helps her mother face some of her own issues and grow as a person.

WHY DO YOU THINK NICK IS SO ATTRACTED TO LAUREN?

Beyond the superficial elements of attraction, I think that Nick sees a kindred spirit in Lauren. Nick, himself, had an awkward childhood, and beyond that, faced the challenges of having to deal with what is by all rights a crazy family: an overbearing mother and two scruple-less brothers. He's used to being the responsible one, and he recognizes those tendencies in Lauren. She's also generally in the eye of the hurricane acting as the person who often holds things together but rarely gets credit.

WHERE DO YOU LOOK FOR INSPIRATION FOR CHARACTERS AND SCENES?

Everywhere. Absolutely everywhere. Friends, family, the news, books. Nothing is safe from me.

HOW DID YOU LEARN TO WRITE? WHAT DREW YOU TO WRITING?

I have always loved to read. My mom often tells the story of the day I first learned to read in preschool. That night we rushed to the bookstore to buy my first books, and she kept the car light on all the way home so I could read aloud. I've never stopped loving to read. That's the root of writing. You have to be a reader before you can be a writer.

Then don't miss these other great books from Downtown Press!

HOW TO PEE STANDING UP
Anna Skinner
Survival Tips for Hip Chicks.
(Available June 2003)

WHY GIRLS ARE WEIRD
Pamela Ribon
Sometimes life is stranger than you are.
(Available July 2003)

LARGER THAN LIFE
Adele Parks
She's got the perfect man. But real love is predictably unpredictable....
(Available August 2003)

ELIOT'S BANANA
Heather Swain
She's tempted by the fruit of another...literally.
(Available September 2003)

BITE
C.J. Tosh
Life is short. Bite off more than you can chew.
(Hardcover Available September 2003)

Look for them wherever books are sold
or visit us online at **www.downtownpress.com.**

Great storytelling just got a new address.
Published by Pocket Books